Book 42 – GARRO
James Swallow

Book 44 – THE CRIMSON KING
Graham McNeill

Book 43 – SHATTERED LEGIONS
Various Authors

Other Novels and Novellas

PROMETHEAN SUN
Nick Kyme

THE PURGE
Anthony Reynolds

AURELIAN
Aaron Dembski-Bowden

THE HONOURED
Rob Sanders

BROTHERHOOD OF THE STORM
Chris Wraight

THE UNBURDENED
David Annandale

THE CRIMSON FIST
John French

BLADES OF THE TRAITOR
Various authors

CORAX: SOULFORGE
Gav Thorpe

TALLARN: IRONCLAD
John French

PRINCE OF CROWS
Aaron Dembski-Bowden

RAVENLORD
Gav Thorpe

DEATH AND DEFIANCE
Various authors

THE SEVENTH SERPENT
Graham McNeill

TALLARN: EXECUTIONER
John French

WOLF KING
Chris Wright

SCORCHED EARTH
Nick Kyme

CYBERNETICA
Rob Sanders

Many of these titles are also available as abridged and unabridged audiobooks.
Order the full range of Horus Heresy novels and audiobooks from
blacklibrary.com

Also available

THE SCRIPTS: VOLUME I
edited by Christian Dunn

THE SCRIPTS: VOLUME II
edited by Laurie Goulding

VISIONS OF HERESY
Alan Merrett

MACRAGGE'S HONOUR
Dan Abnett and Neil Roberts

Download the full range of Horus Heresy audio dramas from
blacklibrary.com

Aaron Dembski-Bowden

THE MASTER OF MANKIND

War in the webway

BLACK LIBRARY

For Savannah Lily Dembski-Bowden, who decorated my shoulder with vile, milky baby vomit only five minutes before I wrote these words. Thanks, Scout.

A BLACK LIBRARY PUBLICATION

Hardback edition published in 2016.
This edition published in Great Britain in 2017 by
Black Library,
Games Workshop Ltd.,
Willow Road,
Nottingham,
NG7 2WS, UK.

10 9 8 7 6 5 4 3 2 1

Produced by Games Workshop in Nottingham.
Cover by Neil Roberts.

A CIP record for this book is available from the British Library.

ISBN 13: 978 1 78496 536 5

See Black Library on the internet at
blacklibrary.com

Find out more about Games Workshop
and the world of Warhammer 40,000 at
games-workshop.com

Printed and bound by CPI Group (UK) Ltd, Croydon, CR0 4YY

THE HORUS HERESY

It is a time of legend.

The galaxy is in flames. The Emperor's glorious vision for humanity is in ruins. His favoured son, Horus, has turned from his father's light and embraced Chaos.

His armies, the mighty and redoubtable Space Marines, are locked in a brutal civil war. Once, these ultimate warriors fought side by side as brothers, protecting the galaxy and bringing mankind back into the Emperor's light.
Now they are divided.

Some remain loyal to the Emperor, whilst others have sided with the Warmaster. Pre-eminent amongst them, the leaders of their thousands-strong Legions are the primarchs. Magnificent, superhuman beings, they are the crowning achievement of the Emperor's genetic science. Thrust into battle against one another, victory is uncertain for either side.

Worlds are burning. At Isstvan V, Horus dealt a vicious blow and three loyal Legions were all but destroyed. War was begun, a conflict that will engulf all mankind in fire. Treachery and betrayal have usurped honour and nobility. Assassins lurk in every shadow. Armies are gathering.
All must choose a side or die.

Horus musters his armada, Terra itself the object of his wrath. Seated upon the Golden Throne, the Emperor waits for his wayward son to return. But his true enemy is Chaos, a primordial force that seeks to enslave mankind to its capricious whims.

The screams of the innocent, the pleas of the righteous resound to the cruel laughter of Dark Gods. Suffering and damnation await all should the Emperor fail and the war be lost.

The age of knowledge and enlightenment has ended.
The Age of Darkness has begun.

~ DRAMATIS PERSONAE ~

Hierarchs of the Imperium

THE EMPEROR	The Master of Mankind
MALCADOR	The Sigillite, High Lord of Terra
ROGAL DORN	Primarch of the Imperial Fists, Praetorian of Terra
MAGNUS THE RED	Primarch of the Thousand Sons, Lord of Prospero
KOJA ZU	Minister of the Anuatan Steppes

The Legio Custodes, 'The Ten Thousand'

CONSTANTIN VALDOR	Captain-General
SAGITTARUS MALACQUE	Warrior of the Moritoi
RA ENDYMION	Tribune of the Hykanatoi
DIOCLETIAN COROS	Prefect of the Hykanatoi
ZHANMADAO NAVENAR	Prefect of the Tharanatoi
HYARIC OSTIANUS	Warrior of the Kataphraktoi

The Silent Sisterhood

JENETIA KROLE	Commander of the Silent Sisterhood
KAERIA CASRYN	Vigilator, Steel Foxes Cadre
MAREI YUL	Vigilator, Fire Wyrms Cadre
MELPOMANEI	Proloquor of the Soulless Queen
VARONIKA SULATH	Mistress of the Black Fleet

The Martian Mechanicum

ZAGREUS KANE	Fabricator General-in-Exile of Sacred Mars
TRIMEJIA DIADANEI	Fabricator Locum
THE ARCHIMANDRITE	Executor Principus
IOSOS	Archwright of the Ten Thousand
ARKHAN LAND	Technoarchaeologist
SAPIEN	Artificimian
HIERONYMA	Magos Domina, Ordo Reductor
ALPHA-RHO-25	Sicarii Protector
NISHOME ALVAREK	Legio Ignatum, princeps of the *Scion of Vigilant Light*
ENKIR MOROVA	Legio Ignatum, princeps of the *Black Sky*

The Mongrel Court

ZEPHON OF BAAL	Warrior of the Crusader Host
JAYA D'ARCUS	Baroness of House Vyridion, Warden of Highrock
DEVRAM SEVIK	Courtier, Scion of House Vyridion
ILLARA LATHARAC	Courtier, Scion of House Vyridion
TOROLEC	Sacristan Apex

Imperial Personae

SKOIA	Ancestor-speaker

'Hell is empty, and all the devils are here.'

– from *Tempestium,*
by the heretic Ariel Sycorax of Old Earth

PROLOGUE

The Herald

'FATHER.'

He whispered the word against the wailing sirens. Lightning arced in panicked flashes between overloading generators, killing men, women and other machines with impunity. His presence was a violation, a profane corruption of the most sacred ground, yet the burden of confusion paralysed him. Weakness flooded his flame-wreathed form as it never had before in his demigod's lifespan.

The cavern before him was only a laboratory in the most poetic sense. He looked with flaming eyes upon the inside of a god's mind, where a cityscape of machinery and snarled utopia of cables reflected the synapses and sections of a human brain. At the core was a throne of gold, once coldly serene, now spitting acetylene sparks bright enough to sear even eyes made of fire.

He felt the heat of pursuit behind him, the ripples of the warp's billion predators spilling into the latticework of tunnels in his wrathful wake. They came in a laughing, howling horde, inexorable as any flood, inevitable as the rolling slide of lava.

And he knew, then, what he had done.

He had led them here. The only being powerful enough to breach the final barriers around the Imperial Dungeon had carved a path and paved a way for them. The warning he had come to give faded from his lips.

The sirens. The sirens howled on and on. Warriors of the Ten Thousand, clad in gold and ringing their king, shouted and fired skywards. Their incendiary rounds dissolved within his towering form, their rage coming to nothing. Even the Custodians didn't know him. He knew each of them by name – there was Constantin Valdor, there was Ra Endymion, there was Amon Tauromachian – yet they levelled their spears at him and opened fire. Good men, men with philosophical souls and unbreakable loyalty, seeking to destroy him.

His father stood at the heart of the storm, looking up at him, looking up at the burning herald of humanity's end. Every other soul in the chamber – the menials and workers and scientists not already aflame or fleeing the cascade of klaxons – stared up with their king. The fiery form was the last thing many of them saw, for its violent luminescence stole their sight forever after.

The Emperor looked upon him – His son, His creation – with eyes that had seen countless suns and civilisations die.

'Magnus,' He said.

'Father,' breathed the avatar of burning misery in reply.

PART ONE
MAGNUS' FOLLY

ONE

The first murder
Thirst
Hunger

TWO MEN CRY out in a forgotten age. The roar of the slayer harmonises
with the scream of the slain. In this earliest epoch, when humankind
still fears spirits of fire and prays to false gods for the sun to rise, the
murder of a brother is the darkest of deeds.

Blood marks the man's face, just as it marks the spear in his clenched
fists and the rocks beneath his brother's body. The wound gouts and
sprays – the man tastes the red wine of his brother's veins, feeling the
blood's heat where it lands on his bearded skin, tasting of metals yet
undiscovered and seas yet unseen. As the hot salt of spilt life burns
his tongue, the man knows with impossible clarity:

He is the first.

Mankind – in all its myriad forms on the thousandfold path from
wretched lizard-thing to warm-blooded mammal – has always fought
to survive. Even as hunched ape-creatures and brutish proto-men, it
waged insignificant and miserable wars upon itself with fists and teeth
and rocks.

Yet this man is the first. Not the first to hate, nor even the first to
kill. He is the first to take life in cold blood. He is the first to murder.

His dying brother's thrashing hand reaches for him, raking dirty nails across his sweating skin. Seeking mercy or vengeance? The man doesn't know, and in his rage he doesn't care. He drives the wooden spear deeper into the yielding hardness of meat and against the scrape of bone. Still he screams, still he roars.

The scream of the first murderer cuts through the veil, echoing across reality and unreality alike.

To the things that wait in the warp, mankind will never sing a sweeter song.

BEHIND THE VEIL, the scream takes a carnival of forms, riotous and infinite in variety. The frail laws of physics that so coldly govern the material universe have no power – here, those binding codes fracture into their separate fictions. Here, time itself goes to die.

On and on it plunges, crashing and dissolving and reforming in the endless storm. It ruptures a cloud-burst of other screams that haven't yet been cried aloud. It punctures the fire-flesh of shrieking ghosts, adding to the torment of those lost and forsaken souls. It knifes through a disease that was rendered extinct by man-made cures twenty-six thousand years before.

And on. And on. And on. Clashing with moments that haven't yet happened, that won't happen for half an eternity. Grinding against events that took place back when the earliest Terran creatures exhaled water and – for the very first time – raked in lungfuls of air.

Behind the veil, there is no *when* and *then*. Everything is now. Always and eternally now, in the shifting tides of an infinite malignance.

Lights shine in that malignant black: the lights of sentience that draw the darkness closer. The same lights flare and shriek and dissolve at the merest touch from the forces around them. Dreams and memories take shape only to shatter amidst the claws and jaws manifesting within the nothingness.

The scream plunges on through every whisper of hatred that will ever be spoken by a human mouth or thought by a human mind. It cracks like lightning above the sky of a dying civilisation that will expire before ever grasping the wonder of space flight. It breaks the stone city-bones of a culture gone to dust thousands of years ago.

From its genesis in breath and sound the scream becomes acidic nothingness, then fury and fire. It becomes a memory that burns, a whisper that rends and a prophecy that bleeds.

And it becomes a name. A name that means nothing in any language spoken by any species, living or dead. A name that carries meaning only in the strangled, misfiring thoughts of humans breathing their last breaths, in that precious and terrifying moment when their spirits are caught between one realm and the next.

The name of a creature, a daemon born from the cold rage of one traitorous soul in one treacherous second. Its name is the deed itself, the first murder and the death rattle that followed.

IN THE CREATURE'S shrieking journey across the warp, it touches the minds of every human who ever was and will ever be, from the long dead to those yet to be born. The daemon is tied to the species with such primal intimacy that every man, woman and child knows its caress – deep in their blood and bones – even if they know nothing of its name.

Billions of them stir in their sleep across the many ages of man, writhing against the unwanted touch of the creature's birth back in the mists of time.

Millions of them wake, staring into the darkness of mud huts, palatial bedchambers, housing complexes and any one of the countless other structures that humans build for themselves across a million worlds and thousands of years.

One of them, a sleeper on Terra itself, wakes and reaches for a weapon.

HER HAND SLID along cool silk, inch by subtle inch, until she grasped the familiar ivory handle. Something mechanical was purring in her chamber, a droning song in the shadows.

'Do not draw the weapon,' said the voice of her killer. 'You are said to be an intelligent woman, Minister Zu. I had hoped we might avoid such futility.'

The minister swallowed with a click in her throat. She didn't release the pistol grip. Her hand felt glued to it by sudden night sweat.

How could he be here? What of her guards? A palace's worth of warriors waited below, armed to the teeth and paid far beyond the threat of her rivals' crude bribery. Where were they? And what of her family?

Where are the gods-cursed alarms?

'Rise, minister.' The voice was too low, too resonant, to be human, nor did it convey anything in the way of human emotion. If statues could speak, they would speak with this assassin's voice. 'You know that if I am here, you are already dead. Nothing will change that now.'

She sat up slowly, though she refused to slacken her grip on the gun. 'Listen,' she said to the golden shape in the darkness.

'Negotiation is equally futile,' the killer assured her.

'But–'

'As is begging.'

That set off a spark within her. She felt her features harden as her temper ignited her courage. 'I wasn't going to beg,' she said, her voice cold.

'My apologies then.' The figure made no move.

'What of my guards?'

'You know what I am, Koja Zu. You can choose to die alone, or you can resist the inevitable and I will leave this palace only after killing everyone who resides within it.'

My son. The thought welled up, bleeding and hot and savage.

'My son.' She said the words aloud before she could help herself.

'He is of an age to serve the Emperor.'

Koja Zu's hand trembled as it gripped the gun.

'No,' she said, and how she loathed herself for the shake in her voice. 'He's only four. Please, no. Not the Legions.'

'He is too young for the Legions. There are other fates, minister.'

Her eyes were adjusting even as her blood ran cold. In the half-light of the hours before dawn she could make out the ornate, overlapping edges of his burnished armour. The suit of golden plate emitted a low thrum, the source of the mechanical purr. In his hands was a long spear, lowered to aim at her. Affixed above the weapon's arm-length blade was the bulky chassis of a boltgun, clad in reinforced wirework.

None of this surprised her. What surprised her was that the killer stood unhelmed, showing a face that had once been human.

'I've never seen one of you like this,' she said. 'I wasn't even sure you had faces.'

'Now you know otherwise.'

Koja Zu watched as the assassin tilted his head slightly, hearing the whisper of priceless mechanics in the collar of his golden armour. Though his towering form was scaled-up by whatever genetic meddling his master had performed to enhance the brute's intellect and physicality, no gene-weaving could hide his roots. He had been human, once. An Albian heritage, perhaps, going by his features beneath the weathered flesh and battle scars.

'May I at least know the name of my killer?'

He hesitated, and she dared to believe she'd caught him with an unexpected question. Yet his dark eyes never wavered.

'My name is Constantin Valdor.'

'Constantin,' she repeated slowly. Her schooling in Old Earth's mythology had been extensive, and she often hearkened back to old tales and legends in her speeches. All the better to inspire the teeming masses of godless, hopeless dregs who served her. Now the minister found herself smiling, no matter that her son was to be stolen away to a fate of genetic torment; no matter that her own death was mere breaths away. She smiled a madwoman's smile, all teeth and wide eyes. 'I am to be killed by a man with an ancient king's name.'

'So it seems. If you have any last words, I will ensure they reach the Emperor's ears.'

Koja Zu's lip curled. '*Emperor.* How I loathe that title.'

'He is the ruler of this world and the master of our species. No title is more appropriate.'

She bared her teeth in an expression too ugly and defiant to be a smile. 'Have you ever considered just what kind of creature you serve?'

'Yes.' The dark eyes stared on. 'Have you?'

'The "Master of Mankind".' She shook her head, feeling the welcome flare of righteousness. 'He isn't even human.'

'Minister Zu.' The golden warrior made a warning of her name. One she didn't heed.

'Does He even breathe?' she demanded. 'Tell me that, Custodian. Have you ever heard Him breathe? He is a relic left over from the Dark Age. A weapon left out of its box, now running rampant.'

Valdor blinked once. The first time she'd seen him blink so far. That rare human movement was unnerving – to her it felt false, like it had no right taking place upon his statuesque features.

'Terra,' he said, 'is a thirsty world.'

She knew, then. With those words, she knew which of her many crimes she was to die for. The one she'd least expected.

A laugh, queasy and unwanted, tore itself from her throat. 'Oh, you vile slave,' she said, unable to keep the sick grin from her face.

'Other worlds suffer a similar thirst.' The golden killer's eyes had glassed over with an inhuman serenity made all the more uncomfortable by the living intelligence shining behind it. 'Yet none of them hold the war-scarred, irradiated honour of being mankind's cradle. This world is the beating heart of the Great Crusade, minister. Do you know how many men, women and children now make their slow way back here – to humanity's first home? Do you know how many pilgrims wish only to see the ancestral Earth with their own eyes? How many refugees flee their flawed and failing worlds now the veil of Old Night has been lifted? Already it is said that unsettled land on the Throne-world is the most valuable commodity in our nascent Imperium. But this is not so, is it? One resource is far more precious.'

She clutched the autopistol tighter as he spoke, breathing slowly and calmly. Even knowing she was to die, even knowing she had no hope of drawing the weapon, the body was reluctant to surrender its survival instincts. Instinct demanded she fight to live.

'What I did,' she said, 'I did for my people.'

'And now you will die for what you did for them,' he said without malice.

'For that alone?'

'For that alone. Your other treacheries are meaningless in my master's eyes. Your cleansing pogroms. Your trade in forbidden flesh. The army of gene-worked detritus you have sequestered in the bunkers beneath the Jermanic Steppes. The prospect of your rebellion was never a threat to the Pax Imperialis. Your crimes of apostasy are nothing. You are dying for the sin of your harvester machines drinking the Last Ocean.'

'For stealing *water*?' She felt like laughing again, and the sensation wasn't a pleasant one. The laughter was creeping up through her blood, seeking a release. 'All of this… *because I stole water?*'

'It pleases me that you understand the situation, Minister Zu.' He inclined his head once more, with a curious courtesy and another subtle purr of machine-muscles. 'Goodbye.'

'Wait. What of my son? What is his fate?'

'He will be armed with silver, armoured in gold and burdened by the weight of ultimate expectation.'

Zu swallowed, feeling her skin crawl anew. 'Will he live?'

The golden statue nodded. 'If he is strong.'

In that moment, her trembles subsided. The fear bled away, leaving only naked defiance somewhere between relief and hope. She closed her eyes.

'Then he will live,' she said.

There was a bang, throaty and concussive, and she was falling, drowning, choking in thunder. There was pressure and heat and grey, grey, grey. And then mercifully there was nothing.

Nothing, at least, for her.

✠ ✠ ✠

The creature formed from the twinned screams of the first murder clawed its shrieking way free from the womb of the warp. It dragged itself through a wound in the universe, breaching reality with all the exertion expected of a being forcing its own birth. Once away from the nurturing tides of the Sea of Souls, its flesh steamed and shivered. Reality immediately began to eat its corpus, gnawing at the beast that should not exist.

It rose, stretched out its limbs and senses, and shook off the slick, wet fire of its genesis.

It hungered.

It hunted.

True to its nature, it hunted alone in the cold of this sunless realm, ignoring the jealous, wrathful and fearful cries of its lesser kin. It had no capacity for kinship even with those monsters that shared similar births, considering them – insofar as it had the intelligence to form any thoughts at all – as lesser reflections of its primacy. Their existences, and the weaknesses they suffered, were nothing and less than nothing.

Had any Imperial scholar managed to pry open the daemon's skull, and were there a brain within to dissect for answers, the creature's mind would have been laid bare as a node of punishingly sensitive perceptions. An animal might hunt by a prey's movement or the smell of its blood, but the daemon didn't comprehend such miserable trails of scent and sight and sound. It hunted not by the crude mechanisms of its prey's bodies, but by the very light of their souls.

The monster moved unseen through the great tunnels and chambers, its tread spreading corrosion through the arcane material that made up this unnatural realm. It clutched no weapon. If it needed a blade or a bludgeon, it would fashion one from its own essence, using them to break open the brittle shells of its victims and feast on the life within. More likely it would rely on its strength, its talons and its jaws. These would suffice for all but the toughest prey. They had survived when the creature had incarnated itself in the past for other hunts on other worlds.

It crawled along the shattered walls of the expansive tunnel, reaching out with its impossible perceptions. The daemon listened to the song of souls nearby, the chorus of human emotion beckoning like a siren call. The Anathema was somewhere in this realm, as were its childlings, the Golden. The daemon would find them, and rend them apart with weapons shaped from its hating heart.

The boiling oil of the creature's thoughts locked on to the promise of prey. Instinct dragged the daemon west.

On it crawled, sometimes moving through tunnels so large they defied the daemon's senses, seemingly great empty expanses of nothingness. It stalked through the knee-deep golden mist that pervaded so much of this realm, and it shifted as it moved, its flesh rippling and solidifying, crusting over in scales of burnished metal.

Pinpricks of life needled against its senses. The creature slowed, halted, turned. Saliva, hot as magma, dripped from between its bared teeth.

It launched forwards, shadow-silent, faster than the eye could follow.

A boundary servitor sensed the creature's approach. AL-141-0-CVI-55-(0023) was a tech-slave, a woman who for fifteen years had been answering to a numerical signifier in place of the name she no longer remembered. She'd earned her sentence through the murder of a forge overseer during a food riot. Now she turned what was left of her head towards the scanner anomaly.

'Tracking,' AL-141-0-CVI-55-(0023) said aloud.

That one word began an awakening among the other servitors nearby. They stalked closer with the pathetic grace of the half-dead wretches they were. Immense weapons rose. Clouded eyes squinted through targeting lenses. Razor-thin tracer beams lanced out from cannon muzzles and targeting arrays.

As rudimentary as they were, the servitors were primed for sentry duty. They were aware that many of their number, once linked to the shared vox-grid, had fallen silent. They knew, in their own simple way, that their kin were being killed.

In a different breed of ignorance, the daemon didn't know what a servitor was. It knew nothing of the lobotomising process that scraped a criminal's brain free of deeper cognition, or the grafting of crude mono-tasked logic engines in place of a reasoning mind. It knew only what it sensed, which was that the diminished souls in this hunting ground were just alive enough to bleed, and the running of blood was all that mattered.

It drew closer. Their clockwork-simple machine thoughts whispered against its essence. It tasted the warp-scent of their weapons – not the fyceline primer or the vibrating magnetic coils, but the weapons themselves. Instruments of destruction with their own spiritual reflections. They were caresses of pressure prickling at the monster's mind. The daemon sensed anything that had shed blood or taken life. A creature of murder knew its own kind, whether it was formed of aetheric ichor, mortal flesh or sanctified metal.

'Tracking,' said AL-141-0-CVI-55-(0023) again. Three of the others repeated the word, slightly out of sync. Her head snapped this way and that on an augmented spinal column, seeking, hunting. Prickles of sensory data buzzed at the sides of her slow consciousness. It was enough. 'Engaging,' she voiced.

'Engaging,' the other three repeated, still out of time, as the sensors in their skulls registered the approaching creature a moment later.

AL-141-0-CVI-55-(0023) devoted her stunted brain processes to two subroutines. The first was to pulse a three-beat signal of white noise across an unclosable vox-link, notifying her handler of her heightened state of alertness. The second was to brace her bionic foot against the unseen surface of the tunnel's floor. The immense heavy bolter that replaced her right arm clunked twice, weighty with purpose. An ammunition feed rattled from the weapon's body to where it connected to her bulky backpack.

The daemon – still nothing more than a nebulous threat throbbing at the edge of her sensory input feeds – ghosted through the shattered buildings thirty-two degrees to the left. The servitor pivoted with a snarling melody of mechanical joints and opened fire with her heavy bolter. It bellowed its roaring staccato, shaking her entire body with the force of a seizure. After a second and a half the crude recoil compensators fused to her muscles and bones kicked in to keep the weapon aimed true. The cracked fragments of her teeth had already crashed together with enough force to start her gums bleeding. She felt no pain from this. The nerves in her gums had been stripped away to immunise her from that very reaction.

The other servitors followed her lead, bracing their feet and opening up with their own salvos of explosive bolts. None of the four units registered the impacts of accurate fire. Each of them recorded their misses in the simplified data engines at the cores of their skulls.

When their weapons cycled down with the target lost, the total number of successful hits tallied at zero.

'Committing to scout-predation subroutine,' AL-141-0-CVI-55-(0023) vocalised. She walked ahead, her auspex vista narrowed and focused in search of the surely wounded foe. Even her blunted brain could process the anomaly at play. Her targeting computations suggested the creature should have been struck by between twenty-nine and forty-four .998 calibre shells. It should no longer be moving at all, let alone moving swiftly enough to ghost away into hiding again. AL-141-0-CVI-55-(0023) vox blurted this anomalous detail to her handler.

She never acknowledged the reply. The daemon propelled itself from somewhere beyond the detection of her sensory array with a single contortion of its unnatural muscles, burying a claw-spear of ichorous cartilage into her torso, destroying every mono-programmed engine acting in place of her removed organs and annihilating her sole biological lung, which had miraculously survived unaugmented for over a decade.

'Enemy sighted,' the servitor tried to say. Blood and chips of broken teeth left her lips instead, gouting across the taloned arm that had killed her. The claw-spear lashed back from her body with a whip-crack of abused meat. The servitor fell to the ground in several wet, suffering pieces.

'Enemy sighted,' the largest of her component pieces tried to say once more. Her torturously primitive thought processes couldn't fathom why her primary weapon wasn't firing. She lacked the capacity for diagnostic function and her nervous system had been chemically rethreaded after her sentencing, so she had no idea that she had been torn asunder.

Bolters roared, utterly silent to the daemon, whose senses knew nothing of sound. The beast lunged three more times, jaws grinding shut on flesh spiced with artificial oil, claws lancing through brittle armour plating to the softer tissue beneath.

The blood that ran was impure and unsuited to beat through a human heart, corrupted by the nature of the cyborging procedure, but these impurities were irrelevant to the creature. It savoured the sensation of murder, wearing different skins and shapes until it adopted a form capable of crouching over and nuzzling at the streams of blood snaking their way across the mist-shrouded ground.

Two of the downed servitors protested voicelessly and limblessly, straining to go about their duties unto their dying breaths. On the ground, half lost in the low mist, the dismembered torso and head of the lead servitor miraculously survived – in no small amount of agony – for almost two minutes. The only thing she could sense beyond the pain of her damaged mechanical organs failing to sustain her was the proximity of the entity that had destroyed her.

'Enemy sighted,' she tried to warn her handler across the vox, though without functioning lungs or most of her throat she was unable to make any sound at all. The last thing she heard, recorded by her fading cognition core, was her killer feasting on the remains of her counterparts.

The beast, ruled by its illogical and depthless hunger, spread its great wings with aching crackles of ragged sinew. The blood of the slain servitors was saturated with chemicals, tasting grey upon the tongue and failing to hold the creature's interest. Hunger was pulling at the threads of the creature's form.

Far from satisfied, it ached to devour stronger souls and fresher blood than that of these false, reforged humans. Driven by murder-lust and blood-need, the daemon born of the first murder turned its array of inhuman perceptions towards a dead city that had, in recent years, been claimed by new invaders.

Sometimes it mattered very much from whence the blood flowed.

TWO

The boy who would be king
A false god's name
The Impossible City

THE BOY WHO would be king held his father's skull in his hands. He turned it slowly, running his fingertips across the contours of skinless bone. A thumb, still browned with field dirt, traced across the blunt ivory pegs of the gap-toothed death smile.

He lifted his eyes to the stone shelf where the other skulls sat in silent vigil. They stared into the hut's gloomy confines, their eyes replaced by smooth stones, their faces restored with the crude artistry of clay. It was the boy's place to remake his father's face in the same way, sculpting the familiar features with wet mud and slow swipes of a flint knife, then letting the skull bake dry in the high sun.

The boy thought he might use sea shells for the eyes, if he could barter with the coastal traders for two that were smooth enough. He would do this soon. Such things were tradition.

First he needed answers.

He turned the skull once more, circling his thumb around the ragged hole broken into the bone. He didn't need to close his eyes and meditate to know the truth. He didn't need to pray for his father's spirit to tell him what happened. He simply touched the hole in his father's head, and at once he knew. He saw the fall of the bronze knife from behind; he saw his father fall into the mud; he saw everything that had happened leading to this moment in time.

The boy who would be king rose from the floor of his family's hut and walked out into the settlement, his father's skull clutched in one hand.

Mud-brick huts lined both sides of the river. The wheat-fields to the east were a patchwork sea of dark gold beneath the eye of the setting sun. The village was never truly quiet, even after the day's work was done. Families talked and laughed and fought. Dogs barked for attention and whined for food. The wind set the scrubland trees to singing, with the hiss of leaves and the creak of branches forming their eternal song.

A ragged dog growled as the boy passed, yet fled yelping when he gave it no more than a glance. A carrion bird, hunchbacked and evil of eye, cried out above the village. A pack of other ragged children moved aside when he drew near, their ball game fading away and their eyes lowering.

His barefooted walk took him unerringly to the home of his father's brother. The man, darkened and hardened by his years in the fields, was sat outside the mud-brick hut, threading beads onto a string for his youngest daughter.

The boy's uncle uttered the sound that meant the boy's name. In response to this greeting, the boy held up his father's skull.

Many centuries after these events, citizens of even civilised and advanced cultures would often misunderstand exactly what a myocardial infarction was. The savage, constricting pain in the chest was due to blood no longer flowing cleanly through the heart's passages, causing harm to the myocardium tissue of the heart itself. Put simply, the core of a human being runs dry, trying to function with no oxygenated lubricant.

This happened to the boy's uncle when he set eyes upon the skull of his murdered brother.

The boy who would be king watched with neither remorse nor any particular hostility. He looked on as his uncle slid from his crouch onto the mud, clutching at his treacherous chest. He watched as his uncle's sun-darkened features pinched closed, ugly and tight in supreme agony as the older man shook with the onset of convulsions. He saw the necklace slip from his uncle's grip, the necklace that was being made for his young cousin, and would now never be finished.

Others came running. They shouted. They cried. They made the noises of language that spoke of panic and sorrow in a proto-Indo-Europan tongue that would come to be known as an early precursor to the Hyttite dialect.

The boy walked away, heading back towards his family's hut. On the way, he turned to the figure – the giant – clad in gold who walked nearby. Nordafrik war-clan tattoos curled on the towering warrior's face, curling from his temples to follow the curves of his cheekbones. The serpentine ink-curves, white against his dark flesh, ended upon his chin just beneath his mouth.

'Hello, Ra,' the boy said in a tongue that wouldn't be spoken on this world for many thousands of years. The language was called High Gothic by those who would come to speak it.

The golden warrior, Ra, went to one knee, dazed at the sight of a Terra that hadn't existed for millennia, a clean and fertile place still untouched by war. This world wasn't really Terra at all; it was still Earth.

With the giant kneeling and the boy standing before him, it was far easier to meet each other's eyes.

'My Emperor,' said the Custodian.

The boy rested a hand on the giant's chestplate, the fingers dark against the royal eagle. The boy's farm-worked palm, already rough despite his youth, ran along one golden wing. His expression was reflective, if not entirely serene. He didn't smile. The man that this boy would become never smiled either.

'You have never shown me this memory before,' Ra said.

The boy stared at him. 'No, I have not. This is where it all began,

Ra. Here, on the banks of the Sakarya River.' The boy turned his old eyes to the river itself. 'So much water. So much life. If I have been disappointed by the galaxy's wonders, it is only because we were fortunate enough to grow in such a cradle. There was so much to learn, Ra. So much to know. It pleases me for you to see what it once was.'

Ra couldn't help but smile at the boy's distracted, contemplative tone. He had heard it many times before, in another man's voice, as familiar to him as his own.

'I'm honoured to see it, sire.'

The boy looked at him, through him, and finally lifted his hand from the eagle sigil upon the Custodian's breastplate. 'I sense you have suffered a grave defeat. I cannot reach Kadai or Jasac.'

'Kadai is three days dead, my king. Jasac fell two weeks before him. I am the last tribune.'

The boy stared, unblinking. Ra noted the suggestion of a wince; the boy flinched at some unknowable pain.

'Sire?' the Custodian pressed.

'The forces unleashed in the wake of Magnus' misjudgement grow stronger. First a trickle, then a tide. Now, a storm's wind, unremitting, unceasing.'

'You will hold them back, sire.'

'My loyal Custodian.' The boy wheezed, soft and slow, his throat giving a tuberculosis rattle. For a moment his eyes unfocused. Blood ran from his nose, lining the curve of his lips.

'Sire? Are you wounded?'

The boy's eyes cleared. He wiped the blood away on the back of his dirty hand. 'No. I sense a new presence within the aetheric pressure. Something old. So very old. Drawing nearer.'

Ra waited for an explanation, but the boy didn't elaborate. 'You must do something for me, Ra.'

'Anything, my king.'

'You must take word to Jenetia Krole. Tell her...' The boy hesitated, taking a breath. 'Tell her it is time to enact the Unspoken Sanction.'

'It will be as you command, sire.' The words meant nothing to Ra. Once more he waited for elaboration. Once more he was denied.

'How did Kadai die?' the child asked.

'The outward tunnels are falling, my king. Kadai had advanced far from the Impossible City when the horde struck. I tried to reach his vanguard to aid their withdrawal.' Ra exhaled softly. 'Forgive me, sire. I tried.'

'What of the enemy in the outward tunnels?'

'Traitors from the Legiones Astartes have joined the Neverborn. The Eaters of Worlds, the Bearers of the Word, the Sons of Horus. Our outriders have witnessed Titans in the mist, and entities the size of Titans. They flood the main arterials and secondary capillaries.'

Unimaginable thoughts dawned and died behind the child's dark eyes. 'It was inevitable. We knew they would gain access to the webway before the war's end. You have Ignatum with you, Ra. You have the *Scion of Vigilant Light*. You will hold.'

'I am withdrawing all remaining forces to the Impossible City. The outward tunnels are lost, my king. Overwhelmed beyond retaking.'

'So be it,' the child allowed. 'Make a stand at Calastar. Sell every step as dearly as you are able. Is there more?'

'I am sending Diocletian to the surface to requisition more warriors. Whatever he can muster. My king, the Ten Thousand bleeds and the Silent Sisterhood bleeds with us, but if you could leave the Throne for even a brief time, sire, we could press deep back into Magnus' Folly. We could cleanse hundreds of tunnels.'

'I cannot leave the Golden Throne,' said the boy, curt, sharp. 'That will not change.'

'Sire...'

'I cannot leave the Golden Throne. Every route between the Imperial Dungeon and the Impossible City would shatter and flood with warp-born. You would be alone, Ra. Alone and surrounded.'

'But we could hold until you reached us.'

'Kadai made the same demand, as did Jasac and Helios before him.

Each one of the Ten Thousand represents genetic lore acquired over many lifetimes. Each one of you is unique. A work of art never to be repeated. I am miserly with your lives, when I spend so many others without a thought. I would not order the Ten Thousand into the fire if there was another way.'

'I understand, sire.'

'No. You do not.' The boy closed his eyes. 'The moment I rise from my place here, mankind's dreams will die.'

'As you say, my king.'

The boy held a hand across his face, cradling his pained features. 'What of the Mechanicum's work? What of Mendel?'

'The Adnector Primus is dead, sire. He fell when the outward tunnels began to collapse.'

The boy met Ra's stare, dark-eyed and cold. 'Mendel has fallen?'

'At a nexus junction in one of the primary arterials. He was part of Kadai's vanguard. I fought my way through to recover his remains.'

The boy's eyes lost their focus. It was like looking at the shell of a child, the preserved cadaver of a boy lost too young.

'My king?' Ra pressed.

'This is your war,' said the distracted boy. 'The Ten Thousand and the Silent Sisterhood must hold the webway. If you fail me, you fail humanity.'

'I will die before I fail you, Highness.'

Again, the boy winced. A cringe this time, the revelation of pain – fearless but true – flashed in the child's eyes. It drew him back to the present. 'Malcador and the Seventh are losing the war for the Imperium,' he said. 'That is a tragedy, but it is a tragedy that can be undone as long as I draw breath. The Imperium is ultimately just an empire. Empires can be reconquered, whether saved from ignorance or pulled back from the clutches of traitors.'

Ra's grin was a crescent of weary misery. 'We face a great many traitors, my king.'

The edges of the boy's mouth deepened. Not a smile. Never that.

A twitch perhaps. Another wince. 'There are always traitors, Ra. After the Ten Thousand performed the Asharik Silencing, I told you all that there was one sin far graver than betrayal.'

'Failure.'

'Failure,' the boy concurred. 'That holds true now, just as it did then, just as it always has. You cannot fail here, Ra. This is the war for humanity's soul. The webway is its battleground.'

Ra said nothing, for no words would do. He turned to look at this paradise of primitive humanity with their mud huts and their fields and their weaponless hands. Such innocence. Such unbelievable, terrifying innocence.

'The Sixteenth sails for Terra to crown itself king,' said the boy. 'Can you imagine if I allowed that to happen? A weapon, held in the wrong hands, installing itself as the lord of a whole species. Terra would be in ashes before the first sunrise.'

Ra swallowed at the sudden chill in the child's words. 'Sire, are you well?'

The boy cast a slow gaze across their surroundings, across the rows of tall crops, around the village where every other man, woman and child was ignoring them as though they no longer existed. 'This is where I spent my youth, working the soil and bringing life from the ground.'

The Custodian inclined his head, causing the servos in his collar to purr. 'I have given you my report, sire. Why do you keep me here?'

'So I may illuminate you,' the boy replied, speaking with a patience that bordered upon the preternatural. 'You watched that man die, did you not?'

Ra looked back over his shoulder, where the village folk were gathered around the fallen man, weeping and comforting in a loose, unwashed herd.

'I did.'

'That was my uncle. My father's brother.'

'You killed him,' the Custodian said without judgement.

'Yes. He struck my father from behind with a piece of sharpened bronze too poorly made to even be called a knife. Men had killed one another for generations before my birth, but this was the first slaying that had resonance to me, that changed my existence. It was illuminating.'

He paused for a moment, following Ra's gaze back to the noisy villagers. 'The very first murder was also a fratricide,' he said without emotion. 'Thousands of years before this, when men and women still owed as much to apes as to the form we know now. But it is curious to me – brothers have always killed brothers. I wonder why that is? Some evolutionary flaw, some ingrained emotional fragility written into mankind's core, perhaps.'

Ra shook his head. 'I have no way of knowing the emotions at hand, sire. I have no brothers.'

'I was being rhetorical, Ra.' The boy took a breath. 'This night was significant not for the murder, but for the deliverance of justice. For my uncle's deed, I stopped his heart's function and forced him to die. In eras to come this will be called the *lex talionis*, the law of retaliation, or more simply "an eye for an eye". It is justice itself. Hundreds of human cultures through time will embrace it. Some will do so out of brutality, others from ideals that they believe to be fair and enlightened, but it is a precept that runs through the marrow of our species.'

Ra pulled his gaze away from the weeping humans. He heard his sire's words, he knew the history and philosophy behind them, but the reason for them yet eluded him. His doubt plainly showed on his face, for the boy inclined his head in recognition.

'I told you that this is where it all began,' the boy said.

'Culture?' the warrior replied. 'Civilisation?'

The boy's momentary silence told Ra that he had guessed wrong. 'We are not far removed from those beginnings, Ra, either in distance or time. You could walk to the cradle of civilisation from here, where men and women made the very first city. When I leave this village, that is where I will go. That journey is coming soon. But no, that is not what I mean when I speak of beginnings.'

The boy turned the skull over in his hands, just as he had done in the hut before. 'This is where I first learned the truth behind our species. This very eve, as I held my father's skull and considered how to restore his features according to our burial rites. When I learned of his murder, it was a revelation into the heart of all of mankind. This is a world that has no need of you yet, Ra. It has no need for Imperial bodyguards, for it is a world that knows nothing of emperors, or warlords, or conquerors. And therefore it knows nothing of unity. Nothing of law.'

'You speak of leadership,' the Custodian said.

'Not quite. Every village already had leaders. Every family had patriarchs and matriarchs. I speak of kings. Givers of law, rulers of cultures. Not merely those who give orders, but those whose decisions keep a civilisation bound together. This was the night I realised that mankind must be ruled. It could not be trusted to thrive without a master. It needed to be guided and shaped, bound by laws and set to follow the course laid by its wisest minds.'

Ra breathed in the humid air of a land that knew nothing of the ravages it would suffer in the centuries to come. He smelled the sweat of the workers and the minerals in the river water, feeling his blood sing at the sensation of a truly unspoiled world. He didn't admire the crudeness of a people that lacked all but the rudiments of technology, but he felt awed at the species' humble genesis. To think that the Emperor, revered above all, had risen from such beginnings.

He looked the boy in the eyes, meeting that dark and knowing gaze, and spoke with a suspicion that curled the war-clan tattoos on his cheeks into a slight smile.

'Did this truly happen, sire? Were you really born here?'

The boy who would be king turned the skull over in his hands, his voice already distant with distraction. 'I shall barter with the coastal traders that come at the high moon. I will use shells for my father's eyes.'

'My king?'

The boy turned to him and spoke in the voice of the monarch he would one day become. He touched his fingertips to the Custodian's forehead, delivering a jolt of force.

+Awaken, Ra.+

RA OPENED HIS eyes. He hadn't slept, he had merely blinked. A half-second's span, within which he saw back to the Emperor's childhood in a time of almost primeval purity. He exhaled slowly as his senses returned to the here and now, among the monuments of a dead empire, within the necropolis of Calastar.

The eldar cathedral was silent around him. Its shattered dome let in the realm's ceaseless, sourceless light, casting shadows at inconsistent angles and reflecting oddly against the Custodian's golden armour. Something like mist clung to the ground with a greasy tenacity, whispering when disturbed by the tread of intruders.

And they were intruders here. Of that, there was no doubt.

A statue of an alien maiden stared down at Ra as he trained. She stood in silent reverence, her streaming robes and features sculpted from the same pillar of songspun wraithbone. One of her slender hands was outstretched in pleading benediction, the other rested, palm against her chest, perhaps warding away some unknowable heartache, perhaps simply conveying some alien torment that had once mattered to her worthless, dying species.

The spear in his hands, gifted to him by the Emperor, cast slashing silver reflections against the cathedral's walls. Its blade showed the scratches and scrapes of endless use with the perfection of ceaseless repair. He ran his fingertips along the flat visage of his own reflection in its mirrored surface, seeing the unmasked image he so rarely presented to the world.

Unease prickled at his flesh beneath the gold war-plate. He felt the weariness of the last five years clinging to him, the way cold wind slows the bones. Exhaustion wasn't alien to the warriors of the Ten Thousand – their strength lay in enduring pain and weariness, not banishing it – but he felt as he had in his initiate days, when the trials had seen him drained of blood by the Emperor's *vitafurtam* machines before subjecting him to the rigours of Custodian training.

Disgusted with himself at his failure of focus, Ra resumed the sparring briefly interrupted by the Emperor. His spear spun and whirled, singing its bladed song in the cold air. He lashed out with fist, boot and elbow, losing himself in the harmony of emptying his mind of all else.

Ra moved before the altar, forcing his muscles through the motions of the Fifty Forms, seeking the absolute focus that came through the alignment of body and mind. He shut out his surroundings, paying no heed to the pillared cathedral or the great altar, banishing the sound of his snarling armour joints and the thudding of his boots on the cracked wraithbone floor.

Soon he was perspiring freely, rivulets of sweat painting his dark features, following the lines of his cheekbones and the tattoos that snaked from his temples to the edges of his mouth. His spear whistled and whined, cutting the misty air. Its high-pitched slicing passage joined the melody of his heaving breaths.

Midway through the Third Form, the whirling spear slipped in his grip. The hesitation was miniscule, a fractional shift of the haft in his clutches, invisible to the observing eye. Ra clenched his teeth, leaning harder into the movements, chasing the elusive serenity.

He thought back to the Emperor's words, spoken in the memory dream of where the Master of Mankind had first risen among the fields and mud huts. Words of promise, of responsibility. The necessary command of humanity, to bring about law and progress.

He thought of his own words to Diocletian and Kaeria before sending them to the surface. *Scarcely one in ten of the Ten Thousand remain here.*

He thought of–

The spear slipped a second time. Ra tightened his grip before the blade could fall from his hands, but the damage was done.

He stilled in his movements, breathing heavily. The stone alien maiden still stared down at him, imploring without meaning. He turned from her, looking up through the shattered dome ceiling.

With no sun there was no day. With no sky there was no night. The Impossible City – none of its defenders used the eldar name except in amused derision – stretched on for kilometres in every direction. In *every* direction: to look to the east and the west was to see a cityscape of winding streets and crumbling towers rising at unbelievable angles, as though the ground curved in the shape of an unimaginably vast conduit. To look directly up was to see yet more districts of the ancient wraithbone city, kilometres distant and difficult to perceive through the realm's haze of mist. Those tall towers of smoothly curving alien architecture reached down just as the spires on the ground reached up. In truth, once a traveller approached the city there was no way of knowing where the true ground was; gravity was unchanged no matter where one walked. None of the Mechanicum's instruments could explain the phenomena, but precious few Martian instruments had worked reliably in this realm since first entering it years before.

It was here that the primarch Magnus had led an ocean of daemons in his wake, in his quest to warn the Emperor of Horus' treachery. And it was here, with the naivety of a proud and wayward god-child, that Magnus had set a sword to the throat of the Emperor's dreams. The catacombs of Calastar led directly to the Imperial Dungeon. If the Impossible City fell, Terra fell with it.

No one knew what cataclysm had ravaged Calastar in epochs past. Whatever had driven the eldar from the Impossible City was a mystery that the Imperial vanguard had no capacity to solve. Much of Calastar's core was a labyrinth of Mechanicum-born sections bolted into place, bridging the divide between the Imperial Dungeon and the dead hub-city itself, great spans of tunnels, bridges and channels forged by the blood, sweat and oil of countless priests in the Mechanicum's sacred red.

How the Emperor had first conceived this inconceivable project was a similar mystery, but the Mechanicum's greatest minds had followed the many hundreds of pages in each exacting schemata nevertheless. In reverence of his vision, a new caste of tech-priest had risen unseen by Terran and Martian eyes alike: the Adnector Concillium, the Unifiers.

And they had done it. They had bound Terran steel and Martian iron to avenues of senseless, unnatural materials previously shaped by long-dead, long-forgotten alien overlords. They had unified physical machinery with the psychically resonant matter of another dimension, and rebuilt the heart of an alien city.

The Impossible City was a gateway to the webway beyond. At its borders, the web began: thousands of capillary tunnels and great thoroughfares worming through the ancient alien network, leading to other worlds and regions in the galaxy. Every junction, every tunnel, every bridge, every passage leading out of the city – whether too small for anything but a lone human or vast enough for a Battle Titan – was held secure by entrenched Mechanicum thrall-warriors, Oblivion Knights of the Sisters of Silence and the Emperor's own Custodians.

Calastar was not made up of roads and sectors as the human mind would contextualise urban order, but was formed into winding pathways across plateaus and rises, all leading to apex structures of presumably great import. Each bridge spanned a stretch of infinite abyss. The Mechanicum's seers had reported that anyone falling from the bridges of Calastar would die of old age before reaching the bottom. Looking down into the nothingness, one could easily believe it.

A great spire rose highest of all in this district, the long promenades on the rising approach to it lined with eroded statues of what were initially believed to be eldar heroes.

'Gods,' Diocletian had said half a decade before, bluntly correcting the Mechanicum overseer responsible for the initial scouting probes. A hololithic map had cast flickering half-light across his features at the time. '*I have studied their profane and foolish lore. These are not merely statues of heroes. Many of them are depictions of the aliens' false gods.*'

And so it was named the Godspire. Tribune Endymion and the Soulless Queen now used it as a command centre.

The approach was once a scene of stunning, if alien, beauty. An eldar traveller in the time of that star-spanning empire's glory would have made a long, sloping ascent through gardens of luminescent singing crystals, across arcing bridges that curved over the bottomless void between tier platforms, before standing at the gates that led into the tower at the city's heart. Now the crystal formations were melted remains on their floating pedestals, many supporting the weight of automated Tarantula gun batteries. Most of the bridges were broken, their spans long since fallen into the nothingness below the Impossible City. The courtyard's once-open expanses housed a bustling hive of Mechanicum arming stations, supply depots, prefab barracks and landing pads.

In the cathedral, Ra levelled his gaze at the statue of the alien goddess-maiden once more. A filthy creature, forever staring with her slanted eyes. Who was she to judge the species that fought this new war in the ruins of her city? Her time, and the time of her people, was over. The eldar had been weighed by the implacable whims of the universe, and they had been found wanting.

His spear began its singing spin – the first blow shattered her reaching hand, sending sundered wraithbone clattering against the floor; the second cleaved through the goddess' neck, toppling her hooded head to the floor with an echoing ring. A great crack lightning-bolted across her pale features from forehead to throat. Her severed neck steamed from the vicious kiss of the spear's power field.

'A fit of temper?' came a gentle voice from the temple's entrance.

Ra turned slowly, irritated that he'd not sensed his visitors' approach. Truly, his humours were more unbalanced than he had realised if it was so easy to enter his presence undetected.

A woman and a girl. He hadn't expected them so soon.

'Not quite,' he admitted. 'I disliked how the alien stared at me.' He braced himself as they took the last few steps, resisting a hissed intake of breath at the pressure squeezing its cold fingers inside his skull. 'Commander,' Ra greeted the first figure, and 'Melpomanei,' he greeted the second.

The commander of the Silent Sisterhood had come accompanied by her aide – a girl-child of nine or ten years, her head shaved bare and marked with aquila tattoos, clad in a simple adept's robe of white, and beribboned with trailing parchments listing observances and rites that Ra had no desire to know of.

He immediately looked away from the soulless child. The Sister-Commander was bad enough alone, but these two together threatened to steal all hope of concentration. Breaking eye contact helped. Barely.

Krole's presence was even harder to tolerate, yet impossible to dismiss. She was a tall figure, clad in contoured silver plate and cloaked in the grey-brown fur of some great off-world beast; it was a struggle for Ra to fix his attention on her, yet difficult to concentrate on anything else. She ate at his thoughts the way the night eats light, dulling and dimming everything else around her. The sensation was far from pleasant – she pulled at the Custodian's focus not because she outshone everything else, but because she drowned and eclipsed it. To stand near her was to be near something hollow, something starving, something that sucked at the inside of Ra's skull.

She was empty. Nothing in the form of Something. A void masquerading as a presence.

Jenetia Krole greeted Ra with a nod, her eyes gently closing for the gesture. Her mouth remained hidden behind a great silver mouthpiece, surgically bound to her jaw and cheekbones. As she dipped her head, her high crest of red-dyed hair swayed gently. Ra knew of that ritual; the Sisters of Silence never cut their hair from the moment they took the Oath of Tranquillity. Krole's mane, even bound at the roots into a topknot, was long enough to reach the base of her spine.

If anyone could ever be in doubt as to her authority – were the evidence of their senses somehow not enough – all lingering misunderstandings would be banished by the Zweihander sword *Veracity* sheathed along her cloak, its hilt and grip showing over her shoulder. The lord of an entire species had once wielded that blade, before making a gift of it to the maiden who now bore it on her back.

'Greetings, Ra Endymion,' said the child at the Sister-Commander's side. Her voice was a delicate lilt at odds with the armoured warrior-maiden towering above her. Jenetia kept her sharp, dark eyes on the Custodian's. She lifted one hand, performing an artful series of gestures with her gauntleted fingers in the air before her chestplate.

The girl-child spoke for her mistress, staring just as brazenly as the older woman. 'You have received word from the Emperor.'

There was no accusation in Melpomanei's tone, nor in Jenetia's stare. An accusation would imply the possibility of doubt.

'I have,' admitted Ra. He didn't bother to ask how Jenetia knew.

Jenetia signed her reply, her dark eyes fierce but her gloved hand moving patiently and slowly. Many of the Ten Thousand no longer required their Silent Sister allies to employ the signs and gestures of thoughtmark at all, having fought at their sides for years and learnt to interpret their moods and meanings from even the slightest movements or facial changes. However, no one could claim that degree of familiarity with Commander Krole. Necessity demanded that Melpomanei remain a constant presence at her side. Something in Krole's appearance slid greasily from the senses, refusing to remain in his mind. He would be looking directly at her, watching her hands move in patterns he knew as well as any spoken language, yet sense and meaning came in fragments, as though he were hearing the barest scraps of any conversation.

'The withdrawal proceeds apace,' translated the bald girl. 'All forces are en route to the Impossible City.'

'He was so weary, Jenetia. I fear news of our failure only added to His burdens.'

'The failure was Kadai's,' replied the girl-child, watching her mistress' hands. 'Not yours. Not mine. Kadai reached too far, with too much pride, against your counsel and my wishes. Regardless, even Kadai could not have known of the hordes infesting the outward tunnels.'

Ra found precious little reassurance in that, no matter how true it might be. Krole noticed his reluctance. 'You and I will hold this vile city until it falls, tribune. And when it does, we will go back to fighting tunnel by tunnel, as we did when we were first ordered into the web. There is no other choice.'

Ra nodded and said nothing. There was nothing to say. Defeat was inconceivable.

'What are our master's wishes?' the child asked.

Ra forced the tension from his muscles, his armour joints murmuring at the subtle change in demeanour. 'He commanded me to tell you that you must enact what He referred to as the Unspoken Sanction.'

Krole's pupils were pinpricks in the alien light. 'He said this?' asked the young girl. 'You are truly certain?'

Ra knew better than to ask what the command might mean. The Sisters were an order apart. They had their secrets just as the Ten Thousand had theirs. Such was the Emperor's will.

Ra met the Sister-Commander's eyes. Sensing his sincerity, Krole nodded and signed a reply.

'Sister Kaeria Casryn will accompany Diocletian on his return to the surface,' said the young girl, 'in order to enact the Emperor's command.'

'As you wish,' Ra agreed.

Jenetia followed this with a question, her eyes darkly urgent.

'Will He join us?' Melpomanei asked.

'He remains bound to the Golden Throne. The forces besieging him outside the webway are growing in strength. He won't stand with us.'

Melpomanei watched her mistress' hands with a distant gaze, her mouth moving all the while. 'What He commands, we will enforce.' As she finished signing, Jenetia shifted once more. Rather than gesture a full sentence, she merely reached up over her shoulder, close to the back of her neck, and tapped her fingertips to *Veracity*'s long grip. It was enough for the child to translate. 'Is the Emperor well?'

'The pressure torments Him, but He remains resolute. Beyond the assault against His psychic defences, He spoke of a new presence, drawing near. Something old. Something already in the webway.'

Jenetia cut him off with a gentle wave of her hand. The motion moved seamlessly into more sign language. 'That is why I am here,' said Melpomanei. 'If you have finished your meditations, will you please come with me?'

'As you wish.'

The Custodian followed as the commander strode from the cathedral. Together they looked across the mist-wreathed vista of Calastar as the Impossible City stretched before them, around them, above them. Gone were the times such an insane view triggered disorientation in even Ra's enhanced senses. Now when he looked at the eldar ruins, he saw a bastion of Mechanicum-armoured and gun-platformed towers and bridges that would be infinitely easier to defend than several hundred separate tunnels – but with no margin for error. Withdrawing to the city itself meant losing any fallback point.

The entire city was an unlikely hybrid of Imperial technology grafted onto time-eaten eldar wraithbone. When it came to the Impossible City, Ra's awe had long ago been replaced by cold calculation and concerns of logistics.

And there stood the Godspire, where a golden Stormbird swinging in to land was silhouetted by the mist of middle distance. Three propellered Mechanicum ornithopters flapped in a slow arc above the landing gunship. The Koloborinkos flyers were mercifully silent at this distance. Up close, the machines' flapping wings and spinning rotors gave off a brutal roar.

Scarcely even a quarter of the Godspire's height, yet standing as a colossus above the marshalling Mechanicum forces, was the *Scion of Vigilant Light*. Freshly returned from one of the widest and tallest tunnels, the Warlord Titan was crawling with repair crews and maintenance servitors, who swarmed over its armour plating like ants clustering over a kill.

'Are you troubled?' Ra asked the Sister-Commander. 'I cannot read your expressions.'

Jenetia Krole elaborated with several gestures for the girl to speak aloud. 'Have you heard the reports of Thoroughfare HG-245-12-12?'

Ra nodded, paying heed to the background murmur of the dimmed vox reports playing at the back of his focus, whispering of the unfolding war. Fighters at the barricades fighting, falling, launching counter-attacks. The endless cycle. He had dulled them to near-mute while sparring and meditating upon the Emperor's will, yet he knew at once of which report the Sister-Commander spoke.

'I have already requested the Mechanicum send one of the Uridia-caste patrols,' Melpomanei qualified. 'They are less efficient since Adnector Primus Mendel was slain, but they assured me it would be done. Now you tell me the Emperor Himself has sensed this being's approach. A Protector and its war machines may not be enough. What would be powerful enough alone for the Emperor to sense? What could be out there?'

'There are a million things out there,' Ra replied, 'each more impossible than the last.'

Jenetia Krole signed her reply slowly and very clearly. 'This,' said Melpomanei, 'is something different.' She hesitated then, almost awkward as she signed once more. 'May I ask what form the Emperor's message took?'

Ra found the concept of what he'd seen, that pure and ancient world, difficult to frame in simple words. Jenetia noted his hesitation and stared, intrigued.

'He showed me His childhood,' the Custodian admitted, 'and told me of the moment He first learned that humanity needed rulers.'

It was gratifying, in a way, to see Sister-Commander Jenetia Krole – the Soulless Queen of the Imperium – show genuine shock. As much as Ra felt discomfort at the sight, it was still a revelation to witness. Her hands hesitated in the air before her breastplate before moving into another series of smooth signs.

'His childhood?' the young girl said. 'Elaborate please, Custodian.'

Ra felt the cold of Krole's fierce adamance. 'I saw Terra. More accurately, perhaps, I saw Old Earth.'

'Neither Kadai nor Jasaric ever spoke of receiving such a vision. The future, the present, the recent past, yes. All of those. Never a reflection of Old Earth.'

'I saw what I saw.'

'Yet why would He show you this?' the girl asked, her neutral tone conveying none of Jenetia's mute amazement.

'You ask a stone why the wind blows, commander. I don't know.'

'I must think on this. Thank you, Custodian.' The Sister-Commander clicked her fingers, beckoning the girl, and offered Ra a polite bow of farewell.

He didn't return it. He bowed and knelt only to one man. He did however force a weary smile to Melpomanei, aping the pleasant expression in an attempt to be disarming.

For the first time, Melpomanei spoke without her mistress signing. 'You look monstrous when you pretend to be human,' said the little girl.

Ra kept smiling. 'As do you, soulless one.'

THREE

Sunlight
First of the Ten Thousand
War council

DIOCLETIAN COROS STOOD upon the wall of a fortress that shouldn't exist, bathed in a halo of unwanted sunlight. While the first natural light to grace his skin in over five years should have been a blessing, he found himself pained by its unwelcome glare. His eyes were far too used to the sunless, skyless half-light of the realm below the Palace.

He wore weariness as a cloak, dulling his senses and pulling at his limbs. Exhaustion burned off him in an aura. The battle was over for now, yet still it leeched his strength. This weakness was new to him. He found that he loathed it.

Here on the high walls, Diocletian scarcely recognised his surroundings. The curving, graceful spires of the Palace's Ennara Towers were gone, replaced by a grey bastion of rockcrete and plasteel. Its minarets, once things of such stark wonder that pilgrims had been speechless upon seeing them, were ground down into rigid, armoured gun towers with rows of turrets and laser batteries aiming up at the sky. Crews of maintenance servitors, ant-small at this distance, worked under the guidance of robed tech-priests.

It was a truth seen across the city-sized Palace. Walls had become ramparts, towers had been rendered down into battlements, and what had once been the most glorious celebration of human ingenuity now stood as a monument to the species' capacity for betrayal.

Rogal Dorn and his stone-hearted Imperial Fists had done their work well – the Imperial Palace had been broken apart and reborn as a fortress beyond reckoning. Exalted architecture constructed in dozens of styles over several generations had been ground down under Dorn's cold gaze, reprocessed into something blunt and crude and inviolate.

A pair of Imperial Fists sentries marched past Diocletian and Kaeria, bolters held at rest. They saluted the Custodian and the Oblivion Knight with the symbol of Unification, banging their fists to their breastplates. Kaeria returned the salute.

Diocletian did not. He watched the two soldiers march on and felt discomfort at the sight of their pristine armour, the very same unease he'd felt upon first seeing the Palace's horizon turned into an endless ocean of grey battlements.

'How proud they look,' Diocletian said. The words came out as a murmur. His voice was still suffering from the blow that had almost severed his head the day before. 'Our noble cousins.'

Cousins. It was true, if one employed a generous licence with the truth. The warriors of the Space Marine Legions were raised through a similar process to the Ten Thousand, albeit in the coldest and crudest imitation. Diocletian had been reshaped at the fundamental level, with perfection threaded through his blood and bred into his bones. In contrast, his lesser cousins among the eighteen Legions were cut open by knives and implanted with false organs, relying on surgical ingenuity and genetic rituals to mimic the end result of better, more painstaking, more complete, work.

Kaeria said nothing. She shifted slightly, meeting his eyes with her own.

'True,' Diocletian allowed, replying as if she'd spoken. 'They have the right to pride. They have never failed, after all. But there's no honour in innocence.'

She raised an eyebrow, tilting her head just so.

'No,' Diocletian replied at once. 'Why would I?'

Kaeria's expression shifted to one of patient doubt.

'I don't envy them for their innocence,' Diocletian admitted, 'but I'm beginning to hate them for it.'

Kaeria raised an eyebrow.

'I know it's petty,' Diocletian snapped. 'That's enough of your judgement, if you please.'

With their faces bared, the Terran melange of their heritage couldn't be denied. Diocletian was a child of the Urshan Steppes, with the dusky skin and curiously light-brown eyes of that region's males, the latter standing as evidence to pre-Unity programmes of genetic processing. In paler contrast, Kaeria had the sun-bronzed olive flesh of the Achaemenid region, light of eye and dark of hair. The high topknot atop her shaven head showed tawny streaks in the thin Terran daylight.

Both bore the scabbed gashes and discolorations of recent battle. The walking wounded, returning to the surface with a grave tale to tell.

Diocletian held a stolen relic in his hands, dirtied by the very fact he had to touch it. Once more he fought the urge to grind it beneath his boot – an urge he'd been resisting since the trophy first came into his possession. He left it on the battlements, relieved to be rid of it even temporarily. Soon he would leave it with the Captain-General. Let Valdor add it to whatever archives were being collected by those still on the surface.

Mere years ago, it was forbidden for any to set foot here but the Ten Thousand, the Sisterhood and their mutual king. No others were permitted to walk where the Ennara Towers had risen into the polluted sky, for here the Emperor liked to contemplate the heavens, speaking to His most loyal warriors of His dreams among the stars. Now the battlements that had risen in the tower's place were swarming with gun-servitors and Imperial Fists overseers. The stars were eclipsed by a forest of drifting searchlights, hundreds of them aimed skywards at the gently toxic clouds. Each stabbing beam of light hunted the sky for foes that couldn't possibly be anywhere near Terra, but their readiness was unquestionable.

'So much has changed,' Diocletian said, looking across the vista of squat gun towers.

Kaeria started, surprised at his tone.

Diocletian fixed his companion with a neutral look. 'Never that,' he said. 'I don't mourn the loss of the Palace's beauty. I mourn what all of this represents. Dorn and Malcador have both conceded that Horus will reach Terra no matter what stands in the Warmaster's way. This is not precaution. This is making ready for war.'

Kaeria turned to look across the newborn battlements once more.

'What?' Diocletian asked.

She favoured him with a brief glance, the light of challenge in her eyes.

'I have no time for your disapproval, Sister. The tribune is not here. I am. Let that be the end of it.'

A low purr of servos and pistons cut into the silence that followed. Kaeria nodded towards a doorway in the nearby battlement tower. An archwright stood there, cowled by the cloak of her order. Three bronze-plated artificers with metalsmith tools rising from prehensile servo-arms linked to their hunched spines flanked the priest in silent vigil.

'Golden One,' came the tech-priest's greeting. 'Honoured Sister.'

'Archwright,' Diocletian replied. Many souls even among the Imperium's hierarchs would greet such a consummate artisan with no small gravitas. Kaeria bowed out of simple respect, but no warrior of the Custodian Guard would bow to anyone but his sire.

The archwright was an iron-boned elder, locked into a posture harness to keep her withered muscles upright, her cybernetics and bionics draped in a robe of Martian red and Terran gold. Whatever was left of her original face was surgically buried under reconstruction plating and an insect's portion of ferrotic eye-lenses. She was female only insofar as her original biological template had been female. That is to say, in the mists of centuries past, she'd been born as a girl-child on Mars. The frail construct that approached both warriors now had evolved far beyond notions of gender.

'I am Iosos,' the decrepit genius stated. 'I have been appointed to attend you before tomorrow's war council.'

'We need no attending,' Diocletian replied at once. 'We have artificers already deployed where we do battle.'

'The Captain-General believes that the sight of one of the Omnissiah's Custodians wounded and with his armour damaged will harm morale among the Palace's pilgrims and defenders.'

For a moment Diocletian couldn't even frame a response. He would have laughed had the notion not been so impossibly tragic, as if the morale of the refugees sitting safe within the Palace's new walls mattered one iota. The war was being fought and lost far from Terra, without any of those dregs even raising their weapons against the foe.

'Their morale,' he said with patience he didn't feel, 'is beyond irrelevant.'

'That may be so,' Iosos conceded, 'but the Captain-General insisted, Golden One. As First of the Ten Thousand, his command takes primacy.'

Kaeria gave her companion a sideways glance. Diocletian backed down, clenching his teeth to prevent himself speaking the dismissal on the tip of his tongue. Kaeria was right: this wasn't a fight worth having.

'You may work,' Diocletian said, his tone passionless in acquiescence.

The archwright drew nearer, leading the three servitors. Diocletian held himself motionless as the archwright ran skeletal metal digits across his war-plate. The shaking of the tech-priest's limbs ceased as liquid-pressure compensators in her arm supports adjusted for stability. Several of the struts in her harness vented tiny breaths of cryo-steam in a song of quiet hisses.

'Golden One,' she said again. 'I wish you to note the honour I take in being appointed to your service.' The vox-bleating that passed for her voice was entirely starved of emotion. Diocletian stood still as her black iron fingertips circled a ragged puncture in his breastplate.

Machinery clicked in her sloping, elongated skull as she calculated the necessary repairs down to levels of exactitude far beyond the human eye. The scratching and scraping of her meticulous inspection made the Custodian's teeth ache.

'Such incredible brutality,' said Iosos, 'inflicted upon such fine work. Such distinctive signatures in the ruination. Each wound in the auramite is something singular, something unique.'

A murmured hum filled the air around her augmented skull as its internal cogitators struggled to process the impossible findings.

'Incredible,' the archwright said at several intervals. And then once, 'Do you see, here? These lacerations in the auramite layers are quite literally impossible. The carved segments at the manubrium bracing could only have been caused by something that violates the laws of physics. Something that moves in and out of corporeal reality, appearing inside the metal, dissipating matter rather than breaking it.'

'Fascinating,' Diocletian replied, his tone dead.

The archwright's bestial allotment of eye-lenses cycled and refocused. 'It is, isn't it? And this, here, the metal itself is diseased. This isn't damage, it's infection. A contagion at the clavicle supports, taking root in the auramite layering as though it were flesh.'

'How much longer will your inspection take?'

'Impossible to calculate.' Three of Iosos' many hands reached for a particularly savage rent in Diocletian's shoulder layering, their fingers quivering in fascination. She caressed the ripped plating with the sound of knives scraping over stone. 'I understand you are forbidden to speak of what transpires in the Imperial Dungeon. But may I ask of the Omnissiah? How does the Machine-God fare since He exiled Himself to His sacred laboratory? What works of genius will He bring back to the surface when He once again deigns us worthy of His presence?'

Diocletian and Kaeria shared another glance. 'The Emperor is well,' the Custodian replied.

Iosos froze, her fingertips resting at the edges of the wound she'd been examining. The cogitators in her elongated skull whined as they struggled with what she had just heard. Before she could speak, she blurted a screed of mangled machine code.

'Your voice patterns,' she said, muted and low, 'suggest you are deceiving me.'

Diocletian bared his teeth in an expression that wasn't a smile, nor a grimace; it was a flash of fangs, the expression a lion might wear as it was backed into a corner.

'The Emperor lives and works on,' the Custodian said. 'Does that reassure you?'

'It does.'

When Diocletian picked up the war spoil from the battlements, three of Iosos' many hands reached for the relic, the tech-priest's inhuman fingers quivering in all-too-human awe. Diocletian pulled it back, refusing to let her steal it.

'Where are your manners, Martian?'

The archwright was respiring heavily. 'Where did you come by this?'

'I am forbidden from answering.'

Kaeria interrupted with a curt hand gesture. Diocletian turned, as did Iosos.

'You look exhausted unto death,' came a cold voice from the arched door.

Constantin Valdor, First of the Ten Thousand, strode towards them. The bitter Terran wind breathed against the side of his nationless features, carrying the scents of distant forges and the chemical tang of the great cannons lining the battlements. The Throneworld had always borne the alkali scent of history, from the dust of a million cultures waging war upon one another down the many millennia. The cycle was now mercilessly set to begin anew. For the first time in its long history, mankind's cradle had known peace. The Emperor had conquered all, and the Pax Imperialis rose from the rubble. Rather than do battle upon the already-wasted soil, humanity had sent its greatest, mightiest armies into the void, to wage war far from their home world.

And yet war was coming, against all reason. Terra's peace had been nothing but an illusion, born of false and foolish hope.

Kaeria greeted the Captain-General with a brief series of hand gestures. Diocletian saluted with the symbol of Unity, fist against his heart, a salute that Valdor returned.

'Where is Jasaric?' Valdor asked at once.

'Dead.'

'Kadai?'

'Dead. He died with Adnector Primus Mendel.'

Valdor hesitated. 'Ra?'

'Ra lives. He is overseeing the defences in the wake of Magnus' ignorance,' said Diocletian. 'I am here in the tribune's place.'

'Ra, then,' Valdor said at last, as if weighing the name and the consequences that came with it. 'So be it.'

Iosos and her artisan servitors worked on scanning, repairing and resealing Diocletian's battered plate. Sparks sprayed from the acetylene-bright fusion tools in the tech-priest's fingertips where she pressed them to the wounds. The servitor standing at his back had removed the auramite layering and now worked on reattaching the severed fibre bundle cabling around his right shoulder blade. Once glorious, Diocletian now looked closer to scorched, filthy bronze than Imperial gold.

By contrast, Valdor stood resplendent in wargear that bordered on ceremonial. Although thousands of scratches and scars marked its surface, and although each one spoke of a battle won in the Emperor's name, they were old wounds long healed. Artificers like Iosos had worked their arcane craft on each armour plate in the months since the Captain-General had last seen war, restoring it to a state of near perfection.

'What has happened?' asked Valdor. Hunger for knowledge of the Emperor's fate was writ plainly across his stern features.

Kaeria answered with a series of brief hand gestures.

'Routed?' Valdor shook his head at the madness of her explanation. 'How can the Silent Sisterhood and the Ten Thousand not be enough to deal with this threat?'

Kaeria repeated the gestures, a touch more emphatically.

'That's why we're here,' said Diocletian, adding his voice to her avowal. 'We need more warriors to hold the Impossible City.'

'What of the Ten Thousand?'

Kaeria and Diocletian exchanged glances. Weary of formality, the Custodian shook his head. 'There is much I can't say. So much is forbidden to be spoken here on the surface, even where no disloyal ears might hear. The last few months have taken a brutal toll, moreso than any of the preceding years. The Ten Thousand is gravely depleted. The Silent Sisterhood fares little better.'

He offered the trophy to Valdor. 'And then there is this.'

It was undeniably a Space Marine helmet. Which was, of course, impossible.

Constantin Valdor turned the relic over in his golden hands, examining every inch of its construction. The helm belonged to no Legion that Valdor could name, and its battered, cracked ceramite was a red worn by none of the eighteen Legions on the battlefield. Sanguinius' noble sons of the IX were clad in the rich red of arterial blood; Magnus' traitorous dogs of the XV wore a paler, more austere shade of crimson.

This helm was neither. Its ceramite was a proud scarlet, chipped away to reveal the gunmetal grey beneath and edged with a bronze-like metal so rife with impurities that it resembled brass.

The faceplate was a Mark IV design with significant variation. Its mouthpiece was rendered into a snarling maw, with the respirator grille crafted into clenched iron teeth. The helm's crests were a twin rise of rigid ceramite reminiscent of the angel wings of the First Legion's officer elite and the high curves of XII Legion champions, yet these were cruder, straighter than either Legion's crests, and emblazoned with brass bolts hammered into the red plating.

Each of these elements was unusual but not unprecedented. There were as many variants in armour mark design as there were foundries and forge worlds producing the arsenals of the Legiones Astartes. In that vein the helmet was marked with its forge of origin, but the stylistically jagged rune imprinted behind the right aural receptor wasn't one that had yet been seen in the Solar System.

'Sarum,' said Valdor at last. 'This was forged on Sarum.' He looked at Diocletian and Kaeria, though he didn't hand the helmet back to either of them. 'World Eaters.' He breathed the name like the curse it was becoming.

Diocletian nodded in agreement. 'The dead legionary wore the devoured world on his pauldron, and the back of his head was wretched with the cybernetics so prized by the Twelfth Legion.'

For a time, Valdor said nothing. What was there to say?

'Tell me everything,' he ordered at last.

Kaeria's hands wove a reply in the air.

'Then tell me all you can.' Valdor's voice was cold. 'Tell me whatever you can before we convene the war council.'

MALCADOR THE SIGILLITE, Regent of Terra, wore the unadorned robes of a Terran administrator. He led the war council, leaning on his eagle-topped staff as if he truly were the ageing councillor he appeared to be.

They gathered in the Sigillite's private sanctum, a tower that had thus far managed to evade the extensive reconstruction engineered by the Imperial Fists. Its ringed balcony was still open to the Terran night sky, and the shadows of great stone spheres drifted around the spire-top chamber in elliptical orbits, casting their shadows through the tall stained-glass windows. Nine primary globes drifted on heavy anti-gravitic suspensors, each one shaped of Albian whitestone. Dozens of secondary spheres, moons formed from dark basalt, orbited them in symbiotic turn, as though the tower's highest chamber were the Sun at the heart of the Solar System.

Malcador referred to it as his study. He liked to have select meetings here at the heart of a three-dimensional astrolabe, claiming it gave him a perspective too easily forgotten in the bowels of the Imperial Palace. He'd refused the tower's reconstruction on the principle of needing somewhere 'less militant, less miserable' to think when he was alone.

Despite Dorn's rank as Praetorian of Terra, Malcador's will had won through. It remained a rare needle of artisanal beauty in the Palace now reborn as a fortress.

Several of the most powerful men and women of the loyal Imperium stood around the circular hololithic table in the heart of the tower-top librarium. They were surrounded by the priceless scrolls and relics of a hundred lost cultures, from the oldest of Old Earth to the many that had faded out of existence during the Dark Age of Technology. Wooden carvings, broken statue fragments of white stone and black rock, scrolls encased in stasis fields, pistols and rifles and swords long since given over to rust and the patina of time's mercies – it was an eclectic collection to say the least.

Six souls stood opposite one another. Six souls deciding the fate of an empire. Whatever was decided here would go on to be disseminated throughout the Imperium's byzantine hierarchy, or sealed away behind seals and sanctions forever.

Diocletian looked at each of the hierarchs in turn, gathered around a table with no sides, so that all were rendered equal: Fabricator Locum Trimejia of Mars; Malcador, the Imperial Regent; Primarch Rogal Dorn of the Imperial Fists; Kaeria, Oblivion Knight of the Silent Sisterhood; Captain-General Constantin Valdor of the Ten Thousand; and Diocletian himself.

He had not seen the Mechanicum's new high priestess before. Trimejia was a stick-thin revenant hooded and cowled in Martian red, showing nothing but her skeletal silver fingers at the ends of her robe's sleeves and a featureless faceplate in the shadows of her hood. She spoke only through the vox-grilles of the three servo-skulls orbiting her on tethered, hazard-striped cables. Three voices in unison, all artificially female.

'The Fabricator General requests word from the guardians of the Great Work.'

'We bring word,' Diocletian replied, gesturing to the World Eaters helm on the central table. 'And evidence.'

'The Adnector Primus no longer conveys reports to the Fabricator General,' Trimejia pressed. 'Zagreus Kane, blessings upon him, believes our representative in the Great Work has met his end in the course of service to the Omnissiah.'

'Kane believes right,' Diocletian replied. 'The Mechanicum forces within the webway answer to their divisional overseers now. Adnector Primus Mendel was killed several days ago in the fall of a tunnel nexus.'

'Inconvenient,' said Trimejia's three servo-skulls.

'Tribune Endymion led a counter-attack to bring aid to the survivors. He recovered Mendel's body.'

'An irrelevancy,' the tech-priestess blurted back. 'His mortal remnants are of no value to the Mechanicum. At most, his organic matter will be reprocessed for servitor sustenance fluid packs.'

Diocletian bared his teeth, resisting the urge to curse at the Martian witch. Good men and women had died in that counter-attack.

Dorn, a warrior-king among the Space Marine Legions, wore no armour. In his pale robe he looked monastic and austere, radiating a halo of impatience. He had his battles to plan and fight. He had his own wounds to lick. The stern patrician of the Imperial Fists, adamant in his cold-eyed sincerity, never lifted his gaze from the Custodian and the Sister, side by side.

'Report in full,' he commanded them.

Diocletian bristled at the order and caught sight of Kaeria's subtle shift in posture. The Sister stood with her arms crossed over her breast-plate, moving a single finger in a miniscule twitch. Her fingertip rested against the lightning bolt engraved on her bicep plating.

'You think me blind to your coded warnings to one another, Oblivion Knight?' Dorn asked Kaeria.

Kaeria showed no sign of attempting a reply. Diocletian answered for her. 'She was merely cautioning me against a show of temper at your presumption, Lord Dorn. Only one man may give me orders. You call that man "Father".'

The primarch watched them both, unblinking, before finally nodding with the curtest gesture of his head. 'A thousand matters pull at my mind. Your point is made. Please continue.'

'There is little to say,' Diocletian admitted. 'The last waves that struck the tunnels reaped a significant toll. All of the ground we claimed within Magnus' Folly is swarming with the aetheric invaders, and we are being beaten back to the walls of the Impossible City. We can hold Calastar far more easily than we can maintain our grip on the outward tunnels. For now, the link between the webway and the Imperial Dungeon remains stable: the Mechanicum-made routes through the city's catacombs remain sheathed in the Emperor's protection and cleansed of aetheric activity.'

'For how long?' asked Dorn.

Diocletian steeled himself. He gestured to the helm on the table, knowing it would offer a far finer explanation than mere words. 'You know what this portends. The Traitor Legions have gained access to the webway. Behind them march silhouettes of Titans. We were already hard-pressed, but now our foes have multiplied. We are losing tunnels in Magnus' Folly at a faster rate than ever before. We have lost our grip on the wider web and no longer have the numbers to advance. For now, the Impossible City's catacombs are safe. We can hold the reconstructed walls of Calastar for as long as we must.'

Malcador, silent until now, dipped his hooded head. 'Where is Tribune Endymion?'

You know, thought Diocletian. *You know Kadai and Jasar have fallen. You know Ra is the last tribune. Ah, to catch one of your spies, you cunning creature.* 'Ra is engaged in battle,' the Custodian said. 'I am here in his stead.'

During Diocletian's retelling, as brief as it was, Dorn had moved to the wide windows, watching the great metal globes passing by in their elliptical drifts. The daylight sky was darkened by the passing of one of Terra's orbital plates, leaving the primarch's features in shadow. His face was stone, betraying no hint of emotion.

Valdor said nothing. Trimejia was equally silent. Even her skulls had

ceased their circling, now bobbing in the air by her shoulders, looking at Diocletian with eye sockets filled with sensoria needle clusters.
The Sigillite leaned more heavily on his staff, making no attempt to
reclaim control of the command briefing in the wake of Diocletian's
confession.

Dorn turned from the window. Diocletian hated the sudden emotion that lifted the primarch's features and brought light to his eyes.

'If you need warriors,' he began, 'then my Legion…'

'No.' Diocletian said the word the very same moment that Kaeria
signed a curt *Negative.*

'No?' As ever, Dorn was calm.

'It is the Emperor's will that the Imperial Fists remain outside the
Dungeon.'

'That was my father's will when He had the Ten Thousand and the
Sisterhood at full strength,' Dorn countered. 'When He is starved of
soldiers and the Traitors mass within the webway, how can His command remain the same?'

'How many of your Fists even remain on Terra?' Diocletian countered. 'Four companies? Five?'

'I have several companies stationed in the event of rebellion from
among the conquered territories.'

'And the rest of your Legion, Rogal?'

'Scattered across three segmentums, and principally deployed in the
engagement spheres of the Solar War. Even so, I offer what I can spare.'

'Which is next to nothing.'

'Even so.'

'It is the Emperor's will,' Diocletian repeated, 'that the Imperial Fists
remain outside the Dungeon.'

'Tell me why.'

'I can only guess,' said Diocletian. His gaze flicked downwards to the
deactivated helm taken as a trophy.

'You believe that my men cannot be trusted?' Dorn replied, perfectly
calm. 'That they would turn their coats as Angron's dogs turned?'

'*Trust*,' said Diocletian, laying into the word. 'I am not free with my trust these nights, Rogal Dorn. If we could *trust* the warriors of the Legions, the galaxy wouldn't be aflame and severed in two by a primarch's ambition. I won't argue with you, Praetorian. I merely bring the Emperor's will back to the surface.'

Dorn leaned his knuckles upon the table and breathed through closed teeth. Although all knew him as a soul of majestic composure, his dislike of Diocletian and the Ten Thousand's secrecy was deeply etched across his being. Malcador's exhalation was subtler, slower, somehow more tense. Only Trimejia showed no emotion whatsoever; her faceless visage was capable of none. Her hood dipped slightly. Something clicked behind her faceplate. The three skulls began drifting around her in a reversed orbit.

'What of the Omnissiah?' her three skulls asked in harmonic monotone.

'He is unchanged. He remains enthroned and unmoving, unresponsive to any stimuli. He has not spoken since taking the Golden Throne. The forces He battles in the wake of Magnus' ignorance are beyond reckoning. We know no more than we already knew.'

'If He remains unspeaking,' Dorn's colourless voice enquired, 'how has He requested more warriors?'

'The Ten Thousand speaks for the Emperor,' Diocletian replied at once.

'We require more information,' said Trimejia's drifting servo-skulls. 'More quantifiable data on the Omnissiah's will. Speak. Enunciate. Explain.'

'The Ten Thousand speaks for the Emperor. What we ask for is no different than if our lord asked Himself. It has ever been thus.'

Silence reigned.

Dorn looked back to the overcast sky. His voice was softened by the moment's immensity.

'Magnus, my brother, of all your mistakes this one is by far the most grievous.' Once more he looked over his shoulder at Diocletian and Kaeria. 'I see now why you came in person.'

Diocletian nodded. 'If the Traitors reach Terra–'

'It is a matter of *when*, prefect, not *if*.'

'As you say. When the Traitors reach Terra, Lord Dorn, you must be ready to defend the Palace without the Emperor's guidance.'

If Dorn was tormented by the notion, he showed no sign. The one implacable son, stone and stoicism in moments when all of his brothers would be fire, spite and honour.

'I'd dared to hope the Emperor's secret war was going well. The audacity of such optimism seems foolish in hindsight, does it not? That I dared to imagine, come the final day, we might only face annihilation from the skies above Terra, not from beneath its surface as well. Horus and his forces are already in Segmentum Solar. Now the Imperial Dungeon is at risk of falling. Tell me, Diocletian, could we lose this war before Horus even sets foot on Terra?'

'Yes,' Diocletian answered at once.

'Is it likely?'

'If all remains the same? Yes, we will lose. If our requisition demands for new warriors are not met? Yes, we will lose. If the enemy is further reinforced? Yes, we will lose.'

'Then what is your plan? Where will you find these soldiers?'

'I will aid them in this matter,' Malcador said. 'There are possibilities beyond the obvious.'

Rogal Dorn, even calm, was relentless. 'Does the Emperor's edict of secrecy remain in force?'

Kaeria signed a brief affirmation, to which Dorn nodded. 'Then you are consigning any volunteers to death,' said the primarch. 'Sacrificing the Mechanicum's servitors is understandable. Culling them, if necessary, is a loss but hardly immoral. Euthanising any human survivors you pull down into the webway is a far bleaker proposition.'

Kaeria's reply was nothing more than a glance to Diocletian and the subtlest gesture of one hand. The Custodian translated: 'The Lady Kaeria's point takes primacy here, Praetorian Dorn. We may not need to cull any survivors at all if we continue losing ground.

The enemy will see us all dead, and your concerns of morality will be meaningless.'

Dorn's jaw tightened. 'Listen to yourself, Diocletian. Hear the words you are speaking and the course you advocate.'

Necessity overcomes morality, Kaeria's hands signed in the air before her breastplate. *Never without regret. Never without shame. Yet even immoral victory must outweigh moral defeat. The victor will have a chance to atone if conscience demands. The vanquished lose any such opportunity.*

'You quote my own brother at me?' Dorn narrowed his gaze. 'Roboute is not here, Oblivion Knight. Would that he were. In his absence, I am Lord Commander of the Imperium.'

Diocletian resisted a flare of temper at the performance unfolding before his eyes. 'This is base hypocrisy, Lord Dorn. How often have your Imperial Fists prided themselves on enduring conflicts that proved to be flesh-grinding stalemates to other forces? Now you object to the execution of... chaff... to keep the Emperor's greatest secret. How is this even worth discussing?'

Dorn's armoured gauntlet crashed onto the central table, causing the hololithic image of the Sol System to jump and flicker. 'We are speaking of more than my own sons. Their lives are coin I may spend as I see fit, but you have been underground for five long, long years, and the Ten Thousand isn't the only force to have bled itself dry. This isn't the Great Crusade, Custodian. You cannot annihilate loyal souls on a whim. The meaning of "necessity" has changed now that we draw near to the final days of this war, Diocletian.'

The words echoed in the air between the gathered hierarchs, as solemn as any confession of guilt.

We will not argue this matter, Kaeria signed, though even she seemed hesitant now.

'We will gather the army required,' said Diocletian. 'With the Sigillite's aid, if he sees fit to grant it. And I will bring your reservations to the Emperor when circumstance allows.'

'That is all I ask,' Dorn acquiesced with grim consent.

Trimejia closed her left hand, summoning the servo-skulls to drift together and dock with the ports on her hunched spine. Malcador made no reply at all. Diocletian wondered how much of this the Sigillite had already known.

'If that is all,' said Malcador, 'I believe we are finished here.'

Trimejia vocalised a spurt of irritated code.

'Is that an objection, archpriestess?'

The docked servo-skulls thrummed, a chorus of skinless faces desperate to speak. 'Mars,' the three probes voiced at once. 'The Mechanicum beseeches the Omnissiah for permission to retake Sacred Mars.'

Dorn stiffened. 'Not here,' he said, curt and clear. 'Not now.'

'The Fabricator General is aware of your refusal, Praetorian. He bade me take my request directly to those waging war at the Omnissiah's side.'

She leaned closer to Kaeria and Diocletian, spindly and inhuman, so frail for one who commanded such authority. 'Mars must be retaken.'

Malcador's staff thudded upon the floor. 'Mars will be reconquered when we have the resources to do so.'

Diocletian and Kaeria remained silent throughout the exchange. They shared a glance, hardly blind to the tension. Malcador's gesture was a plain request for them to leave.

'This meeting is concluded,' said the Regent of Terra. 'You have our gratitude, Sister, Custodian.'

Before any of the hierarchs could argue otherwise, Diocletian and Kaeria strode from the room. There was a great deal yet to do before they could return to the Dungeon.

FOUR

Anomalies
Bodies in the mist
End of Empires

ALPHA-RHO-25 DIDN'T CONSIDER himself burdened by any particular degree of sentiment. Even so, there was a pang of loss as he came across the dead servitors. Whoever had constructed them had done so over many weeks, with painstaking care and expertise, to serve in the Omnissiah's name. And now they were reduced to… this.

Such a waste.

As one of the Mechanicum Protectors assigned to the Unifiers, his role was simple. He was to stalk through the webway, overseeing the Mechanicum's restoration work and shoring up their defences in the outward tunnels – that region known by the vanguard as Magnus' Folly. It fell to him and those like him to defend the outskirts of the Impossible City and guard the Unifiers working in the tunnels leading deeper into the web. Now it fell to him to watch over the retreat.

A decision that had been too long in coming, by the Protector's analytic perceptions. Casualties had risen starkly in recent months. Too few defenders stretched too thin through far too many tunnels. Falling back to the defensible bastion offered by the Impossible City was the logical course of action.

Alpha-Rho-25 had taken part in one thousand, six hundred and eighty-three individual skirmishes since being brought into the Imperial Dungeon five years before. His recordings of individual foes destroyed were accessible to the archpriests who coded his orders, but he didn't like to review them himself or tally the totals. That kind of behaviour seemed close to self-satisfaction – what a full-blood human might call smugness – and therein lay danger. To be satisfied with oneself was to consider oneself perfect, to abandon all hope of refinement and improvement. A tragic delusion indeed. Perfection did not exist outside the Omnissiah Himself.

No, one must always evolve. To consider the stasis of satisfaction was nothing more than a vaguely amusing heresy.

Nor did Alpha-Rho-25 find himself burdened with the weight of superstition. These creatures he had fought now for five years were hardly 'daemons' in the terms referred to in human mythology. They were entities of incorporeal origin, breaching the barrier between the unmapped tides of the aether and the material universe. Aliens, then. A xenos breed from the warp. It was quantifiably true.

If pressed to be truthful on the matter, he found the relentlessly warlike entities no more or less disgusting and unnatural than the perfidious eldar, in whose ruins the Imperial Vanguard had made their fortress. All alien breeds suffered from the unholy imperfections of their forms. That was the beginning and end of the matter.

Still…

Still.

These 'daemons' were violent beyond any other species Alpha-Rho-25 had encountered. And they took a great deal of effort to extinguish. The fact they bled was no guarantee they would die. Many of them refused to even bleed at all. That was quite galling.

He hunted alone in the dayless and nightless flow of time that shrouded the Impossible City. His hunting grounds on this operation were far from the Godspire, a full forty kilometres away, where the eldar ruins grew ever more decayed. Contact had been lost with the boundary servitors guarding one of the many thousands of capillary tunnels leading deeper into the webway, which was by no means unusual.

However, questions remained. These boundary servitors had been guarding a far-flung passageway with significant defence batteries and gun emplacements. It shouldn't have fallen at all, let alone so swiftly and with so little warning. Subsequent contact had been lost with the reinforcement servitors, their handler and then again with the three squads of Thallax war machines sent forwards from the tunnel's second barricade to ascertain the gravity of the situation. All of this was less than typical.

And so, while the rest of the Imperial vanguard withdrew and abandoned the outward tunnels, Alpha-Rho-25 went hunting back through them.

He loped onwards, lens-eye scanning, panning. The sloping walls of this tunnel were glossy white, something that seemed a cousin to clean marble and polished enamel, yet was entirely unrelated to either.

Like walking through the marrow of something's bones, thought the Protector, finding the notion disturbingly organic. Who had they been, those that ruled here before the interloping eldar colonists had even dreamed of setting down foundations? Had the original creators of this realm used the bodies of their immense, fallen god-foes as material for its construction? Nothing would surprise Alpha-Rho-25 about those long-dead entities' intentions or methods. He had seen too much in the last five years to cling to surety about anything here.

En route he passed Mechanicum Unifier priests and their battle-servitor defenders in droves, returning to Calastar. The mist swirled with the passage of bulk conveyors and tracked lab-platforms, yet it never dissipated.

Even the vastest tunnels, their sides invisible to visual or echolocating perception, had a clinging oppressiveness that sat ill within the Protector's mechanical guts. As honoured as he was to have been activated and deployed within the labyrinth of the Great Work, he would not miss the eerily human pressures it placed upon his thoughts. Discomforts he'd believed himself long past pulled at his perceptions every time he left the web's Mechanicum-engineered sections.

Troubling reports crackled across the vox of warden servitors in other outward tunnels committing sacred prayers of violence and failing to destroy their target. Something – a single entity – was testing their defences, then drawing back each time. Tunnels that had long since been repaired and which had seen no battles in years were reporting the expenditure of horrendous amounts of ammunition. Many then ceased reporting at all. Other Protectors were being released to cover the webwide retreat, but Alpha-Rho-25 was the first, already close to his destination by the time the Godspire unleashed more of his kindred.

With his back-jointed legs propelling him into a ragged sprint capable of outrunning a Triaros conveyor, he reached the outward tunnel barricade swiftly after setting out from the Godspire. A series of Mechanicum-constructed barriers and gunnery platforms faced away into the tunnel's mist, the empty cannons tracking on unoiled mechanics, panning left and right over a vista of eldar rubble. Perhaps it had once been a smaller outpost far from Calastar, in the age of eldar supremacy. There was no way of knowing. There would never be a way.

He found AL-141-0-CVI-55-(0023) first, which was fitting. She had been the lead servitor of the boundary team. Her torso lay across a low broken wall of eldar architecture – *wraithbone*, they called the material, with their species' pathetic sense of melodrama – with her skull cracked open and leaking into the ground mist. The mist possessed some kind of preservative properties for the destruction had occurred hours ago, yet the cranial residue was still wet. Another reality deviation that wasn't the Protector's duty or place to analyse and codify.

Alpha-Rho-25 crouched by the remains, the claws in place of his feet finding easy purchase on the rubble and his piston-legs hissing as he lowered himself. His cloaked robe rippled briefly in a sourceless breeze. Another anomaly. He ignored it, drumming his taloned metal fingers on his sphere-jointed knees as he mused.

The nearby passageway leading deeper into the webway was ringed with what seemed to be eldar bone plating and their ridiculous gemstone circuitry. Alpha-Rho-25 had seen the Mechanicum's analyses describing the extent of eldar colonisation within the web. The original creators of this realm had constructed the webway from psychically resistant materials that defied corporeal understanding, but evidence of eldar habitation and restructuring was evident throughout the web. The sprawling necropolis of Calastar was only one of its kind, albeit the largest yet found, and eldar ruins lay throughout many dozens of outward tunnels.

The bodies of the other battle-servitors were in similar states, as were the Thallaxi robots several dozen metres to the north. Intriguingly their lightning guns' chainblade attachments, fallen from slack hands into the mist, still sniggered in idle activation.

The servitors were dismembered but undefiled by further punishment. The Thallaxi's body-shells were broken, their cranial domes shattered, and the organic cognitive slurry within now ran out, congealing greasily in the golden fog.

The daemon sensed movement. Motion prickled at its perception, jabs knifing against the searing muck of its thoughts. It abandoned its idle prowl, turning away from its explorations through the outward tunnels, drawn back to the site of its first hunt in this cold realm. It had to feed. Already its flesh steamed with the slow smoke of threatened dissolution. Stalking the infinite tunnels was, thus far, achieving little. Boundary servitors were chemical-blooded and grey of soul – their deaths offered scarce sustenance, yet they flooded the tunnels in numbers beyond the creature's crude reckoning.

The soul it sensed now was brighter than those it had devoured before. The light of this new spirit gleamed through air and stone alike, a beacon amidst oily black vision. The pain of starvation lent conviction to the creature's movements. It moved faster and faster, wraithing through the tunnels, between the ruins that populated them.

With no one else nearby – no one capable of intelligent conversation, at least – Alpha-Rho-25 allowed his annoyance to show across his angular and not particularly attractive features. In public, he looked like a man always on the edge of scowling. In private, he crossed over that edge and consistently indulged.

Servo-skulls drifted around him, scanning, always scanning. Their anti-gravitic gliding dispersed some of the higher tendrils of mist in their wake. Alpha-Rho-25 paid scant heed to the drones' empty readings scrolling in Martian hieroglyphs across his vambrace monitor. If the osseous probes found what had done this, well, then he'd pay attention.

Instinctively, the prehensile mechadendrite attached to his spine slipped free from the bottom of his robes. The tail-whip gleamed with an armoured dataspike at its tip, more than capable of punching through a daemon's ectoplasmic corpus. Alpha-Rho-25 let the coccyx-bonded tail rise up, scorpion-like, over his left shoulder.

Five years, he thought, stalking away from the Thallaxi and back to the slain servitors. Five years since he strode across the red dunes of Sacred Mars. Five years since he filled his respiratory tract with the metal-tasting holiness of Martian air.

And soon the conflict would be over, one way or another. All the violence and loss of life and materiel to reach beyond the Mechanicum's sections of the webway, at last establishing a fortress at Calastar – meaningless. Each crusade vanguard that pushed out from Calastar to fight through the outward tunnels – meaningless. Tribune Kadai Vilaccan had led the most recent foray, and all calculations had signified a crushing victory. Yet not every qualifying factor had been available to insert into those equations. How could they have known what was streaming towards them through the outward tunnels?

Triumph had been torn from their grasp by sheer weight of numbers.

Severe casualties had been expected given the nature of their foes in this fascinating realm, but Alpha-Rho-25 had high enough clearance to know the truth. Their losses were far beyond the point of sustainability. The last five years had practically bled the Mechanicum's Unifiers and their defenders dry, while the Ten Thousand could – at best – call upon perhaps a thousand remaining warriors. The Silent Sisterhood kept their numbers a mystery to all outside their order, but it was irrelevant – they had always been the rarest of breeds. They, like the Legio Custodes, like the Unifiers themselves, were a precision blade. Not a bludgeon.

Tribune Endymion had sent ambassadors to the surface but Alpha-Rho-25 was a pragmatic being. Reinforcements from outside the Imperial Dungeon, if they were even acquired, would be from weaker souls far less trustworthy than the vanguard's current elite.

The fact that they would have to be extinguished for the secrets they had seen in the webway was irrelevant to the Protector. Let them die. There was no greater testament to a life than to lay it down for the Omnissiah's Great Work.

Still, they might make useful daemon-fodder. Reborn as he was for the holy act of slaughter, the possibility of more briefly warmed him.

AND THE DAEMON sensed that warmth. It hunted a soul that knew death, one that had reaped life in the long years of its existence. Every butchered life was a scent and a flavour in its own right, needling at the meat of the daemon's mind.

The creature latched its senses upon those memories of violence now, reaching for those bloodied edges of the soul's aura, and its stalking sprint became a shrieking wind.

ALPHA-RHO-25 CROUCHED BY AL-141-0-CVI-55-(0023) once more, scanning her with the ectoplasmic detectors in his palm-auspex. The cyborged woman had been thoroughly dismembered. Torn apart not by bladed weaponry but by brute strength. The wounds were rife with aetheric signifiers.

Alpha-Rho-25 began the process of harvesting her final cognitions, which necessitated sawing through the brain pan and plunging a data-spike into one of her internal cranial connectors. Intriguingly, in all the info-feeds that spilled out in numerical echo of the servitor's last thoughts, there was nothing identifying her warp-born assailant. She hadn't been able to make out any visuals of her killer. For all intents and purposes, AL-141-0-CVI-55-(0023) and her cohorts had been firing at nothing.

There was more – somehow, the lobotomised woman's very last thoughts had been of her human life, and the weeping children that had been pulled from her hands as she was hauled away, screaming, on her way to reprocessing. Alpha-Rho-25 discarded the data as irrelevant: a tediously emotional misfire of a dying, imperfect biological engine.

The Protector rose and stalked over to the next slain servitor, his bloodied saw still whining.

One of the servo-skulls ceased its circling, turning to stare out across the eldar ruins. A few seconds later it started emitting a lengthy vocal chime. A screed of data spilled across Alpha-Rho-25's vambrace screen, none of it giving any insight beyond the detection of unspecified inhuman movement, though in this case that was detail enough.

The Protector stood straight, closing his human eye as he focused through his chunky bionic lens. His false eye immediately began to flash with warning pulses of its own, vision filters clicking and purring as they overlaid one another. All he could see was the detritus of the dead eldar settlement scattered across the tunnel. Its low, time-eaten walls were an amusing monument in the webway to a race too arrogant to realise it was dead.

Although it had deeply offended his sense of competency, Alpha-Rho-25 had brought some companions with him via Triaros conveyors. Without looking, he keyed a series of commands into his bracer's runepad. The cohort of nine Castellax battle-automata at his back began active seek-and-destroy protocols, circling him with their great iron strides shaking the ground. The belt-fed cannons on their shoulders panned around with hydraulic whines. He didn't like them – the smoother-hulled Kastelan robots were far more reliable and not born of erratic mongrel intelligences – but a man worked with what he had at hand. He'd recognised the potential need for firepower, and the automata provided it.

Movement drew his gaze to the east, though his focusing lens wouldn't align and his scanning reticule kept slipping its locks. Something was there in the distance, defying his scrutiny.

Alpha-Rho-25 cycled through vision filters, overlaying display upon display, negating those that showed no new data. During this round of perplexed and increasingly irritated staring that took, by human perceptions, almost no time at all, he deployed all four of his primary weapons from all four of his arms: two long-taloned chordclaws thrumming with hostile sonic fields, two transonic stabbing blades scraping against one another in anticipation. The propulsion vanes on his back-mounted power unit began to spin, setting his cloak rippling.

The last vision filter he tried was a confused blend of thermoptical intensifiers with echolocation results rendered as precise binaric data instead of a visual impression.

That one worked.

Behind him, with their sensory feeds linked to his, the Castellax automata saw what he'd just seen. They reacted with the savage crashing of nine mauler-pattern bolt cannons opening up in brutal harmony.

THE DAEMON TOOK form at the hunt's apex, coalescing into a thing of claws and blades and spines – the idea of evisceration made flesh. It roared its name as it descended on burning wings, a name that was a sound and a memory as much as a word. It screamed the hot-blooded yells made by the first man ever to take another man's life, and in the same chorused cry was the gurgling death-rattle of the first man ever to fall to murder.

Alpha-Rho-25's aural receptors registered the sound as a shrieked series of syllables very close to language.

His first and last action upon seeing the entity he had come to hunt was to beam audiovisual data through a tight-lance signal back to his overseers in the Godspire. Sending the pulse took less than the span of a human heartbeat, yet he had no time to do anything else. The jaws and claws of the creature closed in an impossible alignment of rending snaps, wrenching him into almost thirty pieces even as he was being swallowed.

The component chunks of Protector Alpha-Rho-25 tumbled into the monster's several gullets, throat-muscled down to splash into the acid of its guts, still twitching and bleeding as they started to dissolve. Unfortunately for Alpha-Rho-25 there was just enough of his consciousness left to know a brief, searing, transcendent moment of pain as digestion began.

THE PROTECTOR'S MESSAGE reached its destination less than a minute after it was sent – simultaneously as his destroyer was standing amidst the wreckage of nine Castellax battle-automata, regurgitating the melted slag of the Protector's bionics.

The message spurted from the speakers either side of a blank viewing monitor, manifesting as a distortion-flawed approximation of what the daemon had shrieked as it descended for the kill.

The speakers crackled and squealed with the same words roared three times, eerily close to a bellowed chant from some heathen ritual. They came with the rhythm of a heartbeat, in no language known to humankind.

I

Harvest

This is not now. This is then. This is when she was seventeen years old.

Moonlight bathes her as she lies in the long meadow grass and stares up at the stars. Around her, the night insects sing their clicking songs.

The wind is faint tonight but she hears the voices within the breeze, their murmured lilt at the very edge of her senses. Her father's fathers and her mother's mothers are murmuring softly this eve, the spirits lulled by the calm night. It isn't always this way. The dead are rarely quiet. Sometimes – even often – the voices plead with her or rage at her, desiring that she carry their wishes to the living. A rare few even threaten her, though she doesn't know what a mere spirit might do to cause her harm.

The girl stares at the three moons in their ascendancy, at their familiar, cratered faces. Thunder peals far away, rumbling over the southern mountains and drowning out the evening's subdued voices.

She rises, turning south, seeking the storm. Instead of the black-grey thunderheads she expects, the sky over the mountains glows with flames. The clouds churn, orange-bellied as they writhe above the peaks, flickering with inner torment that lights up the distant night.

A spaceship, *she thinks.* A spaceship is landing.

It streams through the clouds, black-hulled and streaming smoky fire, shaking the entire world as it roars overhead. A castle in the sky, descending, drifting down towards the villages and the great city beyond.

The spirits coalesce around her, their murmuring voices coloured by an emotion she has never heard in their tones before. She didn't know ghosts could feel fear.

She hides in the forest, not far from her village. Not far enough, not as far as she wishes to be, but as far as her legs will take her. Like a panting beast she half digs her way into the wet earth, curling herself into the shadow of a fallen tree. Her throat is raw with straining breath. Her lips are cracked and dry.

'The Imperium has returned,' her mother had said. Her eyes were wet, her voice was shaking. 'They are gathering the shamans and the spirit-speakers from every village.'

'Why?' the girl had asked. She heard the fear in her voice. Never had she felt less like a revered witch-priestess of her people.

'A tithe. Another tithe. One of souls and magic, not wheat and grain.'

'Run, Skoia,' said her father, looking into her eyes. 'Run and hide.'

The mothers of her mother and the fathers of her father had besieged her with agreement. The spirits, all of her ancestors, screamed at her to flee.

Skoia fled, white dress streaming, hair loose, into the forest.

Her people are part of the Imperium, so they are taught. Her grandmother told her of the Crusaders' Coming, when the warriors from the Cradleworld landed almost a century ago and brought the word of peace from humanity's Emperor. The First Earth, now called Terra, silent all these thousands of years, wasn't a myth after all.

The First Earth warriors had demanded compliance, and it had been given. They demanded tithes, and these were also given. Every year the grain haulers carry great portions of the annual harvest into the heavens, to dock with the orbital platforms and await collection. This, it has always been believed, was enough. Mankind has been brought back together, each rediscovered world a jewel in the unknown Emperor's crown.

But no Imperial spaceships have made planetfall since the Crusaders departed all those years before. Not until now.

Skoia hears dogs among her pursuers, barking and growling. The fear is enough to force her to her feet once more, staggering into a weak run. The spirits are hissing and agitated, yet she can scarcely hear them over the heaving of her breaths and the beat of her straining heart.

Through the trees ahead she sees one of the hunting dogs, as much machine as beast, its fur stripped in places in favour of robot parts, as though it had suffered in an accident and its owner had the credits required for expensive machine-fusion. Its jaws are locked open with a weapon pointing from inside its mouth. Behind it stands a woman, an Imperial woman, her head shaven, her flesh marked with tattoos of eagles. She wears gold and bronze beneath a red cloak. Her eyes are as dead as the gaze of a body upon an unlit funeral pyre.

Skoia turns and stumbles west. It's no use. She hears the dog bearing down behind her, its machine parts whining. It shoulders into her, throwing her from her feet. It stands above her, growling. The weapon in its mouth aims down at her face.

The gold woman with the dead eyes draws nearer, and – for the very first time Skoia can remember – the spirits fall silent.

No, not just silent. Banished. Gone.

'Leave me alone,' the girl manages to say. 'Please. I've done nothing wrong.'

The older woman says nothing.

Skoia breathes raggedly in the silence left by the spirits' absence, staring up into the ice of the woman's corpse-eyes.

'I see nothing inside you,' she murmurs through trembling lips. 'You have no soul.'

FIVE

Bringer of Sorrow
Refugees
Requisition

ZEPHON'S HANDS BETRAYED him, as they betrayed him every day. The metal fingers lifted from the hair strings of the antique harp, their shuddering subsiding as he ceased focusing on them.

Zephon was familiar with the science behind this malfunction, having memorised the reports on the various failures of biology/technology linkage taking place where his stumped arms met his bionic limbs at both elbows. The pathways of nerve and muscle were poor at conducting the information from his brain. A common enough failure of fusion surgery when dealing with crude implants grafted to the human form, but to his knowledge he was one of the only living Space Marines to suffer such complete augmetic rejection.

That was why he was here, of course. He knew it, even if his brothers had been too compassionate to call it exile. You couldn't fight in a Legion, let alone lead a strike force, if you couldn't pull a trigger or wield a blade.

And so he had come, willingly to all outward perception, to Terra. He'd accepted his exile, pretending it was an accolade, as part of the Crusader Host. He stood with the other representatives of each Space

Marine Legion, garrisoned on the Throneworld and charged to speak for their brothers.

In Hoc Officio Gloriam, read the words on the Preceptory's basalt declaration plaques. *There is honour in this duty.*

A dubious honour at best, Zephon knew. Especially now that the Throneworld no longer trusted the eighteen Legions. He was one of only two Blood Angels present in the thirty-strong monastic ambassadorship that the Crusader Host represented. Of the other warriors, even his Legion-brother Marcus, he saw no sign. He had retreated from the hollow duties of the Preceptory, content no more to work through the unreliable lists of the dead and record their names. With the galaxy burning, no reports reaching Terra were anything close to reliable. Of his Legion and primarch, there was no word at all. Was he to painstakingly etch the name of every single Blood Angel into the bronze funeral slabs in the Halls of the Fallen?

Madness. Worse than madness. Futility.

Sanguinius lived. The Legion lived.

So he had retreated to his personal chambers, where other work awaited him.

It was a truth known to relatively few souls that many of the most beautiful works of art in the entire Imperium – indeed, in the span of human history – were displayed only in the bowels of Blood Angels warships and frontier fortresses. Stained-glass windows that would never see the flare of true sunlight; statues of metaphorical gods and demigods at war with creatures of legend and myth; paintings wrought with forgotten and rediscovered techniques rendered in agonising detail, going unseen amid orchestral compositions of instruments that would never be played for human ears.

The warriors of the IX Legion didn't strive in the same way as the soldier-artisans of the III. The Emperor's Children sculpted, painted, composed to achieve perfection. They crafted great works to bring about something superior to anything shaped by lesser hands. In the act of creation, they exalted themselves above others.

This external, proud focus was anathema to Zephon and many of his brothers. The creation of art in song, in prose, in stone, was to reflect on the nature of humanity; a step forwards in understanding the distance between mankind and their Legion-evolved guardians. Like all of the Legions, the Blood Angels were born and shaped for battle, with rolls of honour a match for any other, with valour beyond question. But away from the eyes of their cousin Legions, they celebrated a culture of enlightenment: a quest not merely to understand the nature of man, but to understand their distance from the root species they were destined to fight and die for.

Zephon, a tribal boy who had eaten dust in the starvation seasons and slaughtered mutants with packs of his kindred before his twelfth summer of life, had learned to play the harp. For a century he'd excelled, his gift for harmony a match for his talents on the field of war.

Until a single battle had stolen both of his gifts. All hope was swept away by the alien sword that had severed both of his arms, mutilated both of his legs and cut him down in indignity.

After the ninth bionic surgery, the Legion's Apothecaries had bade him face the unwelcome reality. The grafts had taken as well as they would take. His physiology was simply not suited to the process of augmentation.

He still practised his music, jangling out discordant melodies with his shaking, slipping metal fingers, just as he still trained with his bolt-gun, able now to fire one in five times when he tried to pull the trigger. That was a significant improvement.

His aim was similarly ruined. Though his new arms had the strength of his old limbs, even their microtrembles threw off the razor precision of his former marksmanship. His blade-work suffered just as savagely. All of his precise balance and easy footwork was lost in the random tenses and spasms of his reconstructed leg joints.

Hence his exile. Hence this assignment to Terra.

In Hoc Officio Gloriam. There is honour in this duty. How those words made him smile.

His hands rested on the fine strings once more, their twitching just beginning again when the door klaxon gave its monotone whine.

Zephon froze, instinct pulling his eyes to the where his weapons were racked against the wall. He'd had no visitors in well over a year, since his last meeting with the Sigillite, when Malcador had refused yet another of the Blood Angel's requests to be granted command of a small frigate and set out in search of his Legion. The thirtieth such request.

Zephon rose from the seat, laid the harp aside and moved across the spartan chamber to turn the door's wheel lock. His left leg whirred with smooth mechanics where his thigh and knee had once been, the four-taloned claw that had replaced his right foot clanking down upon the floor.

When the door swung open on hinges badly in need of oiling, Zephon was faced with the towering figure of a Custodian, a four-metre tall guardian spear clutched at the warrior's side. The immense suit of armour hummed. The eye-lenses of his conical helmet blazed.

'I seek the Bringer of Sorrow,' the Custodian said.

Out of his armour and clad only in a black tunic, the Blood Angel felt curiously at odds with the warrior in full battleplate. 'You have found him.'

'You are far from my expectation,' the Custodian admitted. He disengaged the seals at his collar and removed the helm, revealing an ageless face with Urhan ritual scarring, like rivulets of saliva running in five lines down his chin and throat. 'I am Diocletian. Are you truly the Bringer of Sorrow?'

The title stabbed at Zephon harder the second time. He wasn't sure why. 'That was my title when I led men into war,' he replied. 'You sound disappointed.'

'That's because I am. I expected a champion in exile, and I find a bionic cripple. However, my disappointment is irrelevant. Activate your arming servitors and make ready for battle.'

Zephon hated the palpable sense of hope that surged through him with those words. The shame of it burned him. 'I assume you are aware that the Sigillite has forbidden any of the Crusader Host from acting without his seal of authority.'

'I will spare you a lesson in where the Sigillite's authority begins and ends regarding the Custodian Guard and the actions we may undertake. In this instance, he was the one to commend you to our service. Now arm yourself at once, Bringer of Sorrow.'

With reluctance, the Blood Angel lifted his hands, showing his arms composed entirely of metal struts, plating and muscle-cabling from the elbows down. His treacherous fingers twitched as if on cue.

Diocletian looked for several seconds. He blinked once. 'Is there some significance in your mutilation that I'm supposed to acknowledge?'

Zephon lowered his hands. 'I cannot fire my bolter. My hands do not obey me.'

'Can you at least hold a sword?'

Zephon wondered if he was being mocked, though he couldn't guess to what purpose. 'Not reliably,' he admitted.

'Your invalidity is noted. Now activate your arming servitors. Once you're ready, you'll come with me.'

'To where?'

'First to the Seberakan Isolation Compound via the Ophiukus Colonnades, then to the Halls of Unity Memoria.'

'I do not understand. Why?'

'Understanding will dawn in time. Let obedience come first.' Diocletian gave another of his long, emotionless stares, marred by only a single blink.

How, Zephon wondered, *could these golden avatars ever be considered more human than us?*

'Custodian?' he asked.

'I'm waiting for you,' Diocletian replied. 'My patience isn't infinite, Bringer of Sorrow.'

Zephon moved to the wall-comm, keying in the code to summon his armoury thralls. 'Given the circumstances, "Zephon" is fine, thank you.'

'If you prefer. I agree that the title is unbearably theatrical, especially for a cripple.'

Zephon felt the first stirrings of anger, and by the blood of Sanguinius it was a welcome thing indeed.

'You are the first Custodian I have ever spoken to,' he said. 'Are all of your kind so direct?'

'Are all of your kind so intoxicated with self-pity?' Diocletian looked almost as if he might smile, but the expression was stillborn. 'Now be swift, please. You aren't the only lost soul I need to reclaim today.'

'Lost soul?'

'I told you we are bound for the Seberakan Isolation Compound.'

The Blood Angel narrowed his pale eyes. Seberakan was home to traitors who had marched beneath the Warmaster's banner. 'Perhaps I am missing some aspect of humour in your words, Custodian.'

'There is never any humour in my words. Now come with me. You and I are going to free some prisoners.'

TOGETHER THEY STALKED through the Imperial Palace. Diocletian was displeased by all he saw. He and Zephon walked side by side through the bustling hallways, scattering pilgrims and refugees before them. Helmed, the two warriors had the option of immunising themselves against the sweaty salt-stink of unwashed skin and unclean breath. Diocletian grunted in disgust as he sealed his vox-grille, relying on his armour's internal air supply. The processional halls of the Ophiukus Colonnades were choked with the homeless detritus of war, coughing and sniffing and muttering. In some cases, weeping.

He felt their eyes upon him. Their judging eyes, doubtless wondering why Diocletian and his brethren hadn't saved them all and won the galactic war already. He felt their ignorance as a weight on his shoulders. That, at least, was a response that edged upon nobility. Far less honourable was his irritation at the moronic, animal weakness in their helpless gazes. Why were they here? Why were they not still among the stars, fighting for their home worlds?

'Something ails you?' asked Zephon.

'This detritus,' Diocletian replied. He regretted his honesty at once, for the Space Marine gave a dismissive grunt, and the Custodian felt himself suddenly at risk of being drawn into a conversation.

'This *detritus* is what we fight for,' said Zephon. The Blood Angel gestured with his gauntleted hand, forcing a snarl of armour servos. Several of the humans nearby flinched back, their awe briefly turned to fear. 'These men and women,' Zephon continued. 'They are what we fight for.'

Diocletian snorted, the sound wet and ugly. 'I fight for the Emperor.'

'We fight for the Emperor's dream.' Zephon replied at once. 'For the Imperium.'

'Semantics. Without the Emperor, His dream could never be realised. He alone can bring it to pass. No other.'

'Then we are both right,' Zephon replied.

You are deluded as well as crippled, thought Diocletian. 'It seems to me, Space Marine,' he ventured, 'that too many of your kind decided they were fighting for the Imperium rather than the Emperor. Perhaps if more of you thought as the Ten Thousand do, we would not stand where we stand today, preparing for the end of all we know.'

Zephon fell blessedly silent.

Diocletian took in the great hall – once a place of ranked statues and great, wide windows, now a place of huddling scum and cowards who should be issued with lasrifles and packed into transport ships back to the front lines. He let his gaze – and the accompanying target locks – drift across the crowds of filthy refugees lining the processional hall's sides. Clusters of them were gathered around servitors carrying pallets of dried rations and dehydrated protein potables.

But the Blood Angel's silence was short-lived. 'You say we fight for the Emperor, not for His Imperium. The natural question then is to wonder: without Him, would we still fight? Is there any reason to raise this great empire if He is the only soul capable of leading it? We would be committing ourselves to a futile battle.'

'You speak of impossibilities,' Diocletian chorused, loyally adamant. 'Mankind must be ruled. It has a ruler. Let that be the end of it.'

Yet his flesh crawled at the unfamiliar philosophising. Without the Emperor, who would rule? What lesser minds would take up the mantle of command in His place? In what thousands of ways would they fail to meet the Emperor's vision?

Such thoughts were unwelcome and distracting. He felt slowed by them, felt them running like black poison through his veins.

Both warriors snapped to mechanical halts as two figures manifested before them. Diocletian's spear was free in a blur of ruthless precision, levelled down across one of the refugee's throats. Its keen edge sang with a soft metallic chime from cutting the air so swiftly.

'Sacred Unity!' Zephon hissed the curse across the vox. 'What are you doing?'

Diocletian looked down into the wide eyes of a young boy, no more than seven or eight Terran standard years old. The figure at the youth's side was even more diminutive: a girl, the boy's sister by the uniformity in skin tone and facial structure, a year or two younger. Diocletian had no talent for estimating the ages of unmodified humans. She looked up at the Custodian with wide, terrified eyes. A scream sounded from the crowd, the plaintive cry of their mother. Both children's mouths were wide, their lips shaking.

Diocletian lifted his blade away from the boy's throat and reactivated his helm's mouth grille to speak aloud. 'My apologies,' he said with grave formality. The children flinched at the rawness of his vox-altered tones.

Zephon moved slowly, reaching up to remove his own helm. He stood bareheaded before the two children as their mother reached them. The boy, resisting his mother's attempts to herd him, tore free and stood before Diocletian once more.

'Are you the Emperor?'

Diocletian stood motionless. 'Is that a jest?' he asked, making the boy flinch at the tone.

Zephon's smile was bittersweet as he looked down upon the boy.

He lowered himself slowly, his red war-plate grinding loudly through the motion, until he was on one knee before the child. Even then, he was still thrice the boy's height.

'No, child,' the Blood Angel replied. 'He is not the Emperor. Though he knows the Emperor very well.'

Tears ran from the edges of the boy's eyes. The immensity of the armoured giants before him filled his senses, from the assault of overwhelming red and gold to the thrum of active battleplate. Awe was writ plain across his young features. Awe and desperation and an expression of fearful need.

Diocletian would have voxed his irritation had Zephon still been wearing his helm to hear it. Zephon was blind and deaf to the Custodian's annoyance, or simply chose to ignore it.

'What is your name, young one?'

'Darak.'

'Darak,' the Blood Angel repeated. 'My name is Zephon. And as grand as my companion appears, he is not the Emperor. What is wrong, child?'

The boy stammered his words. 'I... I want to ask the Emperor when we can go home. My parents are still there. We left them behind. We had to get to the evacuation ships.'

Diocletian glanced to the woman protecting the little girl. Not their mother, then. Her facial structure bore the signs of familial resemblance, so there was some genetic linkage. An aunt or older cousin, perhaps. He removed the target lock playing over her filthy face, dismissing it along with his cursory interest.

Zephon wasn't as compelled to move on. 'I see,' the Blood Angel said. 'And what world do you call home?'

'Bleys. We're from Bleys.'

Zephon nodded as if he knew the world well. Diocletian doubted that any of the IX Legion had ever set foot upon it, useless backwater that it was. 'Then you've travelled far,' said the Blood Angel. 'Welcome to Terra, Darak. You're safe here.'

Safe for now, Diocletian added silently.

'What are your parents' trades?' Zephon asked the boy. 'If they were fighting, they must be soldiers?'

The boy nodded. 'They were fighting the grey machine men from Mars.'

'My parents are warriors, as well,' said Zephon, neglecting to mention that they had died over a century ago on the radiation-choked deserts of Baal's second moon. Their ashes would be nothing more than blight dust on the wasteland winds by now.

The boy, Darak, turned his eyes up to Diocletian. 'Are your parents soldiers?'

'No,' said Diocletian. 'They are long dead. My mother was a slave who died of intestinal flux, and my father was a barbarian king executed by the Emperor's own hand for opposing the principles of Unity.'

'The... what?'

'I've finished speaking with you,' Diocletian told the boy.

Darak narrowed his eyes at Diocletian before returning his gaze to Zephon. 'I want to go back for my parents. I want to ask the Emperor to send the Space Marines,' he vowed with painful conviction. 'The Emperor could send you, couldn't He?'

'He could,' Zephon agreed, 'and perhaps He will. I will ask Him of His plans for Bleys the next time I stand before Him.'

The hope in the boy's eyes made Diocletian's gorge rise. He was all too aware of the many eyes upon them at the heart of this ludicrous exchange.

'Our duty awaits,' he said, his tone terse.

'Indeed,' replied Zephon. 'Now, Darak, I must do my duty to the Emperor. Thank you for taking the time to speak with me.'

The boy nodded, mute. Zephon replaced his helm. His voice emerged through the harsh, drawling rasp of his vox-grille. 'Look after your sister, Darak.'

Darak moved to his aunt and sister, the latter weeping softly after the scare Diocletian had given her. Diocletian walked on with Zephon at his side. If the refugee herd's stares had been an irritant before, they were practically boring through the Custodian's armour now.

'You are a creature of pointless sentiment,' Diocletian voxed to his new companion.

He heard Zephon's sigh as they walked onwards. 'You said I disappointed you, Custodian. I assure you that the feeling is mutual. I had not imagined conversing with one of the Ten Thousand to be such an exercise in soulless discourse.'

Diocletian didn't believe that deserved a reply.

He hoped Kaeria was having better luck with the Fabricator General.

Intruder.

That was Kane's first thought. Not the intruder's identity, nor how long it must have taken this defiler to reach his inner sanctum. He didn't even consider the severity of any event that would drive an outsider to venture this far into the catacombs. The trespasser's materialisation alone occupied his first, hostile thought. The audacity of her presence.

Intruder.

Intruders disrupted the music. They were flawed notes amidst the rhythm of crashing hammers and the breath of the forge flames. And this one was a disruption uglier than most.

Zagreus Kane let himself drop from the harmony at the heart of the foundry's song of iron and fire. It was a detachment that took place on three levels – spiritually, physically, cognitively. First he exloaded his conscious focus from the noospheric dataclusters that allowed him to oversee the administration and management of several thousand menials at once. The abrupt loss of infinite information was a hole in his soul, as the Voice of the Great Work was sucked into sudden silence.

Then he physically removed himself from his command cradle, hauling himself along the overhanging steel beams using his four mechanical arms, and lowering himself into the waiting tank treads that comprised the lower half of his body. The lancing pressures of connection/reconnection stabbed dully through his nerve-numbed innards as the metal tendrils of union snaked their way into his augmented guts. The racked volkite and graviton weapons snaked their linkage feeds into his back, shoulders and spine. Each one of them powered up, folding close to his tracked thorax or aligning against his hunched back.

Lastly, as the armoured tank treads ground their way along the gantry, bringing him on his juddering way closer to the visitor – *the intruder* – he readied himself for the tedium and inevitable inaccuracies that came with dealing with those unenlightened souls forced to communicate through the impurity of uncanted language.

As the foundry hammered and roared and clanked and crashed around him, the overseer came to a shuddering halt before the slender figure of an Oblivion Knight. She wore the overlapping gold armour plating of her order over the traditional bronzed mail bodysuit, which was to be expected. Her hair was crested into a warrior's topknot, which also ran according to his expectations; similarly, her portcullised rebreather mask was entirely in keeping with the equipment customarily attributed to the Sisters of Silence. She had marked her face with designs of ink – an Imperial aquila tattooed in red upon her forehead – as if her allegiance were in some way not entirely obvious.

What he found interesting, however, were the signs of wear and tear upon her wargear. The sensoria cluster in place of his left eye flickered a brief hololithic beam across the Oblivion Knight's armour plating, recording signs of unfamiliar damage inflicted upon the various layers. Intriguing. Very much so.

She greeted him with a series of hand gestures. He was impressed that she included all twelve of his long-form titles. That was a formality few outside the Martian Mechanicum would know to offer.

Zagreus Kane looked down at her. His voice emerged from an augmitter in his neck, shaped from human teeth mounted in a framework of black steel and polished bronze. It gave him a snarling grin in the middle of his throat.

'State the necessity of your intrusion.'

She made three brief gestures with a single hand.

'I do not consider myself to have "changed" at all,' said the Fabricator General of Sacred Mars. He adjusted his forge-blackened, ash-darkened red hood with one of his four hands. 'Change implies the possibility of degeneration. My alterations are evolution, Oblivion Knight. Each one a step towards divinity. Now, I repeat, state the necessity of your intrusion.'

She told him her name without saying a word. Her identity was an irrelevancy, but one that Kane let pass. Still, frustration burned. Had they been linked to the noospheric data array, this exchange – and every single nuance within it – would already be over, rather than lurking at the very beginning of the pleasantries.

'I am overseeing the disposition, deployment and armament of several million troops and several hundred fleets, Kaeria. In addition, Fabricator Locum Trimejia is transbonded to me in accordance with the New Precepts of Mars. I am aware of all that took place at the hierarchs' council and the loss of Adnector Primus Mendel. Your expositional formality is a drain on my time.'

She replied in hand gestures, none of which were an apology. At last, they were cutting to the matter's core. As her hands moved, Kane's iron-sealed mouth – his true, human mouth – trickled oil-lubricated coolant saliva as he wheezed, briefly taking over from the auto-respiratory processes of his cyborged lungs. The gesture made the heavy graviton cannons wired into his spine cycle in a brazen sign of his speculation.

'I understand,' he said. 'Supply me with the specifics.'

Kaeria offered a data-slate, which Kane took by deploying one of his many secondary multi-segmented abdominal servo-arms. Three thin fingers snatched it from the Oblivion Knight's grip and immediately drew it into the folds of his robe, slotting it into a data-inload cavity between his ribs.

For the ghost of a second, information danced behind his eyes.

And for the first time in many months, Fabricator General Zagreus Kane hesitated. 'This is a significant order of requisition,' he stated. He made no move to return the data-slate in the wake of his understatement. In a single requisition demand, she was requesting as much battle-iron and war-flesh as the Mechanicum had supplied to the Great Work in the last two years alone.

Kaeria nodded, asking a question with her hands.

'Yes,' was the reply. 'Ammunition is the easiest to provide, and it will be done. We can also harvest forge workers for the thralls and battle-servitors you require. A recall of Cybernetica cohorts will be issued at once from all unthreatened systems within Segmentum Solar, and a clarion call can be raised to attract Myrmidia cultists in nearby systems, in order to replace the significant drain you are proposing. But it is of immense import that you understand what you are requesting. This will severely and potentially gravely deplete the Mechanicum's forces on Terra, as well as our involvement in the active spheres of conflict in the Solar War.'

Kaeria signed her understanding, resolute in her motions.

Kane paused, calculating, calculating...

'The divine armours you request can also be provided, though not in the numbers you require. Those numbers simply do not exist on Terra. And they will be salvaged or otherwise remastered from war spoil, requiring reconsecration in the Omnissiah's name. Even House Terryn has sent its divine armours into the stars to engage the Warmaster and the false Fabricator General.'

Kaeria signed a reply.

'Your acceptance is noted,' said Kane. 'And I return a question of my own – what of the Legio Ignatum forces already deployed to aid in the Great Work?'

Kaeria's reply was curt and simple. Kane felt the synthetic fluids in his veins heat briefly in reassuring warmth. The Fire Wasps yet functioned. Good, good.

'So be it. I shall admit, then, that there are no Legio Titanicus elements remaining upon Terra at this time. As with the Knight Households, all are deployed and garrisoned off-world.'

Kaeria hesitated, then signed her understanding.

'Now,' said Kane, 'to the final element in your order of requisition. This is a request of particular magnitude.'

The Sister's hands moved in a graceful query.

Kane mused over his answer. He didn't like the effortless confidence in her eyes. Perhaps ordering Trimejia to raise the issue of Mars' reconquest at the gathering of hierarchs had been an error of tact. The Fabricator General retreated into the shadows of his hood, thinking, considering, processing.

It could be done. Of course it could be done. And with that hidebound fool Mendel dead, beautiful new possibilities were suddenly dawning.

He turned in his socket, twisting his torso to look back over his shoulder at the seemingly endless production lines in the hellish amber light of dancing forge flames. He would need to retake his place in the omni-cradle to oversee the fulfilment of the requisition order, and he would need the genius of his trusted kindred to complete the list's last element.

Someone would have to submit to reforging. Someone would need to be reforged on a level so absolute and fundamental that it bordered on rebirth – if Kane agreed to arrange it.

If.

Such power in such a little word.

Swivelling back to face the Oblivion Knight, Kane looked down upon the warrior, amusement shining in his remaining human eye. To outward appearances, it was all that was left of the man he'd been only five years before.

'No.'

Kaeria was under no similar compunction to hide her surprise. She signed another query.

Kane emitted a crackle of code. 'The Mechanicum's ability to comply is not the question, Oblivion Knight. Its willingness is. Am I able to fulfil this last element of requisition? Yes. Am I willing to do so? No.'

She was more cautious now, her hands moving slower, her eyes locked to his shadowed features.

Kane's spinal-linked weapons deactivated in sympathy with his rising confidence. 'Then it is my pleasure to enlighten you, Sister. The Priesthood of Mars has been instrumental in the webway's reconstruction. The Omnissiah has shared many of its details with those of us wearing the Holy Red, whom He took into His service within those tunnels. But He is silent now. He has been silent for some time. So much has gone unspoken. You ask a great deal of the Martian Mechanicum, and we give. We provide. We supply. We feed our iron and toil into the webway. Now the time for answers has come.'

Kaeria's caution crystallised. Her signed reply was lengthy, her glare laden with accusation.

'So we have been told,' Kane replied. 'And none of my priesthood doubts that the Omnissiah's Great Work will be the salvation of the species. I am not holding the Great Work to ransom. I am making known my desire for enlightenment.'

Kaeria signed nothing. After a long moment, she gave a curt nod. Kane continued, sensing how close he was coming to the truth.

'These orders of requisition come from the Ten Thousand and the Sisterhood of Silence, not the Master of Mankind. Not even from the Sigillite, who speaks with the Omnissiah's voice. You desire the final, most vital element on this list for your war. I will grant it, at the price of a single answer.'

Another nod. The Oblivion Knight could have been carved from sandstone for all the emotion she showed on her dusky features.

Kane leaned down. His tank treads grumbled as they turned him slightly. 'The webway is a resource beyond value. Tactically. Logistically. It is recorded in my predecessor's archives that the Omnissiah Himself spoke of its passages being used to return to Mars. Will this avenue of return be made available to us in the near future?' Kane heard the too-human emotion in his vocalisation. He didn't care. A momentary weakness was permissible. The answer meant everything.

Kaeria's reply was both blunt and brief. *Unknown.*

Kane had expected no less – but *unknown* was not *forbidden,* and he would take every shred of hope he could salvage from the situation. He'd recorded Kaeria's ocular and respiratory response to pore over later, whereupon he would run the dilation of her pupils and the sound of her breathing through myriad filters to determine even the slightest determinant.

'Mars must be retaken,' he said softly, slowly, as if hypnotised into sounding human. 'The alternatives are unacceptable.'

Kaeria said nothing, did nothing, merely looked up at him. Kane felt an all-too-familiar frustration tighten its clutch around his innards. The Sigillite had refused many times to launch a full reclamation of Sacred Mars. The Seventh Primarch mirrored that refusal. But Kane was no longer a Locum trailing at Kelbor-Hal's heels in the dark forges of the Red Planet. He was Fabricator General in his own right, the rightful lord of humanity's twin capital Mars, and his rank matched theirs in influence and authority.

It was time he was respected and heeded in accordance with his position.

'The Mechanicum will supply your war on this single condition – the Omnissiah Himself once spoke of a route within this alien webway that reaches back to Sacred Mars. Adnector Primus Mendel named it the Aresian Path. No matter the cost, no matter the effort, you will see it reinforced and held, ready for use once the Omnissiah's Great Work is completed. Even if thousands of other routes and passages must fall, you will ensure that the way to Mars remains in Imperial control.'

To his surprise Kaeria replied at once, signing a simple affirmation. She signed a question of her own.

'Yes,' Kane replied, feeling the prickling creep of suspicion. 'That is all I require. For now.'

Kaeria nodded, signing her thanks.

'How easily you give your word,' Kane vocalised with an emission of crackling background code.

Her reply was far longer this time, her hands weaving for several seconds.

Kane watched, seeing her assurances, allowing himself to be appeased by them. He did not know whether to believe her – or indeed if her kind could lie at all – but it was of no consequence. The first and most crucial step had been taken. Opportunity had at last presented itself and been firmly seized.

That poor, mind-stunted fool Mendel. So proud of his place at the Omnissiah's side, now achieving in death far more than he ever had in life.

'Then the last element on your list of requisition will be carried out at once, Kaeria of the Silent Sisterhood. The Mechanicum will provide you with a general.'

SIX

Faith and fear
Unity
Mortis-pulse

THE BOY WHO would be king was a boy no more. The Emperor in His ageless adulthood walked the war-scarred tundra, cloaked against the cold. He held a naked blade low in one hand. The sword was dull in deactivation, the circuitry lining the blade cold and unlit.

Evidence of battle lay strewn in every direction, from the churned earth of shell craters to the remains of warriors on both sides. He walked between the bodies, knee-deep and in their thousands, as the snow began to fall in a miserable grey spill. Around Him, warriors in clanking, crunching armour plate strode among the fallen, dragging comrades from the corpse-heaps and executing wounded foes with swift plunges of cackling chainblades.

The Emperor paid heed to none of this. The theatre of a battle's aftermath held no claim on His attention. He walked on, stepping over His own injured men who called for His aid, approaching a ring of His elite warriors. They guarded a lone, grey-haired figure, clad in an unreliably cloned fur cloak. The captured man hugged himself against the biting cold, standing a little hunched over from his wounds.

He looked up as the Emperor approached. He smiled without mirth, showing bloody teeth.

'So this is how it ends.'

The Emperor stood still, saying nothing. The wind pulled at His long hair. The weak sun glinted in flashes from His lowered sword.

'Why?' the captive asked bitterly. 'Why annihilate my people like this?'

'Your people will be allowed to live on,' replied the Emperor. 'Your army, and you yourself, could not.'

'The "Emperor of Terra",' the grey-haired captive said with a laughing sneer. Blood ran from the corner of his mouth. The wound in his gut was eating him alive.

'No,' said the Emperor. 'The Emperor of Mankind.'

The prisoner hawked blood onto the snow. 'Of mankind now? One nation wasn't enough for you, nor even one world, so you'll take your cancerous touch to the stars.'

'Your defiance is ill-placed,' the Emperor replied.

'Arrogant beast!' He wheezed through the ruination of his chest. 'Hubris beyond reckoning. Madness beyond definition.'

The Emperor turned into the wind, narrowing His eyes as He looked across the ravaged battlefield. 'And yet, victory.'

'Tyrant!' the captive screamed. 'Butcher of the enlightened!' Spit sprayed into the evening air, steaming where it landed. 'Apostate! Heretic!'

The Emperor endured this spittle-punctuated tirade with a quiet patience somewhere between dignity and immunity. 'I bring illumination,' He said.

'You bring damnation!' the captured warlord raged.

'I warned you, priest,' said the Emperor. 'Long ago, I warned you. We stand here now because of the choices you made.'

'I pissed on your warnings then,' the captive snapped back. 'As I piss on your enlightenment now. Let the sword fall! I go to my god's embrace. And with my last breath, I will curse the blood in your veins.'

One of the Custodians encircling him moved forwards, pounding the butt of his guardian spear into the side of the man's head. Though he pulled the blow, scarcely seeking to injure let alone kill, it was enough to break the man's eye socket and burst the orb within, turning it to shattered jelly.

The captive warlord went down into the snow, howling, clutching his savaged skull.

'Restrain yourself, Sagittarus,' the Emperor said. The Custodian hesitated, bowed his head to his master, then returned to the ranks.

And then, as the kneeling prisoner cried out and pressed frostbitten hands to his broken face, the Emperor spoke to a soul that shouldn't be there at all.

'Greetings, Ra.'

Ra remained back from the gathering, his gaze drifting between the Emperor and the Custodians. The latter wore suits of armour far less ornate than the one he wore himself. These were his kindred in the years before he joined them. They still waged wars against the techno-barbarian hordes claiming dominion over Terra, before the rise of the Legions and the commencement of the Great Crusade.

'Sire,' he greeted the Emperor. As ever, nothing about his surroundings felt like a dream or a vision. The wind whipped at Ra's royal crimson cloak. The charnel house reek of the battlefield threaded its way through his helm's filtration systems. Somehow, it always did.

His master turned, leaving the Custodians ringing the wounded prisoner. The Emperor's face was serenely troubled – within it, Ra saw several shifting visages: the worried concern of the boy who would be king; the stern resolve of the Great Crusader; the tranquil caution of the Ruler of All Mankind.

'You received a mortis-pulse, I suspect.'

'From the Protector,' said Ra. 'You sensed it?'

'No. I sensed the entity in the outward tunnels. The ancient presence drawing nearer to the walls of the Impossible City. I sensed when it struck. No Protector could survive that. When it struck, I sensed its name. I imagine your slain Protector sought to inform you of this in the only way he was able, via his mortis-pulse. Most likely the mes-sage conveyed the creature's name.'

'The Protector's audio transmission was nothing more than aetheric shrieking.'

'You have heard the warp-creatures speak Gothic in battle, Ra. They draw such knowledge from the minds of the slain, leeching human thought to form threats, challenges and the like. Yet they lack language and identity as human cognition recognises such things. The aetheric shrieking was its name. I heard it, felt it, myself.'

At Ra's boots, a fallen warrior – one of the crudely armoured Thun-der Warriors who had once marched at the Emperor's side – sought to crawl across the frozen ground. Ra ignored the dying man, doubt-ing he even existed to the wounded warrior.

The Emperor noted the Custodian's hesitation. 'Do you doubt me, Ra?'

'I don't know if it's doubt, sire. More a lack of comprehension.'

'Your comprehension of psychic and aetheric principles has never been as effortless as Jasaric's or as accepting as Constantin's, but this concept should not be beyond you.'

Despite their surroundings, Ra snorted a brief laugh. 'How you flat-ter me, my Emperor.'

The Emperor ignored the weak attempt at sarcasm. 'When I speak to you, to others, am I speaking aloud? Does my mouth move and form the shapes of human language? Does a human voice emerge? Or is it merely how mortal minds process my presence and my psychic will?'

Ra nodded. This, at least, was familiar ground. Many were the times that the Emperor had faced allies or foes, speaking countless tongues without hesitation, and even those with no grasp of the same languages and lexicons had perfectly understood the Master of Mankind's words.

'It is a similar principle,' the Emperor stated.

'Why would a daemon cry out its name?'

The Emperor's dark eyes flickered at his bodyguard's choice of words. 'They do so almost unceasingly. They emanate the concepts and moments of emotion that gave them form. Humankind interprets those emanations as sound – the shrieking and roaring you hear when you do battle with them. They are declaring what they are. You hear it as who they are. The one we speak of now is the entity born from the first murder, when a human first took the life of another outside of the need to survive.'

Ra said nothing. The Emperor's eyes unfocused, as if He looked back to that very moment in antiquity. When He spoke again, His voice was softer, mellifluous with distraction. 'So many minds look to the taming of fire as the moment humanity tore itself apart from the melange of biological life on Old Earth, elevating mankind above the level of beasts. They point to many such moments and no two insights agree – fire, the wheel, gunpowder, jet propulsion, the Navigator gene... All wrong. It was that moment, Ra. A deed that even false, inane, insane religions have cursed throughout history. That one act set humanity irrevocably apart, feeding the beings of the warp, putting us on the first step of a long, long path.'

The Emperor's eyes cleared. He looked at Ra once more, not through him. 'And here we are, so much further along the path. Still seeking to leave it.'

Ra stood in silence, feeling the wind caressing his face with unwanted fingers. The Ten Thousand were blessed above any others and philosophical discussions with the Emperor were hardly unknown to them, but the bleak severity of his master's words turned Ra's blood slow, sluggish and cold.

'The End of Empires,' the Emperor said.

'My king?'

'You cannot reweave warp creatures' names from base concept to human language without an element of psychic adaptation in the translation. As close as it can be rendered into Gothic, that is what the entity's name means. The End of Empires.'

Now, truly, Ra's blood ran cold. Ice flooded his veins in its place. 'Sire, why did you summon me again so soon?'

The Emperor turned, and Ra followed without needing to be beckoned. Together they walked back through the battle's aftermath, accompanied by the cries of the wounded and the snap-crack of execution gunfire. As they approached the circle of Custodians and the kneeling, bleeding warlord, Ra couldn't help but look at the past incarnations of his own kindred. There was Jasaric, tall and proud; Constantin, stoic and observant; Sagittarus, choleric and wild.

To human eyes each of the gathered warriors would look scarcely different to any other, but to Ra each was as distinct as separate songs. How humbling it was, to see them like this, walking the scarred earth of Terra in the time before he stood among their number. A handful of years after this moment, Constantin Valdor would come for him, taking him as a child from–

'Tell me, Ra,' said the Emperor. He aimed His blade at the kneeling warlord. 'Tell me what you see.'

Ra followed the silver sword down to the wounded man. He knew of this battle from the archives, had seen picts ripped from primitive helmet footage of the conflict playing out. He had even seen a few rare surviving murals depicting the man in robes of flowing red, addressing vast crowds. Ra knew who the defeated warlord was.

'The Priest-King of Maulland Sen,' Ra said. 'In the moments before you executed him.'

'That is a title and a moment in time. What do you *see*?'

'A man. A man kneeling on the snow.'

'That is better,' the Emperor agreed. He stepped closer to the kneeling man, activating His blade. Fire cobwebbed down the circuits lining both sides of His sword. None of the gathered warriors paid any notice, nor did the warlord himself.

'I met him long before he was the priest-king,' the Emperor said. 'He began as a holy man, a mendicant preacher wandering the northern wastes, gathering untainted food and purified water, giving it freely to those in need. He claimed it was his calling, and that his god lived in his kindness. It was a calling, of course. A call that was answered by the beings of the immaterium. They gave him the power to feed his beleaguered tribe and heal their ills, and his clan grew. When savage winters ate away at the other tribes, his clan sheltered beneath the protection of his power. He kept them fed, protected and unseen from the eyes of their hunting foes. Soon, hundreds of men and women were huddling for warmth within his mercy, and offered their thanks to the god that he believed he served.

'Yet each miracle took more effort, Ra. More sacrifice. The end always justified the means. First the conundrums were moral in nature. What does it matter if another clan starves, if it allows his tribe to survive? Soon enough the rituals grew more occult in order to achieve their ends. What is the murder of a rival, if that death guarantees another ten years of peace? What is the life of one child, if the offer of its bloody, beating heart will ensure a monarch's immortality? Do you see?'

Ra saw. Just as he had seen the monuments to massacre in the pict archives, from the fall of Maulland Sen.

'The warp rarely makes itself known in manifest form. The damnation flooding the webway is the crescendo of its siren song. Its immensity and physicality is what makes the threat so unprecedented. Far more often, the warp seethes behind the veil, it curdles thoughts inside a skull, it inks the blood in men and women's veins. And that is enough. More than enough. It brings us to moments like these, in the company of ambitious, faithful men, too proud to see their own deception.'

Ra stared down at the kneeling, bleeding priest-king. Gone were the gene-abominations and witchcraft-marked men in their thousands that had formed his ragged armies. He was alone, moments from breathing his last. Soon his sick blood would taint the Emperor's blade.

'Think of this man's clan,' continued the Emperor. 'As a holy man he had begun with offers of food and the promise of survival. Sensing his susceptibility, the warp darkened around the candle flame of his life's light. He prayed, and the warp answered.

'Soon his people were too numerous to hide. Other tribes came for his clan's riches. This man, this revered holy lord, led his people to the machines of the Old Ages, cloning and replicating and gene-forging flawed warriors to wage war for territory.

'The clan branded their own flesh and ran to war alongside these genetic brutes, crying up to the sky for the same power their overlord enjoyed. And how far they had fallen. Committing any act in the belief of their own righteousness. All from superstition. All from ignorance.

'All because one charismatic man believed that the powers that heeded his calls could be trusted. By the time he realised they could not, he believed himself powerful enough to control them, independent enough to resist them. What harm in one more gift, if it allowed his clan to thrive? What harm in one more sacrifice, if it ensured a strong harvest or victory in a coming war? And when it came time to die, what would this powerful, independent man do? Would he go silently into the ground? Would he slumber upon a funeral pyre? Or would he – for the good of his people – reach for longer life at any cost?'

Ra still stared at the defeated monarch. The Custodian knew all there was to know from the archives. He knew of the barbarity practised by the Maulland Sen Confederacy. He had seen pict evidence of the bone pits, those golgothan barrows; every day of his adult life he had fought alongside other gold-armoured warriors who had been there for the dismantling of the confederacy itself.

'Superstition and ignorance always attract the warp's denizens,' continued the Emperor. 'For the core of religion is the twinned principle of arrogance and fear. Fear of oblivion. Fear of an unfair life and an arbitrary universe. Fear of there simply being nothing, no great and grand scheme to existence. The fear, ultimately, of being powerless.'

The Custodian narrowed his eyes. Rarely did the Emperor elucidate His reasoning in such stark terms. And why now? To what end? Ra felt the prickle of unease making its threading way up his spine.

'Look at him, Ra. Truly look at him.'

Ra looked. The priest-king could hardly have appeared less like his treacherously magnificent depictions, with his red robes of office reduced to scorched rags hanging at the edges of his broken armour, and the cloak of cloned fur blackened from flamer burns. The great demagogue stared up at the Emperor with the unshattered half of his face dirtied by blood and matted hair.

'Sire, I don't...'

But he did. Talons rippled in the shadows cast by the man's cloak, glassy and obsidian, impossibly liquid in their caresses. Claws clicked and scratched against one another inside the wide pupil that looked like a hole drilled into the yellowing white of the priest-king's remaining eye. Bulges wormed their maggoty way through the man's veins, bubonically swollen.

The defeated warlord, this impoverished and humbled ruler, was riven from within.

'What am I looking at, sire? What is this?'

'Faith,' said the Emperor. 'You are seeing his faith, through my eyes. Maulland Sen's massacring priest-king is... what? Another of the Unification Wars' warlords? Terra had hundreds of them. He died beneath my executing blade, and history's pages will mark him as nothing more.

'And yet, his life is the path of faith in microcosm. Once a wandering preacher feeding the weak and the lost, ending as a blood-soaked monarch overseeing pogroms and genocides – his teeth stained by cannibal ritual, his skull a shell for the toying touch of warp-entities he does not realise he serves. Every act of violence or pain that he performs is a prayer to those entities, fuelling them, making them stronger behind the veil. What he believes no longer matters, when everything he does feeds their influence.

'This is why we strip the comfort of religion from humanity. These are the slivers of vulnerability that faith cracks open in the human heart. Even if a belief in a lie leads us to do good, eventually it leads to the truth – that we are a species alone in the dark, threatened by the laughing games of sentient malignancies that mortals would call gods.'

Ra wiped his snow-flecked face with a gauntleted palm. His breathing was calm. His heart was slow. Yet his fingers trembled.

'Are they gods?'

'What is a god?' the Emperor replied at once, though without challenge. He sounded curious, not defiant.

'I don't know, sire.'

'A being of great power, perhaps. Am I then a god?'

'Of course not.'

'Is a god the focus of prayer and ritual, then? You are named in a god's honour. Ra – a god of the sun. How many cultures have worshipped the sun or given its arcing journey into the responsibility of a godling's care? More than even I can count. More than even I have seen. Each sun god or goddess bore a different name, and was revered by different people. The sun rose and fell, as it always has. Did it do so because of their prayers and offerings?'

Against all odds, Ra gave a mirthless, unpleasant smile. 'No, my king.'

'Look at the sky above us now, overcast with the coming storm. Most humans would name the shade of the clouds grey, in various languages. How are we to know if the grey one man sees is the same hue seen by the woman at his side? Or the grey his mother and father saw? A blind woman would see nothing, but she still feels the storm's approach on the wind. She knows the sky is grey because she has been told it is so, yet she has never seen it. What, then, is *grey*? Is it the shade I see, or the hue seen by another man's eyes? Is it only a colour, or is it also the feeling of the wind against your skin, promising a storm?'

Ra exhaled. 'I understand.'

The Emperor seemed suddenly weary. He shook His head, a rare moment of human expression. 'Beings of varying sentience and influence exist, given different names by different cultures and species. Gods. Aliens. Entities. It matters not.'

'I don't think I want to know these things, sire.'

'Your wishes are irrelevant, Ra. You will fight harder once you understand what you are fighting for. That is why I tell you all of this.'

'A matter of practicality?' he asked the Emperor, taking no offence. 'Not trust?'

'A matter of victory. You still see the war in the webway as the battle for my dreams and ambitions as a ruler. But I have told you – it is the war for humanity's survival.'

The sudden crack of an aggravated power field snapped Ra's focus back to the snowy tundra. Blood sizzled on the Emperor's blade. The priest-king's headless body toppled, neck stump steaming, into the dirty snow.

Sagittarus gripped the severed head by its long hair, holding it up to the miserable sky. He roared, and thousands of Thunder Warriors roared with him.

The Emperor cleaned His deactivated blade on the dead man's cloak, then sheathed the sword across His back.

'Always so barbaric, Sagittarus.'

The Custodian tossed the head onto the ground. 'Exultant in victory, my king. That's all.'

The Emperor rested an armoured boot on the priest-king's head. Knee servos thrummed. He hesitated, for the span of a single breath, as all eyes fell upon Him.

Then the boot came down, grinding the trophy into the dirt beneath the snow. When He lifted His tread, nothing but wet, red shards remained, stringy with slick hair.

'Burn the body,' said the Emperor. 'Burn all of their bodies.'

Thunder Warriors came forwards, armed with flamers.

+Awaken, Ra.+

SAGITTARUS DREAMED OF unity, of his days at the Emperor's side. The title itself – *Imperator* they had named him in High Gothic – was still new in those days. The Emperor was a warlord, a battle king, but not yet a king of kings. Terra had yet to be brought to its knees by bolter and blade.

The dreamer was a warlord in his own right, then. He'd breathed in the body-stink and faecal-scent of a hundred battlefields in the hours after victory. He'd felt the caress of charnel winds against his flesh, and carried a golden spear in his bloodstained hands across an entire continent.

Days of strength. Days of glory.

He was the first of his kind to die. And for this indignity, this unquenchable shame, they had actually honoured him.

The Battle of Maulland Sen. That was the last day of joy, the last day before his bones were bound inside a cradle of penetrating cold and his mind set aflame with the shame of failure.

'Sagittarus.'

That had been his name. His prime name. His golden armour had been wrought with etchings of his many names, all earned in triumph and honour, all granted by the Emperor Himself.

The Emperor as He was, not as He became. The would-be Ruler of Terra, still so far from His ascension as the Master of Mankind.

The Imperator was there at Maulland Sen, in the hours before the Thunder Legion met the priest-king's ravening hordes. Armoured in archeotech and anachronism, his armour as much baked leather and bronze as ceramite, He stood upon a high rock as the rising sun turned the eagles on his armour to virgin gold.

His army stood to the south, occupying the low ground. Their march to the enemy would be uphill, moving to ascend the rocky inclines in whatever formation they could hold. To the north were the enemy, a horde of branded zealots and dirty wildlanders on the plateaus of their last mountain fastness, clad in motorised plate armour and cloaked in poorly cloned furs to brace against the cold. Lumbering brutes fleshed out their numbers, more evidence of gene-forging gone awry with witchery instead of vision.

They would bleed. At last, with the fall of Maulland Sen, Nordyc would be brought to heel. That blasted, frozen land. In Sagittarus' memories it was freezing to the bone – and surely it had been that way – but the cold was no surprise to him when he recalled it now. All of his memories were cold.

The Emperor had looked down upon the armoured ranks closest to Him, crudely armoured warriors in patched and remade suits of damaged ceramite. The campaign had been a long one, far more gruelling than predicted. His forces at the final battle were outnumbered by seven to one, though such numbers would mean nothing come the dawn. The enemy's high walls meant equally little, and the treacherous ascent to lay siege meant the least of all. The Emperor's army would sustain casualties, as every army always did. But sacrifice was bred into their bones. Victory would be theirs by the day's end.

The lives beneath His banner were there to be spent in the purchase of peace.

Sagittarus had chafed against promised inaction that day. No warrior was ever truly still before a battle. They shifted, they shuffled. The rattle of so many suits of ceramite plating was a dull, constant clanking to rival an ocean's tide. The angry thrum of fibre bundle muscle cabling and active back-mounted power packs was the drone of a locust swarm, a monotone buzz that drowned out spoken words. The only reliable way to speak was over the radioracle network, which was still flawed by occasional static interference.

The warriors closest to the Emperor – a mere thirty souls with Sagittarus among them – wore layered, precious auramite gold, reflecting the warlord's own wargear. In the years to follow, their trappings would become cloaked in red and bulked by additional plating, but as they stood at Maulland Sen they wore half-suits of sacred gold, and the men themselves were a jewel at the army's vanguard, guarding their master. Their war banner was the eagle's head of their royal lord crossed by four bolts of lightning.

Beyond the Custodians were the ranks of the proto-legionaries in their grim, battered plate. Thunder Warriors. Even then Sagittarus had known what fate these soldiers of Unity would face. Their place was here and their time was now: they would be the conquerors of Terra... and then they would be discarded. Their armour was destined to stand in rows within the Emperor's private chambers and various war museums across Terra, and their deeds would be recorded in rich detail throughout Imperial archives.

But far finer soldiers would be required to take the Emperor's war into the stars. Sagittarus, fallen yet not allowed to die, would be one of the many to spill Thunder Warrior blood.

But not yet. Not today. Not on the morning of Maulland Sen.

Here they would lose seven thousand, five hundred and eighty-one warriors against the defiant tides of Maulland Sen's last defenders.

He recalled how the Emperor ran a gloved hand through His wind-claimed hair, pulling it back from His dusky features. The wind had battered the crests atop the Thunder Warriors' helms.

'Sagittarus,' the Emperor had said in a voice that carried above the drone of armour. Sagittarus, his helm adorned with a rearing eagle, turned to regard his liege.

'My king?'

'It is time. Your spear, please.'

Sagittarus offered it without hesitation, raising his spear for the warlord's reaching hand. The Emperor took the weapon, holding it fast in one gloved fist halfway along the haft, and lifted it high. He held it horizontally, ordering His men to hold position, as officers in the Bronze Epoch and Iron Era of Old Earth had done in the centuries before radioracle systems and the vox-networks that would follow.

Sagittarus felt the army shift, their focus tightening as they turned their attention to the Emperor, watching, waiting.

There was no speech, for the army had its orders set in stone the night before. There were no curses or oaths, for those had already been given and made before the horde assembled. The Emperor said nothing at all. He signalled the advance, punching the horizontal spear three times towards the lightening sky.

And there He remained as the regiments of the Thunder Legion shook the earth beneath their marching boots, advancing up into the foothills. His honour guard of thirty Custodians waited with Him, as did a host of banner bearers, aides, runners, attendants and advisors, each with their own stewards and guardians.

Sagittarus watched the disorganised tide of soldiers making their way up the inclines. Their chaotic advance was as far from the implacable order of the Legiones Astartes as could be imagined. Nor could they rely on the same arsenal of biological enhancements implanted within the true Space Marines. These hordes were a force to crush the techno-savages of the Unification Wars, no doubt, but against the alien breeds of the galaxy? The Thunder Warriors would have been annihilated.

The Emperor was paying scant heed to the battle's opening, His patient gaze resting on the higher peaks. From there, the killing machines would soon rise. He handed the spear back to Sagittarus, who took it with due reverence.

The Emperor checked the ornate bolter at His hip. One of the very first boltguns; a progenitor for its kind – not a relic rediscovered from the Dark Age of Technology but an invention of the Emperor's own design.

'Sagittarus.' This time the Emperor's mouth didn't move. And His voice was low, too low, to be the warlord's true tone. 'Sagittarus.'

What remained of Sagittarus leaned his forehead against the cold surface of his vision lenses, staring out through the greasy red smears of reinforced transplastic.

'Sagittarus,' said one of his own kind, looking up at the armoured cradle that held his revenant bones.

Ra, he mouthed, his toothless, scarred mouth full of a thick, oxygen-rich synthetic oil.

'Ra,' intoned the speakers mounted in the armoured chassis of his walking tomb.

'My apologies for interrupting your reflections,' said the tribune.

The Dreadnought didn't move as a living being moved. It had none of the incidental and unnecessary gestures of natural motion. Its movements were statuesque and reserved, coming between bouts of unnatural stillness. It was easy to forget there was a living warrior interred within, though the exact parameters for a Contemptor chassis to sustain life at the point of death was a philosophical argument the warriors of the Ten Thousand had engaged in more than once before. The life support systems suggested the warrior lived, yet the hull itself cradled a remnant in a sarcophagus that would truly die the moment the biological husk was disconnected.

Internment within a Dreadnought chassis straddled the border between both life and death – an intolerable weakness that required sacred machinery to maintain, coupled with a strength of purpose so unquenchably fierce that it defied the grave.

The Ten Thousand, supremely educated and philosophical souls all, had ultimately reached the only conclusion that mattered: their hesitancies and doubts meant nothing. It was the Emperor's will that His warriors live and fight until they could no longer do either. That very testament was inscribed upon Sagittarus' armoured hull by the Emperor's own carving hand: *Only in death does duty end.*

'Memories,' the great golden machine replied. 'They cling to me, Ra. Sometimes it seems as though the mist brings them.'

Ra had entertained the same thought more than once. The two Custodians stood in the Godspire's courtyard, where whole stretches of the long-dead alien botanical garden were given over to prefab Mechanicum architecture. A shanty town of Martian industrial ingenuity, dark against the pale eldar bone and grey Mechanicum gunmetal of the resurrected city.

Sagittarus was undergoing maintenance within an open-sided engineering-barracks. Sparks sprayed. The air reeked of sacred oils and fusing metal. A coterie of arming servitors and archwrights worked the Dreadnought's shell, repairing the hull and reloading the arm-mounted weaponry. Each of Sagittarus' movements disturbed the technical ballet taking place around him, generating a chorus of complaints that he duly ignored.

Ra stood before the tall Dreadnought shell – which bore enough cracks and pits and dents across its golden surface that it resembled the surface of some asteroid-tortured planetoid – and tried not to see Sagittarus' ruination as a statement for the entire Ten Thousand. Those who remained had all seen better days.

'Sometimes I see ghosts in the mist,' said the Dreadnought.

'There is no such thing, my noble friend. Ghosts are a fiction.'

'Most of them are eldar. I think they're begging. They reach out towards me. Not all of them are alien. I see familiar faces turned to smoke, the images of the Ten Thousand that have already fallen.'

Ra watched as the war machine's weapons cycled, evidently eager to fire. Death hadn't soothed Sagittarus' easy and willing wrath. The Dreadnought turned its hull in a grind of servos, and several of the attending machine-adepts emitted binaric curses. 'Do you ever see ghosts in the mist, Ra?'

'No,' Ra lied.

There came the sound of a machine slipping its gears, the Dreadnought shell's attempt to vocalise the laughter of the revenant within. 'Very well. What do you need of me? There is much to do before the foe reaches us.'

'Nothing more than you already give. I bring a warning for the battle to come.'

The Dreadnought opened and closed its immense fist as if testing its knuckle joints, then rotated its hand at the wrist with a grinding whirr. Ra saw the pale face of the corpse within move behind the murk of the machine's eye-lenses.

'What warning?'

'The Emperor and the Soulless Queen have warned of a warp-entity possessing surpassing strength among the enemy hosts. It destroyed the Protector released by Commander Krole, along with its warhost.'

The Dreadnought shifted with a clanking thud. Protectors, the Sicarian Alphas at least, rarely died easily, but it was the notion of the Emperor's warning that sat ill in Sagittarus' heart.

'Do we know its capabilities?'

'Little beyond its lethality.'

The golden war machine cycled its autoloaders slowly and smoothly, allowing the tech-priests to study the motion for flaws.

'We should destroy it, Ra. Destroy it before it reaches the walls and we lose it inside the city. Once the fighting is street to street, disorder will reign.'

'As it happens I agree, but we can hardly sally forth in a grand charge when we're still evacuating the outward tunnels. The rearguard forces are aware of the threat and the Unifiers are seeking to map the creature's likely routes of attack. If we have that, we can lay an ambush.'

'An ambush, then. Before it's loose in Calastar.'

'Truthfully, Sagittarus, I'm more worried about it slipping past us and reaching the throne room.'

The Dreadnought mused, its knuckles closing and opening, opening and closing, betraying a habit its pilot had performed in life. Within its hollow palm, the magnetic coils of an embedded plasma gun ticked in metronomic idleness. Within the shell, the revenant of Sagittarus was studying the data-streams, seeking reports.

'Did the Protector send a mortis-pulse?' asked Sagittarus.

Ra keyed in a command on his ornate vambrace, the buttons elegantly forming part of the soaring eagle sculpted upon the auramite. He threaded Alpha-Rho-25's final audiovisual transmission across a private vox-link directly to the Dreadnought.

The playback repeated. After several seconds Sagittarus rose to his feet in a harmony of whining snarls. 'What does that mean? That word?'

'You hear a word within that mess?' Ra's surprise was brazen. 'The Emperor sensed it, as well. I hear nothing but Alpha-Rho-Twenty-Five's death.'

'It repeats, like the static of disconnection is breathing. *Drach'nyen. Drach'nyen. Drach'nyen.*'

Ra heard it then. The Emperor's voice came back to him, when his master had spoken of the name's meaning.

'Drach'nyen,' he repeated. 'The End of Empires.'

PART TWO
THE NECESSITY OF TYRANNY

SEVEN

Land's Raider and Land's Crawler
The Twelfth
Disciple of the Unmaker God

ARKHAN LAND CONSIDERED himself a man of peace. He was first and foremost a technoarchaeologist, devoting his life to the rediscovery of schematics and Standard Template Construct data lost since the Dark Age of Technology. He was rather renowned in that field, and accordingly proud of the fact.

Who had ventured for years through the deep crust and mantle vaults of the Librarius Omnis with its horde of lethal traps and hardcoded defensive systems? Why, that would be Arkhan Land. Who had mapped a region of the catacombs beneath the surface of Sacred Mars equal to that of a small nation? Well, that would also be Arkhan Land. Who had uncovered the ancient schematics necessary to reintroduce production of the Raider-pattern main battle tank into the sphere of human knowledge? Once more, it was none other than Arkhan Land.

There was an irritating habit emerging among the Legions of calling it the 'Land Raider', with no regard for the distinction in its rediscovery. Arkhan had penned a long and detailed essay in rebuttal of the trend, entitled *Worthy Notes and Treatises of Direct Relevance to Land's Raider-Pattern Main Battle Tank: The Rebirth of an Ancient Miracle*.

And then when he'd returned to the surface of the Red Planet with the extensive – and thoroughly decoded – plans for the Crawler-pattern agriculture harvester, his awed superiors had requested he give a presentation to various worthies from various forges. The machine wasn't merely efficient in its use, it was also an icon of that trifecta of mass-production utility: inexpensive to construct; simple to maintain; easy for untrained users to safely control.

The Crawler, his patrons assured him, would revolutionise life on the emergent Imperium's agri worlds.

Arkhan Land knew that, though. He didn't need to be told. Why else did they think he'd worked so hard to bring its plans back to the surface?

His presentation speech at the symposium had lasted almost three hours. Some of his peers and patrons considered that degree of self-congratulation to be excessive, but Arkhan Land was a pragmatic man. The Crawler was already seeing use on several hundred recon-quered Imperial worlds. Until his peers had also revolutionised the human race's approach to agriculture, he couldn't care less for their views on what constituted speechworthy achievement.

He had always been a creature of vision. A prodigy, beyond doubt. By the time he'd turned five Terran standard years old, Arkhan was flu-ent in fifty Gothic-variant languages and was passable in several dozen more. When it came to augmentation he was something of a purist; at age eleven he refused mnemonic implantation and cognitive bracing because he didn't want his thoughts to be 'slowed down by someone else's engineering'.

He'd augmented himself as he aged, of course. Every hierarch of Sacred Mars indulged in the practice of engineered evolution. Only through bionic and augmetic improvement could adepts bring them-selves closer to the purity of the Omnissiah. However, he kept his modifications subtle to the point of invisibility, seeming to relish his human form in its original incarnation.

The best reason he gave to support this decision was the example of the Emperor.

'The Omnissiah,' Arkhan would say in response to his critics, 'shows little in the way of outward augmentation. For those of you that worry about my piety, consider just who I emulate with my restraint.'

That tended to silence his critics.

His penchant for collecting archeotech was legendary, as was the length and breadth of his collection. Herein lay his true passion rather than the extensive body reconstruction that enraptured many of his peers. Arkhan Land was deeply fond of his tools, gadgets and instruments, many of which defied current Terran and Martian understanding.

One of these weapons – quite possibly the delightful capstone of his armoury thus far – was a bulky sidearm with a curious array of focusing lenses, rotating magnetic vanes, spiralling accelerator coils and the capacity to spit solid micro-atomic rounds the size of a child's fingertip. He'd re-engineered the weapon with aural dampeners to offset how horrendously loud it was when fired, then attached it to a mounting fixed to his shoulder so he could carry his favourite war relic around without needing to bear it at his hip or in his robes like some tediously self-aware gunslinger out to impress his lessers with a martial aspect.

As a final touch he'd slaved the harness to his hind-thoughts, so once the weapon was activated by a thought command it would then follow every tilt and turn of his head, aiming wherever he looked.

Yes, he considered himself a man of peace, even though he possessed a firearm capable of weaponised nuclear fission every time it fired. In no way did he see this as hypocrisy. The very suggestion would have made him balk; Arkhan Land took his personal integrity almost as seriously as he took his duty.

These days, he was a very busy man indeed. There was, after all, a war to win – and being asked to help win it by the guardians of a living god was rather flattering. He'd been instrumental in designing the gravitic suspensor plates in Legio Custodes' battle tanks, as well as their – rather beautiful, in his opinion – Paragon-pattern jetbikes. How those engines howled! A noisy engine was a sacrament to the

Omnissiah. A machine with silent function was a machine with a weak soul. That's simply all there was to it.

Quite when he had been reduced to the whipping boy of the new Fabricator General was beyond him, but the situation was what it was, and he suspected that complaining about it now would be considered arch and petty.

The new Fabricator General. How fresh that title still seemed, despite Kane bearing the mantle since the fall of Mars. *Perhaps that's because he has done so little with the position,* Land thought. He knew the thought was uncharitable the moment it occurred to him, yet it felt righteous enough. Nor was he alone among his kind in thinking it. As long as Sacred Mars turned in the Archtraitor's grip, no number of triumphs elsewhere in the galaxy mattered to the priests and seers of the Martian Mechanicum.

Sapien rode on Arkhan's shoulder, the artificimian watching the people of the Palace with wide, clicking eyes. Occasionally it hissed at passing servitors, baring its blunt teeth. The little fellow was in a foul mood of late, the reason for which eluded Arkhan completely. Sometimes he regretted constructing his nimble companion with no method of binaric cant or human communication. But then, that would have been a deviation from the historical ledgers in his possession, which clearly described just what a monkey had and had not been, back when there were such things on Terra.

He'd argued with several scholars – Terran, Martian and out-system alike – regarding the veracity of those archives. It seemed everyone had their own viewpoint, backed up by their own research, on just what monkeys had actually been. A particularly misguided rival of Arkhan's had insisted the creatures could hang from trees by their tails, which was patently nonsense. Any serious scholar could see the beast's tail was designed as a lash and a puncturing weapon to deliver venom.

Arkhan's boots echoed across the skyway gantries that linked one tower to another. The bitter Terran breeze was weak even this high, thousands of feet above one of the hundreds of flat plains that had been geoshaped in order to lay the Imperial Palace's foundations. It was said that the Palace had taken almost two centuries to build. Arkhan could believe it.

That meant Rogal Dorn and his Imperial Fists had remade it in less than one-twentieth of the time, turning the regal Palace into a fortress bastion, which – again – Arkhan found easy to believe. Space Marines were ever industrious when they set their limited minds to something.

And therein lay the problem, the very heart of the whole matter. The galaxy burned because of that very fact. The Omnissiah's great vision was under threat, all because of the jealousies of lesser beings.

Arkhan himself had enjoyed the tremendous honour of working with the Omnissiah once. It was at once the most notable and mystifying experience of his life. The summons had come to him on Mars, necessitating a brief journey to Terra, which he'd gladly undertaken. Rather than make planetfall at one of the many star ports, the specific instructions in the summons led his landing craft to the war-scarred tundra of the farthest northlands.

There, he had the supreme privilege of entering one of the Omnissiah's secret, sacred laboratories at the heart of an inactive volcano. There, he had navigated a maze of sealed doorways and active defensive systems, at several points picking through the bones of failed, fallen intruders, until he stood in the Emperor's presence. And there, for the first time, he had seen the Machine-God with his own eyes.

'Do not bow,' the Emperor had said. His voice was as machine-like and pure as Arkhan had imagined, devoid of all tone and emphasis. Such monotone purity usually only came with significant augmentation.

Arkhan rose, as instructed. He didn't see a warlord, as so many claimed to see. He saw a scientist. Gone was the armour of the brazen Terran conqueror, replaced by a protective hazard suit suitable for work in sterile and hostile conditions alike. The Emperor stood in the heart of His great laboratory, where fluid bubbled in racked vials and organs pulsated in cylinders brimming with preservative gel. Machines and engines whose use defied common understanding purred and rattled and hummed. To the untrained eye they would seem to be operating independently, but Arkhan saw the truth at once: they were slaved to the Emperor's will, each of them functioning as part of a harmonic chorus in order to do the Omnissiah's intellectual bidding.

Several of the tables housed meticulously written notes upon fresh paper, neatly layered with printed schematics and thin plastic sheets of blueprinted plans. Others were monuments to the past, with ancient scrolls and parchments held open at the corners by whatever served to hand as a paperweight. Arkhan had expected an eclectic mix of orderly High Science and the disorder seen in the sanctums of many geniuses, and that's exactly what he saw.

'Please accept my gratitude,' said the Machine-God, 'for attending me.'

'The honour is mine,' Arkhan replied, feeling the bitter annoyance of tears threatening to ruin the moment. How irritating emotions could be, sometimes. Still, there was strength in overcoming them, not scraping them away with bionics. In this as well, he emulated the Omnissiah above all else.

'I need your expertise, Arkhan.'

There was something in the way the Emperor said his name. His aural sensors registered no sound, yet he heard his name spoken aloud. Arkhan found it somewhat unnerving and terribly fascinating, promising himself he would enquire as to the nature of the effect. He never did.

The Emperor worked alone, sole lord within this sanctum of forbidden, forgotten knowledge. Lightning drew scars across the night sky far above, followed by guttural peals of thunder. Despite the chamber's depth underground, the lights of the laboratory flickered in gothic sympathy with the storm.

A body lay on the central slab. A hulking thing, a creature of overdeveloped musculature and thumb-thick veins that had deviated as far from the template of humanity as imaginable while still being able to lay claim to mankind as its root species. In truth it closer resembled something from myth: the frost giants of the Ancient Nordycii clans, or the godborn of the pre-Dark Age Jarrish conclaves. What was human about it had been swelled to grotesque and militant proportions. Even in death its scabrous face was twisted into a rictus leer, as if, in life, it had known nothing but pain.

The Emperor, clad as any scientist might be clad, stood by the central slab with one hand upon the obscene muscle topography of the monstrous man's chest. His attention was directed towards several nearby monitors and their constant scrolling data. Each screen showed a digital, binaric or runic variation of biodata in an unfolding stream. Arkhan realised then that the body on the slab wasn't a body after all; it still registered a pulse and a confused distortion of brain activity.

The technoarchaeologist moved from the shadows beyond the harsh glare of downward lighting aimed at the body. He found he couldn't look away from the patient's face, and the crude, vicious cybernetics implanted upon the unconscious monster's skull.

'Teeth of the Cog,' he swore softly.

The Emperor seemed too distracted to note his blasphemy. Minute circuitry on the fingertips of the Omnissiah's bloodstained surgical gloves pressed to the giant's chest. They generated an aura of ultrasound – wherever they touched, crude internal scans of the spine and surrounding flesh drew themselves upon several of the nearby monitors, at various angles. The slumbering body gave a heavy twitch and a grunt as pain spiked through its nervous system.

Arkhan moved around to the giant's pained features. The metal teeth. The furrowed brow. The scars upon scars. The cables tendrilling out from his scalp like cybernetic dreadlocks.

'Angron,' he breathed the name.

'Yes,' the Emperor confirmed, inhumanly toneless. 'I am trying to undo the damage that has been done to the Twelfth.'

The Emperor gestured a free hand, similarly smeared with blood, to three screens that still projected a flickering hololithic of the giant's skull, brain and spinal column. The image was riven with dozens of slender black tendrils that were anything but organic. Arkhan stared

at the scanned images in slow-dawning understanding. His comprehension of human anatomy was absolute, given his experience and
education, but the images on the screens weren't entirely human. Nor
were they in accordance with the sacred and approved pathways to
augmetic ascension.

This was rather more profane.

'It is my belief that you have seen this device before,' said the Emperor.
'Is that so?'

'Yes, Divine One. In my expedition down to the Hexarchion Vaults.'

'Vaults that were resealed by your own decree, ratified by Fabricator
General Kelbor-Hal and all findings within unrecorded.'

'Yes, Divine One. The lore within represented a moral threat and a
potential perversion of cognition.'

The Emperor's fingers pressed to the unconscious primarch's temple.
'But you saw a device like this.'

Arkhan Land nodded. 'The profane texts entombed within the Hexarchion Vaults named it a *cruciamen*.'

The Emperor continued his fingertip scans, saying nothing.

'I have never seen one implanted and operational,' Arkhan confessed.
'And never of this specific pattern and intensity, in the repose of stasis or storage. The devices in the sealed vault were rather more crude
than this construct.'

'That is to be expected.'

'Why, in your infinite wisdom, would you implant this device inside
a primarch?'

'I did not do so, Arkhan.'

'Then… with great shame, I confess that I am not certain what I am
looking at, Divine One.'

'The Twelfth and its Legion call them the "Butcher's Nails".' The
Emperor kept staring at the screens. 'You are looking at modifications
to my original template of the Twelfth. More precisely, you are looking
at modifications of primitive genius. Before these examinations, I had
believed the enhancements performed upon the Twelfth on Nuceria

were the source of its emotional instability. My hypothesis was that they stirred the Twelfth to a sense of perpetual but ultimately artificial rage. Yet the opposite is true. With the alterations made to the limbic lobe and insular cortex, the surgeons have impaired the Twelfth's ability to regulate any emotion at all. Furthermore, they have rethreaded its capacity to take pleasure in anything but the sensation of anger. They are the only chemicals and electrical signals that flow freely through, and from, its brain. All else is either dulled to nothingness or rewired to inspire a supreme degree of agony. It is a testament to the durability of my primarch project that the Twelfth has managed to survive this long.'

'His own emotions cause him pain?'

'No, Arkhan. Everything. Everything causes it pain. Thinking. Feeling. Breathing. The only respite it has is in the rewired neurological pleasure it receives from the chemicals of anger and aggression.'

'That's vile,' said the technoarchaeologist. 'Perversion of cognition, rather than purification.'

The Emperor showed nothing but passionless interest. 'Such rewriting of physiology certainly hinders the Twelfth's higher brain function. The device is cunningly wrought, for something so crude.'

'Can you remove it?'

'Of course,' the Emperor answered, still looking at the screens.

Arkhan did his best to hide his surprise. 'Then, Divine One, why would you leave it there?'

'This is why.' The Emperor rested both hands on Angron's head, one with the fingertips pressed to the primarch's temple and cheek, the other pressed to the crown of his shaven head where the cable-tendrils joined the flesh and bone. The images on several screens immediately resolved to a clearer imprint of a brutishly dense skull miserable with crude cybernetics and the bone-scarring of powerful surgical laser cuts.

'Do you see?' the Emperor asked.

Arkhan saw. The tendrils were sunk deep, rooted in the meat of the brain, threaded to the nervous system, and down in roughly serpentine coils around the spinal column. Every movement must have been agony for the primarch, feeding back into the base emotions of anger and spite.

Worse, the brain's limbic lobe and insular cortex were more than just savaged by the pain engine's insertion; they had been surgically attacked and removed even before implantation. The device hammered into his skull hadn't ruined those sections of the brain – it had replaced them. Ugly black cybernetics showed on the internal scans, in place of entire sections of the primarch's brain tissue.

'They are the only thing keeping him alive,' Arkhan said.

The Emperor lifted His hands from the somnolent primarch's skull. Most of the screens instantly went black. He spoke as He removed His surgical gloves. 'This has been educational.'

'I don't understand, Divine One. Can I be of use to you?'

'You have been of immense use, Arkhan. You have confirmed what I suspected regarding the cruciamen's origins. No one else could have done so. I am accordingly grateful.'

Arkhan had expected the Omnissiah's dispassionate demeanour, but to witness it in so intimate a context was inspiring in the extreme. So neutral. So inhumanly neutral.

'Divine One,' he said, before he knew he was going to say anything at all.

'A compromised primarch is still a primarch,' the Emperor mused, still distracted. 'What is it, Arkhan?'

Land hesitated. 'You are more sanguine than I would have imagined in this moment, even knowing of your holy detachment from emotion.'

'What would the alternative be?' The Emperor laid the bloodstained gloves on a nearby surgical trolley, where red-marked knives and other instruments lay wet and freshly used. 'That I might mourn the Twelfth as though it were my injured son, and I its grieving father?'

'Never that, Divine One.' Arkhan chose his words with care. 'Though some might expect that.'

The Emperor unlocked the sealed vambraces of His hazard suit, then removed the surgical mask that had covered His face until now. 'It is not my son, Arkhan. None of them are. They are warlords, generals, tools bred to serve a purpose. Just as the Legions were bred to serve a purpose.'

Arkhan looked down at the sleeping demigod, watching Angron's facial features twitch and tense in painful harmony with a ravaged nervous system.

'With your blessing, Divine One, I would ask something of you.'

The Emperor turned His eyes upon Land for the first time. Falling beneath the Omnissiah's gaze made the Motive Force in Arkhan's bloodstream flow faster, tingling like weak acid.

'Ask.'

'The primarchs. It is said they have always called you father. It seems so… sentimental. I've never understood why you allow it.'

The Emperor was silent for some time. When He spoke, His eyes had returned to the hulking form on the surgical slab. 'There was once a writer,' he said, 'a penner of children's stories who told the tale of a wooden puppet that wished to be reborn as a human child. And this puppet, this automaton of painted, carved wood that sought to be a thing of flesh and blood and bone – do you know what it called its maker? What would such a creature call the creator that gave it shape and form and life?'

Father. Arkhan felt his skin crawl. 'I understand, Divine One.'

'I see that you do.' The Emperor turned back to the body on the slab. 'The Twelfth's lifespan and tactical acuity may be reduced but the pain engine amplifies its effectiveness in other ways to compensate. I believe I will return the Twelfth to its Legion. You have my gratitude once more, Arkhan. Thank you for coming.'

It had been the first and only time he'd stood alone in the Omnissiah's presence. He could have clutched at the singular honour of the moment, bringing it to light and riding the resulting fame. But he hadn't. Arkhan Land, for all that his detractors called him vain and pompous, kept the truest honour of his life a secret from all others.

It would've cheapened it to milk the moment for personal gain. He was content to keep it as his private hour of joy, that glorious evening when a living god had needed his knowledge.

The rattling of the elevator brought him back to the present, where the descent into the Ordo Reductor's stronghold had finally ended. The tri-layered doors unbolted with an opera of metallic crunches, then moaned open one by one. Hazard striping slid away in every direction as the last of the airlock doors finally parted.

Kane was waiting for him on the concourse beyond. The Fabricator General had sanctified himself with severe weaponisation since Arkhan had last been in his presence. *It suits you,* Arkhan thought, *in your blunt and uninspired approach to existence.*

'Fabricator General,' he greeted the exiled ruler of Sacred Mars.

'Arkhan Land,' replied his lord and master. 'Come with me.'

'At once, dominus.' *You tedious gargoyle.* 'May I enquire as to your need?'

'All will be revealed.' Kane turned, backing up on his grinding tracks, curling his arms close to his red cloak. 'Follow.'

'Where are we going?'

'To converse with the Bringers of Blessed Ruin. No more questions for now. Merely follow.'

KANE JUDDERED ALONG on his armoured tank treads, roving between the power generator columns. The air was thick with incense, and humming filtrators pumped carbon dioxide and argon into the entire complex, thinning the nitrogen and oxygen to unpleasantly breathable levels analogous to the terraformed Martian atmosphere. Kane greedily sucked the artificial smog through his respiratory filters. Each breath he took was a holy observance.

The temperature had a tendency to fluctuate this deep in the complex's innards, with the climate controls regulated by overworked processors running to figures that changed by necessity from chamber to chamber. In this particular vault, the shift from forge heat to cryonic cold was stark enough to be felt as a physical barrier. His torso shook in its cable-thick cradle as his treads ran over the uneven floor.

Arkhan Land, that monumental irritant, walked at his side. Really, it was a grievous shame that the technoarchaeologist was necessary at all, but Kane would have been a fool not to use every tool at his disposal. Land was a vainglorious and self-serving wretch, but he was a vainglorious and self-serving wretch with an insight – and vital schematics – possessed by few others.

And, crucially, he had been instrumental in the anti-gravitic designs favoured by the Legio Custodes' war machines. The respect granted to Land by the Ten Thousand was more valuable to Kane than any imaginable currency.

Once inside the next vault, Kane pulled back his hood. The wires and needle-cables that replaced his hair were tugged none too gently by the movement. He drove on, red-dot sights beaming here and there as he turned his head, seeking by eye and scanning by internal auspex.

The inhabitants of the chamber scattered before his rolling advance. Miserable things still consisting mostly of flesh, their robes stained by beggars' filth, they should have been beneath the Fabricator General's notice. On Mars they wouldn't have dared approach him, but the loss of their homeland had ruined their sense of decorum as it had harmed the cognitive processes and emotional restraints of so many other Mechanicum adepts. Several of them tried to pray to him as he trundled past, believing him to be the Omnissiah Incarnate, descending into the purgatory of their lives.

Kane caught sight of Arkhan Land's smile. Evidently the blasphemy on display amused him.

If these forge-vermin believed in their weeping praise that their Fabricator General intended to save them, they were grotesquely mistaken. He drew an elegant phosphor serpenta pistol of pseudowood and Martian red gold and casually shot one of the braying miscreants through the chest. That sent the others fleeing.

Kane was far past the ability to smile, but he felt warmed by silencing their petty, mistaken little blasphemy all the same. The rush of brain chemicals triggering a sense of all-too-human satisfaction was a guilty pleasure indeed. He holstered the slim pistol beneath his robes, the secondary arm that had drawn it curling back close to his torso.

'You are such an inspiring leader,' Arkhan Land noted. Kane glanced towards the man, reading his facial features for any sign of amusement. He detected none, though the artificimian on Land's shoulder made a chittering sound resembling primate laughter.

Once we have retaken our homeland, Kane thought, *I will end you.*

'You think me ignorant of your sarcasm?' the Fabricator General asked, gambling that it had been a disingenuous comment.

'No, dominus. Never that.'

Land seemed sincere. Kane suspected a deception but refused to engage with such petty behaviour. On he rolled, the technoarchaeologist at his side, eventually reaching another airlock. They both endured an aura-spray of cleansing chemicals in a fine mist before they were permitted to enter the next chamber. Kane's treads gripped the contoured gantry slope as he descended through the sloped workshop-laboratory that spread before him in a vast expanse. Arkhan's boots thud-thudded on.

Here, hundreds of menials and thralls laboured at the slabs of deactivated automata, building, repairing and resealing armoured carapaces of blessed iron and sacred steel. Adepts and priests, low of rank yet still commanding positions eclipsing their thrall minions, bent their expertise to the construction and rethreading of complicated internal circuitry, or managed the integration and installation of bio-mechanical organ container tanks.

Ranks of half-built war robots lined the walls, slouched by work tables or lying in disassembled repose upon surgical slabs. The recreated Martian air was beautifully spiced with the reek of blood, oil and *toxma*, the holy synthetic petrochemical blend that served in place of either natural fluid.

Head after head turned to regard him. Some of the adepts bowed, some murmured greetings in binaric cant or exloaded welcomes onto the noospheric net as data across the Fabricator General's visual feed. He ignored most and canted back greetings to a few, moving between the hive of dead robots lying on their surgery tables. Emblazoned on every wall in great sigils of dark metal and Martian red gold was the fortress and lightning bolt symbol of the Unmaker God's blessed artisans of destruction, the Ordo Reductor.

He spurted a binaric query to Land, who, to the Fabricator General's irritation, kept choosing to reply aloud in unaugmented vocalisation.

'No,' said Land. 'I've never ventured here before.'

'Impressive, is it not?'

'Oh, yes. Very impressive.'

'The delay and tone of your reply suggests deception.'

'You should learn to accept a polite lie for the value it has,' Land replied, adding Kane's title after another conversationally significant pause.

Sapien clicked its tongue and chittered, a sound quite unlike anything Terran monkeys had ever made, many thousands of years ago when they'd still drawn breath.

Kane's internal curse was a screed of binaric invective that he was far too dignified to transmit.

A circular elevator platform in the floor took them even deeper into the complex. The fortress symbol was repeated on the walls of the elevator shaft, and Kane expressed a moment of revelatory admiration across the noosphere for just how deep his people had dug into Terra's crust, and how tenacious they were in their resolve to have accomplished so much in their brief banishment from the Red Planet.

Land evidently had a different perspective. 'Look how we spread our tendrils, gripping tight to the soil of our exile, the way trees spread roots, never to be moved.'

Kane felt a flicker of camaraderie, at long last. An alignment of vision. 'You fear we will never see Sacred Mars again.'

Arkhan nodded. All sons and daughters of Mars knew that he had left a lifetime of work unfinished. For once there was no suggestion of a snide comeback or disrespectful glance.

'I fear we are becoming comfortable. Complacency will only make this exile permanent.'

Kane vocalised a code of solidarity, the canted equivalent of a reassuring smile, and moved onwards. Another accord between them. This was good. This was promising.

They descended another nine levels, leaving the platform at the bottom of the shaft. Bulkheads whined and groaned open, admitting them with gearborn mechanical songs. Another workshop stretched out in every direction, indistinguishable from the first but for one utterly significant aspect – the temperature was glacial, maintained thus by mist-breathing climate processor units in the low ceiling.

Here the adepts and their minions worked on the most complicated brain function cogitators of the ordo's siege engine automata and anti-infantry hunter-killer machines. Their work involved the preservation and linkage of delicate biological components, bonding man and machine at an inseparable level. The craft on this sublevel was of the highest, most precise quality, and it was here that Kane finally found the adept he had been seeking.

Hieronyma was working alone, which was no surprise; Kane knew her idiosyncrasies well. She stood bent over a surgical slab, all four of her mechanical hands devoted to a bowl of preservative soup that contained a nest of wires and cables binding a human brain. Kane always enjoyed watching her work. Her fingers were designed to divide into three slender sections at the tips, each able to move independently from its neighbours, giving her a level of precise digital control few tech-priests could begin to match.

A great hunch marked her curved back. Whatever augmentations lay beneath her robe were enthusiastically inhuman in nature. Kane greatly approved.

She didn't look up, though she canted a very polite greeting from beneath her red hood. The stream of code not only welcomed the

Fabricator General to her workstation, but also expressed the honour of being deemed worthy of a visit. Would that all of his people were so dutiful, Mars would never have fallen. She greeted Arkhan Land with a much briefer vocalised spurt. The technoarchaeologist returned a shallow bow.

<Magos domina,> Kane canted, spilling the numerical code of her name aloud on an almost subsonic frequency. The barest flicker of her divided fingertips showed her surprise as she worked on delicately puncturing the soaking brain. Around them both, work continued on.

'The event I bring to your attention cannot be trusted to the noosphere,' he clarified, quenching her dignified confusion.

Her reply was similarly quiet, pitched and transmitted for his personal receptors and Land's ears. In the heart of the Mechanicum's fortress on Terra, the most secure way to converse was the most primitive: they whispered.

Her hood twitched as she tilted her head, still focusing on her work. 'What brings you here, Lord of Mars?'

'The Great Work,' he said, trans-shaping the reply so muted, so fine, that it was barely even subsonic.

He was gratified to see another hesitation in her divided fingertips. She was too dutiful, and too aware of the Mechanicum's depleting resources, to risk abandoning her work for lesser hands, but her fascination with Kane's presence was becoming a very real distraction.

'You honour me,' she said, bluntly honest. Her private tone was yearning, practically starving for more data.

'I do,' Kane confirmed. 'The Omnissiah's war rages on. The Ten Thousand and the Silent Sisterhood, praise upon their names for their most glorious of duties, bring the Machine-God's will to us in the form of a requisition list.'

Land raised a thin eyebrow but said nothing. Hieronyma turned her hooded features to face the Fabricator General, eyeing him with a shadowed visage of variously sized green lenses. To compensate, a mechadendrite uncoiled from her spine and aimed its eye-lens tip down at her work. With her vision doubled, she examined Kane and continued working at the same time. Bio-sign monitors hanging from the ceiling in a loose ring showed a spill of data detailing the brain's function as Hieronyma manipulated it beneath her tender touch.

She said nothing, for she needed to say nothing. Not yet. The Fabricator General of Sacred Mars wouldn't come here to trouble her for a requisition order consisting of crates of bolt shells and robots to serve as blade fodder for the enemy. This was something else. Something unexpected.

'And,' Kane added, 'opportunity has arisen at last. Adnector Primus Mendel has fallen. His demise leaves a void in the Unifiers' leadership.'

Still Hieronyma said nothing. Kane appreciated her appropriate reverence and attention. Instinct almost had him exload the requisition manifest directly to her, but he was not ready to trust the noosphere. As united as Mars and Terra were, they were still two empires beneath the same banner, two kingdoms sharing a king. Their interests were not always strictly and perfectly aligned, and Zagreus Kane was a man short on trust these days. Being forced to flee one's home world in panicked disgrace could have that effect on a soul.

Land's psyber-monkey hopped from the explorer's shoulder onto Hieronyma's workstation. It watched the motions of her slender bionic fingers, chittering to itself. Its antics went ignored, even by Land himself.

The Fabricator General continued, 'In addition to thousands of new troops and a forge-harvest's worth of materiel, the Ten Thousand, with the Omnissiah's blessing, have requested the Mechanicum provide their new army with a general to replace Mendel. To meet this demand, your disciples of the Unmaker God will proceed with the Archimandrite Venture.'

Now, against all code and creed, Hieronyma ceased her ministrations. The mechadendrite tentacle lashed back beneath her robe, and her four hands snicked and clicked back into clawed completion. Every single one of her eye-lenses, the only features of her face, whirred and refocused.

'You require this of me, Fabricator General?'

Kane blurted a forceful shunt of code.

Hieronyma bowed deeply. 'You honour me,' she said again with appropriate reverence. 'As you will it, it shall be so.'

'Your work honours the Mechanicum in kind,' Kane replied. 'Harvest the materials you require to enact the process and infuse yourself with the Motive Force. May the Omnissiah bless you upon your ascension.'

Arkhan Land cleared his throat with disgusting humanity. 'As fascinating as this is...'

Both archpriests turned their eye-lenses upon the still-human, far shorter member of their triumvirate.

'...what do you need of me?'

How it galled Kane to admit this. 'Your vision. Your insight into the process of forbidden weaponisation. Your knowledge of the secrets within the Hexarchion Vaults.'

Arkhan turned his head slightly, eyes narrowed. 'What you ask is sealed unto eternal silence, by order of the Fabricator General. You know this.'

'I *am* the Fabricator General!'

Land chuckled. 'The real Fa–'

'Abandon your attempts at humour,' Kane warned. 'Do not even breathe such a sentiment, Technoarchaeologist Land. My patience has its limits.'

Land acquiesced with an amused nod. 'Even so, they ask much of us and offer little.'

Kane responded with a negative/abort chime equating derisive laughter, mocking the very idea. He no longer had enough of a human face remaining to smile, which was, briefly, something he regretted. The effect of biological smugness had its usefully deployable moments.

'They ask much, this is true. Yet in exchange I have secured their word that an avenue to Mars will remain within Imperial and Mechanicum control.'

'Home,' Hieronyma said, hissing and urgent. 'Red Mars. Sacred Mars. Mother Mars.'

Arkhan Land seemed rather less impressed. 'Hollow promises. The Imperium can offer us no such guarantees. We cannot return home while the skies of Mars remain caged.'

Kane emitted an abort code-spurt at the ludicrous imprecision of the technoarchaeologist's hyperbole. 'I speak not of an orbital assault, nor of any other traditional attack. I speak of another avenue. One known only among the highest echelons of Imperial command.'

Amidst the rattle and crash of the repair cavern's ceaseless industry, Kane leaned in close to his confidants, feeling the words caressing their way through his vocabulator. He felt himself drooling. Lubricant stalactited from his mouth grille.

'The Omnissiah Himself once spoke of a route between the Imperial Dungeon and the timelocked gates of the Aresian Vault. I have seen no such reference even among the Antiquitous Archives, but His word to me is All. This avenue lies within a network of galactic thoroughfares and pathways metaphysically connected to His principal soul engine.'

Hieronyma stared at him in silence. By some unguessable miracle, even Arkhan Land had nothing to say.

'I speak the truth,' Kane said. 'I speak the gravest and greatest secret truth in the twin empires of Terra and Mars, and I speak it to those that must hear it. The fate of the Mechanicum rests upon the triumvirate gathered here now.'

And still the others said nothing.

'This is the avenue I have demanded reinforced and defended against all costs,' said Kane. 'Through this "Aresian Path" we shall return to Mars.'

Now, Kane saw Land's thoughts working behind his human eyes. Musing over the principles of flight and distance, of teleportation, of this undiscovered void-lateral technology, too sacred to speak of and too precious to share. He didn't understand the idea of the webway. And how could he? The structure, if it even was a structure, defied explanation.

But he would soon see. Yes, he would.

'How can this be?' Arkhan asked.

'Irrelevant,' replied Kane. 'You shall learn all you need to learn in the fullness of time.'

'You mean you don't know.'

'*Irrelevant.*'

Hieronyma was an altogether more obedient and dignified ally. She said nothing, waiting for her overlord's input. Kane was wearily grateful for that.

'Adnector Primus Mendel was a soul of weak vision and anaemic patriotism,' said the Fabricator General. 'Thus it falls to us to work in the Red World's best interests. We three will oversee the rendering and weaponisation of the Archimandrite's ascension. We will aid the Ten Thousand in their secret war and record the various avenues of this alien webway. And then, once we have secured the Aresian Path, we will lead our people home.'

EIGHT

Imprisoned
Trial upon the battlements
Banners of the III Legion

JAYA STILL COUNTED the days, though it was a matter of instinct rather than intent. Time had little meaning between the unchanging walls of her confinement cell, but the regularity of her two meals a day made for a schedule that couldn't easily be forgotten. Especially since there was nothing else to do but eat and sleep.

And wait, of course. There was always waiting to do.

The servitor that brought her the nutrient paste was mono-tasked to the point of lobotomy, rendering it useless for information let alone conversation. On the few occasions she'd pressed it for details regarding the date of her execution, all that had emerged from its wet mouth were a few wordless grunts. She didn't think the thing had long left to live. It looked halfway dead already with its cataract-milked eyes and black teeth showing between its eternally slack lips.

The cell had been comfortable at first, a fact that had surprised her given the nature of her crime. The sleeping slab was padded, and the walls were a smooth, dry granite with a thermal strip emanating a modest breath of warmth, rather than the dank, moss-covered stone of the prison cells her family had maintained in the dungeons of her ancestral home, Castle Highrock. There was even a chest for her possessions, few though they were in captivity – she used the chest to store the cheap tin pots of nutrient paste they had been feeding her since she arrived. Jaya, at fifty-one years of age, had never been imprisoned before but she was a cautious soul; leaving a little in each pot and building up a stockpile seemed wise, just in case they suspended her rations as a form of punishment.

She could have broken and bent the tin pots, fashioning them into slivers of knives, but as weapons such shards would be flimsy and next to useless. She could slash up the servitor that brought her meals, but wounding the damn thing wouldn't do anything to improve her situation. For one, it might cut off her food supply completely. For two, it would be the pettiest of acts, striking a defenceless and mindless cyborg like that. A truly honourless kill. No war banner would fly in the great hall of Castle Highrock to celebrate *that* little victory.

So she let the thing live.

Her other option was to cut her own wrists, which was no option at all. It wasn't that she found the notion distasteful – it was that suicide could only be sanctioned as penance for sins against the code of chivalry, not to escape the consequences of crime. Honour demanded that she live until her execution.

The fact that her captors left her access to ways of killing herself showed their true disregard. It would likely be a convenience for them if she did end her own life.

She exercised to maintain her health, pushing herself up from the stone floor until the sweat ran from her thinning form, gluing her worn and filthy uniform to her flesh. She ate the thick nutrient paste and drank the brackish, repeatedly filtered water they gave her. She slept in her clothes, refusing to shed her uniform even in captivity. For the first few weeks she'd been appalled and increasingly sickened by the smell rising from her unwashed body, but by the second month the stench had simply gone away. She suspected it was still there, she was merely so used to her own stink that it no longer registered to her senses. Finger-combing her hair had only worked for the first week. Soon enough she'd been reduced to binding it back in a ponytail using one of her bootlaces.

When she went to her cell's metal door, all she could see were the smooth walls of the corridor stretching in either direction, lit by dull and flickering lumen orbs. It wasn't until the third day that she'd realised she wasn't alone down here – a shout, more of a frustrated scream in truth, had echoed down the corridor. She'd called back, her lungs raw from the dungeon's bad air, asking who was out there.

'Baroness?' the reply had come, miserable with hope.

She'd burst into laughter. One of her courtiers was caged nearby. 'Sevik?'

'Baroness! I don't suppose you have a comb, do you?'

One courtier had turned out to be several. They conducted shouted conversations in the days that followed, such behaviour simply ignored by their captors.

They grew quieter over time. What was there to say? How many times could they force good-natured laughter about their fate as they all started losing weight and feeling their teeth loosening in their gums?

The baroness understood. She fell silent too, in the same way, for the same reasons. She withdrew within herself, not to hide but to survive. She refused to be dragged before a firing squad as a ruined echo of herself – so she exercised. She stored her rations, just in case. She composed battle verses in her mind or recited old saga-poems, singing them aloud in a voice that grew shakier week by week. At first she'd tried to sing once a day, and her courtiers had joined in. As their strength failed, the real silence took hold. She'd sometimes hear one or two of them groaning or murmuring in their cells, far down the corridor. Starvation walked among them, caressing with gnawed fingers.

On the one hundred and fifty-first day, the servitor came with no food. It stood before her door, the interface slot drawn back and open, and mimed pushing the tin pot through the gap. Its pale hand was empty but the mimed action was perfect. It behaved as it always did, not acknowledging that it was delivering a handful of stale air.

She watched it from where she'd been exercising, performing slow sit-ups with her boots to the wall. She watched the servitor slide the flask of water through next, no different from usual. She saw the powdery filtration crystals, like silt at the bottom of the flask, spreading their bitter purity through the drink.

And then she watched the servitor leave.

Was this punishment? A mistake in allotting food rations? The possibility passed through her mind, icy and unwelcome, that this was the form her execution would take. Perhaps they wouldn't haul her before a firing squad after all, to let her die proud in her uniform. They'd starve her instead. At best she would be buried in a pauper's grave on Terra itself, a malnourished husk of her former self. At worst they would throw her body into a funereal incinerator along with worn-down servitors and the prisoners who ended their own lives in dishonour.

She took the flask of water, not yet giving in to panic. She had supplies. She had a few weeks' worth of the nutrient-rich gruel built up that she could fall back on.

The shouting started up again as the day passed. The other prisoners were going through the same farce, being served nothing by the servitor jailor too mindlocked to realise what it was doing wrong.

All the baroness could do was wait. If the servitor returned later that night and repeated its hollow actions, then she would know something was amiss. Until then, she wouldn't give in to the rush of fear. Fear was useful: it told you when you should be alert and aware, but it became a poison if allowed to take root. The deeper it nestled in the heart, the more it affected judgement and played havoc with reason.

She passed the hours exercising, meditating and letting the stale water fill her stomach in place of the rationed paste. When the servitor returned exactly eight hours later, right on cue, she rose to her feet and approached, watching the cyborg's pallid hands.

Again it went through the motions of feeding her, with nothing in its grip. This time it repeated the gesture – the flask it offered to quench her thirst was empty. The filtration crystals were piled at the bottom, as dry as desert sand.

No food. No water.

The baroness closed her eyes, listening to the servitor's retreating tread. She could accept the fall of a headsman's axe or the gunline stare of a firing squad. But a life spent sheathed in steel had ill prepared her to feel this helpless.

Her hands closed into fists, slowly, firmly, her knuckles showing white.

'If I breathe, I am unbeaten. If I fight, I am unbroken.'

She raced to the door, pounding on it with the heels of her fists, shouting the words over and over, letting them fill the long corridors of the prison complex.

'If I breathe, I am unbeaten. If I fight, I am unbroken.'

The words echoed back at her, shouted by dozens of throats, taking up the old, familiar banner-cry.

ONE DAY BECAME two. That was all the evidence she needed. The baroness decided to act before two days became three.

There was moisture in the nutrient paste, though scarcely enough to sustain a human body. Soon enough the baroness was looking at her cell through gummy, dehydrated eyes, and clutching a shard of can that she'd shaped into a flimsy knife after all. She was under no illusions that killing her servitor jailor would improve her lot in life, but destroying it might trip some kind of system alarm, letting her real captors know that she and her courtiers were dying of thirst and starvation. If no one came to deal with the slain jailor, then at least she'd know whether this was to be her execution.

It wouldn't be difficult. The servitor lacked any obvious counter-threat systems or retaliatory weapons beyond its cylindrical shock maul, which it was far too slow and rundown to use with any speed. All she'd need to do is drag the jailor's hands into the food slot, stun the thing by crashing its face against the door, then cut its wrists with the crude knife. It would likely go back to its duties, bleeding out along the way and hopefully triggering some kind of prison-wide alarm.

Hopefully.

When she heard the distant thump of its bionic-legged tread, she clutched the knife tight enough that blood ran from her palm. Dehydration greyed out the edges of her senses, dulling her hearing and making every vein in her skull throb with abandon, but she still managed to rise to her feet and – without consciously realising she was doing it – straighten her ragged, sweat-soiled uniform.

'If I breathe, I am unbeaten.' The words were a savage whisper. 'If I fight, I am unbroken.'

'Please stand away from the door,' the servitor intoned from behind the sealed metal portal. The gaoler had never spoken before. She doubted it even could. For a moment she wondered if her thirst-slowed thoughts had conjured the words as an auditory hallucination. It certainly didn't sound the way she'd expected. A flash of gold metal shone on the other side of the food slot.

What the–

That wonder was banished as a metre-long spear-blade rammed through the reinforced door with a ringing crash. It slid back out to be replaced by golden fingers reaching into the wound. She saw them curl and grip, then wrench the puncture open with a horrendous whine of abused iron. The door came free of the wall, sending tremors through the ground. She flinched at the bang of its twisted remains dropping onto the corridor's stone floor.

The figure that entered wasn't the servitor. It had to stoop to fit through the doorway.

'Baroness Jaya D'Arcus, Warden of Highrock?'

'A Custodian. I'm honoured.' Her voice was a parched ruin. It shamed her to show any weakness at all before a foe, but she'd be damned before she stood there in silence. 'Have you come to execute me at last?'

'I'll accept that as an affirmation. My name is Diocletian Coros of the Ten Thousand, Prefect of the Hykanatoi. Come with me please, baroness.'

'I request the right to die in a clean uniform.'

'Very civilised. And I'm sure that one day you'll die in that exact manner. However, I'm not going to kill you. You've been pardoned.'

'The Sigillite would never overturn my sentence.'

'The Sigillite had never sentenced you at all. Amidst the war's endless bureaucracy, I suspect he forgot you even existed until you were needed. You are pardoned in the Emperor's name. Now come with me, unless you want your baronial court to keep rotting in their cells.'

She followed, though cautiously. 'Needed?' she asked. 'We are needed?'

The Custodian didn't reply.

Immediately outside her cell stood another towering warrior, not quite as tall as the Custodian but still two heads above her. He was clad in red rather than gold and carried his helmet under his arm – a crested portcullis-faceplate of a thing, with a green visor dulled in deactivation. Symbols of white wings adorned his armour plating, as did elaborate silver filigree.

His features held nothing of sensuality, yet the truth remained: he was quite literally the most beautiful man Jaya d'Arcus had ever seen. The artistry of living beauty rendered in marble. An angel of myth, stricken by the hauntingly elegant pallor of consumption.

'I am Zephon,' he said with a polite bow. His voice, low yet brutally soft, was made to sing beneath the stars.

Jaya looked between the two warriors. 'Free my court. Then, for the love of all that is holy, please tell me what's going on.'

DOZENS OF THEM stood blinking and sore in the weak sunlight. Clad in the faded and filthy uniforms in which they'd been imprisoned, they nevertheless stood in orderly ranks as they would upon the Highrock parade ground. Jaya's spirits soared to see them muster in such defiant order on the back of enduring such privation. Her hopes sank soon after – with the courtiers were their attendants, several sacristans for every scion, and the robed tech-adepts had seemingly suffered far more than their masters. They gathered in loose, wheezing, shaking packs; it smote the baroness' heart to see that her house's revered engineers had been treated so poorly.

The Court of Highrock, ragged and worse for wear but free at last, stood on the battlements of the mountainous Outer Palace. Thrusting up from among the lance-like spires to the west was the Seberekan Tower, haloed by the watery eye of the setting sun. Jaya resisted the urge to spit at the sight. Engines whined, plaintive and distant, somewhere in the clouds above them.

Three figures faced them as they waited in ranks. Jaya regarded each of them in turn, cautious of each and mistrusting them equally. The Blood Angel watched the gathered courtiers and their attendants, standing unhelmed in the acrid, polluted breeze. The gentle wind's fingers plucked at his golden hair. His arms, both bionic replacements, were crossed over the X made by the reinforced cables across his breastplate. He was at once fiercely focused and utterly serene, making no threatening move. Making no move at all that wasn't inspired by the breeze.

By contrast, the Custodian paced before them, his burnished features set in neutral regard. The long spear that marked his order was held at his side in one gloved hand. Eyes so pale they were practically colourless stared from his oversized tanned features, catching the gaze of every man and woman willing to meet it.

The woman seemed to be their leader, or at least they deferred to her in some unknowable way. She was human to Jaya's eyes, externally unaugmented, tattooed with an Imperial aquila upon her keen features and clad in archaic armour of bronze chain links and golden platework. A hand-and-a-half power sword rode upon her back, the weapon sheathed and deactivated. The power generator in its hilt took the form of a golden eagle spreading its wings to form the quillions.

'I haven't seen her blink,' Sevik murmured beside Jaya. The baroness hushed him with a glance. She still suspected this all to be some bizarre ritual before their mass execution.

The Custodian looked back over his shoulder. The sword-maiden nodded, and the golden warrior began.

'Baroness,' said the warrior of the Ten Thousand. 'Step forwards.'

Jaya did so. She walked towards him, and as proud and straight-backed as she was after over thirty years of leading armies in Highrock's name, she barely reached the Custodian's armoured stomach. The warrior towered three heads taller than her. She held back a little, to maintain her dignified posture and not indulge in the foolishness of craning her neck.

'You are Jaya D'Arcus, Warden of Highrock, Baroness of House Vyridion. Is that so?'

'Actually, I have rather more titles than that.' Since being fed and watered, albeit with a brief and dubious feast of yet more stale water and nutrient gruel, she was finding her voice again. 'Marcher Lady of the Eastern Barrens, First Scion of the Envolius Reach, Crusader of the… Well, I won't bore you with my list of honours.'

'We would be here for some time if she did,' said Devram Sevik with immaculate politeness, from the first rank of courtiers.

Behind the Custodian, the tattooed woman smiled faintly, as did the Blood Angel. The Custodian did not.

'I am Diocletian of the Ten Thousand,' he told her again, this time including all of her court in the proclamation of his name. 'With me are Dominion Zephon of the Ninth Legion, and Sister Kaeria Casryn, one of the Emperor's own Oblivion Knights.'

The latter title meant nothing to the courtiers. Diocletian's sonorous voice carried to them with little effort, even against the wind that pulled gently at his red plume. 'It's said that House Vyridion abandoned the Emperor and turned its cloak to march beneath the rebel banners of the Warmaster.'

Silence greeted this announcement, into which the Custodian cast his lure. 'So tell me, scions of Highrock. Are you guilty or innocent?'

The courtiers stood resolute in silence, dignity incarnate, bound by oaths of fealty considered arcane even here at the heart of the Imperium. The baroness would speak for them. And speak she did.

'Guilty.'

The Custodian seemed to hesitate. He turned back to the Oblivion Knight, who dipped her head, bidding him continue. From the golden warrior's pause, Jaya wondered if her admission of guilt had taken the man by surprise.

'Guilty,' Diocletian repeated her confession. 'And yet your hearth-ship entered Terran skies and you surrendered into imprisonment. That speaks of repentance, or at least a willingness to be punished for your sins.'

'You did not ask of repentance or punishment,' Jaya replied. She stood straight, her hands clasped behind her back, loathing the unwashed smell rising from her dirty uniform. 'You asked if we had marched with the Warmaster's rebels, and we have done exactly that. We have fired our weapons in anger upon souls loyal to the Emperor.'

'I see.' Diocletian rested his spear upon one shoulder guard. The setting sun turned his armour to fiery bronze. 'Your scions marched alongside the Third Legion, conquering two worlds. You are responsible for the destruction of several hundred warriors and war machines of the Iron Hands, as well as innumerable thousands of their Army reserve elements. You personally slew Baron Kells of House Riathan at the Battle of Mount Galheim.'

'In single combat,' Sevik pointed out.

Diocletian's attention snapped to the courtier. 'Are you your mistress' herald?'

'No, Custodian.'

'Does she need you singing her achievements to the sky as if this were some tawdry baronial procession?'

'I suspect not, Golden One.'

'Indeed she doesn't. So be silent.' Diocletian paused again, and then added, 'Slew Baron Kells of House Riathan... in single combat.'

Jaya nodded. 'As you say.'

'That's an impressive roster of treachery for such a brief involvement in the war. Tell me why you fired upon souls loyal to the Emperor, baroness.'

'Vyridion's oldest oaths are to the Children of the Emperor. It was Prince Fulgrim who descended to Highrock, bringing the Emperor's light to spell the end of Old Night. We marched with his Legion throughout the Great Crusade for three generations, as we vowed in our Declaration of Allegiance. When he called us to war again, we answered.'

'A matter of loyalty, then.'

'As you say,' she repeated. 'The war is no clean-cut matter away from Terra. Rumours fly over who is the betrayer and who is the betrayed. Worlds and battles are named with no knowledge of why they were held, lost or fought. The Iron Hands sought to destroy our allies in the Third Legion. We held to our oaths, fighting for the sons of Prince Fulgrim.'

'And attacked several Imperial bastions.'

'A fact I do not deny, Custodian Diocletian. Is this a trial?'

'Yes, of sorts. So let us speak of regret and punishment, baroness. Tell me what brings a very well-armed, well-supplied two-thirds of House Vyridion from fighting at the side of the Emperor's Children to surrendering their arms in the skies of Terra?'

'We were ordered into the field against the remnants of House Kells. We laid siege to their last citadel. Rather than curse us for our treachery as the Tenth Legion had done, they implored us to see reason, transmitting details of the wider war to our hearth-ship. Maps and charts of the collapsing Great Crusade. Reports of other battles. Names of fallen worlds. Word of the Warmaster's apostasy.'

Diocletian snorted, the sound a mechanical bark through his helm's vocaliser. 'And you simply believed them? You weren't concerned that this was enemy propaganda?'

Jaya felt the threat of anger. 'We had no way of knowing for certain. One name emerged, again and again, wretched in its terrible possibility.'

'I can guess that name.' It was Zephon who spoke, his voice soft. 'Isstvan.'

Jaya nodded. 'Isstvan. We could not break the truth apart from the lies. That day we refused to march against Kells. The Emperor's Children fleet fired upon us as we withdrew. Our support fleet sailed to Highrock with our sacred armours, to return them to the Great Vault. My courtiers and I made the long journey to Terra aboard our empty hearth-ship, with a small contingent of our sacristans.'

Diocletian's gaze raked across the orderly ranks once more. 'And when you arrived?'

'When we arrived, seeking answers, we were imprisoned at once. And there we have remained until you freed us.'

Diocletian shook his head. 'You must have known execution awaited you on Terra.'

'Perhaps. We are oathbreakers, thus we knew execution was deserved. Is that why we were being starved?'

Diocletian sighed, but didn't answer. The Blood Angel did.

'No,' Zephon said. 'That was merely the degeneration of unmonitored servitors. The Palace's hierarchs are forced to turn their attention to a thousand matters at once, and the breaking down of your servitor jailors was unlikely to have registered at all, until it was far too late.'

Jaya clenched her teeth. Well. That answered that question. She had almost been executed by the stalled processes of disgusting Terran bureaucracy.

'You were speaking of Terra,' Diocletian prompted her, 'and the execution that awaited you.'

'We knew execution was possible. But the truth awaited us, Custodian, and that meant more than death. Better an honourable end than a life spent wallowing in ignorant treason. We made a choice to risk death rather than become the generation whose entry in the Highrock archives records them as deceived into dishonour.'

Again, Diocletian turned to Kaeria. And again, she nodded. Something in the Oblivion Knight's eyes made Jaya wonder if the silent sword-maiden was granting permission at all. Surely no one but the Emperor held authority over the Ten Thousand. Perhaps she was offering some subtle advice or judgement instead.

Diocletian turned back to the baroness with a whir of active armour joints. 'I can offer you a fate you wouldn't be ashamed to etch into those archives, Baroness D'Arcus. But I will need more than your word. I will need your life. I will need you to march, fight and likely die for the Emperor.'

There was no hesitation at all. 'Send to Highrock for our sacred armours,' she replied, 'and our blood and steel will be the Emperor's coin to spend until the Imperium's last breath.'

'I can't do that.'

For the first time in all of this madness, Jaya felt the creeping chill of an unease that threatened to become fear. 'Please explain yourself,' she said, breathy with restrained panic.

'You made the right choice,' Diocletian replied. 'To bring your war suits here would have risked them being melted down out of hate, or gifted to other houses as war spoil. But we can't send word to Highrock, baroness. Highrock as you knew it no longer exists. It fell to the Warmaster's forces mere weeks after you were first imprisoned. A dead world orbits the sun in its place.'

The stunned silence didn't last long. The unbelievable order and dignity held by the massed ranks slowly dissolved, and the gathered courtiers and tech-adepts became the starving remnants of the Seberekan Isolation Compound once again. Jaya, above all the others, looked ravaged. She fell to her knees, struggling to breathe.

'The whole world. The whole world.'

'The whole world,' Diocletian confirmed. 'The Emperor's Children punished you for seeking the truth behind their treachery. They brought fire and ruin to Highrock. Now Third Legion banners wave in the wind above the ashes.'

Jaya was beyond words. The archives of a noble house that had endured the millennia of Old Night, marching to guard the people whose towns clung to the walls of its fortresses. Hundreds of generations of honourable vigil, defending the weak, adhering to oaths, watching over the sacred armours that had been the lifeblood and salvation of Highrock for thousands of years.

Fourteen million people, in freeholds and fortress-towns, across the world.

Gone. All gone.

Failed by House Vyridion, who had not been there to defend them. Whose refusal to fight with the Warmaster's armies had brought annihilation.

Jaya forced herself to her feet, too hollow to weep. She felt pain in a way starvation hadn't harmed her, deep and cold and cancerous.

Above them, the engine sounds beyond the clouds drew closer. The sun had almost set now, lingering as a thin sliver, murky with pollution, above the horizon.

'We... we will need confirmation.'

'It will be provided to you,' Diocletian promised. 'We have orbital picts and surface imagery for you to study, baroness.'

Jaya nodded, unblinking, flensed to her core.

The Oblivion Knight approached her, then. Kaeria met the older woman's eyes for several long seconds, and the baroness stood before the stare, unflinching.

Kaeria broke the gaze and looked to Diocletian.

'You're certain?' the Custodian replied.

The Oblivion Knight didn't answer. She returned to her place by the Blood Angel's side.

Diocletian looked down into the baroness' eyes. 'I can offer you the Emperor's forgiveness,' he said. 'And I can offer you revenge.'

Jaya cleared her still-raw throat. 'I... we... House Vyridion will take both.'

Diocletian's cold eye-lenses and golden faceplate revealed nothing of his rare admiration for how the human woman fought back her devastating grief. 'I thought you might. You have a week to prepare. Perhaps ten days. We can spare no longer.'

'How are we to fight?' she asked, closing her eyes. 'How can we serve the Emperor without our sacred armours?'

'I anticipated those very questions, baroness.' The sky darkened with the arrival of a bulk lander. Its huge silhouette juddered overhead, great clawed landing gear grinding free of its housings.

'And here,' said Diocletian, 'is your answer.'

NINE

In ambition's shadow
In the mist
Chimaera

Ra scraped an Imperial Army bayonet along his cheek, shaving dark stubble with the spit-wet edge as he watched the input monitors detailing the reports from the last of the outrider forces. The Godspire was heaving with activity as of the last few days, with the Unifiers and their attendant hosts of servitors returned from mapping and repairing the outward tunnels.

Squad after squad of Custodians and Sisters alike were reporting the enemy hordes' advance, divided now across almost forty principal arterials. Grainy pict-feeds showed the hideous shapes of deformed Titans marching behind swarms of marching legionaries, though these were few in number compared to the endless blurred imagery of warp-born entities spilling through the passages.

Most of the warp's creatures were repelled by the automated defences established under his predecessors' ambitious reigns. They had taken their first steps into the webway, originally fighting blade to blade against daemons and devilry, only to turn the defence of the Imperial Dungeon into a gruelling crusade in this secret realm. Now the tide had reached its highest point, and the inevitable backslide was in full effect.

Jasaric, Kadai, Helios. All dead. Slain in the throes of their glorious ambitions, in their assured need to serve the Emperor's will as they saw fit.

Three artificers worked on Ra's armour as he watched the feeds, drinking in all the information the screens could offer. He had always made a point of acknowledging their patience and expertise in all the years they had served him; today he barely noticed their existence at all. Acetylene-bright sparks flickered from their tools as they re-fused and reworked the tribune's battle-worn auramite. He had been out in the tunnels for days himself, overseeing the withdrawals personally and adding his blade to the butchery.

'Tribune?' called a Mechanicum serf from his console.

'Speak.' Ra didn't look away from the three dozen screens. He didn't stop shaving. He didn't disturb his artificers' work by turning to face the speaker.

'Word from Sister-Vigilator Marei Yul.'

'Relay it.'

The thrall did so at once, augmitting a series of acutely timed clicks – the kind of coded burst from a Sister's hand-held messenger. For the first time in over a century of life, Ra Endymion winced and held a hand to his half-shaven cheek, drawing away bloody fingers.

MAREI WAS FAR from the Impossible City when she heard the echo-location chime. The sound was a familiar one after so long dwelling inside the realm of mist-choked tunnels, but its intensity made her skin crawl. She felt it not only in her instruments but humming through the ground, through whatever aether-resistant materials had been used in the webway's construction by whatever xenos ancients had dreamed it into being.

This was new. She'd never felt the Neverborn in such a way before. Always their manifestations were limited to what she could see, hear and kill.

And there should be silence in this section of tunnels. Rare, blessed silence. The evacuated tunnels were stripped of Mechanicum workers and materials, but Marei had appealed to Commander Krole and Tribune Endymion to remain in the tunnels of western descension, for suspicion of the warp entity that had devoured the Protector and its honour guard of war robots navigating their way here.

Map triangulation was its own special nightmare in the extra-dimensional realm in which they waged war, but the officers of the Ten Thousand and the Silent Sisterhood had several possible delineated paths for the creature to take, given the tunnels it had so far retreated from in apparent wounded haste. Marei's case had been simple and clear: the creature was testing the automated defences in several dozen tunnels, seeking a way into the city ahead of the enemy horde. Assassination, she reasoned, not warfare, was its intent. If the automated defences continued to herd it into a path of least resistance, that made one route far likelier than any others. First the tunnels of western descension, then the region called the Bone Garden, where the husks of eldar war machines lay in pitiful state.

Marei had volunteered, with Custodian Hyaric Ostianus, to lead the outriders charged with finding the creature and destroying it if possible. Ra had even sent Titan support, one of Ignatum's precious engines, striding alongside their small warband of grav-vehicles.

The echolocation chime sounded again. Far from here, but webway readings were erratic at best. More than once the Imperials had been confronted by forces that registered as several kilometres away, or chased nothingness that read as an enemy tide.

The first thing she did upon hearing the chime was send a mono-beam spurt to Commander Krole via the thumb-sized message beamer in her belt pouch. Several clicks in one of the Sisterhood's coded non-verbal languages was all it took, rapidly signifying her position and the imminent threat swifter than a spoken explanation.

The second thing she did was go to Hyaric. The Custodian sat in his saddle, his guardian spear over one shoulder, watching his own hand-held auspex. The great Warhound Titan *Ascraeus* stood on station nearby, rotating its top half upon its waist axis, panning and scanning, watching and waiting.

Marei appeared next to Hyaric as if she'd been born from the mist. Her transbonded chainmail whispered with her walk. He looked at her, his rent and restitched face grim.

'My readings cite a single entity,' he said. '*Ascraeus'* auspex confirms it. This isn't the horde.'

Marei and her Fire Wyrms had served alongside Squad Ostianus since their first days within the webway. She had no need to sign; Hyaric could read her as easily as a data-slate.

'Yes,' he replied to her expression.

She glanced to the east, to the endless mist of the labyrinthine tunnels that had brought them here.

'No, remain here and establish a defensive position. We'll return once we have ascertained the truth of the readings.'

She met his eyes, and then his eye-lenses once he had sealed his helm into place.

'Jasaric's death has made Endymion and Commander Krole far too cautious,' he told her. 'I appreciate your warning but there's a world of difference between patience and hesitation, and only one of those is considered virtuous.'

Within moments he was accelerating at a strained whine, the suspensors of his jetbike ululating in protest at the sudden speed. The rest of his squad followed, falling into effortless alignment through ease of habit. They were gone into the mist of the tunnel ahead within the span of a single breath.

Commander Krole's reply set the message beamer vibrating in Marei's hand, against her palm. Receipt of Marei's position and progress, and a warning to redouble her caution.

But that had been an hour ago, when everyone was still alive.

MAREI MOVED THROUGH the mist alone, her blade held before in a traditional garde position, embodying the first form in the Principles of Alertness. She stalked rather than walked, careful that her passage wouldn't disturb the golden fog. Elsewhere within the mist, impossible to know where, she heard the daemon growl. After that came a series of wet cracks and crunches. It was feeding again. If she came upon it now, she might have a chance.

Though now was also her best chance to run.

She found Varujan before long. One of Squad Ostianus' warriors, she came upon his jetbike first, a clawed thing of tormented wreckage, the sleek eagles broken, the engine ripped apart. The Custodian lay not far from his vehicle, unbreathing, missing both legs and one of his arms. His breastplate and the body beneath was lost to ruination, and his guardian spear was snapped midway down the haft where it had sundered on impact at high speed.

Leaving him untouched, she moved on. A shape loomed in the mist ahead, not a wall as she'd first thought but the fallen form of *Ascraeus*. She drew nearer to its cockpit, the great metal canine head crooked where its collapse had driven its chin into the ground. The Warhound's eye windows were shattered, leaving the war machine's corpse staring sightlessly out into the shrouded webway. Marei could make out the silhouette of one of the crew, slumped in a restraint throne.

'Sister...'

She moved closer still, drawn by the voice from the ruptured cockpit. Two of the crew were dead, bent and slouched at unnatural angles. The surviving steersman had removed his helm and stared towards her. Closer now, she could hear the shallow, swift rhythm of his breathing.

'Which... which one are you?' He spoke in a whisper, seemingly from shock and his wounds rather than tact.

She signed her name with one hand and gestured for him to remain quiet.

He didn't obey. Both of his eyes were black with dilation. 'Where is it? Where did it go? Help. Please. Help me, Sister.'

Marei looked into the ruined, slanted cockpit. The steersman's control panel had twisted in the impact, crushing his legs and trapping him in his throne. Leaning in, Marei saw his malformed shins and broken ankles wedged within the wreckage. The pain must have been immense. The fact he wasn't screaming was either a testament to his resolve or to the depths of his shock.

He was dead whether she freed him from the debris or not, and she couldn't even do that without industrial cutting tools.

'Sister,' he said again, louder this time. Marei pressed a gloved finger to her lips, to no avail. 'Help me,' the steersman repeated. Elsewhere in the mist, she heard the daemon cease its feast and grunt, sniffing the air.

'Sist–' He spoke no more. The steersman stared at her for several trembling seconds, unable to do anything more than gurgle breathlessly around the blade lancing through his neck. Marei pulled her longsword free of his throat, letting him fall limp.

The daemon moved nearby. She heard the creaking and crackling of its stretching limbs, smelt the rancid mammalian stink of its spread wings.

She moved again, staying close to the downed Titan, drawing her incinerator pistol. The dead Warhound wasn't silent; its internals still ticked and clicked as they cooled, its joints still gave infrequent creaks and scrapes as the machine settled into what would be its grave.

It had struck *Ascraeus* first. With the Custodians still setting up a perimeter and the Sisters of the Fire Wyrms Cadre taking up defensive positions, a bolt of winged darkness had dropped from the featureless sky, landing atop the Warhound with an insane screech of claws tearing through consecrated metal. The plaintive whine of rent armour plating and the hammer-hiss of bursting pistons ringing through the mist had made the outcome clear even before the immense crash of the Titan's collapse. Reactor-guts and spinal stanchions flew wide from the creature's plunging talons, tumbling through the mist and resonating with metallic bangs as they spilled across the ground.

Marei could scarcely see the thrashing creature's outline. It seemed out of phase with human senses – there and not there. As much as it was harrowing its way through *Ascraeus'* armour plating with great swings of its claws, its very presence seemed to rend corporeal matter apart, leaving reinforced ceramite and adamantium as fluid as protein mush.

It took to the sky, kicking off from the toppling Warhound, and vanished once more into the gold.

The next time it landed, it had started on the Sisters.

MAREI THUMBED HER pistol to a thin jet setting, intending to get close enough that a full spread of flame would be useless. As she reached the Warhound's rear, ducking beneath one of the ungainly raised clawed feet, she heard the thrum of active power armour.

Marei turned, sword aimed at Hyaric's face. The steel point was a finger's breadth from his nose. His stitched face was a mapwork of fresh bruising and blood spatters. His eyes, at least, were undamaged and clear. Judging by the damage to his gorget, the daemon had torn his helmet clean free when it had almost killed him.

She lowered her blade and stared at him. She kept nothing from her expression. Relief, unease, her belief on where they should move – it was all present upon her features.

He didn't reply. He didn't even acknowledge her meaning. That was how she knew.

Sister and Custodian moved in the same moment, both blades coming up as if in reflection of one another. The Custodian thrust forwards with his spear, the Sister spun aside and parried the blade with an echoing cry of steel on steel.

The creature wearing Hyaric's corpse swung uselessly at her, the unpowered blade whistling through the air. Fury lit its dead eyes, the daemon enraged at its own sluggishness.

Marei cracked the pommel of her blade into Hyaric's face, shattering the already crooked nose with a snap. She was already moving away, twisting and spinning, levelling her pistol and disgorging a slick torrent of liquid flame.

It wasn't enough. The guardian spear pounded through her stomach and burst from her back, driving deep into the layered armour plating of the downed Warhound behind her. Her weapons fell from her hands, dropping into the mist.

Pinned in place, Marei still struggled to pull herself forwards, dragging her impaled body along the spear's haft, inch by agonising inch. Gutting herself for the chance to get free.

Hyaric stood there, watching her with a loose jaw showing a spread of lengthening teeth.

'**Anathema's Daughter,**' he said aloud, in a voice that was too wet and slack to be his own, the unformed tone of a child practising speech.

Marei's leeched strength would carry her no further. Blood ran hot and dark from her mouth, cascading in bitter torrents down her breastplate each time she tried to breathe. Weakening hands clutched at the message beamer at her belt, only for it to almost fall from nerveless fingers. She thumbed a brief code before dropping it, the messenger following her weapons down into the ground fog.

Her last thought, as Hyaric stepped closer, was that she would still be alive when he started eating her. Fortunately, she was wrong.

TEN

The way home
Archimandrite
Mistress of the Black Fleet

HIERONYMA, THAT REDOUBTABLE archpriestess of the Ordo Reductor, didn't scream even when they drilled out her eyes. She was a war-priestess of the Unmaker God, responsible for the nerve-stripping torture of countless thousands of prisoners and criminals, binding them into holy robotic shells through sacred rituals. Given her role and authority, she had deadened most of her nerves along with her conscience. It was simply the way of things.

The procedure was never going to be painless. Having been responsible for much of the schematics that her reforging was operating from, she was well aware of the torment involved. Willingly she made the sacrifice, offering up her flesh for transmogrification and ascension. Her operator-surgeons expected her to show her pain; it had been calculated in the factors of reforging, which made her even more eager to show no reaction at all. She couldn't stop the tics and twitches of dead nerves briefly rekindled to life, but she could at least prevent herself screaming aloud.

She had done so with a minor and forgivable deception, however. Before the surgeries began, she had removed her vocal cords during her isolated preparations. The only sounds she could make at all were sighing, weakling huffs.

She had to be awake for the process itself, so her neural activity could be carefully monitored. The physical implants were only a portion of her ascension. The mental implantation was of greater importance.

Arkhan Land was present by virtue of expertise, if not by rank. At his side was Diocletian, the Custodian present by virtue of the fact no one had the authority to tell him to go anywhere else. They remained outside the surgery chamber, with Diocletian watching the operation taking place and Land watching the data-feeds flooding into Hieronyma's mind.

Seven monitors, each fed from separate cogitators, spilled reams of code across their flickering faces. Land stared, scratching his bald head, doing his very best to follow what he was seeing unfold. He had provided the schematics and references for the machinery necessary to cradle unequalled degrees of lore in a semi-biological brain. He had added recovered plans and schema from his personal collection to weaponise the tech-priestess beyond anything her ordo had seen before. It had been with a heavy heart he'd passed over the forbidden texts from his deepest excavations, but truth be told that weight came with no shortage of curiosity. If all went according to plan, those weapon systems would be instrumental in retaking Sacred Mars.

Now all he could do was wait and see if Hieronyma survived.

He doubted she would. Land was under no illusions that she would come through the surgery itself – a staggeringly unlikely outcome – let alone survive long enough to lead them back to Mars via this so-called Aresian Path. Given his doubts, one might then ask why he had agreed to the Archimandrite Venture at all. The answer was deliciously, ambitiously simple. Agreement with the Fabricator General's desperate hopes had been the only way to learn all of the details pertaining to the Emperor's Great Work.

And oh, the things Land was learning.

Much as a painting was formed not only of pigments and water and parchment, but also the individual hairs that made up a brush and the years of expertise at the artist's fingertips, the many layered codes running through the cogitators amounted to one thing.

A map.

A map in impossible dimensions of a realm that couldn't exist. A map that was being poured piecemeal into Hieronyma's mind.

He smiled as he watched the data flood. *'Poured into' is the wrong term*, Land thought. *More like 'etched upon'*.

The pain must have been monumental, even to her stripped nervous system. Having a world's worth of data inloaded like this would send reason screaming from the mortal consciousness. Frankly, he was impressed she was still alive four hours into the procedure. If she survived it would be unlikely that Hieronyma would be able to entertain any other thoughts in her skull. The map would swallow her consciousness and all of her concentration. It was simply that vast.

Through the viewing window, he caught sight of Hieronyma thrashing on the surgical table. The attendants – the Fabricator General among them – were bleating and murmuring about convulsions. The immense metal limbs of Hieronyma's new form crashed and twitched. A huge three-barrelled energy cannon rotated on her forearm, trying to fire, whirring in starvation. A tremor of the nervous system most likely, or a randomly firing synapse in the brain. He doubted she was genuinely trying to kill the surgeons attending her, though... Well. With what was going on in her mind, one couldn't be sure.

Land took no particular joy in the pain she must be feeling, but nor did her torment exactly inspire him to the precious heights of sympathy. She chose this fate, after all. The yearning of homesickness had driven her to it, which Land could understand – and even consider admirable, in its rather petulant earnestness – but she'd also been led by her faith in the Fabricator General, and that was something the technoarchaeologist considered endlessly mystifying.

He returned his attention to the map's code, partly due to the worry it would stop flowing once Hieronyma died. He had to learn what he could while there was still time.

The heart of the map was a city. It had catacombs, which were a labyrinth with several hundred passages abruptly severed or otherwise unfinished, and thousands of other routes leading out from its edges like capillary veins. The city existed in three hundred and sixty degrees, as if it covered the entire inside of a great shaft or tunnel. It called to mind the tales of Old Earth space installations that rolled in the void to create artificial gravity, though this city was ultimately motionless. It merely existed, static, at every angle, including the impossible ones.

Nor were the city and its catacombs the entirety of the map. They weren't even the majority of it. From the city's edges, thousands of capillary tunnels branched out in a seemingly endless and random network, following no sense of human order and leading to no specific destinations.

Land could grasp all of this. That wasn't the problem.

No, the problem was the way the map evolved even as it was being imprinted within Hieronyma's mind. It shifted and changed moment by moment, as if the realm it was mapping had only the loosest relationship with the corporeal flow of time. Since the expeditionary teams had started surveying this hidden region, thousands upon thousands of subtle shiftings had occurred, as if the labyrinth reacted to something – some outward pressure – and sought to stabilise itself. And all of the shifts, in excruciating detail, were being scarred onto Hieronyma's brain.

The map-code's intricacies would have been on the edge of mortal comprehension even in three dimensions. In four, it was almost laughably, terrifyingly fascinating.

In the surgical chamber, Hieronyma's mouth worked in silent futility. Land spared a moment to watch Kane injecting her with something pale blue and milky, something that in no way lessened her thrashing and completely failed to stabilise her spiking vital signs. As her head bucked, its bevy of mechanical replacements bared without her hood, Land saw her staring through the chamber's window, right at him. Her eye-lenses revolved and refocused. He was certain he detected something pleading in her machine-gaze. And, perhaps, something of regret?

Land looked back to the monitors. On and on the data streamed.

Soon the cartography and chronology were joined by archival data that defied belief, let alone possibility. Scans and analyses made by the Unifier-caste tech-priests, quantifying the nature of the realm in which they worked, and... and the foes they faced.

Land's eyes widened. His mouth slowly, almost delicately, parted and hung open. In the chamber, the thrashing, writhing machine that Hieronyma was becoming suddenly fell still, motionless but for her trembling.

'Teeth of the Cog,' said Land. Awe softened his curse to a whisper.

His eyes flickered. A realm of psychically resistant passageways. A realm that existed not within the warp but in spite of it. A realm that allowed travel across vast distances without ever once entering the reach of the warp's unreliable and treacherous tendrils. A realm that shifted as part of its resistance to the warp's corrosive touch, realigning itself to remain immune.

A web. The webway.

His eyes flickered. A realm flooded by warp entities. Beings formed from hatred and madness and emotion. Creatures born of every emotion ever felt, taking form and twisted behind the veil of reality. Monsters formed of the warp's matter and flooding into this ancient, precious sanctuary.

His eyes flickered. A realm shattered by Magnus the Red. A realm gouged open with lethal wounds in its protective psychic sheath. A realm sundered by immense releases of sorcerous power that allowed the infection of these beings – the *daemons* – to spread.

His eyes flickered, shining with the threat of tears. Vulnerabilities! Weaknesses in the process! Signs of decay in the alien-made sections of the webway, and worse, the flaws of incomplete human knowledge in the Mechanicum-built sections. They weren't psychically sheathed, as the ancient and original structures were. The human-engineered halls of the endless labyrinth were protected by...

His eyes flickered, and now he wept. A great machine. A machine of such power and purity as to defy mortal thought. A throne of gold, built to house the Emperor's power. The Omnissiah's Throne, the seat of the Machine-God Himself, harnessing and focusing His psychic might into the webway, bolstering the Mechanicum-made conduits. A soul-engine that roared power into this secret and sacred realm, shielding the Mechanicum's iron and steel against the daemons clawing against it.

His eyes flickered and streamed with awed tears, just as Ancient Terran tales told of men and women weeping before the faces of their false gods. The abandonment of the Great Crusade. The appointment of Horus as Warmaster. The Emperor's retreat into the Imperial Dungeon. The treachery of Magnus the Red. The Custodian Guard. The Silent Sisterhood. The Unifiers. The War in the Webway. The Emperor's Great Work. The magnum opus that was the very reason the Omnissiah had reached up into the night sky and united the two empires of Mars and Terra. It was for this. It was *all* for this. It was all for *this*.

And – through the disobedience of a primarch, the ignorance of a weapon that moronically believed itself a man – the magnum opus stood upon the precipice of failure.

His eyes closed. Finally, as Hieronyma wheezed her last breath upon the table where she had been promised rebirth – at long last Arkhan Land understood.

'I must come with you...' he said, turning to Diocletian. The need in his voice bordered upon begging. He gripped the Custodian's bracer, staring up at the warrior's impassive faceplate. *'I must join you in the Great Work.'*

The Custodian had stood in silence during the entirety of the surgery. He moved for the first time, turning to look down at the technoarchaeologist through emotionless eye-lenses. The whine of flat-lining vital signs echoed in the air around both men.

'She keeps dying,' was Diocletian's reply. 'You said this was the preparatory phase of the surgery.'

'Custodian, please...'

Diocletian looked back into the chamber, his features clear of any emotion.

SOMETHING SHIVERED INSIDE the priestess' skull. It curled and uncurled with revolting physicality, a tendril of prehensile ice dredging her brain matter. Its tremors caused no pain, but the pressure of its presence was the burden of high gravity applied directly to her skull and spine. She felt hunched, compacted, and the moment she tried to stretch to free herself was the moment she realised she wasn't breathing.

Not only that she wasn't, she couldn't. Heaving in to breathe met a wall of solid cold barricading her throat. Her lungs didn't even twitch. Her body didn't answer her urges to rise, to fight, to thrash, to do anything at all, to breathe, breathe, breathe.

'Pulmonary instability,' said a voice. Distant. Dispassionate. Sacred in its serenity. Without identity in the reddening black of her blindness. 'Mark the ninth instance. Illuminate her.'

Code flared through her reddening senses, numerals written in fire upon the wet meat of her mind. Its meaning eluded her.

She screamed in mouthless, breathless silence.

'Pulmonary spasms,' came another voice, just as cold, just as enlightened.

'Teeth of the Cog. She is trying to breathe again.'

'Illuminate her.'

Acid-numerals raked across the inside of her skull again. For all the pain of them, they were more distant now, harder to see, impossible to read.

Strangling on her own silence, drowning in uncolour, she fell silently screaming away from everything.

'Illumi-'

THE TENDRIL UNCURLED slowly through the silt and sludge of her mind, coaxing her back. She felt slow, dense, her blood and thoughts alike turned sludgy with toxins.

Dazed, drained and strangled, she fought to open her eyes.

'Reactivation,' said a voice from beyond.

I can't breathe. I can't breathe. I can't breathe!

'Convulsions. Pulmonary spasms. Mark the tenth inst–'

'Illuminate her before–'

The words weren't fire or acid this time, they were pain itself. Scrawled directly onto the inside of her skull with talons of code.

She stared at them. She felt them. She knew them.

She stopped trying to drag air through the blockage in her throat.

'Stabilising.'

'Praise the Omnissiah.'

She felt air whisper into her system, then flood her, cold and purified and rich in as much incense as oxygen. She could only breathe when she didn't try to breathe. When she tried to work lungs she no longer had, she overrode the automated systems that respired for her.

'Awakening.'

She opened her eyes.

The world exploded in red-stained holy light. Target locks saturated her vision. Prayer text and sacred code bathed her sight in layers of algebraic mandalas. Beneath what she could see was what she knew, a latticework map of impossible spatial distances that defied conventional physics. She shut that madness away and turned from the knowledge for now, needing to focus only on the immediacy of her surroundings.

Hooded faces and surgical servitors looked down at her. No, not down. *Up.* She had thought she would be lying on her back, but the faces tilted towards hers were below her. She was bound to a standing gurney.

Bindings cracked away in sweet hisses of released air pressure. Grinding machinery lowered her the half-metre to the ground as the last cabling snapped free.

Behind the worshipful surgery-priests and their mindlocked cyborg slaves, a heavily augmented corpse lay upon another table. The cadaver was ostensibly female, headless, gored through autopsy, medicae drilling and organ harvesting.

She knew that corpse. Even headless, its remains were brutally familiar.

Hieronyma, the priestess thought. *Me. I.*

Her clawed foot ground down on the polished metal floor. It shook the chamber.

'Archimandrite,' said one of the hooded priests. Tall. Many-armed. Savagely weaponised. *Zagreus Kane Divine Bishopric of the Cult Mechanicum Fabricator General of Sacred Mars my lord my master* – the knowledge was there once she accessed the data-stream, albeit with a slight delay.

'Fabricator General,' she said. Her voice, even to her own ears, was almost wholly human. A vox-simulation of her biological tone. At the sound of her voice, several of the adepts went to their knees, murmuring a mono-note *ohm* prayer, linking their knuckles in the sign of the cog.

'Do you know?' Kane asked, rumbling forwards on his tracked lower half. 'Do you see the way back to Mars?'

Her second step shook the chamber, the same as the first. As did the third. As did the fourth.

As THE WEEKS passed after the Archimandrite's rebirth, Diocletian found himself alone more often than not. Kaeria was gone. He knew not where, only that she was dealing with the secret intricacies of her silent order elsewhere in the Palace. He had little to say to Baroness D'Arcus and her knightly kindred, nor did he find much worth in the stoic computations of the Mechanicum's various overseers.

Two souls consistently sought out his company: the pleading figure of Arkhan Land, and the serenely lost presence of Dominion Zephon. Now that the Archimandrite Venture had succeeded, Diocletian had no further use for the former. He would likely allow the technoarchaeologist to join the expedition back to the Impossible City, even if only on the rare chance the explorator's knowledge would prove useful. And as for the Blood Angel, the so-called Bringer of Sorrow would serve well enough merely by accompanying them into the webway when the time came.

It was the delay that wore at the Custodian's patience. The Mechanicum's requisitioned supplies were already proceeding through in a convey stream, thousands of battle-servitors, tracked conveyors, robots and even the rare sicarii funnelled through to their fates within the Great Work. The first shipments would already have reached Ra by now, reinforcing the Impossible City.

And yet Diocletian waited. Impatient, but without any show of temper. House Vyridion drew ever closer to war readiness; the Archimandrite was adjusting to its new form and its enhanced cognition. Things were proceeding as expected, even if not with a swiftness Diocletian would have preferred.

His place was to oversee every item of requisition, and he wouldn't return to Calastar without doing so. He felt no frustration in doing his duty, only the vague concern that he could better be serving the Emperor elsewhere. Next to Ra on the walls of Calastar, perhaps, or slowing the foe in the outer tunnels, making them pay for each metre of misted ground they took. Something proactive. Something where he felt as though he were contributing to the defence of his master's vision.

The one thing he was not, however, was bored. He spent much of his time isolated within the Tower of Hegemon, the command core of the Legio Custodes' efforts in the Emperor's defence. Here Diocletian watched the continual streams of population data, materiel transport, and the aerial and orbital traffic entering and exiting the Solar System, maintained by bank upon bank of cogitators and life-bonded savant-serfs in robes of Imperial scarlet. These data-artisans – each one tattooed with the aquila – dwelled within the Watchroom, where only those lifesworn to the Emperor were permitted. Rather than the dregs enslaved and augmented by the Machine Cult of Mars, none of the Ten Thousand's serfs were cyborged to their stations or bound to live and die in their life support cradles. These men and women had sworn themselves to the All-Seeing Eye of the Emperor's Custodians;

they wore jewellery of sculpted bone made from the bodies of their mothers and fathers who served before them, and of the grandparents before them. In time their mortal remains would be harvested and ritual trinkets of their own bones gifted to their specifically bred children. To serve the Custodian Guard wasn't merely a life sentence, it was an eternal, generational one.

Much of the Watchroom's information centred on the Palace itself, with Unified Biometric Verification feeds forming a living web of several million souls entering and exiting the Palace's myriad districts.

Diocletian watched this calculation of life taking place. Perhaps another soul might have seen something harmonic or musical in the display. Even among the Ten Thousand, such vigils usually took note of the hundreds of potential infiltration threats that might somehow slip past even the Imperial Fists. Yet Diocletian saw something unexpected in the patternless mess.

He saw diminishing supplies even as Terra itself was broken down for materials, even as the Himalazia Mountains themselves were ground down for rock and ore. He saw fewer and fewer convoy fleets reaching the Solar System as the war raged on. He saw Terra strangled beneath the weight of off-world refugees, devouring their way through ever-diminishing resources. He saw fewer and fewer successful attempts to land reinforcements on Mars or bring materiel back through the Imperial blockade. He saw all of this written as plainly as the eight hundred and seventy-one words of his full name, laser-etched upon the inside of his breastplate, as familiar to him as the weight of the spear in his hands.

Defeat. He was looking at defeat. The rebels were winning the war. Though their conquests across the galaxy were far from absolute, Horus didn't need wholesale victory among the stars; the Warmaster needed only to amass enough support on the way to Terra and deny Imperial reinforcement reaching the Solar System. And, overwhelmingly, these ugly calculations painted a portrait of the Warmaster doing just that.

Diocletian spent several days immersing himself in the reports and cogitations, seeking a wider view of the escalating conflict. It was in studying the movements of the rarest of all Imperial resources – the Ten Thousand and the Silent Sisterhood not currently deployed in the webway – that he discovered something tentative in the millions of cogitations. Something in the pattern was flawed, and it gnawed at Diocletian. Silent sections of code revealed shadows in the streaming figures. Equations were buried in the cogitations that returned half-truths as answers.

Data deletions? he first wondered. But no, no. These weren't holes in the pattern, merely patches of occlusion. Shrouded, not deleted. Hidden, not forbidden.

Diocletian followed the patterns, watching them unfurl with a savant's understanding of mathematic and algebraic principles. At first it seemed the serfs were themselves ignorant of the patterns, but soon enough he realised this wasn't so: they were clearly aware, they were simply not flagging the curious elements for archival examination.

He saw fleets of ships in the numbers. *We have an entire fleet out there, scattered across three segmentums. Sailing the stars, avoiding the war.*

And more than that. Displacement calculations and void logistical data suggested these ships would descend on loyal worlds in the days and weeks before Horus' forces committed to an invasion, yet they extracted nothing of any military significance, they landed no reinforcements and they evacuated none of the established regent-governments put in place by the Great Crusade.

What, then, are they doing?

None of the vessels were accounted for in the Great Crusade's tallies, each one unattached to any expeditionary fleets. Nor were their dealings translated off-world, with no word transmitted by common routes, nothing from the divisions of the Astra Telepathica, and–

There.

Word had come in the form of a cursory transmission by a modest rogue trader fleet returning from the spiral arm of the Halo Stars. Her family's armada had been negotiating for orbital resupply above the capital city of some nameless backwater still going by its allocated colonial code, when one of these logistically occluded vessels showed itself. Despite its obvious Imperial allegiance, it had refused all communication, completed several planetary operations, and left orbit for the system's Mandeville point without illuminating the rogue trader fleet as to its purpose.

The trader scion's report concluded with a message from the planet itself, stating what little dealings its provincial quorum government had managed to have with the ships' commander, including the vessel's intent.

'They came for our psychically attuned citizens.'

Diocletian breathed a disbelieving laugh. *A Black Ship. The Black Ships of the Silent Sisterhood are sailing across three segmentums, unescorted, hiding from battle and harvesting psykers on an unprecedented scale. And they are doing it practically unseen by anyone, oath-binding whole governments to silence.*

Once he knew what ships were causing the flaws in the galactic pattern, the calculations solved themselves. Dozens of similarly shrouded equations noted Black Ships in Terra's orbit, committing shuttles, loaders and transports of cargo to the planet's surface without registering upon terrestrial traffic. And dozens more were drawing towards Terra from across the galaxy.

Diocletian had a fair suspicion of just where Kaeria had gone. He turned to a nearby serf at a cogitation console and narrowed his eyes.

'You.'

The worker halted but didn't look away from his screen. Numeric runes flashed upon his unblinking eyes. 'Golden One?'

'Arrange for a vox-link to the Magadan Orbital Construct. I wish to speak with the Mistress of the Black Fleet.'

IT CAME AS no surprise to Diocletian when, two hours later, he saw a familiar figure on the crackling hololith connection. Kaeria stood at the side of a robed and cowled fellow Sister, the former armed and armoured just as Diocletian had last seen her, the latter with her eyes hidden by the fall of her hood. The Mistress of the Black Ships wore leather gloves with reinforced knuckles and dagger-length knives for fingernails. In the rippling holo image, she seemed to be clicking them together.

'Mistress Varonika,' he greeted the spindly creature clad in black, adding 'Sister Kaeria,' a moment later.

The older Sister wove an elaborately formal greeting with her brutal finger-blades. Kaeria offered no more than a nod.

Diocletian wasted no time. The door to the communications suite was sealed. He was entirely alone, bathed in blue holo-light. 'What is the Black Fleet doing?'

Both Sisters signed a reply at once, curt without rudeness.

'And what is the Unspoken Sanction?'

Another brief reply. One that Diocletian had expected.

'Forbidden,' Diocletian replied. Well, the Sisters of Silence were entitled to their secrets in the Emperor's service. Never would they act without the Emperor's command.

'Where are you housing these harvested psykers?' he asked.

Again, a curt reply from both Sisters. *Forbidden.*

'Be that as it may,' the Custodian replied, 'you cannot ship tens of thousands of psykers to Terra and hide them indefinitely. Have you taken their sustenance into consideration? Half of the Throneworld's granaries already stand hollow. Water farms across the Afrik Swathe stand mute in rainless thirst.'

He expected another blunt, curt response. To his mild surprise, Varonika replied by signing a longer reply with both hands. Diocletian could almost imagine the click-clack of her bladed talons meeting on several of the words.

'Then I will press no more on the matter,' said the Custodian. 'But in the Emperor's name, tell me whether I might expect reinforcements in the webway as a result of your scheming.'

The merest flicker of the older Sister's finger-blades was enough to betray her hesitation. She signed a negative response, but Diocletian found her hesitation intriguing.

'Very well. Am I to assume you will be returning when I lead House Vyridion and the Archimandrite's convoy into the Dungeon, Kaeria?'

The Oblivion Knight bowed her head once more, more formally this time. He needed no sign language to see her respect in the reply, nor any further explanation to note her refusal. She was staying there.

'So be it. Good eve, Sisters.' Diocletian terminated the link and exhaled slowly. He knew better than to pry further into whatever secrets they sought so ardently to protect. If they required his aid, they would ask for it.

The Custodian turned back to the closest bank of monitors, resuming the staring absorption of limitless, scrolling data.

II
Cargo

This is not now. This is then. This is when she was caged away from everything she had ever known.

Skoia sits on the floor, breathing slowly, listening to the voices of those trapped here with her. They don't speak often; few of them know one another and no one has any answers to offer to the others. Sometimes there are brief outbursts of fury that begin with the aggressors beating their hands bloody on the sealed metal doors and end with them sinking, weak-limbed and no freer, to the floor. Others give in to despair and wail, or weep quietly alone, which achieves just as much – just as little – as angry defiance.

At first there had been a sense of community and shared suffering, when the villagers and townspeople came to realise they were all ancestor-speakers and witch-priests, taken in a harvest tithe up into the belly of an Imperial spaceship. But the days became weeks, then months, and the cargo hold grew cramped with more and more people – these spoke in different languages and came from different worlds, and soon enough everyone was weak and weary enough to see out their suffering alone.

'Astropaths,' another man declares. He, too, is from another world. 'Astropaths. We are to be trained as astropaths. You will see. You shall see.

Astropaths.' He repeats the word as if it were talismanic. Skoia isn't certain if he seeks to reassure the others or convince himself. Whatever the truth, she has no conception of his meaning. He doesn't answer when anyone asks him.

The spirits are silent, have been silent since she first looked up and saw the dead-eyed woman above her back in the forest. Not once has Skoia heard their whispers, perhaps because they are the ghosts of her own planet and she's far from home, or perhaps because she has been severed from the Wheel of Life by the soulless women who crew this vessel.

Servitors bring them their food in strange sealed pouches. The food is a rendered brown paste that tastes of nothing natural. Skoia has to force it down with a wash of the powdery water that tastes of machinery and recyc-processing.

The more violent souls among the captive community have tried to kill the servitors before, but several of the soulless women now stand watch each ration hour. They remain by the doors with their blades held in their hands and bulky pistols that eternally sigh with the threat of breathing fire. Approaching them is impossible. Anyone who tries is wracked with cramps and sickness, vomiting onto the deck, seemingly poisoned for hours afterwards. One man collapsed and didn't wake for three days.

'Devils,' some of the captives call the eagle-tattooed women. 'Banshees.' 'Husks.' 'Undead.' Each culture has its own words for the creatures that have captured them.

'They have no sixth sense,' explains one of the others in a bizarrely accented variation of Gothic. Skoia can follow his words if she concentrates. 'No anima. No psychic capability.'

She looks away, saying nothing. His words are without meaning or relevance. She knows the only truth that matters, that these women have no souls.

The ship often shakes around them, buffeted by the eddies of its voyage through the galaxy. It does so now, but more violently than ever before. Nervous voices begin to clamour. Wide eyes meet other open gazes. The turbulence is enough to send the captives sprawling. Some of them collide with the iron walls, and their voices rise higher, bordering upon panic in proto- or post-Gothic languages Skoia can't understand. Those that she can are mumbling of crashes and attacks and their own helplessness.

'We are not crashing,' she says aloud. The men and women nearest to her turn and stare. She swallows her own fear in the face of theirs. 'I think… I think we are landing.'

ELEVEN

Ossuary
A shattered silence
He will live

THEY LAID THE trap in the region known as the Ossuary. Only hours distant from the Impossible City and its main arterial, the Garden of Bones existed in a modest span of the webway where the tunnel walls and ceilings pressed in with vanished into the omnipresent mist. If Calastar was a fallen eldar city, the Ossuary was a ruined monument to that worthless race.

'We only have one chance at this,' Ra had said at a gathering of leaders in the Godspire.

Nishome Alvarek, appearing via hololith and clad in her full Ignatum wargear as she sat upon her princeps throne on the command deck of the *Scion of Vigilant Light,* had resisted the choice of ambush site. It was too small for her Titan to walk, and she had insisted that her Warlord's weapons would be more than capable of destroying the creature in open battle.

'Your zealotry is invaluable,' Ra began. Her perspective had been gently argued down: an ambush was critical and it had to be handled with meticulous care. The larger tunnels allowed too easy an opportunity for the creature to escape or get past the Imperial line.

'You will stay and oversee operations within the Impossible City,' Ra had decided.

'Do you seek to appease me with charitable morsels of honour, Endymion?'

Ra had forced a smile and said nothing. Princeps Alvarek had chuckled, letting the matter lie.

Commander Krole had signed her fervent avowal for Ra's plan, as had her underofficers.

Zhanmadao, one of the Tharanatoi Terminator caste, had noted that the creature remained tentative, seeking easy ingress rather than a frontal siege. There would be no better time, he reasoned, than now. It had been herded far enough, by fortune if not by intent.

Ra had nodded, agreed and let fly the gunships.

THE OSSUARY WAS an aisle, a narrow tunnel path fit for alien processions back when the failed eldar empire had still enjoyed events worth celebrating. Either side of the main roadway, nothing but organic powder residue and gemstone dust remained of whatever botanical and crystalline wonders had once grown in sorcery-touched beauty. Now the misty landscape was given over to broken statuary and the wraithbone husks of unpowered eldar automata. It was as if a culture had brought its funereal artistry here to be forgotten, left in this ill-maintained route of the vast web.

The Unifiers had spent little time here, initially reporting brief and tense encounters with eldar pilgrims and that species' kaleidoscopic high priests and priestesses, yet considering that the eldar were known to still use the webway, they had judiciously and fervently avoided almost all Imperial expansion. Many among the Ten Thousand who had ventured deeper into the web suspected the abruptly fused passageways or sealed gateways led to eldar craftworlds, and the aliens were barring human entry into their far-flung domains. What it must it cost them to seal themselves away from their own means of travelling across the galaxy, however, none could guess.

Ra had originally expected to encounter the eldar a great deal as the

Imperial vanguard ventured beyond the Mechanicum's portions of the webway. Instead he found them recalcitrant and furtive, ghosting back rather than engaging, often sealing themselves away, even to the degree of damaging the webway to enforce their isolation.

The Ossuary was one such mystery. It seemed to be some xeno-logic amalgamation of graveyard and scrapyard, almost in the form of a refuse tunnel. None knew why it existed. Did the eldar not remake and reuse their wraithbone via the sacred art of bonesinging? Was this a deliberate abandonment of tainted material, discarding resources that were flawed in a manner indecipherable to the human eye? Or was it merely a monument to loss, and thus a place the eldar were unwilling to desecrate with even their own presence?

He loathed the unknown, even as he and his Custodian kindred were trained to react and adapt to it, perhaps better than any other living beings.

Ra had studied the eldar in depth, as had all of the Ten Thousand. A wise warrior's creed was to *know your enemy*, but the Custodian Guard lived their lives to an extreme beyond desiring typical insight into their foes. They pushed themselves cognitively as much as physically, learning the languages, cultures and histories of their enemies in order to attain an almost enlightened sense of understanding with every one they faced. All in order to counter and oppose them; to stand against their foes and anticipate every action, answering with commensurate, consummate reaction. It wasn't enough to be able to stop an enemy from doing something – purity of purpose and perfection in duty lay in knowing what they would do before they did it, and what the perfect response would be. By necessity that meant knowing when and why actions would be undertaken at all.

Yet this mindset held little rigidity. Almost nothing was codified. Lore was gathered not only to predict patterns but also to create a fluid sense of potential and awareness. Perceiving potential threats didn't mean adhering to formulaic responses.

There were civilisations in the galaxy, human and alien alike, that had known little but the savagery of Legion conquest or Imperial Army compliance, yet the warriors of the Ten Thousand could speak their local tongues and recite the virtues and pitfalls of their historical military leaders, with deep insight into the cultures' characters. All done in service to protecting the most powerful and important soul who had ever lived.

It was what galled Ra more than anything else when facing the creatures calling themselves Neverborn. These daemons were so varied, so populous, so in flux and so utterly alien that attaining any useful comprehension of them was next to impossible.

The silence of the Ossuary was shattered with the daemon's arrival. It was no longer alone; it led a shrieking, roaring swarm of its lessers, creatures that had started flocking to its leavings, like the carrion-feeders that trailed after predators in the wild lands of countless worlds.

Its shape defied sight even when one looked directly towards it. It appeared as a smear across the vision of everyone who sought to follow its advance. Vast wings stood proud of its back, yet it ran on all fours. Its eyes blazed; the warriors who couldn't describe the creature's appearance at all could still feel when it turned its attention upon them, even at great distance.

It loped from the mist at the tunnel's far end a full kilometre distant, a catalyst for the wretches at its back, sustaining these new followers with its bloodshed. Ra watched through magnoculars, applying filter after filter to pierce the preternatural fog with little effect. Flies surrounded its swollen corpus. Tendrils rose from its back like the curved tails of aggravated scorpions.

The creature nosed, hound-like, at the carpet of broken eldar wraithbone covering the tunnel floor. The lesser daemons kept back from its inquisitions, cowed from venturing too close in case they suffered the apex beast's rage.

Ra lowered his magnoculars and thudded the butt of his spear down against the mist-hidden ground. The sound carried, resonating through the webway's unearthly material, and the creature's head rose with inhuman smoothness.

The Custodians at his side did the same, lifting and pounding their spear butts down in continual rhythm. It was the marching song of some ancient army, echoing for the first time here in an alien realm. Only twenty of them stood together; Ra had refused to risk any more of the dwindling Ten Thousand when the true battle was yet to be fought. Twenty warriors, each drawn from different squads. Twenty souls to serve as bait.

The creatures responded with roars of their own, none louder than the winged monster in their vanguard. They began to charge. The Custodians kept hammering their spears down in cold, rhythmic unity.

Ra's retinal display couldn't lock on to the approaching figures, but approximations of their shrinking distance ticked along the edges of his eye-lenses. He thumped his spear once more, then whirled the blade forwards, levelling it at the charging daemons. The Custodians at his side did the same, in the very same breaths.

'Kill it,' Ra voxed.

THE WRAITHBONE CAIRNS shifted, dead eldar machines slipping and tumbling as they were cast aside. Imperial robots rose from their blanketing shrouds of alien bone, their somnolent life sparks kindling at the behest of their Mechanicum masters. Fifty of them lined the narrow avenue, each one standing in ragged harmony with its cousins, cannons whirring and joints snarling. They wore the red plate of Sacred Mars, dented and battered from so many years of fighting away from their stolen home world, but loyal to the last.

They opened up as one. Castellax, Vorax, Kastelan – pattern after pattern, no two weapon arrays truly alike – each of the robots lit the tunnel with an unremitting salvo of fire. Laser weapons flashed and cut. Energy cannons flared and roared. Spheres of seething plasma spat from scorched muzzles. Torrents of flame belched forth. Maxim bolters thundered and darkfire beams daggered into the heaving pack of charging creatures.

The daemons went down as if scythed. Those that fell were flayed and taken apart by the ceaseless barrage. Those that kept running were forced down a gauntlet of relentless firepower. At the Ossuary's end, Ra and his Custodians fired their spears' bolters, adding to the cannonade.

Battle tanks rolled forwards from the mist on heavy treads, grinding eldar wraithbone into fragments. The Mechanicum's transports added their heavy weapons to the assault, as did three of the Ten Thousand's grav-tanks.

A squad of axe-bearing Sisters leapt from a golden grav-Rhino, led by Jenetia Krole. They moved to take position behind Ra and the Custodians, weapons raised in readiness.

All twenty Custodians reloaded in the same two-heartbeat span. All twenty fired again, straight ahead, aiming for the burning, dissolving creature still racing towards them.

This, then, was pain. This was uncreation. The daemon of the first murder felt itself being taken apart, but keener still was the acid of a thwarted hunt. To be trapped like this, to be unmade by mortal anger. This was pain.

Escape. Survive. What passed for its cognition plunged into a ravenous loop of primal urges. *Escape. Survive. Escape. Survive.*

Still they charged. Hundreds lay dead and dissolving, soon to be thousands, yet still the survivors charged. They answered each of the alpha creature's bellows, peeling off from the collapsing pack and launching themselves at the closest robots cutting off their escape. Automata fell in smoking, exploding husks. Daemons burst apart with them, willingly sacrificing themselves at their overlord's whim.

The creature, the End of Empires, reached the Custodians' battle-line first. There it met the plunging spears and hacking axes of the Ten Thousand and the Silent Sisters, ignoring their first blows as it shifted into a chimaeric thing of thrashing serpent-limbs and curved claws. It killed even as aetheric blood rained from its devastated form. It killed even as hanks of sizzling flesh were ripped from its corpus, laying it bare to where a true beast would have bones.

Several of the Castellax battle-automata lumbered forwards, engaging it alongside the humans, tearing at the daemon's ichorous flesh with their whining buzz saws and industrial fists. They fared no better, their cranial domes and chestplates hammered and mangled, their vital internals torn free in clawed fistfuls of fluid-slick artificial life. They detonated, bathing the daemon in eviscerating shrapnel and petro-chemical burns, and still – *still* – it killed.

It melted its way through forms, shifting and seeking lethality above all, survival-urge and blood-hunger fusing together to force it through change after change, seeking to escape its cage by butchering those that had trapped it here.

The Custodians fell back, the Sisters with them. It gave chase, panic granting it aggression, doing all it needed to do in order to rip itself free of the ambush. It fell upon the very beings slaughtering it because to run from them would only mean swifter destruction. Human blood ran. Golden limbs crashed to the ground. Axes fell from dead hands.

Ra and Jenetia struck in the very same second. The Custodian drove his spear up through the shapeless mass, wrenching it deeper, lodging it within and emptying his bolter inside its body. The Sister-Commander plunged her two-handed blade in alongside Ra's, tearing a mirrored wound. Scalding filth poured upon both of them, steaming on their armour, burning patches of exposed skin.

A snake-like limb battered Krole aside. The creature staggered, then fell, crashing into the metal-strewn debris of dead robot and abandoned wraithbone. It reached a grasping claw from its seething mess of limbs, its structure breaking down into something amoebic and many-eyed.

End of Empires, it said in Ra's mind, using Ra's thoughts. It sounded so weak. Almost fearful, though such a thing could feel no fear. *End... of...*

The daemon rose from the wreckage like a fire cloud above an annihilated city, haemorrhaging thunder as it roared. Debris and machine oil rose into the air in glistening ropes. Inferno heat rolled from its resurrecting carcass. Black smoke and the blood of its kills congealed into muscle and sinew as its presence billowed higher.

Gunfire from the survivors yet tore into it, changing nothing, doing nothing. A head formed at its apex, rows of eyes burning as bolt-rounds ripped harmless cinders from its torso. Plates of mangled armour rose from the wrecks of the war machines, charring to black as they folded over the daemon's form.

Ra stood beneath it, bathed in its heat, the coldness of the wounded Sisters beside him pressing back against the naked hunger of the thing that filled the tunnelway. It opened its mouth and breathed in the golden mist.

'*He will live,*' it rasped in a voice that felt like memory.

'*Kill it!*' Ra cried the order, desperate fury turning his tone to adrenal fire. Yet there was almost no one left alive to obey.

THE DAEMON PULLED reality towards itself, binding wraithbone and iron and even fire into a new form. It ensconced itself in corporeal armour to ward off the rage of corporeal weaponry.

'*Kill it!*' one of the Golden roared.

Escape. Survive. Anathema. End of Empires.

And, for the first time in its existence, savaged almost unto uncreation, it truly fled. The survivors' parting fire tore at its temporary form, breaking armour away, but not enough, not enough. The echo of the first murder fled in bleeding, shambling defeat, puppeting a mongrel form of broken robots that fell apart with each step.

It would find the horde. It would join the war. It would hide among its lessers, and it would survive.

TWELVE

Sacristan Apex
Starved of ammunition
Renewal

WEEKS INTO THE realignment process, Jaya was still struggling. She slid the last five metres down the ladder, tearing off her helmet and breathing in the crisp, hot metal tang of the hangar bay. Torolec, her Sacristan Apex, was waiting for her.

'It's the pressure valves in the left knee's pneumatics,' she said to the robed figure. 'It's affecting the turning circle.'

Torolec was tall and slender beneath his hooded robe, proud to wear the black and laurel-green and rearing pegasus of House Vyridion. He was beribboned at all times by devotional parchments, often fluttering in the heat wash of engine exhaust as he attended to his sacred work. As Sacristan Apex he was the house's foremost machine-seer, and at three hundred years of age, he had known and served Jaya her entire life. He'd refused to return to Highrock with the rest of the fleet, and Jaya had respected the wishes of her family's oldest retainer. Given the circumstances and how events had played out, she was doubly grateful for his presence.

'I have re-attuned them twice now,' the old man replied. Around his words, the breath of the ventilation systems roared on. Air filtration gargoyles breathed in the forge scent and exhaled recycled air, dragon-keen, doing little to diminish the sweltering heat. 'And I say again, baroness – the flaw is with the Merging. You are blaming consecrated metal and obedient mechanisms when all evidence points to a disconnect between scion and Knight.'

Two servitors walked forwards to remove her breastplate and pauldrons, but Jaya warned them back. 'I spent all of last night in meditative reflection,' she argued. 'I feel no such disconnect.'

Torolec moved away, heading towards the idle Knight, giving Jaya little choice but to follow. The sacristan held up two bionic hands extending from the same elbow, placing twin palms on the unpainted Knight's armoured toe-plating.

'You resist its noble spirit. It resists yours. Two stubborn souls locked in discord.'

Jaya pursed her lips. Only Torolec would be allowed to speak to her so. 'My spirit is at ease,' she lied.

'Then I shan't argue with you, baroness.' Torolec looked up at the towering war machine in all its bleak glory. Where proud and bright house colours should show, only bare and scratched metal met the eye. Where war banners should hang, depicting the Knight's own deeds and the honourable service of its scion pilot, there was nothing at all. Soon they would march to war in these cast-offs and jury-rigged exiles from still-living houses, and do battle for the first time without Vyridion's pennants waving in the wind.

'I find you in a mood of rare charity if you are unwilling to argue,' said Jaya.

Torolec's amusement showed on his wizened features, sparkling in his eyes. 'You should reboard, baroness. Perhaps the next exercise will work towards merging you with your new armour. We are scheduled for weapons trials.'

'I have dry-fired that decrepit thing's guns a hundred times.'

'Indeed! Today, however, you are to be loaded for live fire.'

Jaya stared at him. They had been waiting over a week for the anticipated shipment from House Mortan. 'We have ammunition?'

'At long last, being ferried to us as we speak.' He paused, his amusement darkening. 'You will of course be expected to make an appropriate display of gratitude to House Krast for the sharing of sacred resources from their forges.'

'Krast?' Jaya's tone rang with disbelief. 'Those vainglorious...'

'Ah, ah,' Torolec chided. 'Those *generous* and *noble* souls, you were about to say?'

'...but of course. What of their earlier refusal?'

'The Sigillite is said to have leaned upon them in this matter.'

Jaya watched as another gunmetal grey and badly dented Knight stalked past, shaking the hangar ground with its tread. The machine was in dire need of cleansing and re-oiling; the whining of protesting iron was torture on the ears.

Torolec saw her wince. 'Perhaps you might easier win the suit's regard if you stopped referring to it as "that decrepit thing". The others of our court seem to be adapting well.'

Jaya had the grace to accept the rebuke. 'Most are, yes.'

'Your resentment is understandable, baroness. But I know you do not need me to caution you on the vice of ingratitude.'

Again, she nodded. At least they had suits. Even these unmarked and untended exiles were a treasure any Knight House would consider a fortune in their own right. But to have fallen so far, so fast, to be relying on the scrapyard charity of indignant and indifferent houses...

Jaya took a breath. 'Summon me when the ammunition shipment arrives.'

Torolec said nothing. He merely bowed.

THE THRONE ROCKED beneath her, its suspensors worn down through a gestalt of time, damage and poor maintenance. Jaya's spinal plate locked into a groove along the chair's backrest, the connection triggering a flare in the cockpit's red lights and kindling three more monitors. Her weighted boots crunched into their stirrup-locks. Her gloved hands gripped the guidance levers that rose up from the throne's armrests.

Torolec had ascended the gantry ladder after his mistress, and now crouched his emaciated form at the airlock door above her. He reached in with several bionic hands, locking buckles and inserting penetrative interface cables into the baroness' helm. But the sacristan didn't linger beyond his murmured blessings. He bade her well and sealed her in with a ringing, echoing clang.

Jaya watched the hangar through her vision feeds, waiting for the gantries to be pulled away. Three Errants, unmarked and unbannered, were marching back to their boarding cradles for maintenance and reblessing, and far more importantly, for rearming. One of them turned to her as it passed with its ground-shaking tread, its hunched shoulders and faceplate grinding down in approximation of a brief half-bow. Jaya couldn't return the gesture with her boarding gantries still locked in, but she reached for the vox-plate to send an acknowledgement pulse back to the pilot.

She didn't know who it was. Gone forever were the days of knowing each scion by the heraldry their Knights wore and the banners they bore. Even the painted artistry of kill-markings was absent.

Shame burned fresh. House Vyridion and Highrock itself had died under her guardianship. And, with dark hilarity, her shame couldn't even be recorded in the familial archives, for they were ash along with the world that had been Vyridion's home for thousands of generations.

I am becoming maudlin, Jaya thought with a sigh. *Less than a month ago I was expecting execution.*

Torolec was right. Ingratitude was an impious vice.

The cockpit's bleak redness flickered once, twice, then the light around her was suddenly pale yellow instead of oppressive scarlet.

'Gantry cradle clear,' came Torolec's voice across the vox.

Jaya clenched the control levers and eased them forwards. The cockpit tilted forwards in sympathy, leaning with the motion. Jaya's throne stabilisers lagged a few seconds behind, but the heavy tilting and lurching as the Knight began its stride was nothing more than a vague irritation to a scion who had lived her life in the saddle.

And yet, everything was different. The machine didn't walk as her baronial Lancer had walked. Its piston-tendons compressed and extended with different air-hisses and at different speeds. Its gait rattled and clanged and clanked in an entirely different chorus of sound. The throne reacted differently to her weight and movements. The Knight's posture and rhythm required different compensational adjustment when moving at speed. The visual monitors were in different places, and slaved to feeds and target locks and aura-scryers that operated on momentary circuit-lags, or detuned if exerted a certain way. The cockpit even smelt different; rather than the sacred incense of High-rock's iluva herbs, no amount of Torolec's consecrations could rid the cockpit of that scorched blood and burned-metal scent lingering beneath the smell of old corrosion. Every one of Vyridion's new Knights had been acquired from wreckships and unused war spoil from local, loyal houses, and each one of them smelt exactly as one would expect a machine from such a fate to smell.

Even so, it wasn't that she couldn't endure these changes or that cataloguing them led to distraction. The truth was far blunter than anyone not of a noble Knightly bloodline could ever easily grasp. After a lifetime of piloting her own machine, Jaya was living inside a body that wasn't her own. She was wearing someone else's skin.

She walked the still-unfamiliar Knight through the hangar, swaying against the buckles of her throne with its graceless gait. Runic signifiers on her weapon monitors showed her ammunition by weight instead of exact numerals, estimating payloads. She felt her teeth clenching at the prickle along her skin, the blood-rush of bearing lethal armament once more.

For the first time since setting eyes upon this war machine, she felt the tremble of a connection. She could kill again. She could destroy.

This was strength. This was power.

What was your name? she wondered, looking around the cockpit. *Who were you before you were beaten, shamed and left for dead?*

She brought the Knight around towards the hangar's rear, where the massed wreckage of tanks and troop transports was serving as obstacles to manoeuvre around or assault with arm-mounted melee weaponry. Recognising their baroness' approach, two other scions walked their machines back out of the way, giving her the field.

And she swore in that moment that she felt the immense engine block housed in the armoured compartment behind her growl just a little louder.

She glanced to the crackling monitor linked to her left arm's gun-feed. Target locks refused to hold. Alignment chimes that should be ringing in clear, constant signals instead stuttered and hiccupped. How typical of this machine. How–

No. No more excuses. She didn't care. She leaned forwards in the throne, riding the uncomfortable, shaking gait, and guided the war machine's left arm upwards. No trajectory calculations. No aiming. No hesitation. She raised the arm and fired.

Stabilisers kicked in late, subjecting her to two seconds of teeth-clacking shivers, but Jaya scarcely noticed. Her grin was morbid with black laughter as a stream of tracer fire roared forth and pulverised the wreckage of a loader transport, punching molten yellow holes in its scorched hull. By the time her heart had beat six times, the flyer was barely recognisable. In its place lay a steaming mangle of blighted metal.

Jaya strode forwards, her clawed mechanical feet crushing thousands of spent shells into the deck. The sword that formed her right arm thunder-cracked into life, sheathed in an energy-spitting power field. A second peal of thunder rang out across the great hangar as she battered the annihilated wreckage aside with the swinging blade.

Later, she would remember hearing cheers across the vox. Later, she'd recall Torolec's pleased murmurs of benediction. Later, she'd rest well for the first time in months.

The Knight-Castigator overbalanced on the backswing, almost stumbling; Jaya slammed the opposing foot down, catching herself from falling, and immediately reared back up to full height. Another skull-rattling volley spat in a tracer stream from the over-under twin barrels of her primary cannon, stitching a trail across the hulls of three trashed Rhinos.

The blade fell again, swinging down in an impaling execution – a warrior finishing off a fallen foe. Jaya slammed a foot down on the shattered civilian transport beneath her, keeping it in place as she wrenched the sword free again. This time she didn't overbalance. Flakes and scraps of metal sizzled along the sword's edge as they dissolved in the power field's heat.

The towering Knight raised its blade high before an audience of menial hangar crews, servitor slaves and their sacristan overseers; yet the gesture wasn't for them. In ragged mimicry, the active Knights present each answered as best they could. Some raised blades or bullet-starved barrels of their own, others blared raw noise from their bullhorns, while those rendered unarmed and otherwise silent lowered their unpainted faceplates in respect.

Sacristan Apex Torolec consulted the data-slate in two of his four hands, allowing himself a thin smile at the sight of his baroness' cockpit feed. Perhaps this was going to work, after all.

THIRTEEN

What has happened before
The use of glory
Prophecy and foresight

R<small>A OPENED HIS</small> eyes to absolute blackness. A darkness deep enough to penetrate the senses, filling his eye sockets like pools of spilled oil. He waited for his perceptions to align. There was no fear. He knew the sensation of his master's summons.

Remorse sat within his heart, this time. The ambush at the Ossuary still tore at him, its questions presenting no easy answers.

We were so close.

No answer came from the Emperor – if his king had even heard.

Soon, there was light. Faint. Fractured. Tormentingly distant. Light manifesting in pinpricks, the iota-eyes of faraway suns. They speckled the void in a milky rash, glinting, winking, each one staring with a light that took a brief eternity to reach Ra's senses.

He was without form and shape. He merely existed in the void, a presence above a world cradled in the infinite black, a war-eaten planet bathed by the fusion glare of its insignificant yellow sun.

'Terra,' he said, without mouth, breath, teeth or tongue.

+Terra.+ The Emperor's voice thrummed through his skull. Disembodied, as eternal as any star. +Mere centuries ago, in the thrall of the

Unification Wars. Warlords and archpriestesses and magician-kings and clan chiefs fight over the harrowed territory of a broken world. My Thunder Legion marches to war against them. Against all of them.+

'It grieves me not to have fought at your side in those days, my king.'

+Your loyalty is noted, yet your grief is irrelevant.+

'Why am I here?' Ra thought and spoke at once. No discernible sep-aration existed between what was in his mind and what he vocalised into the void.

+Because I will it.+

It was the only answer he required, but he had hoped for more. Whatever purpose this illumination served was, so far, beyond Ra's guesswork.

With a wrenching lurch, the stars spun. Light bent and folded. The infinite blackness at once welcomed and rejected him, embracing his presence but defying his senses as he sought to process the speed at which he flew through the void. Nebulae bloomed before him, around him, as thick to the eyes as the poison gas clouds of forbidden weaponry, yet perfectly dark to all other senses. Worlds turned around god's-eye stars, some seared beneath the fat blue heat of swollen suns, some left cold on the outermost edges of the stellar ballet, travelling almost in exile among the frozen rocks that tumbled through deep and lifeless space.

So many of these globular jewels were not jewels at all, as unsuited as they were to cradling human life. For all of the terraforming pushed upon the galaxy's scattered worlds during the wonderworking of the Dark Age of Technology, an infinity of planets still revolved in the sav-age, storm-wracked, gaseous serenity that rendered human habitation impossible.

The true gems were just as varied in shade and hue. The alkali ochre of desert land predominated, planed smooth by the industry of colo-nisation or shattered in great chasm-rents by tectonic unrest. Oceanic worlds were turbulent sapphires and aquamarines swallowing sunlight beneath their immense depths – and many defied even water's pure hue, instead saturated by endless seas stained chrysoberyl by choking clouds of bacterium life, or rippling carnelian depths playing haven to hosts of aquacarnosaurs.

Colour upon colour upon colour, many worlds blending their offerings together, landmass by varied landmass. And yet the blue-green of unriven Terran antiquity was rarest of all. Such an innocent shade defied inevitability: everywhere mankind set foot, it tore from the earth and sucked from the seas, it harvested and wrought. It claimed. It conquered. It destroyed.

Nowhere was this truer than amidst the worlds turning around Terra's own sun. Ra hadn't been surprised when he first saw Terra from orbit, seeing the Throneworld herself a sickly beige, strangled by pollution, raked by the scars of endless war. Mars, once terraformed into a place of palatial idyll where human ingenuity had brought forth vegetation from dead soil, had been war-torn back into the dustbowl barrenness of its pre-colonisation era.

Ra was far from those worlds now. He twisted bodilessly in the black, facing another cloud-wreathed sphere, this one a Pangaean orb of earthen continents and only modest seas. Cityscapes showed as grey bruising across the landmasses, becoming pinprick-lit beacons as night fell swiftly across the hemisphere. Mere heartbeats later, dawn returned to the visible hemisphere, extinguishing the cityscapes' multitude of lights, restoring them to the grey blotches of any civilisation viewed from orbit. Millions of people must have called the world home. Billions.

'What world is this?' Ra asked the void.

There was no answer. With the ease of taking a breath, he was flung through the night heavens once more, soaring dreamlike without weight or momentum.

A migraine took form before his senses, painting the void with the retinal smearing of terminal brain cancer. Stars burned the nebulaic gases around them, sending streams of shimmering poison back into the void. They burned and strangled in the shifting tides of some alien substance that was and wasn't gas; that was and wasn't real.

The Ocularis Malifica. A warp storm. *The* warp storm, where the alternate reality of the warp had shattered its way into truespace and curdled dozens of star systems in its hostile miasma. Here was where two universes met, and both suffered with the union.

He stared at the rotting eye polluting the void. It stared back, somehow seething, malevolent without sentience.

'Why are you showing me all of this, sire?'

+I am not. Not really. This is merely how you process what you are learning when our thoughts are linked. Your mind is attuning to the scale of what I am imprinting upon it.+

Absolute loyalty meant he took reassurance at the Emperor's words. He did not, however, take much in the way of easy understanding.

'Sire?' he asked the void.

The void's answer was to send him hurling through space, weightless and ethereal, surrounded by the scream of a dying species. Years ago. Centuries ago, when much of the galaxy's human territories sweltered beneath the choking fire of Old Night's warp storms.

Here, among the eldar, all was at peace. He saw orbital platforms of sorcery-spun bone, so delicate that a breath of solar wind would surely shatter their tenuous frailty. He saw lush worlds of vegetation where spires of crystal and psychically sung wraithbone formed great spires and connecting walkways, while webway gates flared with endless use inside the towers of grand bloodlines. He saw a race crying out for more, always for more; for music that stimulated the biology of their brains; for wine that sent fire through their nervous systems; for entertainment and pleasures that replaced dignity with the harmony of madness.

He saw things wearing eldar skin moving in the shadows of their society, caressing with blades, killing with biting kisses, drinking blood and eating forbidden flesh with filed-fang smiles.

The truth burst from pale, alien flesh. It erupted free. Claws tore eldar open from within, doorways of bloody meat ripping open in bodies and minds grown soft by decadence and indolence. Warp-things crawled from ears, from nostrils, from tear ducts, shattering the skulls of their hosts as they swelled and grew. Daemons of hybrid gender, as much scorpion as maiden and man, shrieked – newborn and blood-wet – at the burning skies.

And far, far from such horrors, the human race was locked away in the isolation of Old Night. A million different worlds with no capacity to contact one another, each one alone in the fiery twilight of eternal warp storms raking through truespace. Only as one species died could another rise.

The eldar fall, damned by their own vices eating into the wards around their psychic souls. Warp storms that had wracked every world bleed away, focusing in final clusters: the Maelstrom, the Ocularis Malifica, and others far lesser besides. The human race rises, Old Night giving way to the dawn as the eternal storms recede.

A new godling has been born – '*Slaanesh!*' the eldar weep and cry, '*Slaanesh! Slaanesh!*' – but the rest of the suddenly silent galaxy takes its first breaths in a new age.

Ships begin to sail. Stellar empires form. One of those empires will become the only empire: the Imperium of Man, the twin kingdoms of Terra and Mars binding together to conquer the now-serene night sky.

A crusade, then an empire, all beneath one man's banner.

+Everything that has happened, will happen again. It is the way of things. Yet humanity's death will eclipse the eldar's annihilation tenfold, for we are evolving into a far more psychically powerful race. Uncontrolled psychic energy will tear reality apart. The warp's entities will feed on the carcass of the galaxy. There must be control, and control must be maintained.+

'Control…' Ra repeated. *The scale of such ambition…*

+The necessity of it. Lest mankind face a far harsher extinction than the eldar. Their souls shine bright within the warp, drawing the predations of the beasts within its tides. Soon, every human soul will become a beacon of fire.+

How, Ra wondered. *How can you know? What other unbelievable futures have you foreseen? How can evolution itself be conquered and controlled?*

+Through vision, Ra. We see the warp as an alternate reality, and this is so. It is a mirror, reflecting our every thought and action. Every hate, every death, every nightmare and dream, echoing into eternity. We break into this place, into a realm that harbours the pain and suffering of every man and woman and child to ever live, and we use it to sail between the stars. Because we must. Because until now there has been no other choice.+

'The webway,' Ra murmured into the silent night.

+The webway. Mankind is ascending, Ra. Humanity is taking a great developmental step, evolving into a psychic race. Uncontrolled psykers are lodestones for the warp's touch. A species comprising them would suffer as the eldar suffered. And for the eldar, this evolutionary juncture was their final step before destruction. I will not let humanity be destroyed by the same fate. The eldar had the answers within their grasp but were too naive and too proud to save themselves. They had the webway, which could have been their salvation. But they never fully severed their connection to the warp. Their soulfires drew damnation upon their entire species.'

Ra knew this, yet never had it been related to him in these exact words, flavoured as they were by the promise of prophecy. With the webway, humanity would need no Navigators. They would never need to rely on the unreliable warp-whispers of astropaths. Vessels would never enter the warp to be lost or torn apart by the entities that dwelt within it. But the eldar had done the same, had they not?

+No. They eradicated their reliance on the warp but they never severed their species' connection to it. I will do that for humanity, once and for all.+

Ra twisted in the nothingness, turning to stare at the light of so many distant stars. He faced Terra without knowing how he knew its direction, only knowing that he was right. One of those pinprick starlights was Sol, so far away.

+I have conquered humanity's cradle-world. I have conquered the galaxy, in order to shape mankind's development as it at last evolves into a psychic race. No isolated pockets of our species may remain free, lest in their ignorance they invite destruction upon us all. I have shattered the hold of faith and fear over the human mind. Superstition and religion must continue to be outlawed, for they are easy doors for the warp's denizens to enter the human heart. This is what we have already done. And soon I will offer humanity a way of interstellar travel without reliance upon Geller fields and Navigators. I will offer them means of communicating between worlds without reliance on the warp-dreams of astropaths. And when the Imperium shields the entire species within the laws of my Pax Imperialis, when humanity is freed from the warp and united beneath my vision, I can at last shepherd mankind's growth into a psychic race.+

The primarchs, thought Ra. *The Thunder Legion. The Unification Wars. The Great Crusade. The Space Marine Legions. The Imperial Truth. The Webway Project. The Black Ships, with psykers huddled in the holds, watched over by the Silent Sisterhood. It is all about–*

+Control. Tyranny is not the end, Ra. Absolute control is but the means to the end.+

The hubris... Ra couldn't fight the insidiously treacherous thought, to see the hidden depths of his master's ambitions. *The sheer, unrivalled hubris.*

+The necessity.+ The Emperor's voice was iced iron. +Not arrogance. Not vainglory. Necessity. I have already told you, Ra. Humans need rulers. Now you see why. A single murder is on one end of the spectrum, for rulers bring law. The hope of the entire race is at the far end of the continuum, for I – as ruler – bring salvation.+

Ra stared towards distant Terra, unsure if he was humbled or touched by the alien sensation of something akin to terror.

+You are shedding tears, Ra.+

Surprised, the Custodian touched gold-clad fingertips to his tattooed cheeks. They came away glinting with faint wetness in the light of distant suns.

'I have never done so before.'

+That is not true. You wept on the night your mother died. You merely do not remember it.+

Ra still looked at the faint moisture on his fingertip. *How curious.* 'Forgive the indignity, sire.'

+There is nothing to forgive. The immensity of my ambitions sit ill within mortal minds. Even among mortals that will live as close to eternally as my Ten Thousand.+

And yet, Ra thought in another treasonous whisper, *it is all threatened, coming apart at the seams.*

+The primarchs,+ agreed the Emperor. +Witness them.+

RA DRAGGED IN a cold breath. He was on guard immediately, his spear in his hands, razor gaze flicking across his surroundings, seeking threats. But in every direction, all he saw was a featureless landscape far too flat to be of natural origin. No matter where he looked, the horizon was a pale line of useless, bare land meeting a cloudless sky. Even his retinal gauges registered his surroundings as impossibly even. This was the work of the Mechanicum and their continental geoplaning engines.

In that moment, he knew where he was.

'Ullanor.' His voice echoed strangely. For all he knew, he was the only living soul on the whole world. The wind took his word and carried it away.

'Ullanor,' the Emperor confirmed. Ra turned to see his master clad in the brazen light of layered golden plate, festooned with Imperial aquilas the way a shaman might decorate his flesh with wards against black magic. 'Do you remember when you last walked the earth of this world, Ra?'

How could he not? It had been at the Triumph, when millions of troops had gathered to bid the Emperor farewell from the Great Crusade, in the final hours before He returned to Terra. The day that nine – nine! – primarchs had gathered together at their father's side.

The day that Horus had been proclaimed Warmaster.

A single breath later, Ra was back there once more. The salt flats of geoplaned banality were host to a sea of colours: banners, flags, soldiers, tanks, Titans. The eye couldn't take in the immensity of the sight. The mind couldn't process it. The Martian Mechanicum had cleaved an entire continent to make the procession possible, dismantling mountain ranges, filling valleys, contouring the planet's crust for the most monumental gathering since the declaration of the Great Crusade.

And the sound, the sound. The thrum of so many engines was a living, draconic roar. Regiments of pristine warriors standing beneath remade war standards cried their victories to the sky. A single Titan's footsteps made for infrequent, rhythmic thunder. A battle division's worth of giant war machines made for a storm capable of shaking a city to its foundations. Here walked thrice that number, and thrice again, and thrice more beyond that. The Martian behemoths strode over and through the millions of troops at their ankles, leaving immense footprints that served to finally carve features upon the plain plateau.

The Luna Wolves had mustered in unified ranks at the procession's vanguard, still clad in the pearly white of their nobler incarnation rather than the murky green of their self-damnation as the Sons of Horus.

And with them? Phalanx upon phalanx of warriors from every Legion. Even those without primarchs present still stood proud beneath the million war banners waving in the desert wind.

The primarchs stood apart, occupying the colossal dais erected for their specific purpose. They towered above even the great Imperators and Warmongers that no other war machine could match, and each of the Emperor's geneforged generals variously bathed in or endured the shouted jubilation of the organised masses below.

One by one they walked forwards to greet the assembled host. Angron, raising his weapons high, consecrated by the army's roars just as he had once been exalted by the cries of arena crowds in his life as Angronius of Nuceria, Lord of the Red Sands.

Lorgar Aurelian, Herald of the Emperor, throwing his arms wide and beckoning the millions of loyal souls to shout louder, harder. He was a demagogue presented with a crowd that offered nothing but vindication.

Sanguinius was next, reluctant and wrathful and soulful Sanguinius, the Emperor's eagle-winged son and the living avatar of the Imperium. The cries that met his presentation rang loudest of all, and the tens of millions of men and women gathered below were too far distant to ever see how their near-worship flickered uneasily in the Angel's eyes. Even so, as they bayed and begged, he drew his sword in salute to the masses of humanity arrayed across the plain. They cried their throats raw as he spread his great wings wide. A single feather flew free, descending upon the wind in slow whirls. It would become a sacred relic to the Imperial Army regiment that claimed it, with the image of a single white feather forever after emblazoned in a place of honour upon their campaign banners.

One by one they came and presented themselves, until, at last, the Master of Mankind took His place.

And all of that raucous, rapturous cheering died. Every eye looked to the golden figure holding court at the centre of the dais. Those too far removed, kilometres away from the processional core, looked to erected monitors connected to drifting servo-skull feeds, relaying the images.

The Emperor stood before them all, armoured and armed but never again to march with them to war. Men and women stared up at Him, unaware they were weeping. Even many legionaries' faces would have shown tear trails down their gene-altered features, had they not been hidden by the grilles of Crusade- and Iron-pattern helms.

Horus was declared Warmaster. The cheers returned. Victory was celebrated. Glory to the Imperium. Glory to the Emperor. Glory to the Warmaster.

All proceeded as expected. No one thought the Emperor would speak again at the Triumph's conclusion. What was there that He could say? Every soul gathered knew what He intended to do. He would leave the Great Crusade in the hands of His sons, returning to Terra to oversee the workings of the ever-expanding Imperium. Surely nothing He could say would lessen the blow of His abandonment.

And yet, He had spoken once more, one last time, after all.

'I leave not by choice,' He promised them. His voice carried across the geoburned plateau, aided by the speaker-drones and vox-emitters liberally populating the muster. 'I leave not by choice. I leave only because I must. Know this, and know my regret, but know also that I return to Terra for the good of our Imperium.'

From among the Custodian Guard stationed nearby, in a rank behind the primarchs, two incarnations of Ra stood watching in silence. The first was helmed and at attention, his guardian spear clutched in one gloved hand, the warrior himself a perfect mirror of the Custodians standing at his side. The second was unhelmed, smiling faintly, to so vividly recall this breathtaking moment once more.

The Emperor turned from the crowd, moving through the pack of demigods around Him. Already they were regarding their father, and each other, with newfound caution. One of their number had been elevated above the rest – no longer merely first among equals, but definitively named *first*. Like any family, their reactions and emotions at such a development would prove... variable.

'Ra,' the Emperor greeted him. The worthies around them both continued speaking, no longer paying either of them any heed at all.

'All of this,' the Custodian said. He gestured not only to the primarchs, but the amassed pomp itself – the geoscaped continent, the sky pregnant with dropships, the gathered regimental masses weeping and cheering below. 'Why, sire? I never asked it then, and I have always wondered since. Why all of this?'

'For glory,' the Emperor replied. 'To honour the creatures that call themselves my sons. My necessary tools. They feed on glory as if it were a palpable sustenance. Their own glory, of course, no different from the kings and emperors of old. It scarcely crosses their mind that glory matters nothing to me. I could have had a planet's worth of glory any time I wished it when I walked in the species' shadow throughout prehistory. Only three of them ever thought to ask why I timed my emergence as I did.'

Ra looked at the gathered pantheon of primarchs. He didn't ask which three had questioned the Emperor. In truth, he didn't care. Such lore was irrelevant.

'And so I gave them Ullanor,' the Emperor said. 'They crave recognition for their honour and achievements, and the Triumph was the ultimate expression of that. In that regard, they are just as the Akhean gods and goddesses of Ulimpos were believed to be.'

Ra knew the legends. Zoas Lightningfather. Avena Warbringer. Hermios Swiftrunner. Heraklus Halfgod. Bickering, violent divinities who were powerful enough to act with impunity over the mortals that prayed to them.

'Humanity's perception of god-beings has never been consistent,' the Emperor mused. 'Give any being great power and the largesse to act with impunity, and what you have is indivisible from those ancient myths. The rage of thunder gods. The battle drums of nations that prayed to war gods. The madness and decadence of powerful kings. That is what true power has always done to the mortal mind – elements of humanity become magnified, more human than human. In that light, are the primarchs not deities?'

Ra grunted, noncommittal. 'That is not what I meant, my liege. I mean... how could they betray you without warning? Why did you not foresee it?'

For the first time in Ra's memory, the Emperor hesitated. He wondered if he was the first of the Custodian Guard – perhaps even the first Imperial soul – to ask such a thing. The Ten Thousand had spoken of it amongst themselves many hundreds of times. Consensus on the truth was impossible to reach. Their place was to live in loyalty and die in duty, not question in doubt.

'You ask about the very nature of foresight,' said the Emperor. 'From your words and tone, you suggest it is no different to looking back down a road already travelled, and seeing the places and people you have passed.'

Ra couldn't tear his eyes from the primarchs. Fulgrim, smiling, always smiling; Magnus, stern in the guarded pretence that none must perceive he bore a troubled mind. Proximity to them even in this moment of glory – especially in this moment of glory – sickened the Custodian, heart and soul. How he ached to strike them down.

'Is that not the function of foresight, my king? To see the future before it unfolds?'

'You imply omniscience.'

'I imply nothing, unless by my own ignorance. I merely seek enlightenment.'

The Emperor seemed to weigh His guardian's words. 'I see.'

'I mean no disrespect, my liege.'

'I know, Ra. I take no umbrage at your questions. Think on this, then. I prepared them all, this pantheon of proud godlings that insist they are my heirs. I warned them of the warp's perils. Coupled with this, they knew of those dangers themselves. The Imperium has relied on Navigators to sail the stars and astropaths to communicate between worlds since the empire's very first breath. The Imperium itself is only possible because of those enduring souls. No void sailor or psychically touched soul can help but know of the warp's insidious predation. Ships have always been lost during their unstable journeys. Astropaths have always suffered for their powers. Navigators have always seen horrors swimming through those strange tides. I commanded the cessation of Legion Librarius divisions as a warning against the unrestrained use of psychic power. One of our most precious technologies, the Geller field, exists to shield vessels from the warp's corrosive touch. These are not secrets, Ra, nor mystical lore known only to a select few. Even possession by warp-wrought beings is not unknown. The Sixteenth witnessed it with his own eyes long before he convinced his kindred to walk a traitor's path with him. That which we call the warp is a universe alongside our own, seething with limitless, alien hostility. The primarchs have always known this. What difference would it have made had I labelled the warp's entities "daemons" or "dark gods"?'

'I don't know, sire. I can't see what might have changed. I cannot see into the skeins of fate.'

The Emperor was silent for a moment. 'You speak of seeing the future,' He finally said, 'without knowing the limits of what you speak.'

In a heartbeat the Ullanor Triumph was gone, banished between breaths. Ra and the Emperor stood alone on a rocky shore, ankle-deep in icy saltwater. They faced a great cliff, reaching up hundreds of metres – sheer in many places, sloped in others. Even as Ra stared, loose rocks clattered down its surface, splashing into the rising water not far from where they stood.

'Where you stand now,' the Emperor said, 'is the present. Do you see the top of the cliff?'

'Of course, sire.'

'That is the future. You see it. You know what it is. Now reach it.'

Ra hesitated. 'Now?'

'Climb, Custodian. You questioned the nature of my foresight. I am granting you an answer.'

Ra moved to the rock face, looking over the stone, finding his first grips. He tested them, finding them strong, even against the weight of his armour. The weaker ones, he avoided.

Less than ten heartbeats had passed when a rock cracked and crumbled in his gauntleted hand. Ra skidded, arresting his fall by clutching at the stone; another gave way, sending him the last few metres to the rocky ground in a breathy cloud of white dust.

'You looked for places to safely grip,' said the Emperor, 'yet you have already stumbled. You did not know the stone was weak.'

'It looked strong.'

The Emperor smiled, and it was by far the most unpleasant sight Ra had ever witnessed. Emotion painted across a human face, as false as the grotesques at any masquerade. 'Yes,' the Emperor agreed. 'It did, and you only learned the truth too late. Now climb.'

Ra hesitated once more, a hesitation that bordered upon defiance. As if such an action were even possible for one such as he in the presence of his master.

'It is not necessary, sire. I believe I understand now.'

'Do you? Look out across the water, Ra.'

Ra returned to the Emperor's side and did as he was bid. The water rippled in sedate waves, sloshing around the rocks that lined the shore. At the horizon's very edge, he could see the mirroring lip of another landmass.

'I see another land. An island, perhaps.'

'It is Albia, many thousands of years ago. But that is unimportant. You see the shore. You know it is there. You know you could reach it by ship, or by swimming, or by flight. That is what you know.'

The Emperor's dark eyes lost their focus. He faced towards the distant shore but Ra doubted He was still seeing it. 'So you journey towards it. But all you can see is your destination. You cannot see the beasts below the water that devour travellers. You cannot know if the wind will blow and throw you aside from your course. And if the wind does blow, will it send you east? West? North? South? Will it shatter your craft completely? Perhaps there are rocks beneath the water, impossible to see until they grind and tear at the hull of your ship. Perhaps the inhabitants of that far shore will fire upon your craft before you can make landfall.'

The Emperor turned back to Ra, though curiously His eyes didn't clear. 'But you can see the shore, Ra. Did you fail to predict any of those possible flaws between here and there?'

'Perhaps I predicted them all, sire. Perhaps I factored in the possibilities of each one occurring.'

'Maybe so. And what of the eventualities you could not predict? Each passing moment is rich with a hundred thousand possible pathways. The craftswoman making your boat may suffer a heart failure before she can gift it to you. Or she decides not to offer you the boat at all. You say the wrong words to her. You offer the wrong currency. She lies to you, for she is a thief. An enemy sabotages your boat before you set sail. You reach halfway across this channel of water, only to see a more appealing coast to the east or west. Minute after minute, possibility upon possibility, path after path. All variables you are unable to see from where you stand at this moment.'

The Emperor reached out as if He could crush the coast in His golden gauntlet. His expression was cold in its pale ferocity. 'I can *see* the coast, Ra. I know what awaits me there. But I cannot see all the infinite vicissitudes between here and there.'

At last, He lowered His hand.

'That is foresight, Ra. To know a trillion possible futures, and to be left to guess at the infinite ways of arriving at each one. To map out even one possible eventuality, taking into account every decision that every living being will make that will impact upon the others around it, would take all of the lifetimes I have already lived. The only way to know anything for certain...'

He trailed off, gesturing to the distant shore.

'Is to reach the other side,' said Ra.

The Emperor nodded. 'When the vault was attacked and the Primarch Project compromised, should I have destroyed them all? Or do as I did, and trust that I would be able to restore them to grandeur? If I had destroyed them to prevent their abduction, would the Imperium have risen as it has now done? Or would the Great Crusade have stuttered and failed without its generals? There are no answers yet, Ra. We are in the middle of the sea, beset by strange tides and unexpected beasts, but not yet thrown off course.'

'I won't fail you, sire.'

The Emperor closed His eyes and winced as pain flickered across His dusky features. He touched all ten fingertips to His face beneath the weight of some silent strain.

'My liege?'

'The forces of Magnus' Folly press harder against the Mechanicum's junctions. I do not know how this can be. Their efforts were already relentless and monumental. Coupled with the intrusions within the original web, I fear time is growing short.'

'We've failed to destroy the Echo of the First Murder. Why did it pull back from us? How can it be stopped?'

The Emperor swallowed, His eyes bloodshot and haunted in their distraction.

+Awaken, Ra.+

RA OPENED HIS eyes, his senses immediately attuning to the sound of sirens.

FOURTEEN

ZEPHON'S BANDOLIERS RATTLED as he walked, the bound arsenal of rad-grenades clinking against his red ceramite. He felt like an imposter in his own skin: the volkite pistols holstered on his thigh plates hadn't been fired in years, nor had he sparred with the power sword sheathed on his backpack. Similarly, he'd done nothing more than clean and maintain the bolter he now carried over one shoulder, hanging by its thick strap of Baalite mutant hide-leather.

After an airspeeder conveyance had carried him halfway across Himala-zia to the Palace's high-security core, he walked ever-downwards through the beating heart of the Imperium, occasionally resorting to subterra-nean transit pods or the elevator platforms in constant operation.

He had spoken to Diocletian and Arkhan Land, the former telling him of the dark wonders of the Impossible City and the foes faced by the Ten Thousand, the latter waxing loud and long about the struc-ture of the webway and its potential for mankind. He had reviewed the Archimandrite's implanted map, and yet... doubts lingered. Or perhaps it was hope that lingered. Zephon wished feverishly for such enlightenment to be lies.

The Blood Angel had no idea what to believe. He knew only that the
Ten Thousand had chosen him to serve the Emperor, and he would
do so to his dying breath.

And so, he journeyed to join them.

Through districts that had evolved into librarium archives; through
museum sectors given over to the teeming refugee masses; through storage chambers and arsenals and even old Terran foundries, the Blood
Angel walked in solemn silence, his gait exaggerated slightly by the
bulky twin turbines of his jump pack. The double engines rose above
his pauldrons, wings in intent if not in form. Servo-skulls drifted endlessly past, pausing to aim their sensoria-cluster eye needles at him,
scanning him for Unified Biometric Identification. Inevitably they
would give a satisfied click and drift away.

Towards the end of the first day he passed the first seal. The ever-locked
iris gate wasn't locked for him; he entered without hesitation, passing
a phalanx of one hundred Imperial Fists on one side of the gate, then
five Custodians on the other. The former greeted him with grim formality. The latter ignored him completely.

His descending path converged with those of his fellow pilgrims. A
stream of tracked battle-servitors rumbled along the hallways in their
hundreds, en route to the Imperial Dungeon for whatever purpose the
Custodians had in mind.

Not long after Zephon joined this lobo-chipped convoy, they were
joined by the tall and striding forms of House Vyridion. The great
Knights shook the stone chambers and corridors with their thunderous
march, and Zephon felt his bleak heart stir at the sight of Jaya and her
war court. Gone was the gunmetal grey and bare steel of the unpainted
dregs-machines donated and begged from other houses. Zephon might
have expected the blue-green of their former heraldry, but this too was
absent. Vyridion's armour plates had turned black and gold, and while
they lacked the banners of their past deeds, they once more showed a
sigil on their tilting shields: the Imperial aquila symbolising the unity
of Terra and Mars. The simplest, purest symbol they could have chosen.

Looking at the monstrous form of Baroness Jaya as she strode over and ahead of him, Zephon kindled a shared vox-link.

'Vyridion marches,' he said with a faint smile.

'*Vyridion marches,*' came the crackling reply.

The lead Knight turned, a great bronze aquila hanging on chains from its bolt cannon swaying with the motion, and sounded its alarm horn through the stone hallways. It was answered by the horns and klaxons of every other Knight in the procession as House Vyridion celebrated its march.

By the second day's dawn, the travellers were far from the sun's light. Zephon's trudging tread was marked by the clank of pistons and the thunder of heavy metal feet in silent corridors. Billions lived and toiled within the walls of the Palace, but the procession saw none of them, as though this was not the heart of the Imperium after all, merely an empty realm, a kingdom of stone and shadow.

On they walked. Every few hours they would pass one of the seals, the irises of each gateway open and waiting: unpatrolled, unguarded, unbarred.

They passed the Hibran Arch, vaulted above the fires of torches that had burned through Old Night and burned still. They walked the Processional of the Eternals, beneath the painted eyes of vanquished warlords. They walked until they had sunk into the underworld of the Palace's foundations, gouged into the living rock of the planet's Himalazian spine, and still they descended.

Servitor workers began to appear at infrequent intervals, along with robed adepts tending to machines and engines squatting in the basalt rock. The earthen corridors remained tall and wide – the Knights never once had to hunch or double back to seek another way – and the ground showed the erosion of countless feet and vehicle tracks.

Despite an eidetic recollection, Zephon wasn't certain of the exact moment he realised the convoy was no longer being presented with alternate routes. After the fifth seal? At the sixth? When had the many tributary corridors converged at last into this one final path?

His instinctive sense of direction slowly began to tell another truth – the twists and turns betrayed his route, not always downwards but never ascending, remaining deep within the planet's crust: he was walking a labyrinth. Not one akin to the eclectic garden mazes of the wealthy or the prisons of the mythologically monstrous, but a true labyrinth out of Ancient Terran lore, of the kind once seen in holy temples and places of pilgrimage. He knew them from his studies into pre-Imperial spirituality, when they had been embossed onto cathedral floors or etched upon the earth, forming a path for pilgrims to walk every step until reaching the centre. They were meant to be journeys of understanding, from ignorance to enlightenment. Was this such a journey?

I hear thunder.

Almost as soon as the thought came he realised its untruth. Not thunder at all, no matter how similar in sound. The false thunder grew louder with the passing of time, turn by turn, tunnel by tunnel.

Zephon saw faint markings along the walls and brushed aside the dust as delicately as he could with a sweep of one bionic hand. Simple, primal pictures met his curious touch, resembling the cave paintings exhibited by the most primitive human cultures. He walked on, stopping at random to study the primeval artwork: hunting scenes of simple figures bearing spears against great beasts; a community of shadowy humans gathered around the red-orange curls of a fire; dozens of figures with arms raised in worship to the high sphere of the sun.

It wasn't long before the travellers reached the bridge, and with it, the thunder.

The path before them spanned an abyss. The servitors stalked and rolled onwards. The Knights hesitated, reining their war suits to a halt. Zephon stopped with them, sliding from the conveyor upon which he'd been riding, looking with unbelieving eyes at the source of the thunder pouring down into the infinite black. The water of Terra, harvested for the Palace's underground reservoirs, plunged in vast, roaring falls from the cavern's roof high above.

Zephon found himself first smiling, then laughing at the breathtaking

sight, such was its scale and the deafening pressure of its crashing bellow. He had fought on oceanic worlds, on monsoon worlds, but the
effect was no less majestic to him. He was a child of Baal, and few
planets could claim such a radiation-soaked, thirsty legacy as that distant globe.

Yet on they walked, steps becoming metres, metres becoming
kilometres.

Eventually the thunder receded.

Zephon's focus drifted with uneasy wonder as he ventured through
the labyrinth, beneath the vast stone statues of humanity's first false
gods, over bridge-spanned chasms that cradled the bones of long-dead
settlements. As he traversed another wide stone archbridge he saw the
cold, sunless remains of an entire city. Even from his maddening alti-
tude above the grave-city he sensed movement inside the black eyes
of glassless windows: the ghosts of a distant past, staring up in hollow
and sullen silence at the passing of their descendants and inheritors.

What was this place when it stood in the sun? He wasn't certain whether
he thought the words or whispered them aloud, until he received an
answer.

'*Kath Mandau,*' a voice murmured across the vox.

Zephon didn't tear his eyes from the dead city five hundred metres
below. Impossibly, there was wind here. A soft breeze that tasted of
dust.

'Diocletian?' he voxed back.

'*You asked what this place once was. It was the city Kath Mandau. Capital of the nation Sagarmatha, also called Nehpal. It was once the roof of
the world.*'

'That is very poetic.' *And now it lies dead, part of the Palace's foundations,
remaining only in name in the precincts above.* 'Thank you, Diocletian.'

The Custodian, far ahead at the front of the column, didn't respond
again.

The next bridge was reinforced by support stanchions and black iron
gantries binding the stone pathway to the cavern's far-off walls. The

air itself gleamed orange from the underworld's light. Heat assailed Zephon in a rising miasma.

Molten rock seethed and sludged in the abyss below. The bridge spanned a wound in Terra's crust, seemingly torn open to the planet's mantle. A great lake of the world's liquid blood-fire burned in the darkness far, far below, somehow only breeding more shadows instead of banishing them.

More and more images showed upon the chamber walls as the procession made its way through the labyrinth. Cave paintings of ochre and charcoal became artful mosaics and impressionist vistas. Images of suns, of the heavens, of the blue Terran sky and the black void beyond. Pictographs of satellites, those earliest machines that sung their songs into the silent night.

Then came the artistry of the Dark Age, of Old Night, and the Unification Wars that ravaged Terra. Wars of unrivalled savagery wracked cities that couldn't possibly exist. Men of flesh fought men of stone and men of steel. Zephon swallowed at the sight of Baal among the painted heavens, far too high on a ceiling mural for him to touch. He held his knuckles to his heart in solemn salute and walked on, passing yet more scenes of devastation on a scale never again to be matched, followed in turn by scenes showing the salvation of a species brought together after Old Night by the guiding golden hand of the species' master.

Then came the monsters. Devilish forms conjured from human nightmare waged war in realms of fire and ice and smoke and flood. Horned beasts, red-fleshed and armoured in brass. Carrion-eating skeletal dancers with the faces and features of ancient birds. Zephon saw creatures from his own childhood dreams, monsters conjured by his own youthful, slumbering imagination.

How can they be here?

No answer presented itself.

Soon enough, Zephon noted another change. A shift in the surroundings.

Machines – engines – became far more numerous, set into the ground or half projecting out from unfinished murals and incomplete mosaics. The crash and bang of industry's metallic song grew louder and louder with each twist and turn. Where the artistry of ages had marked the walls, soon space was given over to the primacy of cables and pipes to feed the machines, seemingly pushed into place and bolted to the Palace's stone foundations out of rushed necessity.

Some of the engines spun chemicals the way a centrifuge spins blood. Others juddered as they sucked power, or generated it, or acted as junctions to spit it elsewhere. Towers of crates lined the walls of each chamber, eclipsing the incomplete architecture. Workers, robed or coated or suited, were everywhere.

Zephon removed his helmet to wipe silent tears from his eyes. The agony of the journey, of this entire labyrinth, burned at his core in place of the doubts he'd previously held.

This journey would have been the first step of humanity's life without the warp. This was the route to the webway... Mankind should have walked through this labyrinth as a journey of understanding, bathing in the symbolism, preparing to step into the stars anew. A species reborn, saved from damnation by one man's vision.

Yet it stood darkened and unfinished, so much stone yet undressed, the passageways that were supposed to lead to enlightenment now blighted and defaced by archeotech machines bolted into place in the wake of Magnus' Folly. War had touched this place of last hope.

Suddenly it was all too easy to see this place defiled in the months to come, suffering at the rabid, iconoclastic hands of Horus' rebels when they reached Terra. Would they care for the promise of this unfinished labyrinth, or would they desecrate it with the wrath of the ignorant?

Zephon's smile was a weak, dark little thing. Mere days before, he'd not been sure what to believe. Now he mourned the incompleteness of the Emperor's vision of salvation. He had walked the labyrinth and learned all he needed to know.

He closed his pale eyes.

'Why do you weep, Blood Angel?'

Zephon turned to see Jaya's Sacristan Apex. He'd believed only servitors were nearby in this section of the processional. Torolec, that was the priest-artisan's name. Zephon had only met the man once before, on the battlements weeks ago.

'Loss,' he said, and added nothing more.

'*Are we close?*' Baroness Jaya voxed across the general channel.

'*Close to what?*' Diocletian's reply was blithe.

'*To the Imperial Dungeon. To the Emperor's laboratory.*'

The Custodian's reply was immediate. '*They are the same thing,*' he said. '*We have been in the Imperial Dungeon since passing the final seal. This is the Emperor's laboratory. All of it.*'

Zephon replaced his helm, sealing his collar lock with a snap-hiss of air pressure. He breathed the recycled air of his battleplate and walked on.

Less than an hour later, they reached the Eternity Gate.

THE PROCESSION STOPPED at the heart of the labyrinth.

Zephon stood in the final promenade, surrounded by a multitude of banners standing in honoured rows. A cavalcade of colours stretched out on both sides of the downward-staired marble avenue, each woven standard showing the names, numbers, sigils, worlds or proud avataric beasts that embodied one of the Imperium's regiments. Every regiment that had ever worn the Imperial eagle and fought under the Emperor's aegis was represented by a flag, banner, trophy or pennant. A field of markers stretching in their tens of thousands, all leading ever-downwards toward the door of the Emperor's throne room.

The great doors of the Gate stood open at the end of the descending avenue, their two-hundred metre height reaching up to the cavern's arched roof. Moisture wept from the sedimentary rock sky, painting a thousand shining trickle-rivers down the surface of the metal doors. An image of the Emperor was bisected by their parting: a great embossed mural of the Master of Mankind wielding a spear against the draconic beasts and machine horrors of Old Night.

And between those wide doors, only darkness.

For the first time in several hours, no machinery was bolted to the walls and floor, and no workstations or storage crates obscured the beauty of what lay before him. Yet Zephon sensed the subsonic thrum of power cables beneath his boots, as energy cobwebbed throughout the labyrinth. Ostentation may have eclipsed pragmatism here at the Eternity Gate, but it hadn't replaced it.

Shadows and spectres stood at the edges of Zephon's sight, overlaying the truth of his senses with stories not yet told. Each time he shifted his gaze he witnessed some other echoing ghost, some other suggestion of what might yet be.

The great doors were unguarded, yet there stood two towering Reaver Titans either side of the arch, their armour plating cast in the aggressive blazonry of Mars' own Legio Ignatum.

The ocean of banners stood in windless silence, yet there walked a host of hunchbacked priests dressed in the flayed skin of their forefathers, swinging incense braziers and chanting prayers to the souls of those men and women who fought beneath the icons across the galaxy.

The air above the avenue was empty, yet there circled the ungainly anti-gravitic forms of cherub-like drones, seemingly cloned child-angels wheeling through the air. They trailed banners from their ankles and rang hand-held bells, tolling who knew what.

The doors were wide open, yet they stood closed in their ethereal echo, and the rendition of the Emperor showed Him surrounded by a wheeling cosmos of daemons and mythological beasts. He was haloed by the sun, triumphant above the impaled body of something horned and serpentine.

Each baroque ghost glimpse told a tale from a time when the Imperial Dungeon seemed more of a cathedral than a laboratory, a time when the Emperor Himself was worshipped rather than revered.

And there, last of all, out of tune with the other echoes... An Angel stood before the gate, armoured in bleeding gold, bearing a sword of silver fire. Its great white wings spread wide in defiance, the swan feathers ragged and bloody red.

'Father,' said Zephon through numb lips, but the Angel was gone and the words were fading behind him as he stepped forwards. The gate yawned wide before him.

Alongside rumbling tank-treaded servitors unable to acknowledge their surroundings beyond track/kill subroutines, Zephon entered the Emperor's throne room.

THE DARKNESS WAS a falsehood, one that cleared as soon as he passed through it. The first thing to hit Zephon's senses was a retinal smear of migraine light, bright enough that even his occulobe implant was useless in defending his eyes against it. He narrowed his gaze to a slit, one hand raised against the fierce illumination.

The second thing to strike was the burning machine-stink of overworked metal. He'd fought in manufactories on several worlds, breathing in the charcoal and scorched iron reek of machinery slowly dying, wearing out its moving parts. He knew that same smell at once, even spiced as it was by the acidic tang of charged ozone.

The third element was the sound. The shouting voices. The lightning lash of sparking machines. The primeval *hum* of running engines. He felt it as much as heard it; he felt it in his blood, in his bones.

'*Keep walking.*' Diocletian's voice.

He kept walking, seeing little, sensing everything. Ahead of him, someone shrieked.

'*Keep walking!*' shouted Diocletian across the vox.

Pivoting to find who had called out, Zephon saw only the faintest silhouettes. Maddening. Insane. His genetic modifications were born of the Emperor's own genius; a Space Marine saw in near-darkness and overcame blinding light with equal ease. Yet he could see almost nothing.

Another cry, this time from his side. An unknowable distance away, there was the crash of falling metal beams or perhaps a collapsing gantry. He saw none of it.

Am I blind?

'I cannot see,' he said aloud.

'*You don't need to,*' replied Diocletian. '*Move forwards. Keep walking.*'

His eyes did adjust, though far slower than he'd ever known. Zephon saw the pale stone floor beneath his boots, and the dark bronze of immense, humming machines at the edges of his vision. Pain knifed awkward cuts at his eye sockets as he raised his head to see what lay before the marching procession.

An archway. A door. A portal. A construct of light-stained marble that disgorged golden mist into the chamber. He couldn't make out its exact shape – *Circular? Oval?* – nor its exact boundaries, where the alien mist ended and the structure's sides began.

'*Don't look back,*' came Diocletian's voice once more.

Row after row of battle-servitors rumbled into the golden fog, mind-dead to all but their orders. A Krios tank was swallowed a moment later, its passage doing nothing to disturb the mist.

One of Jaya's Knights strode in alongside another servitor host, enveloped by the portal's exhalations. Another of them stood inactive by the portal's edge, grasped by tendrils of golden fog, half turned away to look back over the rest of the marching column. Zephon could hear the baroness shouting at the courtier, demanding he keep moving.

The pilot's voice came back stammering, shattered. '*The Emperor. My Emperor. The Omnissiah.*'

'*Don't look back,*' Diocletian snapped. '*Baroness, lead your scions through now.*'

Jaya's towering form lurched in a heavy stride, shaking the ground as she clanked forwards. The remaining Knights followed in a ragged march, moving between and stepping over the servitor horde.

When Zephon reached the portal's cusp, the curling wisps of mist formed breathy tendrils against his armour plating. It carried no scent, no taste, no presence beyond what he could see. Above him swayed the idle form of the awestruck Knight. Either side of him, Thallaxi cyborgs marched into the mist. Their blood-filled face domes reflected the golden fog.

Zephon turned – and ceased. What would he see if he looked back? The light's intensity as a sun's flare, ringing a structure raised above the ground? A core of blackness in the heart of a thunderstorm's flickering light? A throne, with a corona of energy, and a figure upon it, a figure that–

'Don't look back!' Diocletian was there, shoving the Blood Angel with the haft of his spear.

But the Emperor... The very Throne of Terra...

'Move, Bringer of Sorrow. Move now.'

Zephon swallowed, faced the golden mist head-on, and took his first step into the webway.

PART THREE
DEATH OF
A DREAM

FIFTEEN

Avenues of the Mechanicum
The true webway
Eternal war

THE PROCESSION TRAVELLED through tunnels of dark metal and glowing circuitry. Arkhan Land, no stranger to the gloom of underground complexes given his chosen profession, yet found it curiously oppressive. It wasn't the darkness, for the walls themselves radiated a weak electrical light from their circuit lines. Nor was it the fog, which seemed to have no source, for once he had determined it carried no toxic potential, the stuff was easy to ignore.

No, what he found oppressive was the knowledge of what waited beyond these ironclad walls. He had faith, of course. He had all the faith a man could possess that the Omnissiah's psychic resolve would keep these passages protected.

But still.

Land had never considered himself given to fits of imaginative excess. When venturing into the ancient catacombs of data-dungeons his concerns were largely centred on dealing with the inevitable slew of automated defences, not worrying what mythological monsters might lurk within the shadows outside his torch beams. Now he found himself endlessly staring at the circuit-etched walls, wincing at every shudder of a passing tank or rattling generator, thinking of the warp – *the warp itself* – crashing in shrieking, monstrous majesty against the outside of the tunnels through which he travelled. He couldn't hear it, he couldn't see it, but he knew it was there. A siege, invisible to the senses.

Like travelling beneath an ocean, he mused without a smile. *Constantly fearful of the transit tubes springing a leak.*

A mind full of these nebulous terrors made for a joyless walk. It wasn't as if he could confide his fears to the rest of the convoy, either. The Sisters of Silence already knew and seemed wholly unfazed. The Archimandrite was impossible to engage in any conversation beyond the status of the convoy, and the battle-servitors lacked any conversational aptitude whatsoever. Baroness Jaya and her courtiers were still in the dark regarding the truth of the webway and the warp beyond. Now there was an amusing thought. *How their limited intellects must be straining to process all of this.*

Zephon knew the truth, of course. But placid, angelic Zephon had spent most of the journey alone, when he wasn't at Diocletian's side. Ah, well.

Occasionally the sections of the circuitry ingrained upon the walls would shatter and emit sparks. Land flinched each and every time, picking up his pace.

Determining any temporal data here had proved impossible. The procession's various chronometers tallied seconds, minutes and hours in both directions with no consistency. One servitor's systems insisted the date was three hundred years before the declaration of the Great Crusade. Arkhan Land's own chron had functioned well enough for almost four hours, at which point it had started counting between seven and fifty seconds for each one that passed. On several occasions it had stopped for an unknown span, only to come back to life of its own accord. He'd ceased trying to glean any sense from it.

He walked knee-deep in the clinging fog, which was either pale gold or smoky azure depending upon the viewer in question. Despite bringing his Raider he was content to let it guide itself as part of the procession, relying on its onboard servitors and machine-spirit core. The webway was something he simply had to experience outside of his battle tank's protective plating.

Sapien rode upon his shoulder, the irises of its eyes endlessly click-click-clicking as it recorded picts that appealed to its primitive brain. Frequently Land paused to make auspex scans and take readings – Sapien would leap from his shoulder during each stop, plunging through the mist, doing the Emperor alone knew what. Land regularly pried the beast's cranium open to review the psyber-monkey's pict-feed, but the images were of nothing but circuit-inlaid walls and floors, or the featureless spread of colour-bleaching mist.

Arkhan was entitled to travel at the head of the procession alongside the Archimandrite and the unwelcoming presences of Kaeria and Diocletian. More often he chose to travel alone, moving here and there throughout the convoy, sometimes even falling back far enough to walk alongside the rattling strides of Baroness Jaya and her marching Knights. They were an inspiring lot, in their own way.

A Vigilator clade of Protectors brought up the column's rear, their claws thrumming with waspish, sonic lethality, curved talons clicking out of rhythm with their augmented tread. He knew better than to seek to engage them in conversation. On Sacred Mars they were known as the sicarii – a dune-stalking, inhuman transmogrification of lesser skitarii warriors – and few of them possessed enough personality to be considered companionable.

At no point did they make camp. The servitors required no rest and the convoy never ceased. Land himself was used to the discomfort of months-long expeditions into subterranean vaults, so stealing a few hours of sleep in the back of a Triaros conveyor or his own Raider tank was luxury enough. Sleep didn't come easily, but it offered the only opportunities to forget what waited behind the curved walls.

The Mechanicum's sections of the webway were much as he expected them to be, albeit with the added occlusion of the strange and sourceless mist. Tunnel after tunnel of sanctified metal, the walls lacerated by gleaming lines of precious circuitry. The wiring was complicated enough to be almost hieroglyphic in nature, covering every surface of the tunnels' insides. Unerringly the procession marched forwards, never pausing even when the passages forked or branched, never journeying along a route that would be too confined for House Vyridion's towering silhouettes. There were several of those.

'Where do these passages lead?' he'd voxed to Diocletian from his Raider's command console.

'*Nowhere,*' was the inevitable reply.

The tunnels are unfinished, then. Or never rebuilt. Or construction was never started after the very first foundations. Curious.

Even so, there was a definite scale to the operation. Arkhan knew from the Archimandrite's map that the Mechanicum-engineered sections were nothing more than tentative tendrils binding Terra to the true web. It justified the modesty of their efforts, including why he could perceive the ceilings of most tunnels through a haze of mist. Yet was it not said that the Legio Ignatum had committed Titans to the Great Work? How could they have walked their god-machines along these routes?

The answer came to him as soon the question occurred. The Great Workers must have brought any larger Titans piecemeal, their disassembled components shipped along these paths upon grav-convoy slabs to be reassembled deeper in the webway.

What delicious sacrilege. And what would be the fate of any machine-spirit given life in this strange realm? Would it display tics and deficiencies unseen outside the webway? Would Titans constructed within the webway fall victim to the realm's unnatural juncture in reality?

So many questions. So few answers.

Kane, dear respected Zagreus Kane, hadn't opposed Land's decision to devote himself to the Great Work. The Fabricator General's accommodating position on the matter had come as a surprise, to say the least. He'd anticipated refusals based on notions of expertise and primacy.

He was after all a technoarchaeologist, wholly unsuited to war, no matter how respected he might be in his vocation.

Land had his suspicions on just why Kane had agreed, however. Oh, yes. He had his suspicions.

Sapien bared his little teeth and emitted a series of chittering clicks. Land turned, looking back over his shoulder as a tall shape emerged from the mist, becoming the Blood Angel Zephon. The twin turbines rising from his back like brutal machine wings swayed with the warrior's gait. Battle-servitors trundled past, blind to anything beyond the Archimandrite's guiding signal at the front of the column.

'Greetings,' said the pale Blood Angel. His portcullis-faced Mark III helm was under his arm, leaving his face bare.

'My Baalite compatriot,' Land replied. He scratched his scalp, where hair had long since lost the war to maintain a colony on the barren landscape.

Zephon slowed his pace to walk alongside Land. 'You must be proud,' he said. 'To see what the efforts of Mars have wrought.'

Proud? thought Land. *Yes, I suppose. In a way. Though the true wonder, the true lore, waits beyond.*

'I am indeed,' he said aloud.

'And it was good that your high priestess survived her surgery.'

'Hieronyma? She isn't *my* high priestess. She falls within the circle of a far different aspect of the Martian covens. She worships the Omnissiah as Destruction Itself. As the Unmaker God.'

'And you?'

'I revere Him for what He is – a genius. I don't hold any one aspect of His genius sacred above any other.'

'I see.' Zephon raised an eyebrow. 'Though I note that you corrected my terminology rather than express relief at the priestess' survival.'

'Insightful fellow. The Archimandrite Venture is a glory, good sir. But it isn't a fate I would ever crave. Trapped inside that hull forevermore? Nerve-stripped and muscle-riven and bone-scraped, bound into amniotic soup to sustain a brain and spinal cord?' Land shuddered theatrically. 'No, thank you.'

'I see,' the Blood Angel said again.

I doubt that, Land thought. *You didn't witness the surgery.*

Zephon turned gentle eyes upon Sapien. The psyber-monkey took it as an invitation. It leapt onto the warrior's pauldron, clinging to the white wing symbol of the IX Legion before scampering up between the jump pack's turbines.

'I trust this creature will not urinate on me?' the Space Marine asked. 'I am not certain my dignity could survive such a blow.'

Land looked up at the Blood Angel, one eye narrowed. He stroked his pointed beard in thought. 'Sapien takes nutrients intravenously. What little waste he excretes is via gel-sac deposits. Therefore, the answer to your question is no.'

Zephon chuckled softly. 'Charming. Here.' He reached a bionic hand back over one shoulder; the psyber-monkey allowed itself to be lifted by the scruff and handed back to its master. It looked at the immense warrior as it settled upon Land's shoulder once more, and clicked an inquisitive little chirping sound.

'I note the instabilities of your bionics,' said the technoarchaeologist. 'Flicker-twitches at the metacarpophalangeal knuckles. The work of a poor surgeon?'

Zephon's smile was gone. 'Graft rejection.'

'Indeed? I didn't think that could happen with your kind.'

'Now you know otherwise,' the Blood Angel replied mildly.

'I'd like to study your bionics at some point, to glean an understanding of their exact deficiencies.'

'Perhaps, if circumstances allow.'

The silence was approaching awkwardness when Land spoke once more. 'Is there something you need of me, Blood Angel?'

'No. I merely wished to ask your thoughts regarding the Imperial Dungeon. The Vyridion Knights witnessed it through gun-feeds and their cockpits' monitors. The servitors were obviously indifferent. You and I were among the only ones to witness it with our naked eyes.'

'And you wondered if, what, I found it some profound and moving experience?'

The Blood Angel hesitated. 'I wondered exactly that. Though the venom in your tone leads me to believe you did not.'

'It was interesting enough,' Land replied archly. *What was he going to do? Admit to some superhuman brute that he had wept with the revelations of that journey? The galaxy burned because of these ceramite-clad fools.* 'But we of the Red World are used to wonders beyond the ken of mortal minds.'

'I see. Then may I ask why you accompanied the expedition?'

Land raised an eyebrow. 'To bear witness. I assure you, nothing could keep me away. Aren't you honoured to be here, warrior?'

Zephon nodded. 'Of course. Prefect Coros chose me specifically, though I confess I do not know why.'

Land looked up at the Blood Angel's statuesque features, seeking any expression or suggestion as to the warrior's thoughts. Seeing no sign of understanding, Arkhan Land smiled a strange smile, one with no warmth that yet lacked any shred of mockery.

He really doesn't know, Land thought. *And yet it's so obvious.*

'Something amuses you?' asked Zephon.

'Oh, no. Never that.' Land chuckled, giving lie to the words.

Reaching the end of his patience, Zephon inclined his head in respect. 'If you will excuse me, Explorator Land.'

'Of course, of course.'

The Blood Angel walked on, his long stride easily outpacing Land's.

Touchy fellow, he thought, watching the Blood Angel's back.

An unknowable time after his encounter with Zephon, a message crackled across the vox, making its way down the processional line. The order was given to brace, to be ready, to detune any aura-scrye sensors and auspex scanners, and diminish any transhuman senses.

'*Ahead is one of the webway's original sections.*' It was Diocletian's voice, as distracted and terse as the Custodian always seemed to sound. '*Adhere to the path at all costs.*'

Land's mouth was dry. Licking his lips made no difference. His tongue was leather. *At last. At last...*

He walked on, staring ahead through the wide manufactured tunnel, feeling the thrill of excitement that always bubbled up before the possibility of revelation. At his sides, the battle-servitors rumbled on. They, however, were lobotomised far past wonder.

WHEN THE IRON walls faded away, they took their circuit-laden gleam and the hum of trembling engines with them. Mist rose in place of defined structure – Baroness Jaya had no idea where the path was, or how those at the procession's vanguard were still following it. The procession's footsteps no longer echoed from walls of Martian metal; instead the golden mist ate all sound and sent it back to them in fragments.

Was this the webway? The true webway? Yes it was, she soon realised. And no, it was not.

Passage walls became evident where the mist thinned: architecture of some arching substance that defeated any auspex rakes. The invalid returns read as something akin to eldar wraithbone, similar in physical density – and according to Land's prattling, 'similar in psychic resonance! Ah, forgive me! You couldn't possibly understand...' – yet comprised of no known material.

She'd known from studying the limited available data that the Great Work, this so-called web, was the creation of a race far older than any living in the galaxy. That fact held little awe for a woman who had taken her first xenos life at the age of fourteen. Species dawned and died with brutal regularity: the Crusade had driven hundreds of such species to extinction, and there had been alien empires at war before humanity itself was a brief, portentous meeting of proteins. No, it didn't matter how old this industrious species had been. What made her skin crawl was the far more visceral reality that her scanners forced her to face.

Illara Latharac, Third Sword Exemplar, had voxed the very same sentiment from farther back in the processional line. Jaya heard her courtier swallow softly. *'Pray to speak, baroness.'*

'Ever and always.'

'My gratitude. Whatever this material is, it came from outside our galaxy. How can that be? How can that be possible?'

Jaya shuddered at the thought. Her Knight's joints groaned in sympathy through their kin-bond.

The tunnels diverged without warning or any impression of which route was worthy over any other. The mist would simply part to reveal two or more alternate passages, each as indistinct as all others. Jaya sent auspex-relays down every passage even long past the point she realised no route would register anything of interest upon her scanners. She switched through focus/refine, through mono-drenching, even through the relative crudeness of colo-scrying, only the latter revealing anything at all. Her instruments measured no life yet a great deal of movement.

'I have motion,' she had voxed the first time.

'I have nothing,' Devram replied at once. The rest of the column reported their own findings, which varied between the silence of Devram's scans and the mess of Jaya's.

The movement ghosted around with each scan, seemingly belonging to no living beings, following no physical possibility. Either an army of spirits danced down many of the tunnels, or the passages themselves were moving in some unearthly, instrument-defeating manner.

Sometimes, she heard her name spoken aloud. It wasn't a voice she recognised, nor did the vox acknowledge transmission receipt despite the telltale crackle of interference that bordered the man's speech. More than once she heard his murmuring directly into her left ear, in a whispering tone that was too faint to make out his meaning. She couldn't be sure if his parched whispers were too soft to understand or spoken in a language she didn't simply know.

'Pray to speak, baroness.' Devram's voice made her flinch.

'Ever and always,' she replied. The formal words seemed stuck in her dry mouth.

'My gratitude. My vox receiver is malfunctioning, or... I'm not certain. Is anyone's vox registering indecipherable whispering?'

Nervous chuckles from throughout the column answered the question well enough.

Faces leered at Jaya from the mist, human, alien, other. She watched them on her gun-feeds and through the god's-eye strip-feed of her Knight's primary vision realiser. One of the faces wrenched in the mist, turning and melting with the hazy impressions of reaching arms. The mist rippled with the suggestion of flame. That was how her father had died, seared alive in his control seat, too weakened by his wounds to operate the ejection bracers. It took Sacristan Torolec three sleepless days to reverently scrape and respectfully flush all organic particulates from the Knight's cockpit. In the end, House Vyridion's courtiers had buried a charred husk still baked into its throne.

Other shadows danced, capered, thrashed in the murk. Jaya did her best to pay them no heed. She kept her grip white-knuckled on the controls. Her hands couldn't shake that way.

'Jaya,' a voice whispered her name with shy care. A youthful voice, one that made her squeeze her eyes closed as if such a gesture could ward her against any haunting. Perhaps it worked, for the voice didn't return. Grunting in dismissal, she did her best not to think of the voice's owner – there had been a boy once, a boy from another of Highrock's monarch-blooded families. The first boy she had ever spent time with, unchaperoned. A lifetime ago now.

She heard several of the others draw in their breath as the column entered the first void. Mist and mist and mist met their eyes and scanners alike.

Objectively, she knew what this must be. Objectively she knew this must be one of the immense regions capable of allowing transit for–
Entities
–eldar wraithbone vessels, the size of Imperial warships. Their own pathway had finally threaded through one of the vast thoroughfares that made up the webway, where–

Alien monsters

–swam through space without need of the warp. She had seen the tale told by the walls of the Imperial Dungeon. She knew what this was. This was the Emperor's hope for the species. These passages were supposed to be safe.

Why, then, am I trembling?

Jaya had ceased forward locomotion and twist-unlocked the seals of her cockpit. She wanted to stand up in her throne and look out upon the nothingness with naked eyes.

The first thing she sensed was the faint smell of ice, as if this passageway led to some clean, frozen world with aspects of precious normality like a sun and a moon and sane dimensions that complied with physics.

The second thing she sensed was the enormity of the absolute nothingness above her. Around her. Beneath her. Pure void existed with her at its heart. Jaya felt as she always did when looking at images of the deep ocean. The endless murk in every direction, forming an entire reality where creatures of impossible size writhed in the salty, silty dark.

She resealed her hatch and enthroned herself once more. The Knight strode on.

Jaya heard music drifting down several of the misty tunnels, as teasingly familiar and ultimately unrecognisable as the murmurs had been. Half-remembered melodies played on instruments she couldn't imagine. This, it seemed, was the harmonic accompaniment to the shadows that beckoned to her. More than once she panned her hull-mounted stubber at the capering, thrashing silhouettes, her gloved finger curled against the trigger, stroking with slow need.

Later passages – *farther into the webway?* she wondered. *Deeper?* – offered indistinct geometries that no pict resolution could refine. Walls veered away at angles that caused the human observers to blink their watering eyes and turn away from the threat of headaches. Buildings stood in the misty shadows, towers and arches and domes wrought by alien thaumaturgy, either lost to time or far along the path to the oblivion of the forgotten. They seemed out of phase and somehow untouchable, as if imperfectly recalled by a wounded mind.

The path rose. Some tunnels sloped sharply enough to almost be considered a fall. Slants and askew angles became commonplace. Even gravity began to follow its own erratic choices: noting an incline of yaw beneath her Knight's iron tread, Jaya cast an auspex probe ahead through the convoy, realising that fully half of the procession was travelling along what she'd believed was the tunnel's westward side, treating it as though it were the floor.

Wonder and adrenaline made for poor sustenance over a protracted period of time. Jaya was tired, having scarcely slept in days. Her leaden limbs were beginning to click and crackle with cramping sinew.

Still she refused to vox Diocletian and ask for an estimation for when they would reach their destination. Vyridion would show no weakness throughout its penitence.

Again the passages divided. Again they branched. Again they rejoined other arteries, meshing into one.

She had advanced to the column's front when the vox exploded in a storm of static, the white noise shrouding dozens of male voices all speaking over each other in deathly calm. A ripple spread through the convoy, section by section. Servitor motors whined. Tanks rattled and growled.

Jaya slammed both boots into their control holsters, switching to active manipulation.

Is that the main army? Are these the voices of the Ten Thousand? She couldn't see anything beyond the ghostly buildings in every direction, at odd slopes as the passageway rose. *Are we here, at last?*

'Diocletian,' she voxed. 'Prefect Coros, are we close?'

'*We are in vox-range of Calastar,*' he replied, distracted. She could almost feel him straining to filter through the conflicting voices.

The Archimandrite entered the channel with a tuning screech of her internal comm system. Her monotone voice followed, '*I have established cognitive grips within Calastar. The city is heavily besieged. Every war-servitor currently engaged reports overwhelming force arrayed against the defenders.'*

Diocletian whispered a curse, some cultural slang from his child-hood that made no sense to her. Nevertheless, it was the first time Jaya had ever heard him swear. *'The walls are already down. The enemy is inside the city.'*

SIXTEEN

War in the webway
Dynastes, the Lords of Terra
The Golden and the Soulless

THE ENEMY WAS without number, an ocean without an end. No two figures in their uneven ranks were exactly alike, each one seemingly born into its own breed, conjured from a unique nightmare. The alien air carried the sounds of crashing blades and waves of searing heat, and above all it brought the creatures' stench, too strong for even respirator masks and the Custodians' own helmet filters.

War had a scent of its own, the spice of human carrion underlying the fyceline reek of spent bolts and the ozone tang of air ionised by las-rounds, but this was a reek beyond reason. The smell of unearthed plague graves, with the killing sicknesses living on in the stripped bones. The charnel stink of hopelessness as blood runs from riven flesh. The salt scent of dirty sweat that lines a murderer's brow. And above all of it, the charred porcine stench of sizzling meat fat, that pyre smell of burning human bodies.

Sagittarus held his ground against this rank tide. Never had he felt farther from the Emperor's light. One thought played out through his mind, again and again.

We're going to lose the city.

The stench of the unburied dead outside the city walls was near toxic. For what seemed like days even in this timeless place, the enemy had hurled themselves at the Ten Thousand upon the walls, achieving nothing but the running of their own blood.

The true battle had begun when the Legio Audax pulled down the Impossible City's walls. Beneath the barrage of fire and plasma and explosive shells spat down from the high barricades, a host of Warhound Titans had done the work almost alone – achieving triumph at the cost of their lives. Each of the war machines staggered and burned beneath burst shields and blistering armour plating, as their harpoons cracked through Calastar's wraithbone walls. In ragged disorder they pulled back, dragging sections of the wall with them, tearing rifts for the masses of infantry to spill through.

Not a single Warhound survived to enter the city. Their smoking wreckage lay as monuments in the great tunnel expanse, amidst the stilled tide of slain Space Marines and rancid smears of daemonic ichor.

A warmer welcome lay in wait once the foe pushed into the city itself. The Silent Sisterhood and Ten Thousand manned every bridge and junction, reinforced by hordes of Mechanicum battle-servitors and the towering colossi of the Legio Ignatum. Every wall and tower still standing had long ago been fitted with turrets, and the city's defenders funnelled the advancing tides into courtyards that became slaughterhouses; across bridges that were detonated beneath the teeming press of daemonic creatures and sent plunging into the abyss; into avenues that became killing grounds.

The streets were winding, maddening routes through a city that already made no sense. Reports rattled at the edges of Sagittarus' perception, some streaming across the red lens of his visor slit, others coming in a stream of conflicting vox voices. He processed all of them with unconscious focus, concentrating on pushing forwards.

The Custodians at his side were veterans of centuries of war at the Emperor's side. They moved in the loosest amalgamation of a squad, more akin to a pride of hunting lions than a squad of soldiers fighting their way through city streets. Yet they never hindered each other – they had transhuman senses and reflexes coupled with absolute familiarity with each other warrior in their midst. Theirs was a unity that needed no artificial synchronicity. It lacked the gene-bred precision of the Legiones Astartes moving in the cohesion of their lifelong squads, but the Emperor Himself had engineered it to be thus. His Space Marine Legions were built upon the principles of tradition, brotherhood and conformity. The Ten Thousand weren't bound by such crude rote and militancy to foster obedience. They were left to possess greater individuality, and their bindings of loyalty took the form of other, subtler restraints.

Sagittarus led Ra's own squad for his strike team. Armed with guardian spears and paired meridian blades, they were Squad Dynastes – called the Lords of Terra by the Emperor Himself, not without a sense of irony. Each one was the scion of now-dead royal Terran bloodlines: the sons and nephews of warlords and witch-queens, taken as tribute in conquest and inducted into the Ten Thousand. Once they had been twenty souls, bled down to twelve after five years of fighting in the webway's tunnels.

They now moved at a dead sprint, their spears reaving through corroded bronze swords and hewing through unnatural flesh. Sagittarus led them, his Contemptor shell more than able to keep pace with even a grav-Rhino.

Somewhere, a Titan sounded out its war-horn cry, abrasively projecting its machine roar through external augmitters. Another railed in answer, beginning a chorus of distant, arguing metal godlings.

We're going to lose the city. Sagittarus had no blood left to run cold; whatever synthetic haemovitae sustained him in his amniotic sarcophagus didn't mimic human blood in such poetic, pointless ways. Without orbital surveillance he couldn't be sure of the battle's wider scale, but the voice-shattered vox was alive with unwelcome revelations regarding the enemy's numbers. More legionaries, more creatures, more Titans than any of the Ten Thousand's outriders had reported. Horus – or, more likely that accursed witch-king Lorgar – had found a way to flood the webway with his minions.

We're going to lose the city.

Beasts with rugged red hides and primitive brass armour howled and spat and cursed in a heaving tide, moving with inhuman vigour on their backwards-jointed legs. The blades in their hands were great axes and swords of primitive metal, marked with runes that made the Custodians' eyes ache just to witness them. Chariots raged through their midst, crescent wheel scythes tearing their own ranks as often as through Imperial formations. Artillery hurled profane payloads upon the defenders, not with the Mechanicum's volleys of massed energy but in mimicry of the battlefields of Ancient Terra, when such skyfire took the form of crude, physical rain. The enemy launched everything at their disposal, from the hulls of wrecked Mechanicum tanks and great hunks of the city's broken architecture, to the severed, ensorcelled heads of the Imperial dead.

They were especially fond of the latter. Skulls rained from above, coming down upon Sagittarus in a crashing hailstorm. They broke upon Dynastes' auramite plating, detonating into clouds of choking blood-mist. Hundreds more burst across the wraithbone buildings nearby or fell to shatter on the rising street.

The mist thickened quickly, rendering automatic vision filters useless and unable to pierce the red fog. Blinded, he sensed shadows in the mist reaching for his hull with gripless clutches, their shadowed embraces ghosting through him. A more superstitious man might have believed them the spirits of whomever had lost their skulls to give the daemonic artillery something to fire. Sagittarus weaved away from the reaching shadows; they didn't register on his sensors the way that the warp entities did, but real or false, he wouldn't let them touch him.

Sagittarus moved, unseeing and unbreathing, fighting by sound alone. He swung his fist at disturbances in the air nearby when he heard the creak of daemonic muscle tissue, parrying with his armoured forearm when the whispery song of blade edges cut the air. He panned his kicking, shell-torrenting cannon down alleyways he couldn't see, butchering daemons he could only sense by their howls.

Some of the creatures could speak Gothic. Sagittarus loathed these most of all. With voices of shrieking fever and drowning gargles, they called out in a language they had no right to know.

'When will the sun rise?' they cried. Could he hear fear in those demands? *'When will the sun rise?'*

Sagittarus gave them no answer beyond the fall of his fist and the hot roar of his Kheres-pattern cannon. He clutched at a horned form in the smoke, lifting the thrashing, shrieking thing from the ground and engaging his pneumatic compression. The beast burst after a mere three seconds, falling to the ground in two pieces. One of the halves was still howling; Sagittarus silenced it with a descending metal foot.

Turning, still blind, he opened the ichor-wet fist and discharged the thrumming plasma gun in its palm. The magnetic accelerators whined and spat a sphere of caged fusion. Another of the monsters collapsed headless at his feet, steaming as it dissolved.

Sagittarus ran on, weaving to the left as the roar of bolt shells passed by on his right. He heard them impact and detonate, felt the wet spattering of ichor painting his hull plating. The foul, hissing fluid sent the temperature gauge on his lens readouts spiking high.

He heard wheels ahead, wheels of metal upon streets of shaped bone. He saw it – it was big enough for its silhouette to show through the mist – a chariot, yet another crude echo from the Bronze Epoch battlefields of Old Earth rattling along the curving road, pulled by thrashing, serpentine creatures. A feminine shadow drove the beasts on with cracking whiplashes from the vehicle's back.

Even as Sagittarus was voxing the warning to Dynastes the driver fell, impaled through the chest by a thrown spear. The vehicle careened from the sloping road, the beasts tangling themselves in their reins as they scattered in bestial indecision. Sagittarus spared a glance for several of his squad plunging their spears through the prone bodies. Whatever the creatures were, they died screaming, sounding almost human.

He covered his men as more of the horned foes drew closer, his assault cannon levelled and groaning as it fired. Above the eternal crackle of the vox he heard the dull crumps of shells punching home.

'Advance!' he voxed to Dynastes. The same word, yet again. How many times had he given the order since the walls fell? A hundred? A thousand? 'Advance!'

His squad broke from the mist at the next junction. Sagittarus took stock of his men as they materialised from the blood vapour. Their armour was marked with molten ichor, their spear-blades smoking as energy fields crisped away the last of the clinging blood.

Eight, he counted. *Nine. Ten. Eleven,* as Mycorian emerged.

'Gathas?' he asked the last warrior.

'Down,' Mycorian replied.

Sagittarus bunched useless muscles on instinct. He was already turning to plunge back into the blood-mist when Mycorian moved to stand before him.

'I would've saved him if there were anything left to save.'

A warrior Sagittarus had fought beside for over a century, one of Ra's own brethren, lost in the mist. Reluctantly they moved on, weapons ready, a hunting party at the heart of an alien city. This was no painstakingly planned siege committed by regimented forces – this was the fulcrum moment of a war, avenue by avenue and step by step.

The sky around the Godspire was miserable with creatures soaring on the nonexistent wind, repelling any aerial approach. Something winged darkened the sky overhead, beating a carrion stink downwards with its leathery wings as it passed. The roaring shape of a Stormbird raged after it on howling afterburners, raining spent shell casings on the warriors far below.

Sagittarus' retinal display dimmed to compensate against the sudden brightness as the Stormbird went nova. Its gold-and-silver hull was torn from the sky with a dragon's roar of wrenching, protesting metal. The daemonic shape that sent it to the ground flew from the falling gunship, its black wings beating to carry it free of the detonation.

He looked across the arching bridges to the Godspire, still too distant to make out individual defenders. Gunships rose from nearby only to be torn down like the first, helpless against the sheer numbers of winged creatures circling the central tower. A convoy of Mechanicum crawlers and battle-walkers was threading its way from the tower's west courtyard, attacking through a thick tide of daemonic blades and flesh.

Sagittarus and Dynastes sprinted across the long bridge, their strides sending echoes through the bone ground. Spears that were growing dull through overuse still cut and carved, blasting their foes apart through the slam of power fields against flesh as much as by the blades' fading capacities to cleave. Sagittarus was reduced to using his empty assault cannon as a bludgeon.

Another gunship streamed overhead, spinning on screaming engines, falling into the abyss between the great city platforms.

We're going to lose the city. It wouldn't detach from his thoughts.

The bridge's previous defenders had been a regiment of Adsecularis thralls, near-mindless but numerous to compensate. As Dynastes advanced upon the daemons laying claim to the span, they stepped over the bodies of the cyborg slaves that had died to hold the bridge for a few minutes longer.

Sagittarus caught a beast's blade against his forearm. The creature shrieked a demand to know when the sun would rise, and he killed it with the returning backhand swing. The foulness that served as its blood bubbled and gushed forth.

Blades and whips lashed against his armour plating, slowing him, sending shivs of pain jabbing into the mutilated limbs floating within his cold cradle. He killed and killed and killed by instinct and rote, too weary now for bloodlust or the joy of battle.

He saw Mycorian on the ground with three jagged swords drilled through his back. Standing over his companion's fallen form was Juhaza, another of Ra's so-called Lords of Terra, his guardian spear long lost, fighting with his paired meridian swords in a swirling dance. He wouldn't leave Mycorian's corpse.

'He's gone,' Sagittarus shouted at his kinsman.

Juhaza had lost half of his face, his features abraded down to the bone. One eye gone, his jaw hanging slack, he didn't have enough muscle left on his face to speak. His acknowledgement of Sagittarus' words came through motion alone, as the other Custodian cut his way closer.

Up close, the damage was far worse. Juhaza's helmet had been wrenched clear, taking a significant section of the back of the warrior's skull and brain matter with it. Blood had washed into the recesses of his pauldrons and soaked his cloak of Imperial red. Yet the Custodian was fighting on, facing the creatures surging across the bridge, spinning his spear and building momentum. The fact he still stood with those wounds defied reason; Juhaza had no idea he was already dead.

Another war-horn sounded. Sagittarus knew it at once, that unmistakable clarion cry ringing out across the besieged city: the *Scion of Vigilant Light* – Ignatum's lone Warlord – fought on, claiming another kill. Risking the clatter and crash of weapons against his hull, the Dreadnought looked up to the mist-hazed sight of the city spread above and beyond in the great tunnel. Those distant streets were just as choked with teeming bodies and the flicker-flashes of discharging weapons. Larger, darker shapes showed Titans – and things the size of Titans – moving between the bone buildings, laying waste to their surroundings as they grappled and marched and fired. Across hundreds of vox-channels, the city's defenders murmured and appraised and coordinated, dangerously cold and calm where human soldiers would be yelling orders and shrieking of their wounds.

Sagittarus ground the dissolving bodies of his foes beneath his iron tread and moved forwards.

His name crackled over the vox, going unheard until the third repetition. A recall. A recall back to the Godspire.

'Dynastes is embattled,' he replied. 'We require a transport.'

'It will be done, Sagittarus.'

'Dio? Is that you?'

✠ ✠ ✠

THE RAIDER TANK resembled a Space Marine Spartan in all but three ways. The first was its increased size: not only did it possess a larger maw and increased cargo capacity, it was also armoured in dense layers of ceramite reinforced with rare Martian alloys considered far too valuable for line service among the Legiones Astartes. The tank was considerably bulkier, turning its smooth red hull into the plated skin of something mythic and bestial. As one might expect, the divided skull of the Martian Mechanicum showed along its sides, along with holy binaric and trinaric scripture painstakingly etched into every inch of its ceramite plating.

The second difference was that it had an armoured servitor-manned turret pod on its roof, giving the massive quad-bound volkite culverin array a three hundred and sixty-degree firing arc.

The third and most dramatic divergence from the mainstay of the Space Marine Legions' vehicle armoury was the fact it lacked any sign of treads or tracks. This Raider skimmed over a metre above the ground, moving significantly faster than its grounded cousins.

It thundered across the bridge, its anti-grav suspensor panels protesting, grinding monsters into aetheric ichor against its forward hull. The sound of the impacts was the beat of a drum, like great hailstones pounding against a metal roof. Those creatures that weren't pulped by its momentum fared no better. They burned beneath its guns, hordes of them igniting into shrieking silhouettes under the screaming beams of the tank's volkite array.

The hardwired servitor spending its existence in the pod itself had been ritually stumped at the knees and surgically fixed into place, mono-tasked with simple – and entirely vicious – find/see/kill protocols. It went about its goal with cold, calculated aggression. It had neither emotions nor nightmares within the shadowy nothingness of its skull, thus the creatures it faced held little clutch on its heart.

Behind the lead tank came three Spartans, hovering on the same anti-grav repulsor fields. These were cast in Imperial gold, marked with the eagle sigil of the Legio Custodes. Ra recognised the squad-specific honour markings along the transports' hulls at once.

Gang ramps slammed down into the mist. Bulkheads whined open. The three gold-hulled tanks disgorged the bulky forms of Zhanmadao and his favoured Terminator squads, each warrior bringing an incendium firepike to bear. They breathed dragons' flame across the beasts that sought to assail them. Daemonic corpus melted as surely as mortal flesh when bathed in pyrochemical fire.

The lead tank, proud in its plating of Mechanicum red, was a monstrosity of wrath and sound. The overcharged squeals of its volkite array overlapped one another as it ignited row upon row of the hunched, horned creatures. Its gang ramp slammed down last. Only two warriors stood within. A familiar figure clutched his spear low, firing bolts from the hip. The other was clad in foreign crimson, aiming a bolter he didn't fire. His hands shook with miniscule tremors.

'Sagittarus,' said Diocletian, reloading his guardian spear. 'Your chariot awaits.'

Sagittarus ordered his warriors – Ra's warriors – into the vehicle. He was the last to board, still fighting, executing the downed Neverborn that clawed at his ceramite-sheathed legs. Behind him, daemonic limbs were ground to poisonous slush in the hydraulic press of the closing ramp.

He had to kneel to fit his chassis within the confines of the Raider, even with its expanded crew hold. He vented pressure from his hydraulics and settled into an ugly crouch.

Within the red-lit confines of the crew bay, he found himself face to face with an inhuman creature hanging from the commander's cupola ladder. His gunlimb was half-raised before Diocletian stepped in front of it.

'It's harmless, Sagittarus.'

Through the scrolling lists of retinal data, Sagittarus saw the creature's wide eyes and slinky, furry form in better detail. Sapien gave an unsimian squawk and scampered away as Sagittarus lowered the cannon.

In the driver's throne Arkhan Land held the steering bars with both hands, peering through the vision slit with an old man's squint. He was shaking, babbling. Spit flecked his chin. He stammered questions that weren't questions, questions that he didn't truly want answered.

'What am I looking at. What is this. What are these things. What am I seeing.'

'Back to the Godspire,' Diocletian ordered the robed man.

'I... But...'

'Stay with us, Land. Focus on your duty. Get us back to the Godspire.'

'I... I... Yes. The spire. The central tower. Yes, of course. At once.'

The tank rattled and banged around them as it tilted in a heavy swerve, crashing through more of the beasts. As Diocletian was greeting his closest warriors, Sagittarus spared a brief glance at the red figure standing slightly apart.

'Blood Angel,' he greeted the Baalite.

'Custodian.'

Sagittarus turned to Diocletian on slow, whining servos. 'Dio. You took your damn time in the Palace.'

The other warrior nodded. 'I see you've made a mess of Dynastes. Ra won't be pleased.'

'We've been fighting for two hundred and ninety-three hours since the walls fell,' Sagittarus pointed out.

'Twelve days of this would explain why you look terrible,' Diocletian agreed. There was no humour in his tone.

Sagittarus took stock of Dynastes and found it difficult to disagree with his kinsman's appraisal. Juhaza was somehow still standing, though his stare was unfocused and he swayed as he held on to the ceiling rail. Solon stood next to him, teeth clenched as whatever corrosive foulness had splashed across his armour still fizzed and popped, unable to eat into the auramite but slowly dissolving the left side of his face.

Solon grinned back at his leader. 'I'll live, Sagittarus.'

Arkhan Land groaned a weak, troubled cry. The tank bucked as the relic hunter rammed something at high speed, and there was a brief rise as the repulsorlift plating carried the Raider over whatever he'd struck.

'I... I can't–'

'Don't stare at them,' Sagittarus interrupted. 'Fear makes them stronger.'

'I...'

'Who are you?' the Dreadnought demanded.

'I... Arkhan Land.'

'I've heard of you.'

'Just get us to the Godspire,' said Diocletian.

THE DAEMON NO longer soared on great wings above the city of arcane bone, nor did it stalk alone in silent predation. The wounds it had taken in its hunts were lessons of pain etched upon its corpus. No matter that it lacked the capacity to truly reason, it had still learned its lessons well. The threat of dissolution goaded it towards caution. Incarnate murder was unsuited to naked war, and even immortals could learn from agony.

Alone among the horde, the daemon was kindred to every other creature. It was the piercing of flesh with a tool of war, and the blood that ran with the first slaying. It was the madness of the mind that comes from murder, and the rotting of a brother's body. It was the savage and guilty pleasure of life triumphing over other life, and the panicked pain of knowing your own death has come. It was the deed that reshaped the destiny of a species.

And thus, it could hide anywhere within the host. No shape was forbidden to it. No part of the ravening horde saw it as a shard of another Power. All were its kindred.

The daemon shifted between forms, discontented with mere beasts of myth and pagan nightmare. It propelled itself as something feathered and winged, a creature of lies given hunched, avian form. It crawled on six legs. It slid across the ground slug-like on none. The cluster of senses that throbbed within its corpus skull acted in place of sight and scent, drawing it towards the next kill.

It thinned its corpus to near-nothingness, becoming a virus within another daemon's ichor sprayed against the faceplate of a Martian war robot. It thinned further, to mist, to air, seeping in through the cracks in the machine's armour plating, infecting the biological cortex cradled in the cognitive soup. A moment later the Castellax turned its weapons upon its own kindred, annihilating them with its cannon and claws.

Amused but unsatisfied, the daemon ghosted free of that semi-living cage and leapt skywards, embedding itself in the cold, cold metal of an ornithopter passing overhead. Small effort to warp the vehicle's iron hull, rippling through it, heating it, swelling it – sending biological vein-threads through its inorganic form and rewriting the machine's essence. The daemon could feel the dull disquiet of the flying vehicle's pilot as she lost control.

The ornithopter exploded at the head of its formation. It didn't scatter or fall from the sky; the daemon kept the spinning, burning shards of jagged metal loosely together, each fragment of debris taking its own shape. A flock of flickering, scorched raptor-things veered and whirled, a host of gargoyles with bodies of shredded metal and fire.

Three other ornithopters veered away from the spreading cloud of burning, clawed homunculi, but it was already too late. The cloud of savaged metal razored through them, a thousand cuts shredded their hulls and wings beyond function, plunging them from the air. The daemon lingered within each vessel long enough to savour the sickly sweet death-thoughts of their doomed pilots, then it was gone, coalescing once more in the teeming horde below.

With a predator's instinct it sensed it was being hunted. Somehow, the Anathema's Daughters could see it no matter the form it took. When it revealed itself they were the ones to give chase. They summoned the Golden, they directed the machine rage of the towering metal constructs striding throughout the city. The rawness of its consciousness knew pain, and it was not supposed to be this way. As strong as it was, it couldn't hold to incarnation if it sustained many more wounds. It bled now. Everything that bled could be killed.

The daemon had killed several of the Anathema's Daughters, finding nothing within to devour. Their flesh was tasteless, their deaths without nourishment or joy. It felt their presence as a devouring chill, their nearness dragging at its incarnated form, unwinding the threads of its essence. With low, hungry cunning it had learned to blend in among its lessers, taking their shape, mimicking the weakness of their forms until the perfect moment at the apex of each kill. Such immersion deceived the Golden and the grey, robotic souls at their sides. But never the Soulless. The Anathema's Daughters always knew. To face them was to fight crippled and weakened; the daemon knew the weary, desperate weakness from its own hunts, seeing the futile thrashings of those it killed most slowly. To face the Soulless was to face the same destruction the daemon inflicted upon all others.

The creature's crude, vicious sentience rebelled at being considered prey. It shifted and changed and drifted, starving itself in the heat of war in a bid to go unnoticed. It ghosted away from the running battles, avoiding those where it sensed the tides of its kindred crashing against the leeching resistance of the Soulless.

In hiding, it took forms beyond the sphere of mortal sight. It became a disease. Then a breath, a death rattle, wet and clicking in a man's throat.

A promise.

A whisper.

A fear.

A regret.

A thought.

It trickled itself into several minds, dividing its consciousness with amoebic mitosis, seeking, seeking, seeking. Many minds were inviolate; they would take too long to overwhelm. These, it left alone. Stars would die before it mastered one of the Golden.

The grey machine-men provided simpler conquests, yet they were uselessly fragile to husk-ride. It settled in the minds of war servitors at barricades across the city, forcing them to turn their weapons upon one another and – in rare, precious instances – to fire into the backs of the Golden advancing ahead. But the Golden destroyed these threats

as soon as they became aware of them, and far worse, there was a pau-
city of thrill, guilt or any emotion at all in servitors made to murder
one another. They felt too little; they killed without passion or panic.
Thus, they offered no sustenance.

It drifted onwards, plunging at last into a mortal mind that had
known enough bloodshed and battle to drench every one of its own
memories in bitter red. This man – not one of the Grey nor one of the
Golden – was enthroned within cold iron. The daemon looked through
his eyes, seeing the compact confines of a piloted vehicle's cockpit;
males and females chattered in their human tongues and machine
codes around him, creating an aura of noise. These weaker mortals
looked upon their master as a king.

The daemon threaded itself through the man's thoughts, twining
around the man's aggressive hungers, riding through the lactic tingle
of adrenaline in his system. Many of the voices and emotions within
his skull weren't even his own; they goaded him with artificial rage,
coming from some synthetic source.

The machine, it knew. The vehicle itself. These were the bond-machine's
emotions colouring the man's mind with artificial rage.

The daemon knew, then, where it was. It closed its invisible tendrils
around the meat of the man's organs, gently squeezing. Life and lore
trickled from the pressured organs, haemorrhaging language and knowledge and insight into the daemon's cavernous perceptions.

'Moderati,' he said, speaking with the mouth of Princeps Enkir Morova of the Reaver Titan *Black Sky*.

'Aye, my princeps?' replied Talla, a woman shorn of hair, haloed in
cables, hardplugged into her own control throne.

Enkir bared his teeth in a wet smile. In harmonic response to its
master's amusement, *Black Sky* blared its war-horns across the embattled city.

SEVENTEEN

The covenant of Terra and Mars
Tribune
Unspoken Sanction

THE COMMANDERS CONVENED at the Godspire. Those who couldn't with-draw from the field were forced to appear in hololithic form, their life-size images diluted of colour and flickering with interference. What-ever purpose the circular chamber had served in the age of the eldar empire was overshadowed by the machinations of its current Imperial occupiers, who met amidst chattering cogitators and medicaes working on the wounded. A central table ran on low power, projecting a thin green holo of Calastar's maddening tubular geoscape. Anti-air turrets hammered their payloads skywards in a ceaseless song, sending shivers through the wraithbone tower.

Even as Diocletian drew breath to address the gathered officers, the image of Princeps Feyla Xan shrank back in her control throne and blinked out of existence. Several of the gathered officers made the sign of the aquila or linked their knuckles in the sigil of the cog, gravely acknowledging Xan's evident demise.

'The city holds,' said Diocletian. There were nods around the table. Most were desperately weary. 'We all have somewhere to be, so let's be swift. Archimandrite?'

The Archimandrite stood hunched over the holotable, the Domitar-like chassis that had become her new form towering above all others present. Her murky faceplate offered an unreliable suggestion of the face within.

'I have inloaded a complete and constantly updating awareness field of the Mechanicum's present forces,' she vocalised from the bronze speaker-gills in her chest. 'This information is drawn from the exloaded sensories of each alpha unit active within Calastar. Lacking any orbitals for requisite scanning and atmospheric intelligence, I am devoting significant data runnage to maintaining an active tactical sensory overview for each of these alpha units.'

'Can you render this information usable by the rest of us?' asked Diocletian.

'Yes, albeit in primitive form.' Unmodified humanity lacked the biomechanical enhancements required to see things in the 'spheric datastreams available to the cultists of Mars. 'Vocalisation and crude holo-imagery will have to suffice.'

'It will,' the Custodian replied.

'I speak with the aforementioned insight in mind,' the Archimandrite augmitted. 'Summation – the Mechanicum has access to the most accurate, evolving overview of the field of conflict, accessible by all unit leaders. Result – cohesion and performance will be accordingly improved. Judgement – as the disposition of forces currently stands, the city will fall. Enemy reinforcement will only hasten the process. This is an unacceptable outcome.'

Dense servos and fibre bundle muscle-cables whirred as Zhanmadao of the Tharanatoi gestured to various points of scathing conflict on the holo. 'They've gained precious little ground so far. Ignatum holds the choke points leading into the repaired arterials, with the majority of the skitarii and the Unifiers' war servitors. Tribune Endymion has the Sisterhood and the Ten Thousand deployed in defensive positions along major thoroughfares, denying the city to the enemy.'

'So the city holds,' Diocletian repeated.

'The city holds for now,' declared Zhanmadao. He was a pale figure, almost unhealthily so, clad in the bulk of his shining Cataphractii armour. His black hair didn't quite hide the faint markings of blue tattoos on his scalp, legacies of a childhood among the coastal tribes of the faraway world upon which he'd been born.

'But the Archimandrite is right,' he continued, 'and this is a shadow of what's yet to come. Outrider reports have been filtering in for the last two day cycles. Troop transports, Titans, hordes of the warp-wrought. The reinforcements you have brought us today, along with those sent ahead in convoys for the last month, are allowing us to stand our ground. But gone is any realistic vision of crusading forth. This entire sector of the webway is flooded with the foe. We can't hold the Impossible City for more than three or four days.'

The Blood Angel finally lifted his gaze from the revolving holo. 'Where, may I ask, is Tribune Endymion?'

'And Commander Krole,' added Diocletian. 'Can no one reach them via holo?'

The Terminator gestured again, indicating a portion of the rotating map on the tunnel's 'ceiling'. If the host of flashing runes was anything to go by, the fighting was thickest there.

'The Sister-Commander has led the forces defending the main entrance to the city's catacombs,' said Zhanmadao. 'The greatest concentration of defenders stands with them.'

Diocletian didn't need to be told why. If the foe broke through to the catacombs, it was a short journey from there into the Mechanicum's sections of the webway. And then, on to the Dungeon itself.

'*I am present, as well.*' This from one of the skitarii alphas, manifested as a hololith. The figure was seated on an unseen slab that failed to project into the image. Hands moved in and out of the holo as tech-adepts worked on the augmented warrior's damaged limbs. A shattered chord-claw was being machined out from his wrist. The hydraulic musculature of his right thigh was being hastily reworked. A scorched chestplate sigil marked him as Echo-Echo-71.

'Has there been word of Ra?' asked Zhanmadao.

'Probes have been dispatched to reach the tribune. He is engaged with the forward elements. The fighting here is spire to spire. Dense. It occludes individuals. Tracking becomes a trial.'

'I am inloading no vision-data from alpha units present near enough to Tribune Endymion or Sister-Commander Krole to relay accurate streams back to me,' said the Archimandrite. The robotic chassis lowered on growling hydraulics, seeming to Diocletian suddenly threateningly ursine. 'Casualties are severe.'

'Acknowledged and confirmed,' the skitarii warlord replied. The four mismatched lenses that served as his face within the hood rotated as they refocused.

This is war without orbitals, cursed Diocletian. It had been different in the tunnels for all those years. Jetbike outriders carried messages and reports to and from the barricaded passages, maintaining easy if frantic lines of communication. But with a whole city spread open and besieged, chaos reigned.

This is one of the webway's principal hubs. Can we afford to lose it? How many years will its loss put the Great Work back?

'What of any updated evacuation contingencies?' he asked.

One of the hololiths spoke, a Titan princeps hardwired into an armoured throne. His faceplate was modelled into the same snarling visage as the Warhound he piloted.

'Prefect Coros! We bled for a year to take this city.'

Diocletian turned to the man's image. 'And that year was merely one of the five we have been consigned within the web. If we are forced back into the Unifiers' passageways, so be it. It doesn't change our duty. What matters above all is that we defend the Mechanicum's tunnels. The enemy must not reach Terra.'

'We can hold the city,' said another hololith. One of the robed and hooded sicarii, the skitarii elite echelon. He, she, or indeed *it* – it was impossible to know with many of them – cracked its taser goad into life. *'Any rumination of evacuation must bear the following factors into the*

final equation. Primaris – that once abandoned, there will be an infinitesimal probability of retaking Calastar again without significant reinforcement, far beyond what currently stands within the garrisons of the Solar System. Dislodging an entrenched enemy here would be a prospect of mathematically ludicrous possibility. Secundus – *the* Scion of Vigilant Light *cannot flee. Evacuation would necessitate the dismantling and reconveying of the god-machine in its component pieces.'*

Zhanmadao shook his head. 'No time. You know there's no time, Protector. The *Scion* would remain, either with its crew evacuated so they might fight another day, piloting another Titan… or ensconced, allowing the *Scion* to fight as part of the rearguard.'

Several of the princeps and skitarii alphas present shared canted exchanges through their linked vox-melange.

'I assure you,' the Custodian Terminator vowed, 'I'm well aware of the sacrifice that your Legio would be making.'

'*Ignatum cannot accept these terms,*' said the aged princeps of the *Empiris Crescir.* '*The* Scion *cannot be abandoned.*'

We are already falling apart, Diocletian thought.

'Look at me,' he said slowly. 'Forget the pride of your Legio, Kaleb Asarnus. Forget the battle-lust of the war machine singing inside your blood. Forget the last five years we've waged war together, the banners of heraldic glory that sway from your Reaver's weapon limbs and the companions we have all lost. Look at me, look at the colour of my armour, and remember whose authority I speak with.'

The princeps' features were masked behind his ceremonial helm. But he nodded.

This time, the Archimandrite growled a retort. 'The Mechanicum has committed resources far exceeding acceptable parameters, sacrificing the retaking of Sacred Mars, in order to defend Calastar. It was made clear to us that this was a focal point within the webway. A spoke-nexus. A route-hub. Our participation in the Great Work on this scale came with the condition of keeping the Aresian Path open for a possible invasion of our homeland.'

'We are doing all we can,' Zhanmadao pointed out through gritted teeth.

'You see those of us among the Cult Mechanicum as lacking emotive responses, but that is base ignorance. All souls, augmented and unaugmented, fight harder with something to fight for. The retaking of Sacred Mars galvanises us, as well as being promised to us. Summation – the Impossible City must not fall.'

'You should have agreed without the need for such assurances,' Diocletian replied, feeling the first stirrings of real anger. 'I suggest you watch your words, priestess. Your *Omnissiah* has need of you. The covenant between Mars and Terra takes primacy over all else.'

One of the Archimandrite's eye-lenses rotated, projecting the crisp, miniature hololithic image of Sister Kaeria. Diocletian knew at once what the image file was: an archived file from the internal picters of Fabricator General Zagreus Kane. The recorded voice overlaying the image confirmed it.

'The Mechanicum will supply your war on this single condition – the Omnissiah Himself once spoke of a route within this alien webway that reaches back to Sacred Mars. Adnector Primus Mendel named it the Aresian Path. No matter the cost, no matter the effort, you will see it reinforced and held, ready for use once the Omnissiah's Great Work is completed. Even if thousands of other routes and passages must fall, you will ensure that the way to Mars remains in Imperial control.'

The image of Kaeria signed her agreement, and blinked out of existence.

'As evidenced,' the Archimandrite said, 'assurances were made.'

'Made when holding Calastar was practically guaranteed, Martian. Now I say again, we will do all we can, but we all have a duty that stands above personal desire. Evacuating the Unifiers and their supplies takes priority. They are the Emperor's own adepts and apprentices. We will begin a convoy but it will need defending at all times. The enemy is likely to infiltrate the Mechanicum's tunnels through any number of capillaries.'

Several of the Mechanicum's officers – skitarii, princeps, Unifier priests and priestess – looked at one another. The air fairly thrummed between them. Diocletian wondered just what noospheric communion was taking place that the unaugmented present weren't privy to. It felt argumentative, though Diocletian only had the subtlest of body language reactions to judge by.

One of them snorted in weak amusement. Arkhan Land sat slouched in a corner, holding a ration pack's fluid phial in shaking hands. He turned haunted eyes upon the others, scarcely noticing them, still seeing the madness he'd witnessed outside in the city.

'I see now why the Omnissiah kept the Great Work bound in absolute secrecy. To avoid this – this pathetic conflict of mortal minds.'

The Archimandrite turned to stare at the hunched technoarchaeologist. The cyborg construct's eye-lenses meted out cold accusation, but the man did nothing but snort again, looking away. His hands hadn't stopped shaking for an hour. Even his irritating ape-creature was bizarrely solemn, sat at his side.

'We'll begin evacuation preparations,' Diocletian said at last. 'Holding the tunnels is what matters now. We will give them the city, and nothing more.'

Zhanmadao took a breath. 'Dio, even holding the tunnels may be beyond us for more than a few weeks. The host besieging the city has every chance of driving us back to the Dungeon.'

'Unacceptable,' repeated the Archimandrite.

We're wasting time. Diocletian was on the edge of unmannerly cursing when another hololith appeared at the table. This one wore damaged armour plating, spinning a spear in gloved hands. Weapons and talons slashed into view at the edges of the holo's range, but the warrior weaved aside from every blow he didn't block. Bladed replies lashed back, killing the wielders of those weapons. The warrior didn't break stride. He was always moving.

'*Reload!*' the holo called out, laden with distortion. He drove his spear into the ground by his feet and immediately pulled his meridian swords, turning and whirling into another phase of his arcane battle-dance.

'Compliance.' A servitor's voice, toneless and obedient. The warrior moved away from the spear, it vanished out of the holo's range.

The swords rose and fell, twisted and parried, thrust and hacked. Blood rained past him in flickering sprays. Endlessly came the crash of energy fields ramming against ceramite, warping the reinforced metal, mangling it, shattering it. The figure of a colourless Space Marine staggered into the holo's view, tumbling to the ground with a blade through his spine. The warrior severed the falling legionary's head from his shoulders without looking, already turning to meet another foe.

'Reloaded,' came the augmitted, mechanical voice again. The warrior sheathed both blades in a smooth motion, weaved aside from a swinging flail, which missed him by a metre, and reached upwards. He caught the spear in the air, bringing it down in another parry. He disengaged with a roar of effort, throwing his unseen opponent back. The guardian spear banged three times, spitting three bolts in succession, only to spin with another frenzied howl of abused energy fields as the blade punched through another legionary's chestplate. The spear tore viscera and shards of armour free in a wrenching burst as he yanked the blade back, one-handed. His other fist discharged a laser-spit of digital weaponry from his clenched knuckles, lascutting through the faceplate of a charging, crested Legion officer.

Another fighter joined him in the whirling dance. A cloaked female wielding a circuit-lit zweihander, guarding his back one moment, then guarded in kind a moment later. They couldn't have looked more unalike – fighting with utterly different styles, at different speeds; male and female, gold and black; towering genhanced warrior in auramite and regal huntress in armour that honoured the most ancient eras of warfare. Yet they moved in savage harmony, never coming close to harming one another. They fought in the spaces created by each other's fighting styles. She hacked overhead when the long spear whirled aside, killing the enemy that fought to slip within his guard.

He thrust over her shoulder, slaughtering the foes that sought to move behind her.

Zephon's pale eyes narrowed, his concentration absolute, taking in the ballet of violence unfolding before him. He had seen the warriors of the Ten Thousand fight before, albeit only in grainy pict footage. He had heard the countless unpoetic comparisons describing their uniqueness as the perfect exemplar of a process that became diluted and rushed to mass-produce the Legiones Astartes. Yet he had never seen them in battle against Space Marines. This warrior reaved through them – reaved through Zephon's cousins from the rebellious Legions – cutting them down, butchering them the way Zephon himself had massacred his way across human and alien battlefields.

How easy, all of a sudden, to see how Constantin Valdor, the Captain-General of the Custodian Guard, was considered an equal of the primarchs themselves in matters of blade-work, when any Custodian could be as skilled as this.

Had the Emperor foreseen this? His thoughts curdled, growing gravid with treason. *Is this what they were made for? This annihilation? This slaughter of legionaries?*

'We're here, Dio,' came the Custodian's words between panted breaths.

Diocletian inclined his head to the embattled holo. 'Salutations, Ra. And greetings as well, Commander Krole.'

KAERIA WATCHED THE first ship descend through the atmosphere. Black even before the scorching of its heat shielding, its hull was unchanged by the shroud of fire that wrapped it.

The command deck of the Magadan Orbital was never quiet. Servitors limped and murmured and bleated code at one another. Robed adepts spoke in austere tones, avoiding all eye contact as they worked the controls, the buttons, the levers that kept the station in a geostationary orbit above the Imperial Palace. Vox-stations rasped. Doors whirred open and ground closed.

Kaeria was the silence at the storm's heart. She watched through the great oculus as another of the Black Fleet made planetfall. There was something beautifully dramatic in how a vessel born within the void caught fire when it sought to land for the very first time. The flames of atmospheric entry served as Terra's welcoming embrace.

Another figure joined her upon the viewing platform. Kaeria didn't need to turn to see who it was.

The Mistress of the Black Fleet greeted her with clicking talons.

Your melancholic gazing is unbecoming, signed the older woman.

Kaeria rejected the rebuke, her hands weaving a response. *Melancholy has no place within me. You mistake dread for discomfort.*

Dread?

Yes. Dread. That it should come to this.

We have always known the drama may unfold in this manner. The preparations have been in place since the very first of us forswore the use of her tongue.

Kaeria met the other woman's stare for a moment, seeking some semblance of emotion, of perspective, beneath the assured facade. She saw no evidence of either.

How resolute you are, she signed, and then gestured to the descending ships. *How can you look upon this without fearing what it portends? The Imperium will never be the same with what we do here today.*

The Mistress of the Black Fleet stroked her metal talons along the guardrail, eliciting a whispery whine of iron against iron. She replied after lifting the claws from the cold metal.

We are not the engineers of the Imperium's change, Sister. We merely react to it. The Imperium changed when Horus set his blinded eyes upon a throne he does not deserve.

Kaeria's eyes burned with sick amusement. *You absolve yourself of the malice we are willingly undertaking.*

We do nothing but the Emperor's bidding. This is His will. This is what must be done. Varonika drew back her hood, baring her olive features. She had the dusky melange complexion of most Terran natives, and her eyes were a dark enough brown to be black. There was curiosity in her eyes, the expression not unkind. *One thousand souls, Kaeria. Is that really so many? Is that such a sacrifice, weighed against the consequences of doing nothing?*

Kaeria met the mistress' eyes and felt a moment of shame. *One thousand innocents, nervously awaiting the soulbinding they were falsely promised. One thousand men, women and children believing they go now to serve their Emperor.*

Varonika's clawed hands gestured a swift reply. *And serve Him they will. Few souls in the entire empire can claim such purity of service. What is this resistance inside you, Sister? Have you become so enamoured of battle that you believe yourself above our true calling? You are a warden, Kaeria. Not a warrior.*

For a time Kaeria watched the second ship descending, wreathed in atmospheric flame. Carrying its living cargo to their service within the Imperial Palace.

I am both now, she signed. *Warden and warrior. The war has made us all both.*

Varonika's expression showed faint distaste. *Perhaps so. I will leave you to your contemplation, Sister, and wish you well for your own planetfall.*

Kaeria knew she should prepare herself soon. Her place was on the third ship. *Wait.*

Varonika waited, her eyes on Kaeria's own.

One thousand souls, Kaeria signed. *What do the calculations state? How long will they last?*

The Mistress of the Black Fleet lifted her hood back into place, covering her silvering hair. *They will burn for one day,* she signed.

With that she turned and walked away, leaving Kaeria to watch the oculus alone.

One thousand souls today, Kaeria thought. *And what of tomorrow?*

EIGHTEEN

Demigod of Mars
Evacuation
Let me not die unremembered

SHE WAS WOUNDED. Hurting. Weary. But she was also a demigod, and demigods did not lament. They endured. They triumphed. They protected those who looked to them in worship.

<Home,> said a voice.

She would never see home again. She would never leave this city alive. She knew these things. Fire burned in her bones. The souls inside her shouted and cried out and fought the flames.

<Home,> said the voice again. The voice wasn't speaking to the demigod, nor to the crew inside the demigod's skull-cockpit. The voice was speaking to those who would live to fight another day.

She stood above the city, the equal of its wraithbone spires, and saw the war taking place between the faithful and the faithless at her feet. In true wars there was always dust from marching feet and falling buildings, great clouds of it that occluded vision and forced her to rely on the blind echolocation of her auspex or the hunting sense of her heat-maps. There was no dust here. The towers of alien bone fell in brittle shatterings. The lesser buildings gave way beneath her tread like flawed glass. No dust. No dust at all.

The mist, though. The mist was worse than the dust. It came and went without pattern or warning. Even when thin, it sent back false echoes of prey with low-power passive echolocation pulses. When thick, it masked the heat signatures of other engines, friend and foe alike, in a veneer of cold emptiness.

The golden mist was thick now. She couldn't see those that hunted her.

She lit her void shields, her internal generators layering them the way a colony of spiders labours together to weave a web.

<Home,> said the voice.

Be silent, she told it. *Ignatum marches.*

The *Scion of Vigilant Light* strode through the mist, war-horning to those beneath her tread. Martian hoplites scattered in tactical dispersion as they had thousands of times before. They knew how to wage war in the demigod's shadow.

The Titan streamed with smoke as she marched. Victory banners swayed beneath her gunlimbs, far above the heads of her loyal infantry. These pennants and standards of red and black marked the *Scion* as one of Legio Ignatum's ducal engines, eminent in name and deed. The extinct wasp of Ignatum showed in scratched and battered pride upon her carapace.

When she had first joined this theatre of war, she had felt loose and unready. Her worshippers had reassembled her within this alien city and told her to guard them against ghosts and phantoms that scarcely registered on her sensors. Active auspex chimes were worthless; they reverberated throughout the wraithbone buildings, mis-echoing and false-bouncing until the *Scion*'s systems insisted the entire city was alive and moving.

The frustration of her human crew had bled through to the *Scion*'s spirit, infecting her with impatience. But she had learned, and so had they. She had learned to rely on low-grade auspex pulses and to fight via naked vision. She had learned to destroy enemies that barely seemed there at all. And, most recently of all, she learned the enemy had brought demigods of their own.

They had wounded her in these last days, wounded her badly. The demigod was hurting now. She was destined to die today, but not yet. Not yet.

Her brothers and sisters were less sanguine regarding her fate. The arguments had raged between crews until she had silenced them with her decision. To die here was an honour. She would not release her crew to flee with the others. She would stand until she could stand no longer, selling her life to buy time for those fated to fight another day.

<Home,> said the voice.

It was the newest voice among her pantheon of pilots and crew and worshipful servants. Home was the sanctum-forges on Sacred Mars, a world riven by civil war, where the foundry fires were now lifeless and cold. Home was the mountain fortress where traitorous souls had plundered the wealth and lore of Ignatum in the Legio's absence. Home. The very word set the demigod's heart-reactor seething with overburning plasma.

What was she to do? She couldn't run with the others. She was to die here, selling her life to save theirs. Such sacrifice shouldn't have to endure homesick keening in spurts of treacherous code.

<Home.> How relentless the voice was. The Archimandrite, it called itself, insisting that it was invested with the authority of Mars. That repetitive authority had been rattling against the insides of the *Scion*'s skull-cockpit for several days now.

<Home,> said the voice.

Be silent! She refused to die with such puling weakness whining in her senses. Onwards she strode. Street by street, lending indifferent rage from her district-killing cannons when a phalanx of tanks or a lone beast of considerable size presented itself as a ripe target.

Presently she halted in her hunt. Minutes later. Hours later. She did not know and it did not matter. She judged the passing of time only by the pain she suffered and the destruction she inflicted.

Her void shields rippled with the incidental fire of infantry shrieking around her feet. This, she ignored. The pain of the fires inside her had dulled to the ache of abused metal. This, she was grateful for.

A low-grade auspex ping rippled outwards, bleakly blind. Her heat-maps showed cold. The *Scion* panned along her waist axis, staring into the golden mist.

Her pilots worked the controls, not only watching but listening to the calls and cries of their kindred in the skull-cockpits of the *Scion's* brothers and sisters.

At her ankles, her hoplites engaged the phantasms, laying in with spears and shields and brief eruptions of volkite anger. The *Scion* sounded her war-horn once more and moved on. She followed the calls of her siblings.

Onwards. Onwards. Onwards.

She felt her brother die. His agony and fury vented across the communion-link that existed outside any general vox-web. By the time she reached him, he was gone.

Ilmarius Novus lay dead in the street, the Warhound's shattered form driven face-forwards into the ground with a supreme lack of dignity. The thousand punctures of overwhelming bolt penetration/detonation told the tale of how he had fallen.

His core was still lit; that a critical detonative event hadn't occurred was something of a grim miracle. Not that it mattered to *Ilmarius Novus* one way or the other. His armour plating was a blackened ruin. His gunlimbs were reduced to bent wreckage. The last and truest indignity had come after his killer had left; his head had been cracked open with power weapons and hand-held meltas, in order for enemy infantry to drag the soft and vulnerable crew away from their hardplugged thrones.

They hadn't gone far. Their bodies lay like spilled tears by the Warhound's cheek, their own cranial wounds showing the manner of their execution. She knew this because her crew knew this. Hardplugged together, they were her and she was them.

Which of the foe had done this? Was the murderer still here? The answer was swift in coming. *Engine!* She yearned with her flawed sensors, staring into the mist. *The foe!*

The enemy saw her first; it was already fleeing as she rounded the corner, striding around a cluster of wraithbone spires. A Warhound, sprint-stalking in the customary hunched run of its kind. Evidently it had detected the approach of bigger prey and sought to evade.

Cheers sounded from the *Scion*'s feet. The enemy Warhound had turned from its kill and had been savaging the surviving Unifiers with massed fire. Now the tide had turned.

Weakling fire streamed up from the divided packs of enemy infantry brave enough to show their faces. Tanks were scattered among the rabble, these vomited hard shells that hammered rippling tremors across her voids. She returned fire from her hull turrets, streaming lascannon beams and high-calibre bolt shells back in return. The weaklings fell silent.

She strode down the avenue, crunching monuments of wraithbone beneath her heavy tread. Her cockpit-head swung on heaving pistoned hinges, expelling air and sucking it back in as she tracked left and right, left and right.

I can't see it. I can't see... There!

Her war-horn augmitted a wrathful bellow. There in the mist, half hidden by the domes of buildings that barely reached the *Scion*'s waist, the enemy engine was flanking around at a joint-rattling pace. Its predatory lean gave it a hungry cast. Its stabilisers must have been straining fit to rupture with the pace it set.

Her gunlimb rose on too-slow joints. The Warhound was faster, clanking its way around the final building and spitting up a twinned torrent of macro-bolter fire from its gunlimbs.

<Die!> it canted up at her in broken code. There was more in the confused mess of its decree: a mishmash of rage and zealotry and loyalty to the Warmaster. Little of it made sense beyond its evocation of hatred.

She was turning to bring her own weapons to bear, turning into the blizzard of burning metal shells. Her voids rippled. Shuddered. Flickered.

Held.

<Die!> the Warhound emitted again, half pleading now, weaving away and striding beneath the arc of her volcano cannon...

...and into her reaching fist. She was too slow, too tall, too wounded to catch the engine that sprint-hunched away, half her height. Her grasping metal fingers clawed great gouges across the beast's back, stealing its balance but failing to hold it in place. She heard its relieved spurt of exalted, shattered code as it lurched towards escape. Its three-toed feet crashed through a regiment of her skitarii. They discharged small-arms fire at its retreating back. Amazingly, one of her hoplites even threw a spear that bounced from the Warhound's carapace. It stuck there, wedged between two armour plates.

A heroic cast, her crew were saying. *And yet useless,* she thought, even as she admired the skitarii's valour.

She knew the Warhound wouldn't return again. Even injured as she was, slowed by grievous wounds, she would see it dead if it showed itself once more.

The *Scion* waited. Trickles of her worshippers began to make themselves known, riding conveyors or journeying on foot, making their way in safety now the demigod stood watch over them.

And here she would remain. She panned on her waist axis, staring, staring. Her motions were industrial thunder. The mist hid all.

Then, a signal. Another of her brothers calling to her. *Black Sky!* One of her noblest kindred. She had precious few siblings left.

Black Sky! I come.

'My princeps?' one of her crew asked, turning in his forward throne. 'Word from the tribune. *Ilmarius Novus* was the only engine on-station to guard the Unifiers' evacuation in this district.'

Princeps Nishome Alvarek opened her eyes for the first time in uncounted hours. 'Ra wishes us to remain?'

'Aye, my princeps.'

'Inform Ra that it is with regret we cannot fulfil his desires. Tell him that we have received word that the *Black Sky* suffers. If we are to die here, my moderati, then we will ensure the escape of as many of our brother and sister engines as possible. *Black Sky* calls,' she said with finality. 'We walk to his aid.'

The *Scion* walked. One of the phantasms danced before her – one of the creatures that sent shivery unease through her crew and hurt their eyes to look upon, yet simply didn't exist to her instruments. Winged, feathered, like some carrion crow warped into spindly humanoid form, it beat the air with great wings, vomiting blue fire upon the infantry below.

She shredded it with turret fire, sending its charred skeleton to the ground. Walking on, she saw engines in the mist. Their hump-backed silhouettes spoke of size and class and weapon loadouts as surely as any scan report. The fog was thinner in this part of the city.

Black Sky stood alone, facing two of the foe. Smoke streamed from his hull, greying the pervasive golden mist. The Reaver retreated in halting strides, backing across a wide bridge over an expanse of golden nothingness. The other engines followed, moving between domes and towers. One Warhound. One Warlord. A hunting cadre, like a primitive king and his faithful dog.

She recognised the excited bleats of code from the lesser engine as the same garbled nonsense of the Warhound that had fled from her before. Of course. Sending a lone Scout Titan ahead to draw prey in pursuit was a common enough tactic.

The *Scion* took position at the bridge's end, raising her gunlimbs on ponderous hydraulics. Aware of her now, the enemy engines remained on the far side of the span. She sensed their weapon locks slipping, thrown loose by the mist. She heard their spurts of aggravated code and knew the frustration well. Her long-range targeting systems had refused to focus since the first day she walked within this realm.

They must not be allowed to cross the bridge. A Warlord would wreak untold havoc among the evacuating Mechanicum. But wounded and drained, she knew her chances of survival were at best insignificant. Even with *Black Sky* aiding her, it would be two gravely wounded Ignatum engines against two fresh foes.

<Retreat,> she canted to the injured *Black Sky.* <Fall back to the evacuation zone. Live! Survive to fight once more on the surface of Mars! I will deal with these apostates.>

So be it. The *Scion* would make her last stand here.

The very heart of the Great Work. As fine a place as any, and far finer than most.

Missiles streamed past the withdrawing Reaver, leaving smoke trails in the mist. Launched in haste by unlocked targeting systems, they had precious little hope of impacting at such a range. None of them even brushed *Black Sky*'s voids.

<Sanctuary,> the Reaver canted as it reached the bridge end. Its code was laden with relief at survival as well as shame at needing to withdraw. Contemptuously, it ground an abandoned Rhino into the wraithbone avenue. Just another smear of wreckage amidst the devastation. Before their arrival, the alien necropolis had been bare of anything but smooth, gleaming bone. Now it was a graveyard for numberless vehicles and unburied corpses. They blanketed the roadways and bridges, a dark swathe between buildings of pale bone.

<Sanctuary,> *Scion* confirmed. *Black Sky* veered slowly away, stalking towards safety.

Across the span, the first of the enemy engines began its approach. The Warlord was undamaged, its sloping and scaled armour typical of forge world Omadan's engines. The open hand of the forge's symbol showed scarification upon the palm, runic scarring in patterns that resembled no known language for the *Scion* to process.

The Warhound loped past and ahead of its slower brother, its hunchback swaying, gunlimbs rising. It crossed the bridge far faster, and the *Scion* noted the riven markings of its own power fist gouged along the second engine's back.

You die first.

She was destined to be left here, but she would choose her own death. With hydraulic majesty, the *Scion of Vigilant Light* rose to her final challenge, war-horn blaring.

The Archimandrite lifted its fist. The rebel legionary thrashing in its one-handed clutch barely even strained the hydraulics of the war machine's grip. Two bolt shells hammered against the durabonded thickness of its facial armour, causing its visuals to grey out for a fraction of a second. With no more ammunition, the Space Marine hurled the pistol with an impact that would have broken a human's spine. It spanked off the side of the Archimandrite's faceplate, as harmful as a kindly caress.

The machine applied pressure, closing its fist by degrees. Purple armour warped, then cracked, then the meat beneath began to bleed through the ravaged ceramite. Bones cracked, then crumbled. Only then did the warrior cry out, as his torso and thighs were reduced to shards of bone and mangled flesh barely held together by a layer of metal. The ruination no longer resembled a man at all.

'You bore me,' the Archimandrite told the Space Marine. After dropping the crippled mess to the ground, it silenced the warrior for good with a press of its clawed foot.

To untuned and untrained senses, the evacuation looked much the same as the rest of the siege. The grinding of opposing forces across the city had changed little on the surface. Only in the catacombs was the evidence of flight more profound, as the Mechanicum's adepts who formed the first wave filtered into the hazy tunnels. War servitors went with them. A carefully cogitated number, a subtle exodus alongside the true evacuation, dispersed almost to the point of being hidden. The Archimandrite oversaw this second dispersal with the same precision it had arranged the first.

A heavy chainsword slammed against the machine's knee joint, the kind of brute weapon that found easy homes in the more savage Legions, capable of rending an armoured man in two. Sparks arced from where the racing, revving teeth met Martian metal. The Archimandrite didn't even have time to kill its attacker. The red-plated World Eater collapsed, headless, beneath a sweep of a Custodian's spear.

The machine, Executor Principus of the Martian Mechanicum's forces here, approached its role with calculating fervour. In its flesh-life it had wrought weapons, infusing them with spirit and purpose before sending them away to wage holy war. Now it was a weapon in its own right. With each kill, Magos Domina Hieronyma of the Ordo Reductor died a little more inside her own mind. She went willingly, subsumed by the cogitations and mathematical processes of annihilating her foes.

The Archimandrite was in ascendance. No longer a high priestess of the Unmaker God, but an avatar of it.

The Archimandrite was only doing as it was made to do. It had joined the Great Work and in-linked to the entirety of the Mechanicum's army. Now it saw through their eyes, accessed their thought patterns, and led them into battle.

<Home.>

It canted the word into the noosphere, that metadigital network of datastreams accessible only to those born of the Red Planet and subsequently fitted with high-grade augmetics. Its transmissive was laden with codes and equations and coordinates of birth-foundries and manufactories, of plateaus where great battles were fought between forges.

<Home,> it broadcast to those capable of hearing it, instilling the concept itself within the minds of the more aware Mechanicum leaders.

Many of them canted back replies of their own – <Home!> and <For Fabricator General Kane!> most commonly – while still more chorused their words out loud, augmitting them as battle-cries into the faces of their foes.

The Archimandrite paid special heed to the Custodians. It was increasingly evident that the Legio Custodes was no unified army. Its warriors fought without formation or Legion-scale order, even at the squad level. Each one was an individual among other individuals, trailed by his own artificers and arsenal thralls, the latter of whom reloaded the Custodians' guardian spears each time a warrior called out.

Their ranks seemed informal, like gestures of respect towards veterans and gifted individuals rather than a command structure to be rigidly adhered to. Few of them, even Tribune Endymion or those who shared Diocletian Coros' rank of prefect, ever gave orders.

They simply immersed themselves wherever the fighting was thickest, slaughtering in silence.

And yet, there was unity. Unity of purpose, if nothing else. Despite the lack of order and the length of their spinning blades, they never burdened one another or blighted the paths of the other warriors around them. Consummate reflexes far in advance of a legionary's own genhanced grace gave them a talent that required years for human soldiers, even Space Marines, to learn through repetitive discipline. Yet the Ten Thousand were masters of it. The Archimandrite watched them whirling and killing, their energised blades passing within a hand's breadth of another golden warrior, yet never once threatening the other Custodian's life. Each one of them existed within his own sphere, a warlord unto himself.

Nor was that all. The Archimandrite's observation revealed an inherent defensiveness in the initial blows of each duel. At first this seeming passivity during the first seconds of engagement made little sense, but further analysis showed the truth. Each Custodian spent those precious moments studying his foe, adjusting his fighting style to compensate, then delivering a killing blow. They could simply overpower their enemies immediately with superior strength, speed and armament. Instead, they learned from each and every fight.

Ra Endymion exemplified this. He would parry twice or thrice, whether it was sword, axe, fang or claw, following his enemy's movements with brief flickers of attention, then lashing back to impale, to cleave, to sever. According to the Archimandrite's datastreams, no legionary had yet lasted more than three blows against his advance.

Bodyguards, the Archimandrite mused. *Praetorians.* This was their purpose, after all. Not to win wars, but to know their master's enemies and destroy them before they could do Him harm. How many thousands of hours of pict-footage did the Ten Thousand study from each conquered or compliant world? Their lives surely consisted of an eternity of preparatory devotion, studying enemy after enemy in case they ever faced them in battle, atop the physicality of their standard training.

Their preternatural reactions allowed them to block bolts and las-fire alike, deflecting it from their spinning spears, but they could still be killed. The Archimandrite had witnessed that itself. They could be overwhelmed by foes and dragged down, or gunned down while already engaged.

The machine advanced at Ra's side, its shoulder cannons tracking independently of its primary attention, groaning with the ear-straining *chooooom* of Martian volkite beams and the heavier staccato crashing of Avenger bolt cannons. Ammunition feeds and power indicators decorated the edges of the Archimandrite's vision. They flashed with sacred depletion; a prayer to the Unmaker God itself. The armoured energy reactor bound to her back seethed with continually replenishing plasma. The heart of an artificial sun powered her weapons and intellect alike. War had never felt so holy.

A particularly brave legionary launched himself at the Archimandrite from the back of a careening Rhino. The machine plucked the screaming sword-bearer out of the air, holding him as the flamer jets in its wrist incinerated the captive fool. All the while, the Archimandrite fired with its free hand, the double-barrelled energy weapon mounted there – one of Arkhan Land's more precious gifts – streaming with the fires of artificial fusion.

<For Sacred Mars!> it canted, projecting its exaltation through the noosphere. <Home!>

They fought along the rising promenades, between the impossible towers. Silhouettes of extinguished daemons showed against the eldar architecture, their images burned onto the wraithbone by the Archimandrite's weapons.

They came from the sky as often as they surged from the ground – creatures falling from the cityscape above onto the advancing Imperials. Diseased things climbed the towers to leap and fall, bursting as biological bombs with smacks of ruptured skin; feathered wreckages of avian mimicry descended on flyblown wings to be lanced through by grav-Raider lascannons and the massed fire of guardian spears. Around the Archimandrite, the wraithbone spires thrummed with an almost metallic resonance each time their smooth walls were struck by errant fire.

The machine calculated as it killed, noospherically assigning more battle-servitors and skitarii to begin the journey into the tunnels beneath the city. The numbers of withdrawing Mechanicum warriors rose subtly, quietly higher than the projected figures the Archimandrite had offered to the Ten Thousand. There were no inloaded questions to mark this discrepancy. No outrage or curiosity at the alterations in the figures. The Custodians and the Sisters of Silence battled on, oblivious.

'For the Omnissiah,' it augmitted aloud. 'For the Unmaker God.'

<Home!> the Archimandrite canted. <For Sacred Mars! For Fabricator General Kane!>

THE SCION STOOD alone.

She swayed on legs blighted by ruptured stabilisers. She leaned askew, the pistons and pressure junctions of her left leg shattered beyond repair. Oil-blood sluiced from severed pipe-veins, gushing fluid and life and coolant onto the bone bridge beneath her. Torsion-bundle cabling hung from her iron guts, a spillage of intestines.

The bridge was hers.

Inside herself she felt fire and death – the former licking at her internal systems and weakening her bones, the latter resonating in the lost and mournful dirges of dispersing mortal consciousnesses. Her crew were dead or dying, their souls fleeing damaged husks, fading away into whatever nothingness awaited their frail and fleshly kind.

But the bridge was hers.

<Scion of Vigilant Light!> she furiously canted across the falling city. <Scion of Vigilant Light!> The outcry was laden with desperate code: let one of her brothers and sisters hear her, let them absorb that coded cry into their datastreams and carry it with them when they fled this place. Imprinted within the code was the pict-feed footage, weapon reports and crew-linked experiences of her last battle and greatest triumph.

The bridge was hers, and her final wish was that her kindred would remember her like this, as a victor, not as a martyred sacrifice.

Duels between engines rarely lasted long. She had walked towards this last battle amidst a breaker of vox noise. The Warhound closed fast. Both of its gunlimbs were given over to anti-infantry mountings, they screeched up with the explosive rage of several hundred bolt shells per second, lighting the *Scion*'s shields in prismatic shimmers, rippling them like a lake in a hailstorm. It scampered ferally aside from her own opening salvo, compacting itself at full sprint to run beneath the Warlord's right gunlimb. This was the way of the Warhounds in battle: to scout and ambush, to harass and to distract.

Indecision tore at her. Behind her, the Warhound might work its evil unmolested, streaming fire upon her rear voids with impunity. Worse, it might even chase the fleeing *Black Sky*, rendering the *Scion*'s sacrifice worthless.

She let it go, trusting in the simple hatred of its princeps. The *Scion* had wounded this engine; she wagered with her life that the Warhound's commander would hunger for the satisfaction of vengeance, not chase the tactical prize of harrying the wounded *Black Sky*.

The first missiles shattered and burst against the layered aegis of her void shields. Their impacts did no harm beyond stripping the first shield-skins away, but the occlusion of dirty black smoke across her cockpit windows was an irritant. She blind-fired in reply, an expression of disgust more than anything else, yet felt an immediate stab of gratification when the modest rocket salvo from her right shoulder set off the discordant jangle of abused voids.

In the same second, alarms and flashing runes within her crew's helms declared the punishment her rear voids were taking. The first Warhound had loped around for an attack after all. She had been right to trust in its stupid hatred.

<*Daughter of the Red Star!*> the Warhound brayed up at her. Her abused voids screeched under its ceaseless clawing.

The *Scion* twisted in a half turn. She began to lower herself, forcing her protesting hydraulics down by venting pressure from her pistons and setting her joints into neutral-passive. An ungainly hunch at best. At worst, a shameful bowing of her head before death. As expected, the Warhound darted away from her firing arc just as before, even as the *Scion's* gunlimb tracked around at maximum extension.

This time she held nothing back. With every safeguard unlocked and shut down, her shoulders erupted with trailing smoke as her missile pods roared themselves empty. As she purged herself of her munitions, her volcano cannon breathed its magma blast – this combined, flaring payload aimed entirely at the ground around her.

To the credit of the Warhound's crew, the lithe engine veered away from the discharging volcano blast, avoiding the certain death of its fusion heat. To the credit of the *Scion's* crew, however, the unleashing of its primary weapon had merely been a way to shepherd the Warhound to where it wished it to go. Dodging the inferno sent the *Daughter of the Red Star* striding directly into the rain of falling missiles.

The first impacts arrested its evading stride, forcing it to brace back on its own hydraulics to prevent itself toppling over. It was already dead, dead the moment it weaved away from the volcano cannon: the Warhound's voids rippled, blistered, sundered, burst in the span of a human heartbeat. The missiles were dozens of falling blades, each one knifing into the *Daughter's* carapace and gouging away great chunks of blackened ablative metal. One rocket shattered its knee joint, another hammered into its sloping canine forehead and ripped away half of its cockpit-head, leaving its crew's burning corpses dangling from its halved skull, still connected to their thrones by their hardplug cables, hanging like executed criminals.

<Foedeath,> the *Scion* canted, coding her tone with silken malice. She received an answer – snarling, patient hate from the Warlord ahead.

She was rising again, forcing pressure back into depleted hydraulics. Restoring pressure to vented metal bones took time, and she had precious little of it. A barrage from the enemy Warlord struck her front shields with punitive whip-cracks.

Alarm chimes became wailing sirens as her voids thinned and buckled. She silenced her internal warnings with a thought; she knew how much pain she was in and the danger surrounding her. She didn't need automated systems caterwauling to drive the point home.

She was at half-extension when her voids went dark. She braced, leaning into the punishment striking her forward arc, shaking even before the sonic boom of her voids finally giving out. Hard las-fire raked and gouged her armour plating, cutting into her, rending her apart while she still stood.

Mercifully, the battering ceased almost at once. The approaching Warlord had expended itself in shattering the *Scion*'s shields. Both engines strained to reload, fresh rockets racking into place, plasma generators roiling as they recharged.

She was deeply wounded now, sparks lighting up the inside of her cockpit-skull through the windows of her eyes. Fire suppressant sprayed through her insides in soothing rushes. Half of her missile racks had jammed, their mechanisms fouled by damage.

Closer the enemy Warlord came, an executioner's confidence in the shieldless tilt of its wounded prey, needing to be within a kilometre to trust the accuracy of its webway-misted firing solutions. Spraying blind-fire and estimating trajectories was no longer enough. The time had come for the killing blow.

The *Scion* started walking. Bleeding fluid and streaming smoke, the way she still rose on her resetting hydraulics gave her a distinct, shoulder-charging hunch. The enemy Warlord ceased locomotion at an approximate kilometre, unwilling to draw closer. No doubt its crew was trying to ordain a hasty, coolant-dump weapon recharge.

She started running. A stabiliser-wrenching, metal-stressing lean as her ugly, stomping stride gained speed. She dumb-fired, systemless and trusting her gunners' eyes, volleying every missile that had managed to reload and lancing a beam from her volcano cannon. Her assault hammered into her foe's void shields in the precious seconds before the enemy Warlord fired. The *Scion* felt the brief, electric sweetness of vindication as her foe's voids stuttered and snap-died with the telltale thunder-crack of overloading generators. Failed shields could be swiftly relit, but overloaded systems required a more lengthy restart. The two engines were as defenceless as each other.

A moment later the return barrage took the *Scion* high in the torso, exploding along her shoulder, detonating the cache of unloaded rockets in a cacophonic fireburst. Stabilisers braced and held. Others braced and tore free of their housing. She was barely a skeleton now, blackened and stripped of a third of her hull-bulk. Where two immense missile arrays had stood proud of her shoulders there now burned a halo of flame. She left her gunlimb on the bridge where it had fallen, blown free of her carapace by the detonations ripping through her.

<Lexarak!> the Warlord canted its name in confident fury. Even so, it began to back away. The *Scion*'s stride-eating charge was bringing both engines dangerously close, and *Lexarak* needed range to use its primary armaments.

The *Scion*'s overburdened ankle shattered, spraying iron and fire across the bridge. She stumbled, grinding down on the stump of a clawed foot, and strode forwards another step.

Lexarak recognised that its backwards retreat was too slow and risked heading into a turn. Too late now, as well as too slow. Incidental, instinctive fire spat from its defensive turrets, too little, too late.

The *Scion* crashed forwards on its final step, her power fist slamming against opposing armoured metal and clenching closed. *Lexarak* fired its volcano cannon at terminal range, careless of the consequences in its need for panicked retaliation. For several seconds the *Scion* stood motionless, disembowelled by the last shot, lightning snaking its way through her innards, beating out from her critical core.

Fortune was with her for a few moments more. Between the *Hexarchon*'s momentum and her own weight, she pulled her fist back on squealing hydraulics, wrenching her prize free of the enemy Titan's body.

The most glorious Titan-kills, and accordingly rare, involved the close-combat taking of an enemy's head, severing it or dragging it from an engine's still-living form. The cockpit-heads of eldar Titans made for the finest trophies in a forge's halls. *Lexarak* had turned aside, preventing such a triumph. Instead, the *Scion*'s armoured hand had plunged through the damaged plating of its upper rib armour, just beneath the armpit of its left gunlimb. When she drew her hand back, in her scorched fingers was the hourglass-shaped, cable-strewn heart of the plasma reactor, leaking with fireflash containment breaches.

She held to it, fingers locked. She couldn't drop it. Her digital gearings had melted and seized.

<Fall, apostate.> Her canting to *Lexarak* was weak, her war-horns even weaker. <Reap the rewards of treason and heresy.>

Lexarak began to topple, unpowered, unbalanced. It fell forwards in a painfully protracted pitch, first shattering the lip of the wraithbone bridge beneath the weight of its legs, then falling – sluggishly, end over end – into the abyss.

The *Scion* watched it eaten by the golden mist.

<Foedeath,> she canted.

As if her words were a signal, the reactor in her fist went critical, the resulting detonation peeling away the armour on her left side and tearing away her remaining arm at the elbow.

She stood stunned and ruined on the precipice of the chasm, weaponless and unarmed, crowned by fire with sparks raining from her joints.

The bridge was hers.

Wounded unto death, the Warlord Titan stood alone now, leaking life and streaming with the smoke of internal injuries.

<*Scion of Vigilant Light!*> she canted in unison with her failing war-horn. *Hear me,* she prayed. *Hear me. Hear the last words of Princeps Nishome Alvarek and the regal* Scion. *Hear us both. Let us not die unremembered.*

She canted the code-laced cry again, again, again. All the details of her last, best victory. She prayed for them to reach the data-halls of proud Ignatum.

<I hear you.>

Who?

The gutted Titan began to turn on ponderous, failing mechanisms. The industrial pistons and pneumatics of her waist axis were locked, the failsafe seals the only thing keeping her upright in a ballet of fragile harmony. If they unlocked now and left her at the mercy of her broken stabilisers, she would overbalance and fall.

Slowly, so slowly, *Black Sky* hove into view. The Reaver Titan had returned. It stood ankle-deep in the wreckage of Legion vehicles and slaughtered war servitors, watching the *Scion* with the dark panes of its cockpit-eyes.

Her reactor-core churned. Her heart lifted. <Brother.> Even her canting was slowed and slurring. Her princeps was on the edge of unconsciousness.

<I hear you.> The Reaver's returning cants were hollow and dispassionate. Even through her dying agonies, the *Scion* felt a battle-queen's righteous anger at her forge-kin's lack of awed respect.

I have slain two engines with my last act. My death ensures your continued life. By what right do you stand in near silence?

Another thought pressed through the melting sludge of her thoughts. *Eject. Eject. Eject.*

She could live. Her princeps could yet live if she could just reach the *Black Sky,* but the ejection manifolds were fouled along with everything else inside her.

<Come,> she canted to *Black Sky.* <Enkir. Aid me.>

The Reaver began to stride closer.

HIS MODERATI WERE dead. Both of them slouched in their thrones in front of him, their slack features staring lifelessly through *Black Sky*'s eyes, both of their uniforms blossoming in red flowers where the blood of their murders had dried hours ago. The female crewmember had reclined into her throne almost innocently, seemingly asleep. The male, who had seen his companion's death and struggled to react, had bled significantly more after being shot through the back of the neck. He'd died halfway out of his throne and now slumped against one side of the seat, his head still bouncing unnaturally with every step the Reaver took.

The daemon that had hollowed out Princeps Enkir Morova and now nestled within the meat of his mortal form was beginning to resemble the proud Ignatum veteran less and less. His eyes were raw and red, having not blinked in several hours. Bony protrusions bubbled beneath his flesh in living, crawling lumps, seemingly searching for places to break through the skin. His lap was full of his own teeth, which had pushed themselves from their sockets in a slow squeal reminiscent of nails scratching porcelain.

In the hours since it had claimed *Black Sky* as its weaponised sanctum, the Reaver had sustained no small damage from enemy infantry and other engines. The daemon lacked the precision and training of the Titan's true crew. Now coming to the end of its skin-claiming ride, the daemon struggled to contain Enkir's mortal knowledge, and though it could feel the creeping temptation to dive deeper into the Titan itself and wrap its essence around the machine's sentient core, even power such as this would feel limiting to the ancient creature after a time. It had no desire to cage itself, even in such a mighty form.

Its lure had worked to perfection, drawing the *Scion* to its aid, then feigning flight. Now all that remained was the moment of cold-blooded vindication, one that even the flensed spiritual remnants of Enkir would enjoy, for the princeps himself was a man of war and no stranger to murder. Countless men and women had fallen beneath his gunlimbs, each one capable of levelling hive spires.

The daemon felt him now, the shredded tatters of the man's soul, screaming in the back of its thoughts as the Reaver Titan drew close to its taller, expiring sister.

The daemon felt Princeps Nishome Alvarek's dying thoughts, translated into emotion through the code-laced transmissions. The exhausted pride in her meaningless triumph. The more honest desperation she couldn't quite swallow, of all mortal beings unwilling to accept their own death. And yet she ached for one thing more than even her own survival: to be remembered, for these deeds to be spoken of by those that knew her name. That was all. What fortune that *Black Sky* had returned.

How much truer and purer this hunt was. How much more satisfying than simply breaking machine-men apart with its claws or duelling the hateful Golden.

The daemon's answer came in a rise of gunlimbs. The shattered *Scion* was too wounded and joint-locked to even turn aside.

Rooting through Enkir's hind-thoughts kept dredging a single word to the surface. The daemon canted it unthinkingly in the moment before both weapons fired.

<Foedeath.>

The *Scion of Vigilant Light* stood motionless as she was speared through the chest with an inferno blast, killed through shameful execution. The Titan followed the falling form of its last kill, its ravaged silhouette plunging into the mist. The daemon, watching, savoured every moment of Nishome's screams.

Its entertainment ended abruptly when, rather than vanish into the gold of oblivion, the *Scion's* detonating reactor core went nova, sending flashes of thunderstorm light flickering through the mist beneath the bridge. The last of the *Scion's* living crew died, consumed in sacred plasma fire.

Black Sky turned in a ponderous arc, and strode off in search of other prey.

NINETEEN

A thousand souls
Just another tunnel
The pernicious spectre of hope

KAERIA FELT PRECIOUS little awe at the sight of the throne room, or at the labyrinthine dungeon that led to it. Even the bannered avenue that so inspired the souls that ventured this far into the Sanctum Imperialis left her cold; she would look at the army of standards and wonder which of these loyal regiments would be next to cast its oaths into the dirt and stand with the Arch-traitor.

She walked with her sisters now – precious few of them, given their deployment within the web and their dispersal across the galaxy – entering the throne room at the head of the phalanx. Coffins followed in their wake, anti-gravitic caskets with reinforced transparisteel facings, revealing the motionless occupants within. A parade of sorts, if one with most of its participants slumbering in chemically induced stasis.

Kaeria had expected a higher-ranking member of her order to be present in the throne room itself and awaiting her arrival, yet she was the senior Sister here. To be met with nothing more than the nervous gazes of Imperial scientists and the dispassionately expectant stares of Martian priests made her skin crawl. Was the Sisterhood really so depleted that this vile duty fell to her?

Well, so be it.

Coffin after coffin thrummed into the chamber on cheap anti-grav suspensors. Each sarcophagus was wrapped in chains, pushed along by the ever-patient guiding hands of a mind-locked servitor. Kaeria let her gaze wander around the vast chamber, where the roar of unknowable machinery was an unchanging song, and the spitting cracks of lightning arcing between generators no longer made any of the labourers recoil.

How swiftly the human mind attunes to madness.

She kept her distance from the Golden Throne. She could see it upon its raised dais, though she chose to scarcely look at it. Kaeria and her Sisters were forbidden from approaching too closely – their presences sucked at the machine's power and destabilised any psychically resonant machinery. She considered it a grim reflection of the way other humans treated her; the way they cringed or looked away or even bared their teeth on instinct, often without knowing they were doing so. Enslaved to the most animal of reactions, responding on some primal level to the presence of a woman without a soul.

What made her useful, what made her strong, also rendered her an outsider to her own species.

Similarly, past experience told her that the blinding majesty and stupefaction others felt in the presence of the Golden Throne were wholly absent for Kaeria and her Sisters. She saw a man on a throne, no more, no less. No radiant halo. No psychic corona.

She would have preferred the majestic ignorance. Better to feel everything and see almost nothing rather than stare upon the naked truth: the enthroned Emperor was just a man in pain, His suffering etched plain, His mouth open in a silent scream. The agonies He endured for the sake of the species had wrought lines upon His features, somehow bringing the passage of time to an ageless face.

Occasionally the tortured features would twitch in a quiet snarl. His fingers would spasm. A golden boot might gently thud against the metal throne. At first Kaeria had hoped such tics heralded the Emperor's reawakening. Now she knew better.

The Sister rested a gloved hand upon the first coffin. A man slept within, his arms crossed over his chest and bound together at the wrists in unamusing mimicry of Gyptus' faraoh-kings The sarcophagus bobbed beneath Kaeria's gentle touch as she guided it towards the wall. The aquila tattoo upon her face suddenly itched. Not that she believed in omens.

All eyes were on her now, scientists and servitors alike. Several of the latter moved forwards to perform their function, but Kaeria warded them back with a raised hand.

It should be me, she thought. The first of the choir should be put in place by a Sister of Silence. Kaeria Casryn wouldn't shirk from the bleakness of her duty at the eleventh hour.

The suspensors rendered the coffin near weightless, and Kaeria lifted it onto her shoulder despite the awkward heft of its bulky shape. She ascended the metal gantry stairs that awaited her, feeling the stares of every living being in the cavernous hall, with only one exception. The Emperor on His distant throne paid her no heed at all. He had other wars to fight.

The socket set into the wall was a two-metre indented cradle of circuitry and dark metal. Kaeria pushed the floating pod into its waiting recess, feeling the seals at the back of the sarcophagus lock tight and bind it into its cradle. The chains were next. These she wrapped around prepared hooks of polished steel, shackling the coffin in place. Nutrient cables and catheters hung like jungle vines nearby; she fixed these in place one by one, locking them tight.

A chime sounded as she linked the last one to the coffin. *Primed,* read the High Gothic rune on the external display.

Kaeria entered a thirty-digit code into the keypad, setting the sarcophagus to draw power from the machinery in its cradle. The suspensors powered down with a lurch – the coffin swayed slowly, moored to its cradle by the sealed cables and wrapped chains.

The man within stirred with the cessation of his slumber-narcotics. He opened his eyes. This young man who had been taken from his home world and told he would be trained as an astropath, woke bleary-eyed and drugged inside his own coffin. He met Kaeria's gaze through the transparent panel.

Whatever he tried to say was lost in the soundproof womb of the sarcophagus. Kaeria stared in at the man, watching the way weariness slurred his words, ruining any hope she had of reading his lips.

'Sister?' called one of the red priests from below. A cluster of her own Sisters and various tech-adepts had gathered together, watching her with unwelcome intensity.

She broke her gaze away from the entombed man for the last time and descended the ladder.

Kaeria didn't even have to sign. A nod was enough to set the hundreds of servitors working, led by the scattering of Sisters and their Martian allies.

She stood in the heart of the Emperor's throne room and watched every one of the nine hundred and ninety-nine other coffins raised into place along the arching walls. The process took several hours to complete, ending with the dark metal pods all staring inwardly towards the Golden Throne itself.

She refused to dwell on the fact that for each active coffin locked inside its cradle, another nine sockets remained empty.

ZEPHON HAD CONSIDERED his exile from his Legion to be the most shameful moment of his life. It made for an unwelcome capstone to over a century of loyal, capable service. Yet being consigned to remain with the non-combatants after he had reached the Impossible City was proving to be a sentence of similar humiliation.

'You can't fight.' Diocletian's judgement had been bluntly absolute. 'You would be useless.'

'I have journeyed for days to get here,' Zephon pressed. The tower's turrets had cleared the skies by then, offering a brief respite to the Imperials using the Godspire as their command centre. The Knights of House Vyridion moved past the Blood Angel and the Custodian in a metallic chorus of protesting joints, striding across the courtyard, marching to join the war. The Blood Angel's eyes snapped briefly towards them.

'You agreed to come with me into the webway,' replied Diocletian. 'And here you are. I never promised you battle, Blood Angel.'

'If I cannot fight, why am I here at all?'

'Your comprehension of the minutiae couldn't be of less interest to me, Bringer of Sorrow.' Diocletian had fixed his helmet into place. 'Farewell, Zephon.'

And with that he had left, boarding a grav-Raider. The gang ramp slammed closed, punctuating the conversation with neat finality.

Days passed. Wounded Custodians and Sisters were brought back in various anti-gravitic vehicles, but Zephon lacked the digital dexterity to even help with their injuries. Any attempts to lend aid failed with his flinching, twitching fingers. On more than one occasion Zephon considered leaving the Godspire alone and joining one of the skitarii forces engaged in the city, but what would be the use? What benefit could he possibly be?

There was no misery or anguish at his fallen circumstances, only cold anger. What was a soldier who couldn't wage war? Who was he? What was his purpose? The same questions that had plagued him after first suffering his wounds decades before now returned to wrack him tenfold.

He walked the catacombs of the war-shaken Godspire, moving among the wounded skitarii and Unifier priests that made up the day's evacuation manifest.

Among the crowds, he found the only other soul as isolated as himself. The man was alone in a circular chamber, bathed in haunting blue eldar light emitted from cracked gems mounted in a twisting pattern upon the ceiling. His head was down, his concentration levied upon a hand-held device resembling an auspex or a signum.

'Technoarchaeologist Land?' Zephon greeted him.

Arkhan Land looked up, as did the psyber-monkey on his shoulder. Zephon found himself smiling at the bizarrely comedic timing of their twinned movements.

'Zephon,' said the Martian distantly. 'Yes. Hello.'

His eyes were bloodshot orbs in darkened pits. His pointed and immaculate little goat-like beard had spread with several days' worth of stubble along his cheeks and around his mouth.

'You look...' Zephon trailed off, not wishing to be unmannerly.

'A trifle unwell, I imagine.' Land turned his gaze back down to the hand-held device. 'Learning that hell is real and that an underworld of daemons will one day eat all of our souls has a way of meddling with a man's sleep patterns.' There was no life to his mockery. The words were spoken with bland indifference.

'I had believed you gone with the initial evacuation columns.'

'Oh, no. Not yet. One of the Custodians noted the firepower of my Raider and asked if I would remain to escort the final column. Something about them standing the greatest risk of attack, if the rearguard is overwhelmed.' His toneless voice murmured on as he stared down at the device.

Zephon approached, going down to one knee by the distracted explorator. The psyber-monkey turned mournful eyes to the Blood Angel's own, as if this towering red-clad warrior somehow held the answers to its master's grief.

'What occupies your attention?' the Blood Angel asked softly.

Land tilted the device to share the viewscreen. Zephon saw along the barrel of an overheating heavy stubber, high above the ground. It shook as it spat rounds in long bursts into the leathery and thrashing forms of horned beasts below.

'Gun-feeds,' Land replied, staring at the images, unblinking. 'From House Vyridion.'

He cycled through them – the views from the carapace stubbers and meltas of each Knight, then the less reliable feeds of their primary arm weapons. These were far more prone to shake-distortion.

'How long have you been watching these images?'

'How long have we been here?' countered Land. He still didn't look up. 'I wanted to watch the *Scion*'s last stand but I suspect she was out of range when the enemy killed her. I saw her once, many years ago now, striding forth from Ignatum's forge. She was a proud lady.'

Zephon gently closed his fingers around the device and pulled it from Land's grip. There was no resistance. The imagifier was laughably small in the Blood Angel's hand.

'Why are you here?' Land asked, finally making eye contact. 'Why aren't you out fighting?'

Zephon didn't want to admit how often he'd tried. Only a mere hour before he'd stood alone in a chamber, weapons in his hands, unable to trigger his own chainsword.

'My arms,' the Blood Angel replied.

'Ah. Yes. The bionics. I remember now.' Land looked around the chamber, showing emotion for the first time as he curled his lip in distaste. 'What ugly sanctums these eldar built. It's no loss, really, that most of them are dead.'

Zephon deactivated the pict-feed, silencing the tinny clatter of stubbers and inhuman roars.

'There is great elegance in their race,' said the Blood Angel, 'but it is coupled with great malice, sadness and even greater hubris.'

Land snorted. 'You sound as though you admire them.'

Zephon nodded. 'Aspects of their existence, yes. The movements of the exarchs of their warrior castes are breathtaking to behold. I can think of few higher honours than being recognised for besting one blade to blade.'

'Have you ever killed an eldar?'

'Yes,' Zephon admitted.

'How many?'

'I do not know,' the Blood Angel lied. 'Many,' he added, spicing the falsehood with some truth.

'Good riddance,' Land exhaled, not quite a laugh. 'Their technology is fascinating but inarguably foul. Interesting in its occasional efficiency, yet ultimately impure.'

Zephon said nothing. He was beginning to regret engaging with the Martian at all.

'Something about you has irritated me for some time,' said Land. 'What exactly is the significance of "Bringer of Sorrow"? What is the meaning of such an outlandishly theatrical name? It's ludicrous, even for a son of Baal.'

Zephon didn't answer. He had a question of his own. 'You said you knew why I was asked to come here. I would like to know what you believe.'

Now Land did laugh, a bleak little chuckle. 'Is it not obvious? Have you ever been inside a mine, my angelic friend?'

'A salt mine, in the compliance of–'

'Yes, yes.' Land waved a hand to silence the Blood Angel. 'Mines are dangerous places, prone to leakages of natural gas. Even resistant servitor labour can suffer, but that's beside the point for now. Think of deep mine work on worlds where expendable servitor flesh is in short supply, or where workers lack access to machinery capable of detecting gas leakages. Those poor, primitive souls take a caged bird or some other beast with little lungs into the deep dark, and they watch it while they work. If the bird dies, the labourers know the mine is unsafe.'

Land's smile showed almost all of his teeth. 'You, Blood Angel, are the caged bird in the mine. Do you see the Imperial Fists here? No, you do not. Because they can't be trusted. In fact the only legionaries you do see are those rebellious dogs rampaging their way across the Imperium. But what better way, hmm, to test the loyalty of the Blood Angels when it is in doubt? Or to see how a Space Marine handles immersion in the webway, confronted by the monsters of the warp? Why, take a crippled one with you. One who can't even fire his bolter. One who would be no danger if he succumbed to whatever treason has proven so appealing to half of the Emperor's Legions.'

Zephon stood quietly. Above them, the Godspire shivered with the siege. 'I should perhaps be irritated at the manipulation involved,' he said.

'Be angry if you like. I'd say you were vindicated, though. Unless I'm mistaken, you haven't spat on your oaths to the Omnissiah just yet. Whatever the game is, you seem to have won.'

'Perhaps.'

Land gazed around the room once more. He seemed suddenly deflated. 'I will be pleased to leave this place, Zephon.'

'This chamber?'

'No, no. This city.' Land reached into one of his belt pouches, producing the flattened and crumbly remains of a foil-wrapped ration bar. The simian snapped it from its master's grip, devouring its powdery treat with bright eyes.

'But we have only been here a matter of days,' Zephon replied.

The technoarchaeologist raised a bushy eyebrow. 'So?'

'So are you not aggrieved that we are already preparing to evacuate?'

'Why would I be aggrieved?' When the Blood Angel had no answer, Land continued, 'I'm a scholar first and a gentleman adventurer second. I could, perhaps, be convinced to consider myself a binaric philosopher third, as I've always had a passion for debating the dual nature of the Machine-God. But I'm no soldier.'

'But we are leaving, having seen so little.'

'Little? We have seen *everything*.' Land narrowed one eye, peering at the tall warrior. 'You are showing terrifying ignorance, Blood Angel. You look around you and you see a city, the first sign of habitation in the webway, yes? You see evidence of civilisation, albeit in the foul architecture of the eldar race. Your perceptions are tricking you, Space Marine. Your brain recognises the presence of urban structure, where life once existed, and attributes undeserved importance to it.'

Land keyed in a code on his vambrace, projecting a scratchy, inexact version of the unfolding, evolving webway map imprinted inside the Archimandrite's mind. Complete scans of the human body's veins and capillaries showed fewer branching pathways than the disorderly maze beaming forth in green holo light.

The explorator pointed at one of the tunnels. One that seemed no different to any of the other thousands revealed in flickering light.

'What does it matter if this city falls?' asked Land. 'Do you think Tribune Endymion truly cares? Or Prefect Coros? They have been fighting for almost five years in the tunnels between Calastar and Terra – the hundreds of passageways that lead inexorably to the Emperor's very throne room. The Impossible City isn't the focus of the war, Zephon. It isn't even the prime battlefield of the war. This entire city is merely within a tunnel like any other. Its only real note of import is that it made an easy strongpoint to defend when the Ten Thousand advanced as far as their numbers allowed. So, no, I am not aggrieved. I wished to see the Great Work, and I am seeing it. With all its wonders and horrors.'

For a time neither of them spoke. The only sound was Sapien's chewing.

'That will play merry havoc with his digestion,' Land noted. And then, apropos of nothing, he narrowed his eyes as he regarded Zephon. 'You really are a beautiful creature, you know. Aesthetically, I mean. And scientifically, of course.'

'It is said that many of my Legion possess aesthetic qualities considered–'

'Not that it means anything one way or the other,' Land interrupted. 'I've never had that drive within me, you understand. No time for those kinds of entanglements – they're a distraction from real work. I merely find it curious that your primarch's genetic legacy manipulates human physiology to produce such mythologically iconic figures of beauty. Not very secular, eh?'

Zephon smiled. This was something he had heard and debated on many occasions before.

'Angels have great cultural significance on Baal. In many ways, Baal-ite culture holds closer religious similarities to Old Earth in the era of the Holy Pax Romanii Empire than it does to–'

'Yes, yes. Spare me the lesson in the exact flavour of your tawdry barbarism.'

Zephon smiled despite himself. 'As you wish, Arkhan.'

'Hmm. I suppose you are here for me to examine your arms before I leave?'

Zephon's angelic features remained carefully passive. He showed none of his surprise that the explorator had recalled the offhand comment from their journey, but nor did he desire to put himself under such scrutiny. Out of pity for the haunted man before him and sensing Land's abiding isolation, he said, 'Yes.'

'Well, there's no time now. The final evacuation column is in three hours and all of my equipment is already loaded.' He hesitated, regarding the Blood Angel with a critical eye. 'You're welcome to ride with me rather than in one of the bulk conveyors this time, if you so desire.'

'I am touched, Explorator Land. I shall consider it. May I ask why my affliction is of such interest to you?'

'Listen to yourself, Space Marine. *Affliction.* Typical Baalite melodrama. The truth is that I've always wondered about legionaries and their bionics,' Land elaborated, evidently warming to the subject. 'You often leave them unarmoured, yet reverently sheathe the rest of yourselves in ceramite. Even statues of your kind show unarmoured augmentation. I can't say I've been interested enough until now to truly look into it. I'd always assumed it was something pertaining to how bionics fail to interface with power armour.'

'Primarily,' Zephon agreed. He felt the conversation getting away from him and wasn't certain he wished to catch up. Of all the conversations to have, in all the places, with all the people who he might speak with.

'Primarily?' Land pressed.

'There is also an element of inspirational pride to the practice. To present us as invincible, enduring warriors to the Imperium and its enemies. To show that we overcome our wounds and fight on in the Emperor's name.'

Land gave a wry sneer. 'Such cheap propaganda. Like the legends of warriors that fought naked so as to show their courage before their allies and their fearlessness to their foes.'

'There is perhaps an element of that as well,' Zephon confessed. 'But as you said, it is largely a matter of interfacing with our armour.'

Arkhan Land rose, dusting his hands on his long jacket. 'Give me back my auspex,' he said idly. 'And let's be away from here. I have a medicae scanner in my supplies, as it happens.'

Zephon didn't move. 'Is there a possibility that you might be able to restore function?'

'Ah,' Land said with a wry smile. 'The pernicious spectre of hope makes itself known at last. Please note that I can't promise an Omnissian miracle. I'm no surgeon-augmeticist or bionic engineer, yet there's nothing else to do until our departure but stare into the screens and witness nightmares given shape. Given that I've checked and rechecked my Raider thrice in the last few hours, you are, at least for now, my only useful distraction.'

He walked from the chamber, towards where the wounded skitarii were being tended by their artisanal priest-engineers. Beyond that lay the chamber where the final convoy made ready for evacuation.

The psyber-monkey remained a moment more, cocking its head as it looked up at the Blood Angel.

'Come along, Sapien,' Land's voice drifted from the hallway outside.

The artificimian bolted, leaving Zephon alone. He looked at the arched doorway for some time, deciding whether or not to follow.

TWENTY

Undivided
War in the tunnels
As then, so now

THE DAEMON SOARED, free of its iron bindings. *Black Sky* had grown unsustainable as a host, with its crew slain and its damage going untended, leading to the spread of noisome madness within Enkir's broken mind. The creature had abandoned the Titan and its princeps with the metamorphic release of casting aside a shed husk. On regrown wings it took to the air.

And so it soared, watching the hordes of the Four Choirs, each one the scarcest shard of something greater, overrunning the city. No mortal legionaries, here. No god-machines or battle tanks or other corporeal toys. The hosts of the warp marched, spilling from a multitude of tunnels. The city was theirs, though in their triumph they cared not at all. Pursuit of the Golden and the Soulless was all that mattered. The immense, fanged willpowers that drove each shard pressed them onwards, ever onwards. The Golden and the Soulless were almost extinct, the last gate almost defenceless. These creatures and their masters were utterly indifferent to the galaxy burning. Here was the true war, and the hour of its end had come. The Anathema's throat was bared.

Many of the Four's child-shards warred amongst themselves. This was simply the Way, the eternal ebb and flow of the Great Game. Few of them rose against the incarnation of the first murder. Undivided, its genesis was in a song sung by all four Choirs. Among the other shard children, even those of the same Choir might tear at one another to sate bestial hungers or in purified expressions of their incarnated principles. They were daemons, after all, and not to be trusted.

The creature turned in the immense tunnel's misty sky. Something pulled at the node of senses within its skull, something that had tasted and revelled in no small measure of violent annihilation. Something still inside the dead eldar city. Something hiding.

There was no conscious decision to turn and hunt. The daemon hungered eternally, and was drained by the skin-puppetry of possession and immersion in mortal thought. It hungered, so it would feed.

It swooped low above the teeming ranks of its kindred, beating its wings to the sounds of shrieking fear, hate and adoration rising from lesser throats.

As with their arrival, there was no boundary to mark their departure. The spires around the evacuating Imperials became more insubstantial, slowly swallowed by the mist, but there was no geographical assurance they were even the same towers that comprised Impossible City.

Baroness Jaya had no idea when she had left the last avenue and entered the first tunnel, but her focus was most assuredly on more urgent matters.

Minutes became hours, and hours lost any shred of the dubious meaning they'd so far managed to hold in a realm without any true chronology. The battle raged down tunnel after tunnel, with the Ten Thousand and the Silent Sisterhood forced into a neverending fighting retreat by the sheer weight of numbers hammering against them. Tunnels branched and divided and rejoined on the route back to the Imperial Dungeon, each passageway thick with rebel war machines, legionary battalions and hordes of the warp-wrought.

The only respite came at the barricades of wrecked vehicles and downed Titans that the defenders pressed into service as fortifications. All pretence of conventional war had been abandoned. At least in the city they had been able to see the assault as a siege. Here, with the foe choking the tunnels, it was like fighting back the tide of Terra's last ocean.

Nor were the attacks limited to the very end of the Imperial column. The evacuees came under constant threat from capillary tunnels where the rebel forces and their daemonic ilk had outpaced the Imperial rearguard to strike deep within the refugee column.

Jaya remained with the Ten Thousand and Sisterhood units making up the rearguard, backed up only by Sacristan Torolec and his small team in their heavily armoured Logrus-pattern munitions loader. The rest of Vyridion's courtiers were scattered throughout several kilometres of webway tunnels, fighting off secondary attacks along the evacuation line.

The fighting was at its fiercest and thickest at the rearguard, with an ever-diminishing number of the Emperor's finest facing the bulk of the foe's horde.

Repeated vox-calls for the Archimandrite went unanswered. Demands for servitors and Protectors to return from further down the line were answered with similar silence.

Gunflare flowered in the golden dark as her cannons chattered their lethal song. Legionaries, and the creatures that added to their ragged ranks, fell before her in droves. The tunnel gave a great heave around her as a Fellblade rolled from the mist, its Legion colours unreadable, belching its main cannons in her direction. The shells erupted against the tunnel wall nearby, shrapnel impacting against her angled energy shield. She knew herself just how worthless targeting arrays were in the mist. The golden fog unlocked and threw off even dead-sight aiming confirmations.

She veered aside as the debris clattered against her shield. Not for the first time she wondered if these tunnels of alien matter could collapse beneath the weight of the violence inside them. They hadn't yet. Perhaps that boded well.

The Ignatum Warhound *Ikarial*, shield-dead and decorated with the scarification of near-terminal wounds, bounded forwards on sparking, damaged legs, its gunlimbs kicking. One moment Jaya's display was lit by the gunflare of its mega-bolters, the next *Ikarial* took an unnaturally awkward step backwards and toppled sideways into Imperial ranks, trailing smoke from where its cockpit-head had been.

'*Baroness.*' She knew the voice of Tribune Endymion, and knew his command before he needed to speak the order.

'Engaging,' she voxed back, slamming her control pylons forwards. Her nameless, inherited Castigator leaned into its loping run with vicious eagerness, kicking through the shrieking infantry at its shins and raising its power sword high in the mist. Lightning raked along the active swordlimb, spitting sparks as it reacted with the golden fog.

Gunner, she thought. Sweat bathed her inside her suit and stung her eyes within her helm. *Driver.*

The Fellblade, *Ikarial*'s killer, fired again, the boom of its shells shaking Jaya's bones at such close range. Even clipping her was enough to overload her ion shield and rock her sideways in her throne. Her nimble Castigator staggered but kept its balance – a heartbeat later she was on the tank, one foot slamming down onto its forward plating to arrest her own momentum, plunging her blade downwards in a smooth thrust.

In and out darted the impaling shaft of lightning-wreathed steel, searing through the dense ceramite of the Fellblade's turret. *Gunner.* In and out a second time, just as smoothly, into the plating directly beneath her. *Driver.*

A third sweep of the energised blade severed the long-barrelled accelerator cannons halfway along their length. *For the sake of it.*

Quad lascannons tore past her as she sprinted back to the line of gold and black, where the Custodians and Silent Sisters were making their stand. She angled her rekindled shield behind her and ran on, risking the sponson fire rather than wade amidst the foe for any longer than necessary. Damage reports showed as angry runes in the corner of her vision. All fine. Nothing critical.

Something winged slapped against her forward hull. Her automated stubber rattled off a chorus of rounds, ripping the daemon-thing from the air.

She strode over the warring forms of Ra and Dynastes Squad, their spears spinning with the speed of rotors. Half turning as she walked over them, Jaya sent another stream of high-velocity bolts from her gunlimb in a shredding crescent through an enemy phalanx.

The smoking cannons whined to silence.

'Falling back,' she voxed to the front line. 'Reloading.'

Torolec was waiting for her once she had weaved between the grav-tanks of the Ten Thousand and the Sisterhood's skimmer platforms. The munitions loader was an ugly tracked vehicle with a humanoid crane mechanism on its back, appearing as nothing so much as centaur of Terran myth formed from a Sentinel cargolifter and a tank. Torolec brought the Logrus around behind her. She locked her stance and waited, tense in her throne, willing them to work faster.

'*Where are the war servitors?*' one of the Custodians was calling out across the vox. His voice was ragged with the effort of battle. '*Where is the accursed Mechanicum?*'

Jaya had no answer. She listened to the heated exchanges, hearing her own scions reporting the absence of significant portions of the convoy's defenders. Hundreds of servitors, tanks and Protectors were simply not there.

The Knight rocked gently as ammunition canisters were crunched into place. A moment later she felt the slight sway of her gunlimb as ammunition belt feeds were reconnected.

'*For Highrock,*' Torolec intoned the traditional words of readiness.

'For the Emperor,' she replied, and slammed her control pylons forwards once more.

An unknowable time later, the enemy fell back. Perhaps more accurately, they failed to pursue the withdrawing Imperials. No more of them drifted from the golden mist; no hunched silhouettes or screaming warriors or ravening beasts emerged from the fog to hurl themselves at the rearguard. Knowing this precious moment of peace wouldn't last long, Ra made ready to repel another wave.

'Fourth and fifth ranks advance,' he grunted into the vox. 'First through third, fall back.'

Most of the exhausted warriors collapsed where they were, seized by muscle cramps in their first moment of peace in untold hours. Grav-tanks and relatively fresh warriors took their places, advancing in place of the exhausted waves of their kindred who had held until now.

Ra slumped to the ground, his muscles in spasm, physically unable to bring himself to rise. The stimms and adrenal-spikes were wearing off at last, forcing him to confront the reality of his overworked body. He was poisoning himself with sleeplessness, his blood rich with chemical stimulants and his thoughts prey to the distortions of a brain refused the mercy of rest.

By his loose calculations he had been awake now for fifteen days, fighting almost every minute since the walls fell, his ears endlessly ringing with a vox-crackling orchestra of conflicting voices. His body was eating itself for nourishment. He struggled to stay aware of how the evacuation was proceeding farther along the passages, but there was no word beyond the Archimandrite's absence and the predation of foes from many of the side-tunnels. His thoughts were dull and slow, his reflexes slower. Everything he saw was stained by the greying haze of exhausted starvation.

Fifteen days. His right shoulder had seized days ago, yet there had been no respite. It throbbed with crippling cramps from the sheer repetitive weight of hammering his spear down over and over again, thousands of times each day and night.

The tall form of Baroness Jaya's Castigator was a motionless statue above them, staring back into the mist. Waiting, just as they were waiting. Diocletian had done well in finding her. Vyridion's Knights were precious assets in the close-quarter brutality of these tunnel battles.

Jodarion, another of the Lords of Terra, collapsed into the road next to Ra, lying atop the last three legionaries he'd slain. Jodarion's trembling hand managed to drag his blade-split helm free, baring his face to the ashy air. The Custodian sucked it in, in great wet heaves.

There was very little left of Jodarion's face. He left some of it on the inside of his cleaved helmet, reduced to a red smear. Ra looked at the gasping, bloody skull next to him, all that remained of Jodarion's head, half of the teeth hammered away, lost at some point in the last few days. The wounds had clotted almost at once, but the damage was done.

Ra suspected he looked little better.

The legionary nearest to him was still alive. A World Eater, bisected at the waist, was dragging himself closer to where Ra kneeled. His armour was more red than white, signifying some unknown change within his treasonous Legion.

'*Blood*,' the warrior murmured through a shattered mouth.

'I was there,' Ra tried to growl at him, but the exhausted words were a snarling whisper. 'I was there the day we saved your mongrel primarch from certain death.'

'*Blood*,' the World Eater mumbled again. His helm had been crushed, savaging the skull and face within. His eyes were glazed, maddened, the pupils mere pinpricks.

'If only we'd left him there.' The Custodian laughed, feeling his reknitting bones and abused muscles stinging afresh with the squirted application of adrenal elixirs from inside his armour.

'*Blood*...'

'If only we'd left him to die in those mountains.' Ra was smiling now. 'The one primarch who couldn't conquer his world. The one primarch who lived as a slave. The one primarch who had to be saved from death.'

'Blood!' The World Eater's eyes resolved with the ghost of clarity. 'Blood for the–'

A spear rammed through the World Eater's spine, driven down between his shoulder blades. The power pack on his back shorted out and died. The warrior himself went into convulsions. Eyes that had so briefly cleared now rolled back into his broken head.

Above him, Solon wrenched the weapon left, then right, and finally pulled it free. The Custodian collapsed a breath later, using the World Eater's corpse as a seat.

'This has been the worst day since yesterday,' Solon said with no trace of a smile in his tone.

Ra rolled onto his back, first seeing the empty mist above, then looking to his right. He saw Zhanmadao, the Terminator forced down to one knee, his firepike lost or broken who knew how long ago. Grinding gyro-stabilisers in the Cataphractii suit's joints sought to bring the warrior back to his feet but Zhanmadao slouched forwards, head lowered. He refused to rise from his crouch, or he simply couldn't manage it, instead adopting the pose of an ancient knight kneeling in prayer before an altar. Blood had dried while running from rents in his battleplate, and from his mouth in a slow trickle. When he lifted his head to look at Ra, a dirty chasm of scabbed blood and broken bone showed where one eye and one ear had been. Bare skull glistened in the gold mist.

Unable to speak, Zhanmadao grunted.

Ra tried to force a nod. Instead, his eyes fell closed.

HE OPENED THEM a second later. An hour later. A year later. The Mechanicum's tunnel was gone, as were his kindred.

He stood in the throne room, the Emperor's laboratory has it had been half a decade before, not as it stood now. The walls lacked the hive-like hollows of thousands upon thousands of recesses awaiting stasis coffins. The machinery spat no sparks. The Emperor didn't sit upon the Golden Throne. That great engine thrummed with automation, independent of the Emperor's presence yet slaved to His invisible will and the ambitious heights of Imperial dreams.

'Hello, Ra.'

Ra turned, feeling the broken-bone grind of his malfunctioning armour. He tried to kneel but the Emperor stopped him, a hand gripping his Custodian's pauldron. The tribune grunted his gratitude.

'Do you remember this day, Ra?'

The workers performed their duties around him, maintaining the rumbling machines, tending to the connective pipelines and power couplings. It could have been one of any number of days in the throne room, before…

No. *There.* There was Valdor. There was Amon. There was Ra himself, one of twenty of the highest-ranking Custodians present in a loose pack, speaking in voices too low, too far away, for Ra's wounded manifestation to make out.

Ra's mouth curled in a tired smile at the sight. *How innocent we were.*

He knew of what those ghosts spoke. He remembered it well. He even followed the movements of Amon's lips, his memory providing the voice he couldn't hear.

'…no word from Aquillon.'

Aquillon. Prefect of the Hykanatoi. The *Occuli Imperator,* Eyes of the Emperor, assigned to watch over Lorgar in the waning years of the Great Crusade. Aquillon, who had never returned from his vigil. One of Ra's own Dynastes Squad had travelled with Aquillon on that long, distant mission: Sythran – a warrior who had also surely fallen to Word Bearers treachery. Perhaps even on Isstvan itself in the high hour of treachery.

Stoic, dutiful Sythran. Ra hoped he had died well.

'I remember, sire,' said Ra. He watched Amon speaking of Aquillon, seeing one of his finest companions mouthing the very last words spoken before the sirens sounded.

The sirens began to sound.

'Time is short, Ra,' said the Emperor.

Men and women were standing still around them. The shouts were starting to rise, accompanying the flashing warning lights. The gathered Custodians spread apart in effortless awareness of each other's killing reach, the most loyal hands in the Imperium reaching for their spears.

'We may not reach the Dungeon, sire.' Even here, Ra's voice was a cracked ruin. 'The Mechanicum has abandoned us and the convoy is near undefended.'

'I know, my Custodian. I know. It is meaningless now.'

More shouting. Workers and scientists were running now, moving away from the overloading machines. The illumination of the throne room took on a strained, desaturated cast.

Constantin Valdor ran to the Emperor's side, oblivious to the fact his master was playing no part in a performance that had all happened before.

The Emperor had turned to him then, Ra recalled, *and said 'Summon Jenetia Krole. Assemble the Ten Thousand.' This time though, he did not.*

'At once, my liege.' Valdor turned away to make it so.

'Something is coming through!' cried one of the human workers.

The Emperor ignored the spreading chaos. 'Hear me, Ra. You must take word to the Ten Thousand and the Silent Sisterhood. I am leaving the Golden Throne. I am coming to you.'

Ra's blood sang. Eyes wide, he felt riven by sudden hope. It struck him with physical force.

'Sire... How...'

'The how does not matter. Hold, Ra. Fight. I will join you in the Mechanicum's tunnels.'

'But, my liege, all your work...'

The Emperor silenced him with a stare.

Behind Ra, the discoloured webway portal vomited incandescent flame into the throne room. He felt its searing heat, just as he had on that long-ago day. He watched himself with exalted, distracted eyes, moving to the Emperor's side, forming a shield of Custodial auramite to protect his monarch from harm.

The machines were detonating around them now. Many of the humans were on the floor, clutching at their bleeding eyes. The hateful radiance emerging from the webway had stolen their sight.

Those still standing were no safer. Shrapnel flew in a lethal, burning blizzard, cutting them down in their dozens, shearing limbs from bodies, severing heads from shoulders. Wreckage clattered against Ra's armour now, just as it rained against the same armour he had worn five years before. A dagger of jagged metal speared into Amon's side, causing the Custodian to grunt across their shared vox.

A bleeding, desecrated behemoth melted through the webway portal. It dripped with the blood of the souls it had sacrificed to reach this point in space and time. Laughter haloed its terrible form, the laughter of mad entities pantomiming as gods. Their laughter formed the silver strings of puppeteers, pulling at the creature's limbs and thoughts.

It said one word, one terrible proclamation with enough psychic ferocity to slay half of the panicking humans still breathing. They warped and thrashed and burned beneath the pressure of that single telepathic damnation, their flesh losing all integrity, their essences devoured from the inside out.

+FATHER.+

Valdor was firing. Amon was firing. Ra, then and now, was firing. He and the image of himself reloaded in temporal harmony, slamming fresh sickle magazines home in their guardian spears, resuming the torrent of upward bolter fire.

The pain of Ra's wounds was gone. He didn't think, didn't care, that this was a memory. He unloaded his guardian spear into the daemonic avatar of Magnus the Red, just as he had done on that fateful day. He screamed through clenched teeth – again, just as he had done before, just as he was doing not two metres away now.

+Awaken, Ra,+ said the Emperor. +Fight on.+

And as ever, His Custodian obeyed.

TWENTY-ONE

That most sacred duty
The end of many roads
Awakening

THE ARCHIMANDRITE CALCULATED with all haste. There were doubts, of course. Hesitations. On some level it mused over the heretical nature of its choice, but to consider its actions heresy would be the result of flawed and limited perception. The Ten Thousand and the Silent Sisterhood, proving themselves untrue to the word given to the Fabricator General himself, were the guilty ones. The route back to Mars had to remain viable. The Aresian Path must stay in Imperial hands. Ensuring that circumstance was as far from heresy as could be conceived. Indeed, it was a sacred duty.

And if it could not, would not be fulfilled by those responsible? Then the answer was not to flee back to Terra. Terra was safe. Terra didn't languish under the traitorous grip of the false cult. Terra needed no reinforcing.

No, there was only one logical answer that conformed to the relevant needs of Martian primacy. Only one course of action to take.

<Home.>

With the webway's cartography playing out in repetitive reassurance within the Archimandrite's thoughts, it had been no hardship to plan the dispersal of the war servitors, robots, Protectors and Myrmidon war-priests that answered to the Archimandrite itself rather than the Ten Thousand. Those that the Archimandrite didn't personally lead were sent with the earliest sections of the evacuation convoy, then granted enough insight into the Archimandrite's mental map to deviate from the line of retreat and journey through secondary tunnels to double back. They drifted away at key junctions, navigating the webway via their overlord's exloaded data.

It had been easier still to filter through the layers of their loyalties through unspoken code exchanges, holding noospheric conversations with hundreds of them at once to ascertain their use and potential within the Archimandrite's growing forces.

It was under no illusions. It couldn't retake Mars with the force accrued inside the webway. No matter. Holding the Aresian Path would be enough. The Omnissiah would commit far greater forces to the web in the next crusade, and the Archimandrite's war convocation would be waiting, indefatigably in command of the most vital passageway in the entire network.

If only Ignatum had been a viable consideration. Even one of the few remaining Titans would have been an beneficial omen, but the Archimandrite had known better than to even make the attempt of gaining their aid. The Titan crews of Ignatum were more flesh than metal, and the Archimandrite sensed their loyalties were as tightly bound to Terra and the Ten Thousand as to the Martian ideal. They ached for home as much as any of the displaced Cult Mechanicum, yet they held warrior-bonds with the Imperials and personal, inviolate oaths with the Omnissiah.

Their skitarii, however, had proved far more receptive. Simple, weaponised creatures that they were, the Archimandrite had siphoned them away from around the ankles of the god-machines they protected, drawing them into secondary conduits and capillary tunnels, keeping them from the destruction being levied upon the Sisterhood and the Ten Thousand.

The Archimandrite had canted its avowal to stand with the last convoy, warding them from harm – and then, as the final Imperials had
battled their way into the tunnels beneath the Impossible City, it had
performed its most calculated gamble and powered down amidst the
devastation. Now it seemed to be nothing more than yet another wreck,
another robot going tragically unsalvaged in the hours after this terrible battle.

And it had worked. No warp beast had come to tear it apart in daemonic anger.

A sliver of life remained within its core during this slumber, enough
to maintain its few biological components. Those precious shreds of
viscera that had once been Magos Domina Hieronyma couldn't be
allowed to rot.

In the deep caves of the Godspire's wraithbone foundations, sealed
within a vault established by the Unifiers to house volatile materials
for their reconstruction work, the Archimandrite reactivated slowly,
sending power throughout its form in a trickle charge.

Home, it thought.

It. She?

It.

Though again… there were doubts. Logically, this yearning for home –
could it be the corrupting influence of the core of Hieronyma within
the machine? And if so, did that stand as testament to the purity of
the Archimandrite's cause, or was this an emotive flaw, a stutter of the
precision of its plan?

Furthermore: consider the role of external manipulation. Had this been
anticipated? Expected? Planned by the Fabricator General? Had she
been chosen to become It in the knowledge she would put her emotive loyalty to her homeland above the needs of the Ten Thousand?

The Archimandrite cast these considerations aside as irrelevant to
its calculations. They were of no consequence now. *The Cog,* as it was
sometimes said, *was already turning.*

The Archimandrite's first order of duty was to re-establish its noospheric network with the alphas and unit leaders it had won to its cause. And from there, on to the Aresian Path.

Powering up completely, the war machine rose and began to cant to its underlings, assembling an internal map of where they were positioned.

<It is time.>

THE ALPHA INDIVIDUAL named and numbered by the signifier KRRJ-1211 (F) could not be said to possess much in the way of personality or ambition. In that regard he was little different from most of the basic-pattern skitarii, all of whom were surgically and chemically crafted for loyalty and obedience. He stared at the world through target-accumulator lenses grafted over eyes that had had their lids removed in order to provide his masters with continual inloads of data from his senses. And in this, too, he was little different from others among his kind.

His lack of distinctiveness made him perfect for the Archimandrite's purposes. Wholly loyal to Sacred Mars and entirely devoid of the higher brain function necessary to determine the action/reaction cause/effect of his conflict in loyalties, he obeyed the Archimandrite's cants of <Home>, <Home>, <Home> with all the drone-like behaviour of a worker insect following a trail of its kindred back to the hive.

In this instance, however, he was leading them. KRRJ-1211 (F) signalled a halt with a raised fist and a spurt of noospheric code. The warriors with him halted with the inhuman precision of gestalt unity. The conveyors carrying Unifier supplies, and some of the invaluable priests themselves, rolled on ahead through the misty tunnels. Queries from the Mechanicum archpriests responsible for building and rebuilding these very tunnels inloaded into KRRJ-1211 (F)'s senses, to which he responded with the requisite deception.

<You are safe,> he canted to them as they managed their conveyors or walked alongside their cargo haulers. This was a lie. <We must return to battle.> This was somewhere between a lie and the truth. They were recalled to battle, yes, but KRRJ-1211 (F) simply had no

intention of canting just where that battle would be taking place. He led his warriors away, leaving the Unifiers to believe he was returning to aid the rearguard.

Not long after, he plunged into the mist of a side tunnel, leading his warband with him. They moved at a dead sprint, their piston legs carrying them at great speed through the winding passageways.

The auxiliary tunnel as laid out on the Archimandrite's map branched in over one hundred places, and one specific route would lead back to the Impossible City. Most notably, it required a brief traversal through one webway gate, exiting back into the material universe before quickly entering a nearby companion gate and continuing the journey onwards.

Unfortunately for KRRJ-1211 (F), less than a day after the skitarii warband had set off on its sprint through the side passages, they passed from the Mechanicum's rattling monstrosity of a tunnel into the psy-resonant material of the true web, and emerged into what appeared to be a long-dead garden, situated beneath the stars. The skitarii alpha paid brief heed to the dusty remains of flowers beneath his iron tread. He paid similarly little attention to the oddly angular statuary placed around the lifeless, grey garden. His focus was almost entirely fixed upon finding the companion gateway and returning the web to complete his journey.

<Location: Craftworld!> one of his more limited underofficers canted in alarm. She had no access to the webway's map. Her limited intellect would have struggled to sustain even a portion of it. <Location: Eldar craftworld. Procedure: Withdraw?>

<Zzzt,> KRRJ-1211 (F) canted back in irritation.

He had his back to the statuary, engrossed in his search, when the statues began to draw their swords. Even if he had been devoting his full concentration, he wouldn't have recognised the lithe alien figures pulling blades of enchanted bone free from jewelled sheaths. He had never encountered the eldar species before, nor their funereal sentinels, the wraithkind.

<It is time,> canted the Archimandrite some time later. The words augmitted across the still garden from KRRJ-1211 (F)'s vox-feed. The skitarii lay in pieces upon the dead grass along with his warriors, but the augmetic portions of his corpse retained enough internal power to receive transmissions.

If the statues heard this static-flawed announcement, they showed no sign. Their swords were sheathed. Their heads were bowed. They waited in silence, wardens over new graves among the old.

A CLADE OF war servitors trundled through the web, following the Archimandrite's precise directions. This particular clade – noted as LAM-Exios in the Fabricator General's archives – was comprised of Martian criminals sentenced to servitoral repentance, not that any of them remembered who they were or what they were convicted of doing.

Each of the lobotomised slaves bore significant firepower in the form of heavy-barrelled plasma calivers, rad-cannons and flamers enhanced by cognis targeting technology. They were perfect examples of the expendable troops that had died in their thousands defending the Unifiers over the last five years, and those that Zagreus Kane had sent in staggering numbers when Diocletian and Kaeria approached him with a requisition order.

The LAM-Exios clade, to their credit, made it most of the way back to the Impossible City. Their journey halted when they encountered the devastated remains of a XVI Legion Reaver Company and its tank support seeking to cut ahead and ambush the fleeing Imperial convoys.

As they were designed and programmed to do, the battle-servitors of LAM-Exios advanced with kill/extinguish battle subroutines, unleashing a withering torrent of firepower on the enemy units charging towards them.

<It is time,> canted the Archimandrite. And indeed it was. By that time, however, a mere seventeen war servitors survived to limp or roll onwards after the battle. These near-mindless victors were slaughtered by the next enemy wave to come spilling through the tunnel, gutted

and torn apart by World Eaters chainaxes, their heads taken as trophies to be skinned and hung from belts like shamanistic tokens.

<It is time.>

Aravolos of the Cult Myrmidia, his bulky form shrouded in tattered robes of Martian red, deactivated his link to the noosphere. Simultaneously strangling an officer of the Emperor's Children with all four of his mechandendrites, and releasing sustained beams of volkite energy at the rest of the sergeant's squad from his fixed gunlimb, he was already engaged in the consecrated act of waging war.

His muddy, bloodstained consciousness lacked the time and focus for the Archimandrite's treason.

Heaving with his mechadendrites he lifted the ceramite-clad warrior into the air. A second application of effort crushed the warrior's gorget, broke his neck and tore both arms from their sockets. Aravolos hurled the remnants towards the ignited, retreating figures of the sergeant's squad, and turned in search of another life to end.

ECHO-ECHO-71 ABANDONED THE convoy and led his warriors into the ancillary tunnels, as ordered. He possessed more autonomy than many of his alpha-kind, even among other sicarii, but held little comprehension of the immensity of the Great Work even after several years of fighting inside its boundaries. The equation of his loyalty ended in simplicity: the representative of the Fabricator General had canted that Sacred Mars cried out for liberation, and that duty overruled any other.

His expedition proceeded far more smoothly than many others. Without trouble, he reached the specific rendezvous locations marked by the Archimandrite, bypassing the tunnels she had calculated as most likely to be stormed by the foe. He sent out scouts to mark the passages yet to be taken, then progressed only when confirmation arrived that they were clear. He moved his warriors in disciplined kill-teams, their stalk-tanks and 'strider units dispersed to repel, with maximum force and response time mobility, any sudden ambush.

<It is time,> came the cant. Never a particularly fervent believer, Echo-Echo-71 nevertheless felt holiness suffuse him at the inloaded voice. He was doing the Omnissiah's work, and leading his warriors in the service of Sacred Mars.

All was proceeding apace until the tunnel through which they marched ended abruptly. They had long ago branched off into the true webway rather than the Mechanicum's purpose-built avenues, and now found themselves facing a tunnel that continued on the map, yet appeared blunted before their eye-lenses.

It ended in golden mist. The advance scouts had entered and immediately fallen silent. Quite what this portended, Echo-Echo-71 couldn't be sure.

He sent in one of his 'striders, warning the female pilot to be high-sense aware and cant back a continual datastream. She vowed obedience, lurched forwards on her spindly legged dune walker as she began exloading a code-flow of perception data, and entered the mist.

Whereupon she immediately fell silent.

Echo-Echo-71 considered this. The Archimandrite's cartography may have been flawed through inexperience or the vicissitudes of this unnatural realm. The original source may have also been flawed, given that the Unifiers focused their efforts on constructing their own routes to link with the established webway rather than wandering significant distances and recording alternate routes. Archival data showed that such scouting expeditions had been part of the initial steps of the Great Work, but such practices ended with the devastating manifestation of Magnus the Red, and the deployment of the Ten Thousand and Silent Sisterhood to defend the Mechanicum labourers.

Whatever the truth, whether out of date or recorded incorrectly to begin with, his map was unreliable.

None of these musings solved Echo-Echo-71's conundrum. Retreating and reconsidering the route would mean deviation from the Archimandrite's plan. Advancing along the unmodified route would mean venturing into this anomaly through which there was no evidence of survival, let alone drawing nearer to his goal.

All the while, <It is time> thrummed through his senses, a pressurised compulsion, demanding he obey.

'Forward,' he commanded in a spurt of code. 'For Mars and the Omnissiah.'

As relatively valorous as a skitarii elite could ever be, Echo-Echo-71 led his warriors into the mist. He was immediately and completely disassembled beyond even the atomic level, wiped from existence as he plunged from an eroded section of the webway into the raw matter of the warp. What passed for his spirit, a machine-thinned whisper of consciousness, ignited in the Sea of Souls and lasted a statistically insignificant amount of time longer than his body.

With no way of knowing their alpha had been obliviated by immersion into the naked daemonic aether that raged behind the material universe, every one of his warriors dutifully marched forwards and shared his fate.

<It is time.>

The words rang out, augmitting to dozens of warbands, most of whom were dead by the time they would have received the message, or trapped in capillary tunnels and fighting for their lives against hordes of the warp-wrought.

In that respect, at least, they did indeed protect the convoy. Their lives were sold to slow the enemy, even if only by the chance of misfortune.

THE ARCHIMANDRITE PROCESSED the spillage of inloading data with a sense of dawning horror. She coded back to her surviving warbands, requesting updated positional information and sending them rerouting cogitations that would allow them to link up with others to form a more cohesive fighting force.

First she attempted to band the surviving regiments together in order to break through. Within seconds of her primary calculations failing, she was settling for demanding they fall back, flee, do whatever they could to escape. Even then she received precious few canted replies. Most of them were already dead.

She – *She?* – stared at the datastreams within her own mind, gripped by a traitor's icy guilt. She had led thousands upon thousands of Mechanicum souls into annihilation. She had failed to hold the Aresian Path despite betraying the Omnissiah's own praetorians to do so.

Mistakes have been made, she thought with a cognition-failing, creeping unreality.

The fate of the Imperials was nothing in light of her own careless treason; there would be no forgiveness for this. The Fabricator General would pull her organics from her body for this sin, and crush them in his hands before her failing vision.

The depleted core of Hieronyma surfaced through the mess of the Archimandrite's ambitions. She heard footsteps in the chamber, which was patently impossible given the seals in place at the containment door, and streamdumped herself from the noosphere in order to turn and face the intruder.

The first thing she saw through the unresolved failures of her target locks was that the door remained sealed. The second thing she saw was a human male, his features hazy, his shadow too long across the floor.

She deployed an army's worth of weapons from her shoulders, her wrists, her forearms, even her chest cavity. Weapons based on Arkhan Land's forbidden lore, many of which still lacked Imperial names.

'Hieronyma,' said the approaching figure. His speech was awkward, as if he had only recently mastered not just Gothic but any language at all. He moved his mouth out of time with the syllables he spoke. *'I sensed you. You have known such bloodshed...'*

His face twisted in something that began by resembling a smile, but was really just a rending of flesh. The thing inside him tore itself free, reaching for her.

All of her treasured, unnamed weapons fired, far too late to make any difference.

✠ ✠ ✠

KAERIA'S CAPTIVES SANG as the machines began their work. In none of the circumstances and possibilities that she had considered would the doomed prisoners sing.

She couldn't hear them, couldn't even be certain they were singing at all. She was only alerted to this unforeseen behaviour by one of the tech-adepts retracting his secondary arms into his robe and turning his sun-starved face to the coffins above. Hundreds of them were bound to the wall, chained in place.

'They are singing,' he said in faint wonder.

Kaeria's narrowed gaze saw a host of emotions on the various captives' faces. Some were shouting in their soundproof pods, beating their fists bloody against the transparent panels. Some were curled in foetal positions and seemed to sleep. Several even seemed to be in silent rapture, utterly calm and composed. Others lay with their heads back, eyes and mouths open, and... Yes. She could imagine, just about, that these last souls with their rigor mortis expressions were tortured singers.

She had believed they were screaming. Given what was being done to them, it seemed far likelier.

What could they possibly sound like?

She could summon one of the young novices who hadn't yet oathed her tongue to tranquillity, to ask on her behalf. Yet as Kaeria stared around the chamber, hearing only the rumble of the Golden Throne's supplemental generators, she felt grateful for the gift of her hollow heart. Some questions needed no answers.

She turned her gaze to the enthroned Emperor, feeling the acid of bitter irony. Here sat her king, committing His consciousness to the machine created to save a species. And yet, chained in place across the chamber and trapped within parasitic coffin-pods, one thousand prisoners screamed in silence and psychically sang their souls away. Batteries for the Throne, so the Emperor might be free. Human lives reduced to sources of psychic power.

Sacrifices. The thought set her scalp prickling.

The throne room's power flickered for a moment on the edge of failure. Machines around the chamber slowed, several of them giving ugly whines of protesting mechanisms until the power stabilised. One of the coffins emitted a hauntingly gentle chime as the data panel on its surface flashed red with warning signs.

The first one has died, Kaeria thought. *Died already, so soon.*

Upon the Throne itself, as the generators around the chamber hummed louder, the Emperor of Mankind opened His eyes.

III
Choir

This is now. All of her memories, all of those thens, *reel to a close. No longer lying on the grass, hearing a distant storm. No longer confined in the cargo hold of a spaceship, treated as a slave. They were then, and this is now.*

Skoia opens her eyes.

She is bound within her own coffin, bathed in tremulous sound. It rises, octave by octave, and she thinks of deep-sea monsters, ship-eating creatures stirring and thrashing upon the lightless ocean beds as they begin to rise.

She breathes in, managing only a shallow mouthful of air. Her heart beats slowly, so slowly.

She presses her hands to the thickness of the vision panel, knowing instinctively that it isn't for her to see out, it's for her captors to look in. To see her, to see if she's still alive.

Her next breath is harder than the first. She has to fight to suck it in, and it scarcely gets past her throat. Already the edges of her vision darken to grey.

She beats her fists against the window, making the coffin sway gently, the motion no different from a rocking cradle.

Her third breath barely comes at all. In that moment she cries out – not with her mouth but with her mind. She screams for the spirits to come to her. She beseeches them for their aid. She curses them for their silence. Panic drives her past holiness into blasphemy, and still she screams.

Other cries join hers. Some, like Skoia's, beseech ancestor-spirits or the memories of the lost, others are offered up as desperate prayers to the Emperor or the false and half-forgotten gods of distant worlds. It is the unified cry of people drawn from hundreds of cultures voicing their psychic gifts in terminal harmony.

Not all are pained. Some are obliviously joyful, others are sixth sense distillations of helpless rage or simple, crude fear. The chorus of outreaching emotion rises, and the battalion of interconnected machines all run louder, harder, in sympathetic response.

She is fading now. Her breaths no longer come, and that only amplifies her silent cry.

She slumps forwards, cheek pressed to the unbreakable glass, her lips trembling, her eyes wide and shivering. The stiller she becomes, the darker her sight falls, the louder she screams inside her skull.

And now, only now, does she hear the melody of the other souls of the one thousand sharing the same fate, suffering what she suffers. Their screams and prayers and panic and fears entwine, unseen by all, and form one sound, one impossibly perfect note. Those outside the coffins may yet hear it, but its true purity is unheard by any but the dying souls themselves.

It is the very first note in a song that will last ten thousand years, and perhaps beyond.

She, Skoia, is its first singer.

TWENTY-TWO

The Anathema's Daughters
Only in death does duty end
Sunrise

ARKHAN LAND WATCHED as Zephon fired his last shot and ducked back into the darkness of the tank's interior to reload. The spent magazine clattered to the deck as he slapped a new one home. Hauling himself back up into the cupola, the Blood Angel braced again and opened fire once more.

The technoarchaeologist, his face bleached with scrolling viewscreen data, veered the tank in a slow arc. Volkite cannons squealed in arrhythmic discord. Small-arms fire rained against the blessedly reinforced ceramite hull, reduced by the dense plating to dull bangs.

The grav-Raider's interior reeked with the porcine scent of burned gore. Wounded Sisters and Custodians lay across the deck of the hold, too injured to keep fighting. Land suspected several of them were already dead.

Zephon ducked back into the tank and slammed the cupola closed. 'I am out of ammunition,' he stated. His eyes glimmered with what Land suspected, quite correctly, was battle-lust – a rather primitive emotion that the Martian thankfully had no experience with whatsoever.

The Blood Angel locked his bolter to hip with a thumbed activation of magnetic seals. He crouched by one of the injured Sisters, who clutched the stump of her arm against her chest. The severance of her left arm was the least of her wounds if the running of blood beneath her was anything to go by. Something had gone badly wrong inside her during the battle. *A sword through the guts, most likely,* thought Land. *A pathetic way to die. A death worthy of a primate in Terra's Stone Era.*

He loathed the female warriors, and couldn't for the life of him fathom why. They were private, yes, but seemed agreeable enough. Yet merely looking at them made his skin crawl. Being near enough to smell one of them, or Omnissiah forbid accidentally come into contact with one of them, was enough to make his bile rise.

He was even more careful not to stare towards the enemy. The Raider's automated and servitor-manned volkite array was more than capable of responding to threats. The last time Arkhan had looked too long out across the enemy horde, he'd been unable to summon speech for several minutes. No aliens, no matter their world of origin, walked as a host of blade-bearing, cyclopean corpses able to ignore the butchery of their own flesh. Many of the horned, graveborn entities seemed animated from Imperial dead. Shattered plates of golden armour still tumbled from their bloated flesh.

Zephon aided the Sister with her wound bindings. His metal hands twitched, but not enough to ruin his efforts. Land knew that the cure, such as it was, wouldn't last long. It was too hasty, too fragile: fixed as it was to the back of the Blood Angel's neck and crudely drill-locked into the meat beneath the armour, to say nothing of the cables and wires running along the outside of his ceramite to link in fifty places across each forearm.

Land had used a biometric current regulator of the kind used to dampen agony-twitches in Ordo Reductor cyborgs. He'd ripped it right from the rib bracing of a slain Thallax. It effectively blocked any sign of their inner spasms from translating visibly to their robotic bodies; reversing its purpose and amplifying its sensitivity was no leap of genius – it was a fundamental principle in the technology used by the very wealthy of many worlds in rectifying muscle wastage and paralysis. Still, Land felt a kernel of pride in his jury-rigged battlefield solution. Fragile as the cure might be, the Blood Angel had been firing his bolter with murderous precision.

'This isn't even language,' Land said, a hand at his earpiece.

'Cease listening to them,' said Zephon.

Land offered a withering look by way of reply. Sweat had turned his clothing rank and his skin sour. He kept licking his dry lips to no avail.

Land guided the Raider into a whirring skid, aggravating its anti-grav plates. He scanned the last of the convoy, seeing damaged vehicles drifting into the curling golden mist. On this side of the gateway, the Mechanicum's ingenuity was masterfully bolted in layers of gleaming metal over the plain hideousness of the original ancient artistry. The arch itself was carved from a material resembling ivory, marked by silver runes in no known language.

Even as Land watched a tracked conveyor crawl through, three skimmers bearing cadres of Silent Sisters raced back out. If ever there was a time for reinforcements, it was now.

The Raider glided between the other advancing tanks, turning and returning to the crash of the front lines grinding against one another. Spear-wielding male warriors in gold moved in bloodied, exhausted harmony with sword-wielding female soldiers in chainmail. They were being pushed back, step by step, each Custodian or Sister falling opened up another hole in the rapidly diminishing Imperial line. Land's Raider vibrated with the squeal of its high-powered volkite arrays. Creatures and legionaries farther back in the enemy horde ignited beneath the beams, spreading the flames to their closest brethren.

Zephon rose again, clambering back up the crew ladder. The metal rungs bowed beneath his weight as he opened the cupola and looked out at the battle.

'Blood of the Angel.'

'What now?' Land barked.

'The Archimandrite. It is here.'

'Unlikely, given that the Archimandrite is almost certainly dead.'

<*It is time,*> she had canted, and Land had mourned her treachery in disbelieving silence. He refused to follow her whims. He wouldn't turn his back on the Omnissiah.

'It is here,' Zephon repeated. He reached for his chainsword, gunning it loudly in the oppressive, red-lit crew bay.

Land turned in his seat, reaching for the periscope. He dragged a sleeve across his face to clean his stinging eyes, and peered into the lenses. The thing he saw was bathing squads of retreating Sisters in coruscating beams of darkfire energy, atomising them in sweeping arcs. Custodian spears broke against its plating. Lascannon fire skewed aside from its flickering shields.

And yet.

'That,' he said, 'is not the Archimandrite.'

DEVRAM SEVIK HAD named his Knight *Aquila from the Ashes*. He had worked on its tilt plate himself, daubing the new sigil of House Vyridion with his own hand. As much as he was a man who revered the peerless work of sanctified artistry-armourers and sacristans in their maintenance of a Knight suit, he was also given to a personal flourish here and there. And so the Imperial eagle upon his tilt plate was more stylised than the stencilled ubiquity of most, with flaring wings and trails of plumage below as it took wing above a field of black ash.

'Engaging,' he voxed to Jaya, to his fellow scions, to anyone still drawing breath and capable of hearing.

Aquila from the Ashes crashed bodily into the Archimandrite at full stride, shoulder charging the machine with a hammer-blow bang and the choral whine of protesting, warping metal. They stood deadlocked, living machine-flesh against industrial piston-muscles, metal grinding, armour scraping, spraying sparks. *Aquila from the Ashes* had size and weight against the Archimandrite's original husk, but the Archimandrite was blasphemously altered now. The fruits of the Fabricator General's vision and the possessing daemon's strength shoved back

against the taller machine, its taloned feet seeking purchase and clawing into the nameless material of the webway's ground.

Devram's cockpit flooded with alarms and warning runes. He felt his
suit's stance buckling as the creatures around his knees began hacking
away at his stabilisers. A strained look at one of his torso-feed screens
showed the Custodians and Sisters fighting their way to him, but they
were fighting through an ocean of heaving, seething flesh with mere
mortal blades.

It was down to him. This deed would mark his shield or mark his
grave.

Enough left for a four-second burst. Devram forced his gunlimb up,
sacrificing his last shot against the beasts around his legs, jamming
the gatling cannon into the Archimandrite's sloping, featureless face.
It cycled live, rotating, spinning–

His knee buckled, burst. He fell, the last four seconds of his ammunition screaming wide, arcing up into the golden mist as wasted thunder.
The sickening lurch in his stomach told him what the failing pict-feeds
didn't, as his Knight toppled sideways. Impact gel squirted from his support cradle to cushion him but the excretors were poorly maintained;
his helmed head slammed against the cockpit wall and something –
the wall? his helmet? – crunched.

His visor went black, denying all input. Unseeing, feeling hot wetness in his mouth, Devram fought to pull his helmet clear. Fingers
that had turned suddenly clumsy scraped at the helmet's bindings as
all around him metal bent, wrenched, tore.

The pressure of enclosing metal was unrelenting, first squeezing him
into his throne, then crushing him into it, breaking his knees, his shoulders, his hips, his elbows, his ribs with vicious slowness. He screamed
as he was compacted beneath the Archimandrite's iron tread, silenced
only when his neck and jaw gave with wet, clicking snaps.

THE CREATURE STEPPED over the malformed remains of the taller machine,
unknowingly crushing Sevik's hand-painted tilt shield into a mangled

ruin. It hunted the Anathema's Daughters now, and all else was but a distraction.

Its lessers among the weaker Choirs lashed out blindly, unable to even sense the human maidens slaughtering them. The weakest of them all, the most wretched and insignificant within their ranks, dissolved even before the fall of the Daughters' killing blades.

The daemon of the first murder was prey to no such gullible weakness. It didn't need to sense them or see them in order to kill them. Its clustered node of hunger-senses flowed outwards over the hundreds of warring bodies, sensing the dissolution of its own kind. Wherever its lessers were drained of their strength, wherever their corpuses haemorrhaged potency, there it turned its guns. Blinded by the Sisters' soullessness, it hunted the holes in its perceptions, firing streaming volleys of solid shot or bolts of dark energy wherever its kindred suffered against foes it couldn't see.

The weapons so preciously crafted by ancient hands and recovered by Arkhan Land did their duty once again, chewing through the embattled Sisters with murderous precision. It raked them with explosive fire or reaved them down with energy beams – one it even managed to destroy by crushing her beneath its foot when it sought to impale the daemon's stolen metal corpus.

The daemon exhaled blackness, its breath staining the golden mist around its maw. Its tongue slithered free, hanging long and undulating in the fog. It wasn't capable of pleasure beyond the fulfilment of its nature, but there was satisfaction here. These hollow impressions of human females were far easier to kill when they could be torn apart with mortal weapons that vomited killing energy.

Though it wasn't born of war, it sensed the ebb and flow of the battle around it. Each of the Anathema's Daughters' deaths was a lessening of pressure against the creature's pained perceptions. Each burst body let the warp's song grow louder once more. Every one that fell allowed the daemon's lesser kindred to rise again, to fight harder.

Floating war machines raged at the creature, blasting portions of its stolen body apart. This punishment scarcely slowed it. Blood, old and new, painted its armour plating. The mist around its towering form was rancid and red with the shrieking of souls torn from their bodies since its arrival in this realm. Flesh-machine growths added to its size, quivering pods and birth-sacs of lesser daemons in rapid gestation, and thrashing tentacles of sinewy, veined metal that drilled through battle tanks to seek the mortals within. Its back-mounted weapon arrays annihilated whole swathes of the front lines, feeding the warfare while the daemon itself paid no heed to it. The creature butchered only the Golden and the war machines that sought to oppose its advance on the Anathema's Daughters.

As the warp's song grew and grew, threatening an exalting crescendo, the daemon of the first murder felt the defenders' desperation gaining a stained, queasy brittleness. It cast its senses wide to see why, and immediately let forth a roar that was half canted across the noosphere and partially bellowed into the webway's relative reality. The Anathema itself was within reach, stilled and crippled and bound to its Throne. These last, exhausted defenders were all that stood in the daemon's path.

Two of the dead Golden approached in their metal shells, weapons crashing, ripping yet more shards of armour-flesh free. The daemon lashed back with its tendrils, hammering one of them away, sending it tumbling into the ranks of the creature's own kindred to be pried open and the meat within devoured.

It lifted the second in its coiling grip, smelling a familiar soul. It knew this one.

'*End of Empires!*' it voxed, screamed and canted. '*End of Empires!*'

LAND MADE A sound in the back of his throat, one he wasn't proud of. He had to swallow before he could speak. Even the Custodians were falling back from what the Archimandrite had become. It had downed Sevik within mere heartbeats. It killed one of the Ten Thousand's Dreadnoughts as quick as Land could blink. It lifted another in its tentacles, and…

'What in the Omnissiah's name will your chainsword do against that?'

'Very little,' Zephon replied. Yet still he gunned it. 'Bring us in closer.'

Arkhan did so, his eyes locked to the visions feeds.

'Baroness D'Arcus,' Zephon voxed. 'I require your aid.'

Zephon climbed out onto the tank's roof. A second later, Land heard the thruster bark of the Blood Angel's jump pack igniting.

Sagittarus was drowning. Or suffocating. He didn't know which. He was struggling to breathe in the womb-fluid of his coffin, each inhalation coming with the coppery taste of blood and a sour tang of oil. Whatever was left of his physical form – even Sagittarus had never been sure how much of himself remained inside the coffin – banged and thumped inside the life support sarcophagus, sloshing in the amniotic fluid but no longer submerged within it.

Leaking. That thought held primacy in the darkening light of his perceptions. *Crippled. Hurt. Leaking.*

He faced ahead, trying to raise arms that wouldn't obey. He had to pull himself out of the monster's tendrils. His weapons clunked, devoid of ammunition for hours. His chassis, alive with warning readings for so long already, was held together only by dumb luck.

Yet he'd charged the Archimandrite. Limping and bleeding and ammo-starved, he'd charged it as it stepped over the dead Knight. There had been no choice. Its cannons were devastating the faltering Imperial lines.

Only in death does duty end.

One blow was all he'd been able to land, a shattering strike from his fist that ripped the plating from the Archimandrite's chest, revealing a subdermal layer of secondary ablative plate. And then, he was in the creature's clutches, hauled from the ground.

To his shame, he cried out when his right arm tore free. He had no nerves in his Dreadnought shell but the synaptic backlash of being mutilated was all too real. The Archimandrite brandished the ripped limb, still spitting with sparks, before hurling it away into the seething tides below.

Sagittarus' world lurched as he was lifted even higher, the whine of protesting metal resounding in his ears through the murky, muffled coffin. He felt the pressure in his thigh as the daemon took a firmer grip, then the wrenching jolt of dislocation that followed. Another crack of synaptic feedback coursed through his revenant flesh. Malfunctioning systems railed at him. Empty weapons cried out for him to fire.

Turbines screamed as a figure in bloody red thudded onto the Archimandrite's shoulder. The Blood Angel, Zephon, cleaved down with a two-handed blow of his chainblade, the sword ripping into a tendril's joint where flesh met machine in unholy fusion. The sword rose and fell, tearing away chunks of bloody metal, spitting its own teeth as its revving track was fouled by gore and dense armour.

The Archimandrite pivoted but the Blood Angel's jump pack spurted stabilising gas jets, long enough for a fifth blow to bite deep into the carved wound. The tendril deformed with the damage, gushing oil and slime as it fell limp, dropping Sagittarus into the melee below.

His last sight before plunging into the battling bodies was the Archimandrite's left hand closing around the Blood Angel's torso, dragging him from his unstable perch.

Sagittarus rolled with all of the grace of an overturned sand turtle, clawing his remaining fist into the ground, and dragged himself back.

'*Five,*' he heard Zephon vox, the Blood Angel's voice marred by strain for the first time.

Four.

Zephon thrashed in the beast's grip, laying into the machine's forearm with his damaged chainsword.

Three.

A lucky nick at the wrist tore a fluid-wet spillage of cabling from its housing, weakening the grip before it fully closed. The Blood Angel fired his jump pack, red ceramite scraping against the Archimandrite's clutching fingers as he boosted free, straight up.

Two.

With a grace any winged being would envy, the Blood Angel twisted in the air, angling his propulsion to veer him back to the Imperial line.

One.

The bandolier of grenades mag-locked to the back of the Archimandrite's head detonated in incendiary harmony, sending shrapnel rainstorming across the embattled lines. Daemons near to the detonation howled at the punishment delivered to their predator-monarch. The Archimandrite, missing a significant portion of its hunchback and both shoulders, staggered forwards, emitting a shriek that the true war machine was incapable of producing.

'*Engaging*,' came Jaya's voice in Zephon's helm.

SHE HAD EXPENDED her ammunition hours before, even depleting Torolec's reserves. Her swordlimb was a cracked ruin; it had shattered against a Warhound after cutting through the bare metal and severing the leg at the thigh. Lacking any other recourse, she was down to clubbing with the broken hilt and her ammo-starved gunlimb, doing her best to guard the front ranks from harm by warding them from the Archimandrite's onslaught with her ion shield.

Zephon sent the signal. Jaya forced her Knight into a sprinting run, charging as Sevik had charged, heaving her Castigator's weight against the staggering Archimandrite. Hunched as she was, she found herself face to face with the Mechanicum's creation, looking down into the broken cranial armour left in the wake of the grenades' detonation. Fluids ran and bubbled in scorched cables. Fleshy matter was burned against the insides of the dome – what had once been Hieronyma's brain and spinal column. The incinerated remnants still quivered with impossible life.

End of Empires, she heard in her mind. In the same second, warning chimes began singing their familiar song. The creatures were swarming around her knees and she had no means of shoving them away. The Custodians and Sisters were too far back to reach her.

Jaya reversed her grip on the control levers, throwing the Knight into a leaping backstep, coming down awkwardly on the flesh of the daemons around her. Freed from the pressure of her weight, the Archimandrite over-balanced and stumbled forwards – meeting the rising energised remains of Jaya's swordlimb. The uppercut blow pounded into the machine's ruptured chest-plating, sinking all the way to Jaya's elbow joint.

'For Sevik,' she spat into her external speakers. *'For the Emperor.'*

The Archimandrite's only reply was to slump, powerless, dead. For precious seconds they remained there together, fused at the point of death. Her cockpit shook as the creatures beneath her began crawling and cutting their way upwards, ascending her Knight's savaged armour plating.

The Archimandrite began to topple, dragging the Knight down with it. Jaya locked her stabilisers and compensator balancers, buying her a few more seconds of standing upright. Her gloved hands scrabbled for the ejection release, but it had either not functioned since its initial repairs or fallen into uselessness during the days of fighting. The seals blew in the hatch above her, but her throne remained locked in place.

She heard the first creature reach the top of the Castigator's carapace, its talons pulling at the seal-blown hatch. Yet when it ripped away, a figure in arterial-red stood silhouetted and haloed in the golden mist. It reached down and offered her its shining metal hand.

Jaya grabbed it, immediately hauled up into the Blood Angel's grip. She barely had time to suck in a breath before his turbines kicked in and sent them skywards, shaking every bone and pulling every muscle in her body.

They hit the ground no gentler. Zephon's armour was built to withstand the pressures of his short-burst flight, but Jaya felt something snap inside her when they thudded onto the misty ground behind the Custodians and Sisters in the front lines. The Blood Angel didn't release her, half carrying her into the dim bay of Land's volkite-squealing grav-Raider.

One-armed and one-legged, Sagittarus lay on the tank's internal decking, taking up almost half of the bay. The stylised helm that housed his sensorium relays stared up at her with shattered eye-lenses.

'Dawn,' he intoned, drawling and unfocused. Jaya had no idea what he might mean.

'Something is...' said Arkhan Land, looking right through the vision slit. His curse was a breathy whisper as he blinked tired, gritty eyes. 'Teeth of the Cog...'

Jaya turned towards the technoarchaeologist. The unhealthy radiance of the viewscreen was gone from the explorator's features; instead he was bathed in white light streaming through the vision slit. Dust motes danced in the beam of illumination.

'What is it?' she asked.

'I don't know,' Arkhan stammered. 'It looks like the sun is rising.'

AND IN A sunless realm, the sun rose at last.

The light of dawn was palpable on Ra's armour as well as his skin. It was a pressure, a presence with searing physicality. The enemy hordes felt it as acid on their skin. The creatures – daemons no matter what secular truths held strong – lost what little order they had ever possessed.

The Anathema! Ra heard their frantic agony as a sick scraping on the edges of his mind. *The Anathema comes! The sun rises!*

His features were those of one born in the wild lands of Ancient Eurasia. His skin was a Terran blend of bronze and burnt umber, His eyes darker still, His hair darkest of all. The long black fall of His hair was held by a simple circlet crown of metal leaves, binding the mane back from His face so He could fight. More practical than regal.

He moved as a man moved, coming through the straining ranks of His guardians on foot, pushing through the press of bodies on the rare instances they didn't instinctively move aside for Him. He wore gold, as all of His guardians wore gold. The same sigils of Terran Unity and Imperial nobility that showed on their armour were cast thricefold upon His own. His armour joints didn't growl with the crude industrial snarl of mass-manufactured legionary plate, but purred with the song of older, purer technologies.

On His back, held by a simple strap against His flowing red cloak, was an ornate bolter of black and bronze. In His hand He carried a sword – one that looked nothing like the blade portrayed in the victory murals and illustrated sagas. By the standards of Terran lords and kings it was inarguably beautiful, but in the grip of the ruler of an entire species it was, perhaps, rather plain. A weapon to wield, a tool for shedding blood, not an ornament to be admired. Impossibly complicated circuitry latticed its blade, black and coppery against a silver so hallowed that it was almost blue.

In other wars on other worlds He had greeted His Custodians with subtle telepathy, speaking their names as He passed them before a battle. Here He was more restrained, moving to the embattled front rank without offering any acknowledgement at all.

Of the Neverborn, some broke ranks and fled. These cowardly shards of their vile masters knew that destruction had come. Some tore into each other, cannibalising their kindred for strength in the face of destruction. Some lost what little grasp they had on corporeality, their forms melting and dissolving before the sword-wielding monarch even reached the front lines.

The strongest raged at the sin of His existence. With a gestalt bellow loud enough to shake the windless air of this alternate reality, they fought to reach their archenemy.

Ra was at the Emperor's right side, spear whirling, lashing out to punch through the amorphous bodies of flailing blue creatures that wailed through their many mouths. Sweat baked his face inside his helm. The blood in his muscles was heavier than liquid lead.

'Orders, sire?'

The Emperor raised His sword in a two-handed grip. As His knuckles tightened, the geography of circuitry ignited along the blade's length, spitting electrical fire and wreathing the sword's length in flame.

He didn't speak. He didn't look at any of His warriors. The sword came down. The webway caught fire.

TWENTY-THREE

Dawn
The reason for illumination
When all that remains is ash and dust

SHAPES RAGED IN the flames – shadows and suggestions doing battle with the daemons, their fiery forms indistinct and ever-changing. The fire-born avatars of fallen Ten Thousand, knee-deep in psychic fire and thrusting with lances of flame. The silhouettes of Space Marines, the betrayed dead of Isstvan bearing axes and blades and claws; half-seen sigils of slaughtered Legions obscured by the ash of their blackened armour. A giant among giants, its great hands bared and ready as it seared forwards at the crest of the tidal fire. The tenth son of a dying empire, so briefly reborn in his father's immolating wrath.

Daemons burned in their thousands, their aetheric flesh seared from their false bones. White flame haloed from the sword in corrosive, purifying radiance. It coruscated in thrashing waves from each fall of the Emperor's blade. To look at Him was to go blind. To stand before Him was to die.

And with a roar, the Custodians followed their lord and master. They reaved the Neverborn, banishing them with each thrusting spear and bellowing boltgun. Their blades carved through daemonic flesh, sending acidic blood raining in corrosive sprays. It wasn't mist that occluded sight now, it was ash from the incinerated dead. Spears flashed silver in the dust-thickened air. The Last Charge of the Ten Thousand.

Behind the golden warriors came their arming thralls, bearing fresh ammunition and armour sealant; warriors in their own right but sheltered from harm by their masters' spinning blades.

It didn't matter that all these years of secret war had depleted the Legio Custodes to a ghost of itself. It didn't matter that they had fought and bled and died for the last half-decade in this sunless, merciless realm populated only by the dead and the damned. Their king had come, the sun had risen and they charged with a cry that far eclipsed the wails of the daemons dying on their blades.

The beasts that survived the Emperor's onslaught staggered and lurched towards the Custodians, raising brittle blades in dissolving hands, uselessly staring through bleeding, blinded eyes. Something dead – a creature hunched and bloated, still bearing within its flesh the plague that had slain it – lunged at Ra. His spear thrust burst its eye and cracked through the malformed skull. Hissing and bubbling blood sluiced across Ra's gauntlets, steaming as it burned away in the Emperor's aura.

He loosed his last explosive bolts, sensing the weapon was empty before the warning sigil flashed on his visor. 'Reload!' Ra cried as he hurled the weapon back towards the armoury thralls, already drawing his meridian swords in its place. The curved blades ripped through diseased flesh, spilling rotten organs to the misty ground. The swords' energy fields spat kinetic aggravation at every impact.

A rune chimed on his retinal display, flickering white. He sheathed the twin sabres in a smooth turn and caught his guardian spear as the ammunition thrall threw it back to him. The moment he had a fist around its haft, he was killing again. This was the way of his kind.

For Ra, time ceased to exist. There was nothing but the beat of his heart and the lactic burn of his muscles. All he saw were the blades and claws flashing towards his face. The ash of dying, dissipating Neverborn coated his armour.

'Reload!' Solon called from behind him. Ra heard the snap-crack of Solon's meridian swords activating, and the rumbled murmur of compliance as the armoury thrall gathered the guardian spear left thrust into the ground.

Ra parried a cut from a heavy brass blade, returning a blast from his digital lasers that blew the creature's face out the back of its sloped head. Daemonic slop from the burst skull rained across the Emperor's back, turning to ash before it touched the monarch's armour.

Torrents of chemical fire marked Zhanmadao's position to Ra's left. Ra could hear the draconic roar of incendium pikes, burning the still-thrashing creatures that had fallen beneath the blades of the Custodians' first rank. The Ten Thousand and their golden king were shin-deep in ash, the smoky spectres of daemonic entities flailing as they were swallowed by the Emperor's fire.

The daemons that managed to reach the Emperor suffered worst of all. The strongest, most savage of their kind, they swung weapons at a man who was no longer there, cleaving through the golden mist that swirled in His place. With thunder-cracks of psychic force, the golden warlord would appear at the beasts' backs, His flaming sword already buried in their spines. Fire erupted behind their eyes, boiling and bursting them from within. Their sizzling gore soaked Ra and the Custodians closest to their sire.

Exaltation quickened Ra's blood, the cure to the weariness that had slowed him. He was tired beyond belief, yet that had never mattered so little. Each beat of his still-living heart was vengeance, vindication.

We're winning. He could feel it in the renewed curses and oaths across the vox as the Ten Thousand advanced. They weren't just holding their ground. Whatever genius the Emperor had worked in order to stand with them in this final hour had worked. Nothing could stand before them.

The Emperor turned to Ra, hurling His sword as a spear. It lanced over the Custodian's shoulder, driving to the hilt in the skull of a creature Ra barely even saw before it was reduced to burning sludge. In a

flare of sun-enriched mist, the blade was back in the Emperor's hand,
spinning, falling, killing.

And still the Emperor advanced. A reptilian canine leapt at him only
to rip through the air where he had been standing. It gurgled molten
blood as the Emperor's sword manifested within its throat. The warlord clutched it in place a second longer before ripping it free and
moving on.

Still the enemy came – a tide, a flood. Ra stole glances back to the
wraithbone gateway, so incongruous against the Mechanicum's machinery, watching robed Unifiers passing into the blue mist, escorted by
packs of the last surviving Silent Sisters.

Soon enough only the Ten Thousand remained at their master's side.

+Be ready, Ra.+

'My liege?'

The Custodian launched himself over the slumping form of the vul-
turish creature that had fallen to his final six bolts, hurling his spear
back behind the front line and drawing his meridian swords while still
in the air. He landed by the Emperor, back to back with his master.
Their blades wove a lattice of silver light, eviscerating everything that
approached their edged web.

+Be ready.+

'For what, sire?'

Ra's retinal display flashed its white sigil. He caught the returned
weapon, spinning it with the force and speed of a rotor blade. The tunnel around them cracked and sparked with the strain of overworked
generators.

+There, Ra. It draws near.+

The Emperor moved on, cutting, carving. He led His guardians into
the very hordes of a mythological hell, and like the paladins of yore,
they followed their king.

Rare emotion spiced the Emperor's silent words. +I sense such purity
of being. Such pure, unadulterated malice.+

Ra weaved back from a swinging axe blade, returning a spear thrust that punched through the creature's scaled throat. He dared a glance left to Diocletian, seeing his kinsman hauling his own spear from the innards of a pot-bellied, horned grotesque, impaling a prize of rotted entrails. Flies droned around the decayed tangle, swarming at the loss of their hive.

Even immortals could tire. Ra's breath sawed between his closed teeth. Inside his helmet, sweat drew lines of wet fire down his face. His retinal display kept auto-dimming to compensate for the fire and light bursting into being with each fall of the Emperor's blade.

'I see only the horde, sire.' He didn't like the rapt fascination in his lord's tone.

+Reveal thyself...+

The Emperor raised His blade, bringing it down in a crescent of fire. A tide of flame bellowed forth in an incinerating arc, bathing the ranks of the Neverborn before him. Mortis-ash blasted back in the windless air, coating the closest Custodians in the dust of dead daemons.

A shadow. A shape in the ash.

A man. Just a man. Long of hair, dark of skin, tribally bearded, wearing jewellery of shaped bone and bearing a spear of knapped flint vine-lashed to fire-hardened wood. A man wearing wounds almost as grievous as those he had inflicted upon so many others. Hundreds of spear slashes and sword cuts marked his flesh. The freshest and bloodiest showed on his chest, the legacy of Jaya's last blow.

One man, leading the ranks of howling madness behind him.

+The Echo of the First Murder.+ The Emperor's words broke into Ra's skull with crushing gentleness.

'The Anathema,' was its sick, slick reply.

Predators always revealed themselves in the seconds before they struck. Wolves howled as they chased; sharks cut the ocean's surface with their fins as they hunted. Here the ashen silhouette moved through the Neverborn's ranks, lesser creatures parting before its too-human tread. Whatever the creature's true form, it wasn't this muscled Stone Epoch war-chief. It merely aped the form of the first humans.

For the first, terrifying time, Ra saw doubt flicker within his master's eyes. The sight flooded him with the unfamiliar taint of dread.

'Sire,' Ra whispered. 'We should–'

But the Emperor was gone. Monarch and daemon ran at one another, sliding in and out of existence, outpacing their lessers on both sides of the battle. And the two entities, one the salvation of a species and the other its damnation, met blade to blade.

Blood burst into the ashy mist. The Emperor arched, the warlord's body taut with the utter unfamiliarity of agony. Five talons, each one the length and width of a spear, dripped red as they stood proud of the Emperor's back.

Ra had heard tell that every man, woman, and child saw a different face, a different skin tone, a different temperament when they looked upon the Emperor. The Ten Thousand had no experience with such an effect. They considered it doggerel from the strains of unready minds when confronted by a true immortal. To Ra's eyes, the Emperor was a man like any other. The Custodians saw only their master.

In that moment, as the claws ran red with his king's blood, Ra saw what the rest of the species saw. *The boy who would be king. An old man, cloaked and hooded, life running from his cracked lips. A knight in his prime, maned with dark hair, crowned with a wreath of laurels. A barbarian warlord, barbarous and strong, grinning through teeth turned red with His leaking blood.*

Images. Identities. Men who once were. Men He might once have been. Men who had never drawn breath.

The Emperor's boots left the misty ground. He barely even struggled as He was lifted, impaled by the five spearing talons. His sword fell from His gloved hands to disappear in the shrouding fog.

'To the Emperor!' Ra screamed the order loud enough that his retinal display blurred for a half-second. 'To the Emperor's side!'

He ran, killing faster than he'd ever killed, energised by an adrenal cocktail of loyalty, hatred and the alien touch of something nameless that tasted foul on the tongue.

Not fear, no, never that. Surely never that.

I am the End of Empires.

The thought wasn't Ra's own. It belonged to the silhouette in the ashes, the Emperor's killer, speaking by twisting the thoughts of the humans in its presence. A wrenching violation, with crude, cruel fingers pulling at the insides of Ra's skull, forcing his thoughts to form the daemon's words.

'Kill it!' Ra shouted, half an oath, half an order. The man-shape turned in the settling ash, still holding the Emperor above the ground. The warlord clutched at the impaling arm. His telepathic voice was raw.

+Stay back. All of you. Stay back.+

I am your death, the creature promised the Emperor.

+Perhaps one day. But not this day.+

Gold light flared bright enough to blind unshielded eyes. The Emperor manifested at Ra's side, down on one knee, one hand clutched to his chest, hair hanging down to veil his features. Blood, human blood no matter what the legends said, ran in runnels from the Emperor's sundered armour.

+Ra.+ The sending was thick with pained defiance. And then, 'Ra,' He said aloud, raising His eyes to meet His loyal Custodian's horrified gaze.

A blade ran through the Emperor's body. An ornate sword, as much sorcerous bone as metal, a weapon with writhing, shrieking faces soul-carved upon the steel. The faces shrieked as they drank the Emperor's divine life. It thrashed as the Emperor clutched it in His hands. It was alive, starving, its form rippling and growing indistinct.

With a cry the Emperor pulled the weapon free, unsheathing it from His own body. He hurled it from His grip, casting it aside with a surge of armour-boosted strength and devastating telekinetic force.

Ra blinked once with the impact, feeling it as a thunder-crack against his chest. He swallowed, finding himself unable to breathe. Blood streamed from his mouth, denying the passage of air.

It was a blade through his body. It was a daemon embracing him. It was a disease in his blood, eating at his bones. It was there and it wasn't there, everything and nothing.

The Custodian fell to his knees, hands curling around the impaling blade. The thwarted rage of the daemon sent nerve pain lightning-bolting through his fingers.

'Why?' Ra asked his king.

The Emperor stood tall once more, looking down, eyes cold.

In that moment, Ra knew. The Emperor's words, spoken what felt like an eternity ago, flashed through his blackening mind, infusing his thoughts with red revelation.

To illuminate you, the Emperor had said, as they looked upon the wonders and sins of the galaxy's past. *You will fight harder once you understand what you are fighting for.*

And now he knew. Ra Endymion, the one living soul shown the entirety of his master's dreams and ambitions. An enlightenment not gleaned for the purpose of waging war, but... for this. To know the truth when all others believed in shadows and fragments, and to suffer that truth until it tore him apart.

Ra rose on shaking limbs, leaning on his spear for support. The sword was gone now. The daemon was within him, caged by his flesh, bound by his agony-drenched will. He felt its tendrils circling his bones, wrenching at them, thrashing in its need to reach the Master of Mankind. The creature tunnelling through his blood would never stop, never die. It couldn't be destroyed, only imprisoned.

The Custodian didn't meet his sire's eyes. He didn't demand any explanation or apology. Ra was born to serve, raised to obey and chosen for the greatest illumination preceding the darkest duty. Inside him raged a beast even the Emperor couldn't kill, the daemon destined to end the empire.

Every step he took away from the Emperor, separating this daemon from his master, would mean another day that the Imperium stood unbroken.

The Emperor still bled, still clutched His wounded chest with one gloved hand. Blood flecked His lips. 'When all that remains is ash and dust,' He said, strained, 'be ready.'

The sword rose, and once more it fell. Fire tidal-waved from its kill-ing edge, immolating all in its path. Clearing the way. The Neverborn dragging themselves over the ashen remains of their kindred tasted the same destruction.

The Emperor spoke to Ra one final time, a single command heard by no other.

+Run.+

Ra Endymion, Drach'nyen's golden gaoler, the son of a water-thief, obeyed the last command he would ever be given.

He ran.

TWENTY-FOUR

The death of a dream

DIOCLETIAN TORE HIS helm from his head, breathing in the ozone and machine-stink of the Imperial Dungeon. Sweat sheened his face. Blood painted his armour, much of it his own. He was the last one through.

'The tunnels are detonating,' he declared, breathless. Golden mist still pulled at his armour from the portal behind him. 'The circuitry is igniting. Whole sections of our tunnels are falling away into the mist. I couldn't see Ra. He didn't die, I'm sure of it. I was at his side. I would have seen.'

He knew he was raving. He didn't care. He spat to clear his mouth, spattering treacly blood-spit on the floor of the Emperor's throne room. Beyond the ringing in his ears he was aware of a sound, some kind of mechanical droning, a hum falling slowly through the octaves.

Diocletian's spear clattered to the ground, deactivating the second it left the gene-coding of his grip. Blood followed it, running from wounds too deep to swiftly seal. The blood ran down his arm and surfaced through breaks in his auramite, dripping from his curled fingers.

'Seal the gate!' he ordered, not even knowing if it could be done. 'They're still coming. Thousands of them. Seal the gate now, or we lose Terra.'

They were already trying, he saw. Adepts and engineers clustered around the machines, working the controls of each system. His war-struck thoughts made the connection with the slowing mechanical drone: the chamber's attendants were deactivating the machinery, but not fast enough.

A single glance at the coffin-pods in the sockets told him what had happened in his absence, and how the Emperor had been able to come to their aid. The Sisters of Silence had enacted their secretive Unspoken Sanction. They fed the Throne with the lives of a thousand psykers. In every pod he could see a corpse that had thrashed in its death throes, raking uselessly against the transparent panels. All of them were dead. Every one of them. None of them looked to have died swiftly and painlessly.

Confusion reigned across the vox and among the gathered warriors as to the source of their salvation. Some had seen a dawning star or a sunrise, others had seen the Emperor Himself. Still others claimed to have witnessed a tidal surge of fire.

Everywhere, men and women were lost and dazed. Baroness Jaya was there on the chamber floor, her helmet in her hands, unblinkingly staring at her reflection in the visor. The Blood Angel, Zephon, was helping carry wounded Sisters from Land's Raider. The technoarchaeologist himself was kneeling on the ground by his battle tank, rocking back and forth, his trembling hands clutching a necklace of Martian prayer beads, his delicate fingers stroking each bauble of volcanic obsidian in turn.

'My Omnissiah,' he was chanting softly, eyes unfocused. 'My God. The Machine-God. My Omnissiah.'

Sagittarus lived, his chassis scored and ruined, the smokestacks on his back belching unhealthily from his overpushed generator. The Dreadnought had his back to the side of Land's tank, leaking vital fluids from its internal sarcophagus in an oily puddle.

Sisters and warriors of the Ten Thousand gathered in monumental disorder, all of them looking to the portal's arch, all of them hearing the slow drone of machinery powering down.

Diocletian was still demanding answers of the others when Kaeria came to him. 'Where's Ra?' he asked her. 'Did he make it back? He didn't fall. I know he didn't fall.'

Her eyes tightened with tension.

'He didn't fall,' Diocletian repeated. 'I was right next to him in the battle line. I would have seen it. He'll be on the wrong side of the gate when it closes.'

Sister-Commander Krole came to Kaeria's side, signing briefly for Diocletian's benefit. He didn't know her as he knew Kaeria – he couldn't read her meaning by expression alone. Her signing was blighted by the fact she had lost three fingers from her left hand. Wounds patterned her features while her armour showed the ruination of too many hours in the front lines.

'No,' said the Custodian. 'I was *at his side*, commander. He didn't die. One moment he was there, the next he was not.'

Machines were going dark all around them. Great engines of the Emperor's own vision – centuries in the design and decades in the making – were cycling down, haemorrhaging power. Slowly, slowly, far too slowly.

Diocletian sought the Emperor Himself, seeing His master ascending the steps to the Golden Throne once more.

'My liege!'

The Emperor enthroned Himself, His grip loose on the armrests.

'Sire! Seal the gate!'

The Emperor waited, staring towards the portal. Even from such a distance, Diocletian could see the intensity of that stare. The Emperor fixed his gaze on the gateway, waiting, waiting. Hesitating to do what must be done? Reluctant to abandon His greatest ambition? Or hopeful, yet, that another figure might manifest from the golden fog?

A shape darkened the mist. Something winged and clawed. Another figure, bloated and horned. And more. Others. A host of inhumanity. The Throne-engines were still cycling down.

'*Sire!*' Diocletian pleaded.

The Emperor closed His right hand into a fist, clenched within His glove. With a harmonious pattern of thunderclaps, every generator within the chamber went dark, their internal mechanics rupturing, starving the Golden Throne of energy.

The archway that led to humanity's doomed salvation was nothing more than an ornate doorway, leading to the bare rock of the throne room wall.

Power failed completely, plunging the Imperial Dungeon into darkness.

ALONE BUT FOR the daemon seeking to devour him from within, silent but for the caged beast's murderous howls inside his head, a golden figure sprinted through the hazy passages of the ancient webway, leaving the Mechanicum's aborted Unification behind.

EPILOGUE

The Desert

THE SUN WAS a hammer, the desert its scorched anvil. Here the world laboured under the draconic swelter of seething heat, the wind slow-whipping in outraged howls across the dune sea. The barren sky offered no shadow. The lifeless landscape offered no hope of shade.

A lone traveller walked this realm, his boots scuffing the powdery grit, his cloak rippling in the alkali gusts. He trudged onwards, leaving tracks that marked his passage across the featureless expanse. He never looked back. There would be nothing to see even if he did.

His journey brought him to the edge of a chasm, a riven slice of the planet's skin where the world's tectonics had once pulled apart after warring in grinding uproar. The traveller descended the ravine's cliff-side while the high sun remained in vigil.

Soon enough, blessedly, he entered a realm of shadow where the sun no longer stared.

Within the ravine lay the broken bones of a dead city. Silent for so long, free from the ravages of the dusty wind, it echoed only with the sound of the traveller's footsteps. He passed through this place of mournful memory, careful not to the touch the ashen smears that its fleeing people had become.

He walked through time-eaten cathedrals to forgotten gods, through fire-fallen palaces that once housed dynasties of kings and queens who laid claim to whole worlds. He walked with no purpose beyond seeing what lay there in the abandoned shadows.

In the deepest lightless reaches of that slain civilisation, the traveller halted at last. He stood within a cavern several days' journey below the surface, where the stone walls showed precious few remaining signs of the culture that once thrived here. It wasn't from here that those ancient monarchs had ruled their realm, but it was the core-place, the heart of their power, that had allowed them to do so.

Thunder rolled. A week away, far above him, a storm tore across the desert. Dust clattered from the cavern roof, clattering soft melodies of desecration upon dead machines.

The traveller turned in the darkness, raising an illumination globe clutched in a rag-gloved hand.

'Hello, Diocletian,' he said.

The warrior stood in the dark, his spear held in a loose fist. He was helmless, breathing in the earthy smell of a million memories.

'My liege,' he said. Somehow his voice was a gunshot in the nothingness, breaking the silence in a way the Emperor's had not. Things moved in the shadows, crawling away from the defiling sound of speech.

The Emperor walked among the stilled enginery – the sand had blighted everything, even down here – running His gauntleted touch along the fire-blackened metal.

'Sire? What is happening? Why am I here?'

'Do you recognise any of this machinery?'

Diocletian let his gaze roam over the cavern's wreckages. 'No, my liege.'

The Emperor kept walking, moving from structure to structure the way a man might browse the aisles of librarium. The thunder that shouldn't be audible this deep in the earth rumbled louder than before.

'There are those in the Cult Mechanicum, among the Unifiers, that surmise I found the core of the Golden Throne here, beneath the sands of Terra. A relic, they venture, of the Dark Age.'

Diocletian wasn't sure what to say. He had witnessed uncountable hours of the Golden Throne's planning and construction processes. Yet, as he said, he recognised nothing here. He didn't know if that was a flaw in his understanding of the Throne's genesis among these machines, or simply because this machine crypt had nothing to do with the Emperor's greatest work at all.

'Perhaps there was merely inspiration to be found, here,' the Emperor mused softly. 'The idea taking form, based not on the successes of an ancient race but the failures of our own.' He exhaled a rueful sound, not quite a sigh, not quite a chuckle. 'Did I see these machines, how they fell short of their intended purpose, and resolve to create a far superior incarnation? There is a certain poetry to that, isn't there, Diocletian? The belief that we know better than those who came before us. That we will suit a throne better than they did.'

'Sire, I… Are you well?'

'Or perhaps the idea was mine in its entirety. Any relics of lost ages that have proven useful for their parts being the legacies of dead species that had the same idea, millennia before my birth. In such an instance, each race envisions its own salvation independent of the others, only to discover that other species, other empires, have already failed to save themselves.'

Diocletian breathed slowly in the dark. 'Does it matter, sire?'

The Emperor turned to him, His eyes focusing on the Custodian for the first time. 'The war is over, Diocletian. Win or lose, Horus has damned us all. Mankind will share in his ignorance until the last man or woman draws the species' last breath. The warp will forever be a cancer in the heart of all humans. The Imperium may last a hundred years, or a thousand, or ten thousand. But it will fall, Diocletian. It will fall. The shining path is lost to us. Now we rage against the dying of the light.'

'It cannot be this way.' Diocletian stepped forwards, teeth clenched. 'It cannot.'

The Emperor tilted His head. 'No? What then do you intend to do,

Custodian? How will you – with your spear and your fury and your loyalty – pull fate itself from its repeating path?'

'We will kill Horus.' Diocletian stared at his defeated monarch, illuminated in emberish light of the lumoglobe in his hand. 'And after the war, we can begin anew. We can purge the webway. The Unifiers can rebuild all that was lost, even if it takes centuries. We will strike Horus down and–'

'I will face the Sixteenth,' the Emperor interrupted, distracted once more by the machine graveyard. 'But there will come another to take his place. I see that now. It is the way of things. The enemy will never abate. Another will come, one who will doubtless learn from Horus' errors of faith and judgement.'

'Who, my king?'

The Emperor shook His head. 'There is no way to know. And for now it is meaningless. But remember it well – we are not the only ones learning from this conflict. Our enemies grow wiser, as well.'

Diocletian refused to concede. 'You are the Emperor of Mankind. We will conquer any who come against us. After the war, we will rebuild under your guidance.'

The Emperor stared at him. He spoke a question that wasn't a question, one that brooked no answer.

'And what if I am gone, Diocletian.'

The Custodian had no answer. Thunder pealed above them, shaking the cavern and jarring loose a rattling hail of falling pebble-dust.

'My king, what now? What comes next?'

The Emperor turned away, walking into the darkness of the cavern while the storm hammered the dead city so far above. He spoke three words that no Custodian had ever heard Him speak before.

'I don't know.'

ABOUT THE AUTHOR

Aaron Dembski-Bowden is the author of the Horus Heresy novels *The Master of Mankind, Betrayer* and *The First Heretic*, as well as the novella Aurelian and the audio drama Butcher's Nails, for the same series. He has also written the popular Night Lords series, the Space Marine Battles book *Armageddon*, the Black Legion novel *The Talon of Horus*, the Grey Knights novel *The Emperor's Gift* and numerous short stories. He lives and works in Northern Ireland.

SHATTERED LEGIONS

Edited by Laurie Goulding

Shadrak Meduson rallies his kinsmen after
Isstvan V, to wage a different kind of war

READ IT FIRST

EXCLUSIVE PRODUCTS | EARLY RELEASES | FREE DELIVERY

blacklibrary.com